CARNAL

MAFIA WARS - BOOK FOUR

MAGGIE COLE

PULSE PRESS INC

This book is fiction. Any references to historical events, real people, or real places are used fictitiously. All names, characters, plots, and events are products of the author's imagination. Any resemblance to actual events or places or persons, living or dead, is entirely coincidental.

Copyright © 2022 by Maggie Cole

All rights reserved.

No part of this book may be reproduced in any form or by any electronic or mechanical means, including information storage and retrieval systems, without written permission from the author, except for the use of brief quotations in a book review.

PROLOGUE

Pina dela Cruz

DARKNESS FADES AS FAINT NOISES GROW LOUDER. A CHILL runs down my spine while sweat breaks the surface of my skin. My heart pounds harder, and the sound of metal slamming together is followed by horns blaring.

A gruff voice heckles, "Stupid motherfuckers. Look at those idiots, Kiko."

Kiko? Who is Kiko?

I blink, and the sunlight blinds me. Hammers pound in my head. I squeeze my eyelids shut, wondering why my mouth is so dry.

Why does my body feel so sore?

A whistle rings in my ears. Another man's voice replies, "That's not getting fixed. Too bad. That Porsche deserves better."

"Good thing I didn't bring my new Vette down to this dump."

Where am I?

I need to wake up!

"Still think you should have gotten red over the blue, boss," Kiko claims.

The other man grunts. "When you pay for it, you can choose it."

"Suit yourself."

I blink again and attempt to sit up then whimper when pain shoots through my entire body.

"Biagio, she's awake!" Kiko exclaims.

The throbbing agony almost convinces me to stay asleep and not face whatever situation this is, but the voice inside my head tells me not to fall back into the dark abyss. I try harder and keep my eyelids open, letting everything come into focus.

Faded, chipped yellow paint covers the walls. A large window with dusty half-open blinds explains the sunlight. A brown door sits open across from me, and the hallway looks as worn as the room I'm in. Two men study me. One appears a lot older. He's maybe late fifties or early sixties even. The bald spot on his head is shiny, as if he polishes it. Several scars indent his face, and he wears a white tank top. So many tattoos run up his arms and neck, I can't see any skin without ink.

The other man could pass for being in his late thirties. Dark, thick hair fills his head, along with a short goatee. He's in better shape than the older man. He has an arm sleeve tattoo and his designer T-shirt hugs his body, displaying his muscles. They're so big and veiny that he has to be on steroids. Unlike Kiko, he doesn't look like a thug. It's clear he's in charge.

Who are these men?

Panic washes over me. A flashback of me at a conference room table, typing, and warm, muscular arms sliding around my shoulders, pops into my mind. The scent of tonka bean, cedarwood, and geranium briefly filters through my nose. However, almost as soon as it appears, it's gone. The present replaces it. I try to sit up again, but the bald man pushes me down.

"Easy," he orders. I assume he's Kiko, based on his voice.

I freeze, unsure if I should try to fight, even though my body feels like I can barely move it.

Biagio lights a cigarette. The sound of his Zippo flicking makes me wince. Smoke seeps into my airway, and I cough. Sharp pain like nothing I've ever felt before erupts in my lungs.

He steps to the opposite side of the bed and reaches for a metal chair. He pulls it closer, turns it backward, and sits. A few moments drag on as he stares at me, never blinking, keeping his intense gaze on mine. Then he leans closer to me. His stale, cigarette breath flares in my nostrils.

"Wh—" I barely make a sound. I try to swallow the raw feeling in my throat, wincing from the pain.

"I've been waiting a long time for you to wake up," he asserts, then moves his hand toward my face.

I flinch, my breath hitches, and more pain assaults my chest. A tiny whimper escapes my lips.

He holds his hands in the air. "Easy. You've got a few broken ribs, a concussion, and extensive bruising."

"What?" I whisper, confused about how my body is so battered. Several beeps come from the machine next to me, and I glance at it.

He cautiously runs his finger across my forehead, tucking a lock of hair behind my ear, causing me to I cringe. He sees it but doesn't move his hand off me. His lips twitch and he slides his palm over my cheek, holding me firmly. "Did you forget who we are?"

My pulse pounds between my ears. *We? What is he talking about?*

My lack of response answers his question. Instead of disappointment flooding his expression, it's as if he expected my reaction, which only adds to the confusion.

My voice cracks as I claim, "I-I-I don't know you."

He nods, insisting, "You do. In time you'll remember."

"Do you know your name?" Kiko interjects.

I tear my gaze off Biagio, turning toward Kiko. The longer I stare at him, the more horrified I get.

What is my name?

Oh God! Why don't I know my name?

"It's okay, baby. The doctor said there's a good chance it will all come back," Biagio declares.

I snap my face toward him and grimace from more stabs of pain. "What will come back?"

"Your memory," he responds.

My heart pounds harder against my rib cage, creating more horrible sensations. "I lost my memory?"

Biagio glances at Kiko and motions with his head for him to leave the room, ordering, "And shut the door."

Kiko obeys, and once the lock clicks in place, more fear pummels me.

Biagio places both palms on my cheeks. "Everything is going to be okay. I promise."

"Wh-who..." I squeeze my eyes shut, needing hydration like never before.

He grabs a glass of water off the table. "Here, baby. Have a sip." He holds it to my lips.

I drink, relishing the moisture in my mouth and throat.

"Better?" he asks, his dark eyes softer than before.

"Yes. Thank you."

He sits the glass down then picks up my hand. He kisses it then tilts his head, reassessing me.

"Please say something," I beg, unsure what question I should ask first and feeling too foggy to put my anxiety into words.

He takes a deep inhale, strokes my cheek, then answers, "The doctor said you have amnesia."

"What?" I try to sit up again, but he holds his forearm against my neck so I can't move. It freaks me out, but I'm too hurt to fight.

"Pina, stop moving. You need to not make any quick movements, or you could hurt yourself further," he directs.

Pina. My name is Pina.

Is it?

Oh God!

I freeze, blinking hard, but tears fall. *Why can't I remember anything?*

"Listen, baby. You don't need to worry about anything right now," Biagio declares.

"Why can't I remember anything?" I sob.

"Shhh. It's okay. The doctor said it's probably temporary," he reiterates.

"But I... I don't..." I squeeze my eyes shut and try to stop the emotions overpowering me, but I can't. More pain shoots through my ribs as my chest heaves with scared sorrow.

He firmly holds my face in his hands and orders, "Pina, look at me."

I manage to obey.

He asserts, "Everything will be okay. I'm going to take good care of you, just like I always have."

"But I don't remember you," I cry out, and more tears roll over his fingers.

His eyes stay in control. There's no emotion in them, only confidence. It strikes me as odd, but I can't pinpoint why. He replies, "Yes. And one day, you will. In the meantime, I'm going to take care of you. All you need to know is that you love me, and I love you."

Love? How can I love a man I don't remember?

I shake my head, and more hammers pound into my skull.

He holds my face tighter. "Stop moving."

I obey again, unable to fight.

"Good girl," he praises, but it makes me cringe inside. The machine next to me beeps faster, and he arches his eyebrows. "Your IV is empty. I'll send the nurse in to change the bag."

"What is it?" I ask.

He shrugs. "Hydration. Vitamins. Everything you need to make you well enough for me to move you."

Goose bumps break out on my arms. I don't know where I am right now, but something about leaving this room scares me. "Move me?"

He runs his thumb over my lips. " Yes. You don't think we live in this dump, do you?"

My eyes dart to the paint-chipped wall and dusty blinds. I refocus on him.

"Well?" he asks.

"I-I don't know," I admit.

He smiles. "You'll love my place. It's unlike this one."

"Then why am I here? Why aren't I in a hospital?" I interrogate.

His eyes turn to slits. He purses his lips for a moment then chuckles. "That's the Pina I know. Always asking smart questions."

His remark sends a bolt of pride through me. I think, *At least I'm not an idiot.*

He adds, "The doctors and nurses are the best in the country. I can assure you that your medical care has been nothing less than superior. I had to bring you here until the risks were over." The machine beeps again, and he reaches for it and then pushes a button. The loud noise stops.

My agitation grows. "What risks? I don't understand."

A dark storm swirls in his orbs. He snarls, "The Marinos."

"Who are the Marinos?" I ask.

"Our enemy," he fumes. He leans down and pecks me on the lips. The hairs on my neck rise. I turn my head and blink hard.

Biagio moves my face toward him again. Arrogance replaces the anger in his expression. He claims, "I'm your fiancé. Soon enough, you'll be all over me again."

My lips quiver. I whisper, "Fiancé?"

He smiles, but nothing about it comforts me. "Yes. We were starting to work with the wedding coordinator to plan our big day."

"We were?" I ask, unable to recall anything about a wedding.

"Yes," he confirms, then releases me and sits back in his chair. "Any more questions before I send the nurse in?"

I take a few breaths, trying to prioritize my thoughts.

"Pina?"

I blurt out, "How did I get hurt?"

His face darkens so much I can see the evil in it. He seethes, "You were on a motorcycle."

I attempt to remember it, but I can't. I ask, "With you?"

His voice oozes with hatred. He responds, "No. With *him*."

"Him?"

He grinds his molars before replying, "Tristano Marino."

Everything stays blank. I ask, "Who is Tristano Marino? And why was I on his bike if I'm with you?"

His nostrils flare into wide triangles. He grabs my hand and traces his thumb over my knuckles, answering, "He attempted to kidnap you. But don't worry, baby. I stopped him."

A burning sensation fills my belly and climbs up my chest. "Why did he want to kidnap me?"

"Because you're mine," Biagio states.

Maybe I should feel good that this decent-enough-looking man is claiming me as his, but I still don't remember anything. So I stay silent, trying to process all of this. I finally ask, "Is he okay?"

"Why do you care?" Biagio barks.

I jump then wince from the bruises on my back.

"Shit. Sorry," he says in a softer voice, but something tells me he isn't.

I reprimand myself for questioning him when he's my fiancé.

In a controlled tone, Biagio declares, "He's still in the hospital. For now, he's alive. But I guarantee you it won't be for long."

My stomach flips. I can't say why. I don't know this man Tristano who kidnapped me. I shouldn't care about his life after what he did.

Biagio kisses my hand and rises. "I'll send the nurse in to change your IV. As soon as I can bring you home, I will."

Too tired to argue or figure any more of this out, I just reply, "Thank you."

He hesitates then arches his eyebrows. "Any more questions?"

I start to shake my head then stop. "Who are you?"

Pride fills his face. He lifts his head and puffs his chest out. Something about his answer sends chills to my bones, but I have no idea why. He states, "I'm Biagio Abruzzo. Son of Jacopo and next in line to rule the family. And you, Pina dela Cruz, will be queen of the Abruzzos."

1

Tristano Marino

A Few Months Earlier

TENSION FILLS THE AIR, MIXING WITH THE SOUND OF THE waves crashing against the docks. A large container ship blares its horn in the distance. Seagulls caw in the air above us.

Dante scowls at Rubio. "We can't be late on our delivery."

Rubio grinds his molars. His eyes turn into brown slits. He replies, "I can't make the ship arrive any faster. We're lucky the Coast Guard let us through the checkpoint."

A few days ago, our shipment of new gems was supposed to arrive from Africa. Our captain called Rubio and disclosed the Coast Guard had stopped him as soon as he exited international waters and entered US territory.

It wasn't our first rodeo with them, but the men my papà pay are always in charge of the searches. It's now been two days, and we still have no shipment. And even though our captain called an hour ago to inform Rubio the Coast Guard cleared him, the time delay puts us at risk with our buyers.

I interject, "Papà needs to talk to our contact. Why weren't we given any warning there was a new crew?"

Dante's nostrils flare. He inhales deeply, staring at the empty space where the ship will dock.

Rubio states, "I've talked to Julio and assured him we can still deliver."

Dante grinds his molars and spins toward us. He opens his mouth, but his phone rings. He glances at it and answers, "Pina, where are you?"

My ears perk up and my pulse increases. Pina's worked with Dante for years. She's always been hot, but I never really gave her much thought until a few months ago. We were in a meeting at Dante's office. Pina came in wearing hot-pink stilettos and a black pencil skirt suit. When she sat down next to me and crossed her legs, the top of her thigh highs and a garter belt clasp peeked out.

I suddenly wondered why I had never noticed her perfectly shaped calves and thighs before. My dick got so hard, I thought it might break my zipper. The scent of her floral perfume tormented me. It was another thing I had never paid attention to in the past. And then she took off her jacket, displaying her defined arms. When she leaned forward, her tank top gave me a perfect view of enough cleavage to make me obsess all day about what it would be like to see and feel the rest of her breasts.

My blood heated so fast that I got dizzy. How had I always seen Pina as only Dante's assistant? Yet that same question is what's stopped me from making a move even though she's haunting my dreams. Each minute I spend with her only builds the torturous thoughts I can't escape.

Something shifted that day with her, too, or maybe it's my wishful thinking. When she looks at me, a light I've never seen ignites behind her eyes. Every time we're alone, I swear we're flirting.

"We're at dock C," Dante informs her and hangs up.

"Pina's coming here?" I ask, unable to help myself and trying not to appear interested in her.

"Yeah. She has gem documents Papà needs," he replies as one of our drivers pulls up in a black SUV.

As soon as he parks, Dante opens the back door. Pina's sexy calves are the first thing I see. My pulse beats hard against my neck as I silently will Dante to move.

The few seconds feel like minutes until they step away from the vehicle. I reprimand my body for reacting to her, but it's useless. All the confidence God could give a woman he gave to Pina, and it's the sexiest thing I've ever seen.

She's always commanded a room with her air of authority. Dante's her boss, yet she's as fierce as he is, which is probably why she's never left his employment. She doesn't take any crap from him. She negotiates better than New York's top-paid attorneys.

I always respected her. Hell, I even tried to steal her like my other brothers to get her to work as my assistant. No matter what they or I offer her, she's loyal to Dante. It's another reason we all respect her. Yet, since the day she caught the attention of my dick, I've become mesmerized by every smirk, cut-throat conversation, and hard-assed remark she tosses at my brothers and me.

She hands Dante an envelope then pins her golden-brown eyes on mine. She purses her pouty lips then ignores me, tearing her gaze off me and turning to Rubio. "Hey there. Long time no see."

Rubio steps forward and embraces her, kissing her on the cheek. To taunt Dante, he boasts, "Pina, my job offer still stands when you've had enough of this guy."

"Shut up," Dante orders.

"Nah, she'd rather work with me," I proclaim.

Dante points at me. "Trying to steal Pina from me has gotten old. Find your own assistant!"

Pina pats Dante's cheek. "Aw, do we have to review how to keep me happy?"

His scowl deepens. "Don't push me today, Pina."

"Oh! You're in a bad mood already?" she ridicules.

Dante ignores her and motions to my SUV, asking, "Tristano, can you take Pina back to the office? I need to get these documents to Papà."

Adrenaline rushes through my veins. I force myself not to look excited. Giddiness overpowers me, so I don't look at Pina, focusing on Dante. I shrug. "Sure. I don't have a lot going on today."

"Maybe you need a better work ethic so you aren't bored," Pina suggests, batting her eyes at me and grinning.

"Just because I know how to delegate doesn't mean I don't have a good work ethic," I declare.

She tilts her head, arching her eyebrows. "Does it?"

"See, these are the things I could teach you if you worked for me instead of Dante," I claim.

Dante groans. "I'm leaving. Pina, when you get to the office, I need you to alert the drivers we're close."

She gives him a little salute. "On it."

He grumbles something incoherent under his breath then gets in his SUV. It leaves the docks, and I tell Rubio, "Notify me once the shipment arrives and you've reviewed it all."

"Done," he replies.

"Ready?" I ask Pina, walking to the SUV and holding the door open.

The twinkle in her eye ignites. She licks her plump lips, punishing me further. Her floral perfume flares in my nostrils as she slides past me and onto the leather seat.

I get in and shut the door, trying not to stare as she slowly crosses then uncrosses her legs.

"Eyes up here," she chirps, catching me ogling her.

"Is there something you're insinuating?" I bait her, teetering close to crossing a line I know I shouldn't. Dante will kill me if I make a move on Pina.

She glances at my strained zipper then pins her orbs on me, challenging, "What would that be?"

Unable to resist, I lean closer, inhaling her perfume and stepping over the line I shouldn't. I murmur, "I think you have some cougar wishes."

She scoffs and turns her head so her face is inches from mine. "Cougar? I'm only two years older than you."

I glance at her lips, wondering what it would be like to kiss her. I add, "Still makes you a cougar."

She drags two fingers from the top of my head down to my jaw. Tingles burst under her touch. I freeze as she bats her eyes and smiles, declaring, "I'd have to fuck you to be your cougar."

All restraint to not cross any more lines flies out the window. I ask, "My place or yours?"

Pina smirks, and two indents pop out on her cheeks. I hold in my groan, damning those dimples that I can't get off my mind. She moves so close our breaths merge. Mint mixes with her floral scent. She lowers her voice, sliding her hand on my inner thigh and stopping an inch from my groin. "I doubt you can handle what I'm into."

I grunt. "Highly doubt it. The only one who'll be unable to handle anything is you."

"That so?"

"Guarantee it," I claim.

She tilts her head and combs her fingers over the side of my head. They graze my ear, and I barely resist shuddering.

What is it about this woman?

This is a very bad idea. Dante's going to be pissed.

Fuck him.

Her lips brush mine as she states, "Tell you what. I'll make you a deal since you can't seem to stop flirting with me."

"I think it's you who can't stop flirting with me," I claim.

"You want to fight about this or know the deal?" she asks.

Don't do it. Stop this conversation now before you do something you regret.

"Spill it," I order.

She traces my bottom lip. In the most seductive voice I've ever heard, she challenges, "You come to my place tonight. I call the shots."

I tap my fingers on the outside of my thigh. I try not to appear too excited about the invite to her place while quieting my conscience.

"Scared?" she taunts.

I fist her hair and tug her head back. She sharply inhales, and I hold my face over hers. The gold in her eyes swirls faster against the brown. She swallows hard, and her breath hitches.

I wait several moments, carefully watching her expression. She opens her mouth to speak, and I lean closer, stating, "I'm the only one who calls the shots, Pina."

She freezes then slowly shakes her head. "Then I guess you aren't coming over. I knew you couldn't handle it."

I pause again, debating how to work my way around her ultimatum. She says, "I'm not one of your—"

I shut her up with my lips, sliding my tongue in her mouth so fast she gasps. Her palms press against my chest as if to push me away, but she doesn't. It only takes a few flicks of my tongue around hers before she glides her hands around my head and laces her fingers in my hair.

A path of fiery adrenaline explodes in my cells. Her minty tongue swipes against mine in circles then darts in and out of my mouth. Her body curves into mine, pressing tighter to me until there's no room between us.

I flip her over me, moving her pencil skirt to her hips and tugging her knees until they touch the leather seat. I continue kissing her while moving my hands past her garter until I get to her hot pussy.

I groan. "You fucking dirty girl." She's wearing crotchless panties. I trace the edge of them, not passing the barrier even though I'm dying to do everything explicit with her.

"I'm not a girl. I'm a woman," she mumbles between my lips, then lifts her hips and grinds on my erection.

I palm her ass and slide my other hand in her hair, tugging her slightly from my lips, goading, "Then stop being a tease and acting like a schoolgirl. I'll redirect my driver to your place."

Her lips twitch. "You haven't agreed to my terms. Only real men can handle it."

I scoff. "Real men? Please." I return to kissing her.

She pushes her palms against my chest and retreats, asking, "What are you scared of, then?"

"I'm not scared of anything."

"Then agree I'm in charge. You drop me off at the office, and I'll send you my address."

I snort. "I already know your address."

"No, you don't," she claims.

I arch my eyebrows. "Oh? Did you recently move and not tell Dante?"

"One, no, I didn't move. Two, do you think Dante tells you everything? Three, I don't have to disclose anything about my personal life to him," she insists.

I slide my hand up the back of her shirt, amazed by her smooth skin. I arrogantly state, "Well, I know where you live."

"I said come to my place, not my house," she points out, giving me an equally cocky expression to match my own.

"That makes zero sense," I reply, then try to kiss her again, but she resists.

She taps my head and says, "Think with the right head."

"Any head of mine is the right one," I claim.

She rolls her eyes. "Spoken like a true Marino."

"Did you expect anything less?" I question, then drag my knuckles down her cheek and neck. I get to her shirt and release a button. "Oops."

She scoots closer to me, gets up on her knees, and jerks my head until her face is over mine. Zings fly down my spine, surprising me. It's a dominant move that no woman's ever attempted on me before. I squeeze her ass harder, and she pecks me on the lips, then coos, "Are you afraid of me, Tristano?"

I mumble, "You do realize who you're talking to, right?"

She pouts her lips, making my cock throb against her heat. She doesn't miss it, and her lips curve into a smile. In that same seductive voice, she traces my nose, whining, "Don't you want to see my place?"

"The place you don't live in?"

"Yes."

My curiosity is piqued. "You have rental properties or something?"

She tries to stop her smile. "Something like that."

"Meaning?"

"Agree to my terms, and you'll see," she states, then leans to my ear, whispering, "Dante and your other brothers will never know."

Her statement only adds more fuel to our fire. This burning obsession with her I can't deny anymore. I'm also interested in seeing whatever this "place" is where she wants to meet.

Maybe it's because my brothers know nothing about it.

Perhaps it's only due to the fact it's something personal with her.

It may be a combination of both. Whatever the reason, my thoughts turn to mush when she claims, "I promise to take really good care of you."

Fuck it. What's the worst that can happen if I give her some power for whatever her game is she wants to play?

Yes, Pina. Take care of me all night long!

"Okay. But when you're done with whatever it is, I'm in charge."

She tilts her head, squinting her eyes. "Mmm..."

This time, I challenge her. "You don't think you can handle it?"

She huffs. "Of course I can."

"Then why the hesitation? Let's go to your secret place. In fact, let's go now," I suggest.

She laughs. "It's two in the afternoon."

"So?"

"I have a job to do," she claims.

"Tell Dante you're sick. I'm sure he can handle whatever is going on today," I order.

She pushes off me until her ass is on my knees. "I take my job seriously."

"Yes, Pina. We all know," I mock.

She swats my shoulder with the back of her hand. "If you think this situation between us means I'm going to take orders from you and shirk my duties, you're wrong."

I wiggle my eyebrows, teasing, "By situation, you mean this deep desire you have to get naked with me?" I tug her back toward me and suck on her lobe, then add, "Or the fact you're dying to slide your wet little pussy over my cock?" I nibble on her collarbone, and she whimpers.

She clears her throat and pushes away again. Locking eyes with me, she demands, "I mean it, Tristano. Dante and your other brothers are to never know about this. And no one—I mean no one—is to know about my place."

"Pina, do you really believe I'll run to Dante and tell him about this? Give me some credit," I assert, a tad pissed she would even question my discretion. I'm not stupid. Dante would go ballistic, and she's an itch I need to scratch. Once we do this, we can both move on with our lives.

"Marinos talk," she declares.

I freeze. "Have you lost your mind? Marinos do *not* talk."

Arrogance fills her expression. She crosses her arms, claiming, "I know more personal secrets about your family than anyone."

"Bullshit. You know confidential things because of work," I insist.

She shakes her head, firmly claiming, "No. I know lots of personal things. Even about you."

"What are you talking about?" I ask.

She untucks a lock of her hair and runs her hand through it. Then she raises her chin. In her kick-ass, confident tone, she attests, "I know a lot, Tristano. And there's no way I'm telling you everything, so believe me or don't. All I'll say is Dante trusts me with a lot of information, and not just business."

"Bullshit," I retort, unable to imagine my brother disclosing anything personal to anyone. He's the future head of our family and more tight-lipped than any of us.

She rolls her eyes and tries to get off me. "Whatever. Believe what you want."

I yank her back on my lap, circling my arms around her so she can't move.

"Tristano!"

"Don't get your pants—well, what little there is of them—in a tizzy," I taunt.

She stays silent, giving me the evil eye. "If you think you're going to boss me around like your brother does, you're wrong."

"Oh, Pina, Pina, Pina." I drag my finger down her neck. "You'll soon find out I'm nothing like my brother, but you'll enjoy taking orders from me."

She opens her mouth and then snaps it shut. She takes several deep breaths.

"What? Nothing to reply?" I goad.

The driver's door slams shut. Pina pushes away from me and slides on the leather. She straightens her skirt and fastens the button of her shirt.

I lean into her, stating, "Last chance to play hooky and make a run for it."

My driver opens the door. I almost curse him and make a note to tell him never to open the door again until I give him a knock.

Pina sits straighter and motions for me to get out.

I groan inside, wondering if I missed my opportunity. I sniff hard and tell her, "Make sure you text me the address." I get out and reach in to help her out.

She refuses to take my hand and shoves past me. "Forget I said anything. Nice seeing you, Tristano. Have a nice night." She smirks and struts away.

I watch her ass until I can't see it anymore, resisting the urge to run after her. I get back in the SUV then text her.

Me: *Address?*

Pina: *Do you agree to my terms?*

The thought of letting Pina be in charge goes against all my instincts. I'm a Marino man. We're the ones in charge. But if this is the only way I'm going to get in her pants and end this obsession with her, I'll set my normal requirements aside...for now.

Me: *I'll agree to your terms, but when we're done, I'm in charge. Understand?*

A few moments pass, making me feel like I might break out into a sweat. She finally answers.

Pina: *I'll send you the address if I'm not too busy tonight.*

Me: *Seriously? Stop playing games. What's the address?*

I wait for a response, but hours pass. When I get home, I pace my wing, cursing myself over and over for blowing my chance.

Nothing I do gets her off my mind. I throw myself into some work tasks then work out and shower. At eight, I pour myself a beer and check my text messages for the millionth time.

My gut drops. There's nothing from her.

Massimo walks into my suite. "We've got an issue at the club. Let's go."

I sigh. The sex club all the crime families belong to has become more of a pain in the ass than the fun it used to be. "Take someone else," I grumble, then finish my beer.

"I don't have time for this. Let's go," he barks.

I begrudgingly get up and follow him, but I barely hear what he says on the way to the club. All I can think of is how to find out where Pina's place is and scratch our itch.

2

Pina

"I NEED TO GO HOME," I TELL MY FRIEND CHANEL.

"What? We've only been here an hour," she points out.

I empty the remainder of my champagne flute and glance over the rail at the high-end sex club. It's the same scene as always.

People range from fully clothed to wearing nothing. More women are naked than men, which isn't new, either. It's rare any man, unless they're a bartender or janitor, is in this club and not connected to some crime family. It's the one place in New York enemies coexist.

Loud music blares out of the highest quality surround sound. The dance floor ranges from scenes you'd see in any ordinary club to couples having sex. At least a dozen people engage in an orgy in the middle of the floor.

Beds, tables, and sitting areas fill the remainder of the first floor. Anything on the dance floor feels tame to some of the BDSM scenes taking place.

"Pina, I'm not ready to go yet. Don't leave me here on my own," Chanel begs, giving me her green-eyed puppy dog look.

Normally, I'd do what I want and have a good time. Years ago, Dante needed me to bring him a gem. Rubio had an emergency to take care of, and I was the only one Dante trusted. Everything about the club was a new experience for me. Once I stepped into it, all the drunk admissions Dante made to me while pining for Bridget made sense. Every gap in Dante's blubbering got filled in.

Seeing the club firsthand only made me want to understand more of it. That night, Dante told me to leave, but I didn't. I got mesmerized by the first-floor activities, and while I didn't do anything that night, I couldn't help but come back.

When Dante found out, he lectured me, telling me how dangerous it could be since all the families were there. He explained the agreements they had to coexist in the club and the rules they had to follow.

Yet, even though he forbade me to return, I couldn't get it out of my mind. So I went back several times. The third night, Dante caught me. But there was nothing he could do. I was in his world, and he put me there. Whenever he'd try to lecture me, I'd ask him if he wanted me to quit, knowing he'd have a hard time if I left him. I had one goal when he hired me, and that was to make myself irreplaceable.

I grew up in the Bronx. My father is a Mexican immigrant. My mother is a second-generation Filipino. Everything about their relationship was taboo, especially in my mother's culture.

When they married, they had no help from either family. To say I grew up on the struggle bus is an understatement. We were poor, constantly moving due to landlords evicting us, and sometimes went days without food. My parents did the best they could, yet there was hardly enough for my four siblings and me. When my oldest brother turned thirteen, my father's friend hired him to run errands. He gave my parents everything he earned, but it didn't make a difference.

My mother pushed us to study hard and get an education. I did well in school, but college was out of the question. We were trying to survive. Still, I vowed to get myself out of poverty. When I was eighteen, I met Dante. He was in his early twenties and interviewed me for his assistant position. No one had lasted more than a few months with him, making me want to succeed more.

I worked for him for over a decade before the night he needed me to deliver the gem to the club. By then, I was making well over six figures a year, getting large bonuses almost equal to it, and loving every second of my job.

So even though Dante kept forbidding me to return to the club, my threat to quit always hung in the air. One day, we got into a huge argument over it. I had gone to the club on and off for a few months, each time resulting in a more heated discussion. When Dante got in my face, I told him I was done and tossed my office keys at him.

He tried to tell me I was bluffing, but I wasn't. I had saved a substantial amount of cash, invested in rentals all over New York City, and didn't need Dante's employment. I was there because I enjoyed what I did. I loved every aspect of the danger I knew I surrounded myself in, even though I had an office job. Plus, I could have gone to any of the Marino brothers and worked for them. They had offered me numerous times to leave Dante, but loyalty is important to me. Yet so was my freedom to be an independent woman and do what I wanted.

When I didn't show up for work, Dante started calling. After two days, he came pounding on my condo door and caved. He gave me a list of suites and people I was to stay away from, and since then, I come and go as I please.

People have always fascinated me, but the night I stepped into the club was the beginning of a whole new world. The danger of working for Dante had long since faded. The Marinos were no longer scary. I was taken under their wing and belonged to their family. So being in the presence of so many dangerous men who weren't them created a new high. And every time I denied a request to join a powerful man in his VIP suite or a private room, my adrenaline spiked.

Plus, I learned there was more to sex than what I had experienced before. Submission and dominance loomed all over the club. Once I saw the power exchange between two people, it fed desires I never knew I had.

At first, I didn't understand what drew me to it. My confusion grew to the point I sought out a sex therapist so I could understand my obsession with digging into different BDSM activities. Through our sessions, she encouraged me to act on them, but I knew it wouldn't be easy in the club.

I wanted to dominate these dangerous men—I still do. Most will never allow it. Maybe working for Dante for so long gives me the urge to exert power over them. Perhaps it's my need to be in control since everything felt out of control when I was a child. And it might be a mix of the two. Regardless of the root cause, when I'm in the dungeon with the shades drawn, and it's only whatever man I've found who agrees to submit to me, I get a high so potent, it could compete with the strongest of drugs.

In some ways, I get as much from not having sex as I do from it. More often than not, I come to the club and don't do anything besides have fun with Chanel. We have some drinks, dance, and flirt with different men. Sometimes I go into the dungeon and watch. I don't get off on it as Chanel does, so I wouldn't consider myself into voyeurism. I watch to find new techniques or learn how to push my subs to new limits without going too far.

Normally, I'm fascinated with the club and I don't leave until five or six in the morning. But lately, my obsession has shifted.

A few months ago, I sat in a meeting and saw Tristano's interest in me. I'd known him for years and not once had we ever flirted.

He's always been Dante's youngest brother, a couple years younger than me, and in my off-limits box. Sure, from their chiseled faces to ripped boxing bodies, the Marino brothers are all sexy as sin. But I don't play in the sandbox where I work. My career is too important to me, and I wanted to always know I got where I'm at from my abilities to do my job and not by sleeping with the boss.

While Dante is technically my boss and not his brothers, it was too close to home. They all call upon my abilities to help them out at times. Then they always reward me with more money than I could ever anticipate, and I would never want to mess that up.

So when Tristano's gaze lit up, lingering on my legs, cleavage, then my eyes, zings flew to my core. It was the same feeling I always got whenever I zeroed in on a new sub. Since that day, all I can think about is getting him into the dungeon but not the one at the club. I want him restrained and at my mercy in my private one.

While I maintain privacy at the club, never letting anyone watch, I had an itch to build my own a year ago. One of my properties had a tenant moving out. I thought it was best to build it there so whoever I invited over wouldn't know where I lived.

I've never used it. All my activities are still at the club, and I wasn't sure why I held off. Then Tristano looked at me. It was the same hungry expression he directed at other women at the club.

And that's another issue. I know more about the Marino men and their conquests than anyone. I've seen every one of the brothers in action, including Tristano, whether it's a woman giving them a blowjob in their suite or their activities in the dungeon.

I know Tristano's always been a Dom. He's one of the best I've watched. He stays emotionally connected to his sub, and it's fascinating. So his ability to submit probably doesn't exist. Yet, I can't get the itch to dominate him out of my mind.

Since earlier today, when we had our make-out session in the SUV, it's only bugging me further. Besides reprimanding myself for crossing the line with him, I can't stop the urge from intensifying. Kissing Tristano was like another new surge of power. Maybe it's because we're both into dominating, but it's as if we were both challenging each other. I've never felt anything like it. And my desire to win at whatever game we were playing was like a shot of heroin. I'm chasing that high tonight, trying to find it, but everywhere I look is a dead end. No one even seems worth my time.

"Let's go into dungeon three. That new girl Roy brought just went in there with him," Chanel states, her hand gripping the rail so tight her knuckles turn white.

Voyeurism is her thing. When she finds a show she wants to watch, she always has to squeeze something. It's like she's trying to regulate herself in some way. She's Massimo's flight attendant, and we hit it off a long time ago. When I saw her at the club a few years back, our friendship grew stronger.

Normally, I'd have no problem going into the viewing room with her. Roy's a good Dom, and I normally learn new tricks from him. Plus, the girl he brought looks as alpha as they come, so I'd normally be interested in how well she'll submit. But everything feels off tonight.

I shake my head. "I'm going to go—" My mouth turns dry, and my heartbeat races as Tristano and Massimo step out of the elevator.

The look in their eyes tells me something is off. They aren't here to have fun. They're here on business even though it's against one of the club's rules.

Massimo steps in front of him and goes into a suite. I'm only on floor two, which isn't where the Marinos typically hang out. Their main suite is on a higher floor.

Tristano's scowl shifts toward me, and he freezes outside the door. His black designer T-shirt hugs his impeccable shoulders and chest. The bulge of his biceps strains the fabric, and all I can think about is what it felt like to straddle him.

My pulse shoots through the roof. He tears his eyes off me, pulls his phone out of his pants, and swipes his screen. His fingers move fast, and as soon as he shoves it back in his pocket, my phone vibrates.

I remove it from my pocket and read the text message.

Tristano: *I have to take care of something. Give me your address. Let's get out of here.*

My flutters take off, but I'm not diving further into Pandora's box unless I'm getting my way. I look up, but he's already inside the suite.

Me: *You didn't tell me you understand I'm in charge.*

Tristano: *Fine. We'll play your game. Then I get to play mine. Address?*

A mixture of excitement and nerves fills me. I've never let anyone dominate me and shouldn't agree. I won't like it. I debate what to do.

"Why did Tristano just pause outside the suite and text you?" Chanel interrogates.

I lift my chin, lying, "Work crap."

Chanel assesses me.

I square my shoulders. "Listen, I have to go."

"Seriously? You're going to bail?" Chanel whines.

I hug her, claiming, "I'll make it up to you. Sorry! I have a lot of stuff going on for work."

She huffs. "On a Friday night?"

"Hey, you work for the Marinos, too. You know how they are," I state.

She rolls her eyes. "Fine. Call me if you want to hang out tomorrow night."

"Will do. Thanks. Stay safe." I hug her again.

"I will. I'm a Marino employee, remember? There's an invisible warning on my forehead," she claims, which isn't totally untrue. I feel it a lot, too, but it's okay. I suppose it does keep Chanel and me safe.

I beeline toward the elevator then text my driver. It's Dante's employee, but I negotiated it into my contract within a few years of employment with him.

I step into the elevator and the doors shut. Too many thoughts race through my head.

What am I doing?

I need to stop this before it begins.

Tristano Marino at my mercy. Oh God!

He's going to want to dominate me after.

I'll get out of it. I'll make another deal with him when he arrives.

The elevator stops on the main floor and the doors open. I step out and try to make my way through the crowded space. Several people I know see me. They all try to converse, but I ignore them, focusing on the exit.

I get to the coat check, wait in line, and curse myself for wearing a jacket while still debating if I should send Tristano my address. I'm lost in thought when a large hand palms my ass. Vanilla musk overpowers the air. The hairs on the back of my neck rise, and I spin.

Biagio Abruzzo, the man next in line to rule the Abruzzo throne, leers down at me. If I didn't know what was in his DNA, I'd think he was decent looking, but he's shot up too many steroids. His size isn't anything a human being can achieve without them.

Any enemy of the Marinos is one of mine. The only time I ever see Biagio is in the club. He's always hitting on me, but I try to stay as far away from him as possible.

He steps into my personal space. "Why are you in this line? I don't see a coat to drop off."

"Don't ever touch my ass again," I warn.

"Or what?" he challenges.

I push him away, but he's like a tank and doesn't move. "You know the club rules," I reply, instead of telling him, I'll make sure Dante ends his life.

His lips curl, and he leans into my ear. Stale whiskey and cigarette breath flare in my nostrils. He declares, "I think it's time you stop playing hard to get."

I step back and into another large frame.

"Pina, what's going on?" Rubio's voice barks.

Biagio doesn't retreat, but Rubio pulls me behind him, next to the woman he brought to the club. Her eyes widen, and I motion for her to move forward in the line. I don't know who this woman is, but she needs to learn that you get out of the way when a Marino and Abruzzo face off.

Two of Rubio's friends step forward just as three of Biagio's guys do the same. My gut drops, and I pull out my phone to text Tristano there's trouble, but Dante and Gianni turn the corner. I didn't know they were here, but their eyes turn to slits, and they rush toward us.

Dante pushes me farther back and then steps next to Rubio. He asks, "What's going on?"

"Seems like Biagio can't keep his hands off Pina," Rubio snarls.

"Gentlemen, is there a problem?" Sergio questions. He's the head bouncer who makes sure the rules get enforced. He also reports any club issues to the heads of the families.

The tension doesn't cease. Dante and Biagio lock eyes, each challenging the other.

"Answer me," Sergio snaps.

Biagio finally breaks. He sniffs hard and turns toward Sergio. "No, man. We're just having a friendly conversation, aren't we?" He arches his eyebrows at Dante.

Sergio steps closer. "Do I need to suspend you?"

Gianni interjects, "No. We're good. Like he said, we're just having a friendly conversation."

"Sure you are," Sergio says.

"All good," Biagio repeats, then pats him on the back.

"Suites only tonight. If I catch any of you outside, you're out of here. Don't test me," Sergio warns.

"Fine. See you later," Biagio states, then checks me out again.

Gianni puts his hand on Dante's shoulder and mumbles, "Easy."

Sergio uses his walkie-talkie and orders, "Escort Mr. Abruzzo and his guests to his VIP suite."

"Yes, sir," comes through the speaker.

Dante spins. "You all right?"

"Yes. I'm leaving. Can you get me my jacket?" I ask and hand him my ticket.

He studies me. "You sure?"

"Yep. Jacket, please?" I smile, just wanting to get out of here.

Dante squeezes my arm and goes to the front of the line. He quickly returns with my jacket and walks me outside, adding, "Pina, this is why I don't like you coming here."

"Don't start. It's a one-off thing, and I'm fine," I insist.

My driver pulls up to the curb. Dante sighs loudly then opens the door.

"Thanks. See you Monday," I say, then slide onto the seat.

When he shuts the door, I close my eyes and lean back against the headrest. The SUV begins to move, and I wait until my heartbeat is normal again.

I open my eyes, and the driver turns toward my home. I put the divider glass down and instruct, "I'm going to my other place on Riverside."

"Yes, ma'am," he says, then gets in the left-hand lane to circle back.

Several more minutes of debate fill my head, but my phone vibrates. I glance at the screen.

Tristano: *Dante just told me what happened. Are you okay?*

Me: *Yes, I'm fine.*

Tristano: *I'm done here. Address?*

More butterflies take off. I swallow hard.

Tristano: *I agreed to your terms. Address?*

I can't do this.

I need this.

I take a deep breath and jump all the way into Pandora's box.

3

Tristano

"Where are you going?" Massimo inquires.

"None of your business," I reply, downing my sambuca shot and passing him. I avoid my other brother's questioning stare. I don't stop, yanking the door to the stairwell open and taking two steps at a time. At the bottom, I push the fire exit door open and breathe in the cold, fresh air.

My driver, Flex, pulls up. It's a nickname I gave him in high school. He was always lecturing me about stretching after a hard weight lifting session. His father works for Papà, and I've known him forever. We've been friends for as long as I can remember, and he acts as my driver and bodyguard at times. If I had to put my life into anyone's hands besides my brothers', it would be Flex.

I hop in the SUV. I give him the Manhattan address Pina texted me then order, "No one is to know this address. Understand?"

He glances at me through the rearview mirror, locking his cold killer's eyes to mine. "Done. Anything I need to prepare for?"

"No. It's a personal issue," I answer.

"You got it." He refocuses on the road, veers out of the alley, and then turns down several side streets. We get to the main road and he accelerates.

I sit back in my seat, tapping my fingers on my thighs. The New York buildings become a blur against the darkness of the night. The closer I get to Manhattan, the more nervous I become. I've never agreed to let anyone take charge before. And I can't deny my curiosity also has the best of me. Pina's always been the strongest woman I know. She's intelligent, doesn't let anyone, including my brothers or me, intimidate her, and has the confidence of a *Fortune* 500 company CEO.

I shouldn't be surprised she has other real estate besides the condo she lives in, but Manhattan isn't a cheap place. It's always been a hot market with high rents and sale prices. The fact she's kept it hidden from Dante and the rest of us surprises me. So my interest in Pina only grows. I want to know more about what she invests in almost as much as I want to know what she plans on doing with me.

Flex pulls up to the front of the building. I glance at the text message Pina sent shortly after the address.

Pina: *I'll leave your name with the security guard. You'll need to show your license.*

I shove my hand in my pocket to double-check my wallet is on me. I have my own place in Manhattan. It's where I crash when I need to stay in the city or just get away from my family for a few days. So I tell Flex, "Go stay at my place on 59th. I'll text you in the morning when I'm ready for you to come get me."

"Have fun," he replies, his wicked grin forming. He holds his fist out, and I chuckle and bump it.

"You, too," I say. One of the things I appreciate about Flex is he understands he's on my payroll, but we've never lost our friendship. He's dropped me off at too many women's places over the years and knows the drill. My personal nights when he's to stay at my place and get me in the morning means he's on call if I need a ride sooner, but that's rarely the case. My night off means he usually gets one, too, and Flex has a handful of women who'll drop anything to be at his beck and call.

"Done, bro," he claims as I shut the door.

I fill my lungs with the crisp air then head into the building. The doorman holds the door open, and I hand my identification to the guard at the desk.

The guard studies my card then scans it and states, "Thank you, Mr. Marino. Here's the elevator key. Please return it when you leave. It only has access once to Ms. dela Cruz's and one elevator ride to this level."

While I know this is a night to scratch my itch and not something long term, it irritates me Pina is making it clear that she's on the same page as me.

It shouldn't. I should be grateful she's not wanting to sink her hooks into me for a relationship. Anything close to it would create a lot of issues with Dante. The rest of my family wouldn't be happy, either. Yet, I can't shake the slight annoyance balling in my gut.

I grab the plastic card and nod. I take ten steps, push the elevator button, and then slide the key into the slot. When the light turns green, I hesitate before hitting button thirteen.

Lucky thirteen, runs through my mind, and I hold in my groan. Since I was a kid, I've always considered seven and thirteen to be unlucky. My mamma died at 7:13 p.m. Arianna was abducted on the thirteenth day of the month. Too many other things happened in relation to those numbers in my life. So call me superstitious, but I'd normally avoid floors seven and thirteen at all costs.

As the elevator rises, I watch the numbers light up. My pulse increases, and I'm unsure if it's about the thirteenth floor or the anticipation of my upcoming night with Pina.

The elevator stops then dings as the doors open. I step into the hallway, glance at the numbers on the wall, and turn right. I go to the end of the hall and stand in front of her door. Flutters fill my stomach, and I wipe my hands on my jeans. I ring the bell and wait, tapping my fingers on my thigh.

Time seems to stand still. The door finally opens, and her floral scent mixes with others I can't pinpoint. Candlelight flickers and sexy music plays in the background. My heart races so fast that I hold my breath.

Pina's wearing a gold leather negligee with matching six-inch stilettos. A brown leather choker with different metallic spikes adorns her neck. Black fishnets connect to a garter belt. Her brown hair is in a sleek ponytail. Her pouty lips are a deep maroon, and her cheeks are perfectly contoured. Blingy eyeshadow matches the sparkle in her eyes.

She takes a sip of champagne from a crystal flute and steps back. Raising her chin, she asks, "Are you coming in?"

"Shit. Sorry." I step inside and shut the door then allow my eyes to dart all over her body. I lick my lips, trying to ignore the raging hard-on pressing against my zipper.

"See something you like?" She smirks.

I swallow hard, tear my eyes off her cleavage, then lock eyes with her. "Fuck, you're hotter than I imagined."

She stays composed, taking another sip while keeping her brown orbs on mine. She orders, "Down the hall, door to the left. Leave your clothes here."

I chuckle, partly out of nerves. "Nothing like getting straight to the point."

"Sorry. Did you need a drink first?" She tilts her head and bats her eyes at me.

I puff out my chest and kick off my shoes. I drop my pants and underwear. The clang of my belt echoes in the air. I step out of them and tug off my T-shirt, arrogantly tossing her statement back at her, "You like what you see?"

Her lips curl as she drags her eyes down my body. They pause when she gets to my groin.

I use it to my advantage, closing the distance between us and circling my arm around her waist. I tug her into me and pull her ponytail so my face is over hers.

She gasps, and her eyes light up.

I glance at her mouth then say, "Is that any way to greet me?"

Her tongue darts between her lips then quickly disappears. "Did you forget I'm in charge?"

"I think you and I both know that isn't really what you want," I state, then kiss her, sliding my tongue in her mouth.

She freezes for a moment, but I don't let her move away from me. Her palms glide up my chest. She grips the back of my head, kissing me back until her knees weaken and my arm is the only thing holding her up.

Everything I felt in the SUV earlier today comes rushing back, yet it also feels more intense. It's like she took a match, lit me up, and I can't put out the flame. My blood runs hotter. I take several steps, moving her to the wall, palming her ass and picking her up.

Her legs wrap around my waist. She mumbles, "Tristano," then returns to kissing me.

The heat from her pussy makes my dick pulse. I lose all sense of control and yank her panties to the side, gliding into her until my pelvis hits her hips.

"Oh God!" she cries out.

"Fuck, you're tight," I groan. I retreat then slide back inside her, creating a slow thrusting pattern. She follows my lead, circling her hips in perfect unison.

"I-I'm in charge," she whimpers and digs her nails into my shoulders.

I lean into her ear, taunting, "Are you? It feels like I am. You want me to stop?" As soon as the words come out of my mouth, I regret them. If she tells me to stop, I'll have to, and everything about her feels like an awakening. Maybe it's because I've known her forever and now obsess over her. I'm unsure if that's it, but whatever the reason, everything about this moment feels different than other women I've dominated.

Yet, I also know Pina well. She isn't one to not get her own way. But neither am I. So, I increase the speed of my thrusts, sucking on her collarbone, trying to give her every reason not to tell me to stop.

Her clenched jaw and hot exhale tease my cheek, sending fresh endorphins through my bones. I scrape my teeth down her neck and slow my thrusts so I don't release too fast. She stays silent except for an occasional moan.

Something in me wants to display my power over her. Whenever I see her, she's the one calling the shots. An urgency to make her submit further takes hold. I grab her throat, tilting her face toward the ceiling, and suck on her lobe before locking eyes with her. "You'll call me Sir. Now, tell me to keep going."

Defiance fills her expression.

I slide my hand between us and circle her clit.

"Oh!" she breathes, closing her eyes.

"Say it, or I'm stopping," I threaten, moving my thumb faster.

Her lips tremble and her breath merges with mine. Her voice cracks as she begs, "Don't stop."

"Please don't stop, Sir," I bark, thrusting harder and working her clit slower.

"Tristano!" she cries out.

"Say it," I demand again, squeezing her throat, then kissing her with everything I've got.

Her glistening body shakes against mine. Her hard nipples press into my chest.

Speeding back up, I bark, "Say it!"

"Please don't stop!"

"Sir!" I remind her.

"Trist—"

"I'm stopping in two seconds, Pina," I warn and hate the thought of it but need her submission like nothing I've ever wanted before.

She finally caves, blurting out, "Sir! Please!"

Satisfaction explodes in me. My testosterone flares and I have to push her further. I edge her back up and stop myself from letting her fly over the cliff. I command, "How long have you wanted me to play with your pussy?"

"Please," she whispers. Her legs tremble harder.

"How long, Pina?" I bark.

"Tris—"

"Sir," I remind her.

She squeezes her eyes shut then tries to circle her hips faster on my hand.

I pull it away from her and shove my thumb in her mouth. "Suck."

She obeys, giving me another wave of satisfaction.

I keep my other hand positioned on her neck and lean into her ear. "I'm removing my thumb and giving you one last chance, baby girl. Tell me how long you've thought about me making you feel like this, and I'll give you what you want. You don't, and I'm leaving." I slide my thumb back to her clit and release her neck, adding, "Decide! Three. Two. O—"

"Since that day in the office," she admits, then buries her face in the crook of my neck.

I tug her head back, locking eyes with her. "You look at me when you come." I speed up everything, pressing and circling my thumb faster and thrusting as deep as possible.

I barely hear her say, "Tristano," as her golden-brown eyes roll toward the back of her head. The walls of her pussy spasm, clenching me like a vise. Every inch of her body shakes, sending my ego higher.

I growl, "Who controls your pussy?"

She moans louder.

"Tell me," I demand, sliding my hand out from between us and gripping her neck again. Then I slow down my thrusts.

"Don't stop," she pleads.

"Your pussy! Who controls it?" I repeat, doing everything I can not to release inside her. I press my lips to hers.

She urgently darts her tongue into my mouth.

I retreat, keeping my lips an inch from hers. I want her full submission, and it includes this. In a firm tone, I order, "Tell me."

"You do," she squeaks.

"Say it again and call me Sir," I demand.

She hesitates, her eyes watering.

"Pina—"

A tear rolls down her cheek. "You do, Sir!"

I kiss her tear and move my hands to her ass. Stepping away from the wall, I kiss her while carrying her to the bedroom. I flip her on her stomach and order, "Lie flat and don't move. If you do, I'll tie you up and leave until tomorrow morning."

She obeys, and every dominant part of my soul sings louder. I wait a moment at the door, making sure she doesn't move. Then I go to the other room, grab my pants, and remove my knife from the pocket. I return to the bedroom and cage my body over hers. I kiss her neck and murmur, "Stay still, or you'll get hurt."

I could just unzip her leather outfit, but everything in me wants to keep displaying that I'm the boss in this situation. In one fluid move, I slash the back of the gold leather then toss my knife on the floor. I push the material to both sides of her body until it rests on the bed then force her legs apart.

She turns her face toward me, the spark in her eyes brighter than I've ever seen.

"Face toward the headboard, hands pressed against it," I demand.

She hesitates.

I add, "Or I can leave."

She exhales a deep breath then presses her palms against the brown suede. Her tongue swipes across her mouth, and she turns her head as instructed.

I leap over her, nudging her legs wider, then pressing my skin to hers. Her floral perfume flares in my nostrils, and I breathe deeper. The tip of my cock teases her wet heat, and I kiss the back of her neck, deciding there's no way this is a onetime event. She's more perfect than I anticipated. This isn't an itch that can quickly get resolved. I'm going to have her past tonight. I state, "I require your full submission. Not just tonight but going forward. Do you understand me?"

She tries to look at me.

I hold her head in the forward position, asserting, "When I order you to do something, you do it. And I never permitted you to move, did I?"

The sound of her short breaths gets louder.

I push, "Answer me. Did I permit you?"

She replies, "No."

"Then you're ready to submit fully?" I question.

She closes her eyes and inhales deeply.

I drag my hand down her spine, and she shudders. "You want me to stay or go? I need a clear answer," I declare.

The internal fight within her continues. She stays frozen, not saying a word.

Everything about her reaction increases my excitement. This is the Pina I know, headstrong and always trying to be in control. I threaten, "Three. T—"

"I understand," she cries out.

"Good girl," I praise, then suck on the curve of her neck, hold her hands against the headboard, and thrust inside her.

Her moan echoes in the air. Every time I pound into her, the muscles in her arms strain from her pushing against the headboard, which helps me go deeper. Endorphins rip through my body, creating so many sensations, I have a hard time keeping it together.

Pina's whimpers get louder. The smell of her arousal swirls with her floral perfume. Her sweat mingles with mine as my body slides over hers.

It doesn't take long before she climaxes. Her frame trembles underneath mine. And there's no more holding out. I release into her, harder than I ever remember. My orgasm pummels into hers, creating a euphoria so powerful, I could die happy right now.

When it's over, I stay hovered over her as we try to catch our breath. My heartbeat slows, and I roll on my back and tug her into me.

Too many thoughts race around my mind. Before tonight, she was an obsession—a mere fantasy of what seemed impossible. I thought I could have her and everything would be solved. We could both go our separate ways, and no one would be any wiser.

I couldn't have been more naive. I should have known that a woman like Pina isn't someone you get out of your system. And now that I've had her, there's no returning to normal. We did this—both of us. Now we know how good we are together, and it's an entirely new can of worms. Yet strangely enough, I don't regret any of it. Whatever the consequences are with my family, I tell myself I'll deal with them.

Pina slowly sits up and drills her gaze into mine.

I wiggle my eyebrows and, in an arrogant tone, state, "Want to show me the rest of your place?"

She reaches back and slaps me. The sting sprawls across my cheek as she seethes, "You liar."

4

Pina

My insides shake with rage and confusion. It's a gun aimed and fully firing not only at Tristano but also at me. I curl my hand into a fist, jumping off the bed and going into the bathroom.

What the hell did I just do?

This wasn't supposed to happen.

Where was I? Since when do I submit to any man?

How did he turn me into a begging submissive without even restraining me or using any other tools?

Why did I love it so much?

"Pina! What the fuck?" Tristano barks, following me.

I get to the sink and splash cold water on my face, wishing I could erase everything that just happened.

I was supposed to dominate him. He should have been the one pleading with me.

"Pina!" Tristano repeats, grabbing my shoulder and spinning me into him.

I jab the skull tattooed on his chest. "Don't! Go home."

He jerks his head back. "What's happening here?"

So much anger ignites in me that my lips tremble. It only irritates me further. I'm always in control and especially around the Marinos. I don't need them thinking they can run all over me like they do with everyone else. And now Tristano will see me like I'm one of his women he uses then throws out. I step to the side, but he matches my move and cages me against the counter. I seethe, "Get out of my way."

His dark eyes burn hotter, turning into slits. "You're acting like I did something wrong."

My voice shakes, displaying none of the confidence I usually have, which makes me more humiliated. "We had a deal."

"I asked you if you wanted me to stop. Several times. So don't act like I did something against your will," he states in a harsh tone.

My cheeks heat. I hate that he's right. I despise that I lacked the ability to tell him to stop and regain control of the situation in the heat of the moment. I look away, blinking hard and willing myself not to cry in front of him. The last thing I need is to display any more weakness in front of a Marino.

He turns my chin and forces me to face him. In a softer tone, he asserts, "It was good, Pina. No. It was the best sex I've ever had. We're good together, and I know it wasn't only me who enjoyed every minute of that. So whatever this is about, let's get past it."

Butterflies explode in my stomach, fluttering as if they're trying to escape.

The best sex he's ever had?

It was mine, too.

No, no, no! It doesn't matter if I enjoyed it. I shouldn't have. Plus, I submitted to a Marino.

More dread fills me. I hiss, "If you ever utter a word of this to anyone, especially your brothers, I'll kill you, Tristano. I mean it. I'll hunt you down and make anything you've ever done to your enemies look elementary."

Shock floods his chiseled features. "You think I'm a schoolboy who goes around and discusses my personal life with others? Wow. Have you ever heard me bragging about anyone I've been with?"

My heart thumps against my chest cavity. I try to think of a time, but I can't.

Disgust emanates so intensely that I cringe inside. He snarls, "Thanks for letting me know your impression of me." He steps back and goes to the shower. He turns on the water. Tension creeps into his muscular shoulders.

Anger turns to guilt. I try to tear my eyes off his sculpted backside, but it's impossible. I suddenly feel like a fly bouncing around a room, unsure which of his features I like the best. His broad shoulders have the Marino crest perfectly inked across them. It takes up his entire back, ending near his toned ass. And his thighs and calves of steel are the definition of unattainable magnificence for the normal male.

He steps into the shower and announces, "I'll leave as soon as I finish. Forget this night ever happened. One thing I won't do is chase after someone who doesn't want me, so let's just return to how things used to be. And no one will know I've been here, so stop worrying. I don't talk, regardless of what you think." He grabs my bottle of body wash and pours it into his hand.

Panic fills me. I take several breaths, trying to convince myself it's for the best, but the voice in my head keeps telling me I screwed up. I don't understand it. He agreed to my terms then the opposite happened. Yet I didn't tell him to stop. Nor did I dislike any moment of what happened between us.

Do I want him to leave like this?

Have I become a woman who has sex with a man and then accuses him of things because I'm confused over what I allowed him to do?

Crap!

I go to the shower and step in behind him, circling my arms around his waist.

He freezes.

"Tristano."

He doesn't move or speak.

I kiss his back then slide in front of him. I glance up at his clenched jaw and hurt expression. My insides quiver harder, but it's no longer from anger. Fear has replaced the rage. I don't want him to hate me or feel bad about what happened between us. I gave my permission when I didn't tell him to stop and begged him to keep going. I reach up and place my hand on his cheek. "I'm sorry. I know you don't talk. And you didn't do anything wrong. I could have told you to stop, and I didn't."

He doesn't respond, continuing to give me his wounded puppy dog eyes.

"I mean it," I declare, wanting to smooth things over more than anything.

He sniffs hard, glances at the tile above my head, and states, "I meant what I said. No one will ever know about this. Not only because that isn't what I do, but I have too much respect for you. I always have. And I'm sorry you have this fucked-up notion that what we just did somehow makes you anything less than what you are." He steps out of the shower and grabs a towel.

I freeze, watching him dry off and processing his statement. My heart falls further when I realize he's right.

He storms out of the bathroom.

I turn off the shower, wrap a towel around me, and call out, "Tristano! Wait!"

"I'm not into these types of games, Pina," he asserts, then continues to the main room.

I rush after him.

He bends down and picks up his underwear.

"I freaked out for a minute. I'm sorry," I admit, my anxiety building in my chest.

He puts on his pants and then pulls his T-shirt over his head, avoiding me.

I grasp his arm. "Tristano!"

"Don't," he warns.

I close my eyes, trying to figure out how to rewind this conversation and watching him slide into his shoes. I plead, "Please. Just wait a minute."

He spins then crosses his arms. "You know what's super fucked-up?"

The hairs on my arms rise. I meekly reply, "No. What? Tell me."

Darkness floods his expression. "When you were lying in my arms, I actually thought maybe this could be something. Obviously, I'm delirious. I apologize for everything. I shouldn't have crossed the line with you. Have a good night." He turns and reaches for the doorknob.

He thought we could be something?

No, we can't. I work for Dante.

What if we could though?

It's impossible.

I grab his bicep. "Tristano, wait!"

He shrugs out of my hold and opens the door. "Have a nice night." He steps out into the hallway.

"Stop!" I cry out, but he bolts to the elevator and slams his finger on the button.

I rush over to him. "Don't leave like this."

He angrily spins. "Go back inside. You're in a towel."

I clasp my arm against my chest. "Come with me."

The elevator doors open. "See you later." He steps inside and slides the key into the reader.

"Please. We need to talk," I insist.

He pushes a button, asserting, "No. We don't."

"We do," I claim.

The doors shut, and he disappears.

My stomach flips. I suddenly feel like I might throw up.

How did this get so screwed up in a matter of minutes?

Shit, shit, shit!

I return to my place, lock the door behind me, and turn off the lights. I go into the bedroom and crawl into bed. The aroma of tonka bean, cedarwood, and geranium flares in my nostrils, and I groan. To punish myself further, I bury my face into the pillow, smelling as much as possible.

All I can think about is how much I screwed up and hurt him. And was he serious when he said he thought we could be something? What does that even mean? Why do I find that appealing?

Confusion continues to swirl. He's a Marino. It's taboo on so many levels and is everything I've always tried to avoid. I don't sleep with the boss. Even if he technically isn't mine, he sometimes pays me to do things for him. I've mixed business and pleasure, and that's a big no-no for me.

Visions and the memories of the sensations of our encounter flood me.

Why did I submit to him?

Why did I like it so much?

As disturbing as it is for me to admit, he's right. We were really good together. There's a chemistry between us I've never experienced, even if he dominated me. All I want is for him to come back over, forgive me, and do it all over again.

How am I going to get him out of my system?

I curse myself for reacting how I did. I can't blame him for being angry and hurt. Making this right isn't even about our professional relationship. I insulted his character in many ways, and it was wrong of me. All I feel now is regret.

I grab my cell and text Tristano.

Me: *I truly am sorry. Can we please talk about this tomorrow?*

I wait for a response, but it never comes. All night, I toss and turn, unable to stop my mind from spinning. When morning comes, I check my messages and a new panic ignites.

Dante: *I need you to come to the house as soon as possible.*

My stomach drops like I'm on the first hill of a roller coaster. I jump out of bed and pace.

Does he know?

I text him back.

Me: *What's going on?*

Dante: *We need to discuss last night.*

I put my hand over my mouth, closing my eyes.

Did Tristano tell him what happened even though he agreed not to?

Did Dante somehow figure it out on his own?

Unlike my normal behavior, I choose cowardice.

Me: *Can I call you and we can talk over the phone?*

Dante: *No. We need to speak in person.*

"Shit!" I exclaim, the air in my lungs turning stale. If I lose my job, I'll be financially fine. But I love working for Dante and the rest of the Marinos. And I've spent my entire career trying to become irreplaceable.

Have I fooled myself? Am I not as valuable to Dante as I thought?

It's not my nature to worry about things until I have concrete facts. Right now, I have zero ability to not freak out. I pace my room several times, attempting to calm down. My phone vibrates.

Dante: *Bridget and I have a meeting with the wedding planner later this morning. When can you get here?*

I swallow the lump in my throat and reply.

Me: *Give me a half hour to get ready, and I'll be on my way.*

Dante: *See you then.*

My panic builds while getting ready. I text my driver and am soon sitting in the back of the SUV, attempting to think of things to say to Dante to save my job.

Part of me wonders if I can deny what happened between Tristano and me and somehow lie my way out of the situation. Yet, I know it's impossible. Dante isn't stupid. It's one of the reasons I love working with him. Like the rest of the Marinos, he's one of the sharpest men I know.

All the worrying has me feeling super off-balance. I need to buy some more time and pull myself together. I instruct my driver, "Get off at this exit."

"Is there another stop?" he asks.

"No," I admit.

"It's two exits too soon," he states, as if I haven't been at the Marino compound hundreds of times.

"I know. Get off this exit," I repeat.

"You're the boss," he says, then veers onto the ramp.

For the rest of the ride, I stare out the window, but nothing registers. The gates come into view, and my stomach somersaults. My driver pulls in front of the main entrance, and I wait for him to open my door.

Every move I take up the steps feels like another step toward my death. I remind myself that whatever happens, I'll be fine. All I feel reminds me of a schoolgirl waiting to see the principal after getting into trouble.

The bodyguard nods. "Ms. dela Cruz. How've you been?"

"Good. Thank you." I force a smile and hold up my chin, trying to feign confidence.

He opens the door, and I enter the impressive foyer. The ornate decor, rich golds, and darker reds always felt warm and welcoming. The grand staircase I always admired. Right now, everything feels intimidating.

Angelo steps out of his office. He smiles and pulls me into him, hugging me and kissing my cheek. "Pina, it's good to see you."

He must not know.

Over the years, Angelo's been like a father to me. Every year on my birthday, he sends me a six-figure check with a nice note. This past year was especially heartfelt. He wrote:

Pina,

Happy birthday!

Thank you for all you do for our family. I hope you know that you're as much a Marino as my sons or daughter. Go buy something nice for yourself.

All my love,

Angelo

I'VE NEVER TOLD ANYONE ABOUT THE NOTE OR CHECK. I suspect Angelo knows I haven't, but we've never discussed it. But regardless of how good he is to me, I've only had the utmost respect for him.

I choke up and swallow my emotions, imagining how disappointed he'll be when he finds out what I've done. I hug him tight and manage to reply, "It's good to see you, too."

He retreats. "What brings you here on a Saturday morning?"

"I need to speak with Pina," Dante's voice booms.

I freeze, my pulse pounding so hard in my neck that I wonder if it's visible. I take a deep breath, squaring my shoulders.

"Anything I should be aware of?" Angelo asks in a concerned voice.

"I'll fill you in later, Papà," Dante answers.

My insides shake harder.

Angelo glances between us then nods. "Okay. I'm running late to my workout. Arianna's in town, and even though she's pregnant, she's not letting me slack."

Even in my predicament, I can't help but smile. Arianna worries a lot about his health since their mamma died of a heart attack. She made Angelo revamp his diet and start working out. I say, "Tell her I said hi."

"I will." Angelo pats me on the arm and walks away.

"Pina. Let's talk," Dante orders.

I briefly close my eyes then put on the most confident expression I can muster. I spin, and he motions for me to go into the sitting room.

I obey, crossing the doorway, then freeze.

All the Marino brothers are in the room. They all have a slight scowl. Tristano locks eyes with me, and I wince inside. His expression screams he's pissed, but it matches the rest of the Marinos.

Did he tell them?

"Pina, have a seat," Dante instructs.

The only seat free is the armchair across from Tristano. I sit, feeling like I'm on trial and waiting for a verdict.

Dante sits on the armrest next to Tristano. "We need to talk about last night."

I don't say anything, not sure what the appropriate response is.

"Rubio said it's not the first time Biagio's approached you at the club," Dante states.

My anxiety diminishes.

Is this what this is about?

Does Dante not know about Tristano and me?

How could I have forgotten about the incident?

My lack of a response upsets Dante. He seethes, "Pina, why didn't you tell me?"

I glance at all the Marinos and catch myself lingering too long on Tristano. I refocus on Dante and clear my throat. "He's hit on me but never touched me until last night."

"You didn't think I deserved to know?" Dante questions in a hurt but authoritative voice.

I take a deep breath. The club has always been a sore spot between Dante and me. I avoid anything to do with it unless necessary. I admit, "You get worked up when we discuss the club. And lots of men from many families say inappropriate things to me. It wasn't a big deal until last night when he grabbed my ass."

Dante's face turns red with anger. He hisses, "Which families?"

I shrug. "All of them. What does it matter? You know how the club works. They've tried to get my attention but never crossed the line."

"You should have told me," Dante insists.

I glance at the ceiling and take a few deep breaths.

Tristano seethes, "She needs to stay out of the club."

I snap my head toward him. "Excuse me?"

"I agree," Gianni asserts.

I keep my gaze on Tristano. "I didn't do anything. Nothing happened."

"But it could have. If Biagio has his eyes on you, it's not safe to put yourself in that scenario," Tristano claims.

Rage floods me. *Is this his way of getting back at me for last night?* I open my mouth to accuse him then shut it before saying something I'll regret.

"No more club, Pina. And I want a written account of every man from another family who's approached you. I want to know what they said and did," Dante claims.

I turn my focus on him. "You're blowing this out of proportion. And that's impossible. I've been going to the club for years."

"They all know you work for me. You're a Marino. Anyone who's hit on you knows it's out of line," Tristano adds.

I glare at him, seething, "It's a sex club. That's what happens there."

"Pina, you're not allowed back until I say. If I find out you went, I'll have a permanent ban placed on you," Dante states.

Too shocked to respond, I stare at him, speechless. This isn't fair. I've always followed all the club rules.

Dante softens his voice. "As soon as I feel the threat is over, I'll let you know."

"I didn't do anything wrong," I insist.

"No one said you did. But Biagio isn't someone who backs down. If he has his eyes on you, he'll attempt something else," Massimo interjects.

"I can handle myself," I claim.

"Damn it, Pina! This is serious," Tristano barks.

My chest tightens. I shake my head at him then rise. I address Dante. "Is there anything else, boss?"

"Don't be like that," Dante says.

"How do you expect me to react? Should I be happy you're acting like I'm helpless? Should I point out how hypocritical the four of you are? You never wanted me there anyway.

Well, you finally got your way. Congrats," I seethe, then turn to leave.

Dante grabs my arm. "Pina—"

I spin. "I'll have your list to you Monday. Or do you want me to do it over the weekend?"

He sighs.

"We need it sooner rather than later," Tristano answers.

All the remorse I had about the previous night disappears. As far as I'm concerned, Tristano Marino can kiss my ass. I snottily remark, "Fine. Boss."

"Pina," Dante tries again.

"Anything else?" I repeat.

He slowly shakes his head. "No."

"Great. Have a nice weekend." I hold my head high and leave as quickly as possible, vowing to never do any more favors or jobs for Tristano. He crossed a line. He made this personal so he doesn't have to see me in the club anymore. From now on, I'm steering clear of him.

5

Tristano

"Well, she took that better than expected," Massimo mutters.

My stomach somersaults. I'm still pissed about what happened last night, but I didn't want to add more fuel to the fire. And I want to see this list. Pina should have told one of us what was going on at the club.

My blood boiled when Dante told me what happened between Biagio and Pina. The thought of that thug talking to her is bad enough. Touching her is another level of rage.

Dante runs his hand through his hair. "When I get Pina's list, we need to meet again."

"What are we going to do about it?" Gianni asks.

Dante crosses his arms and goes to the window. He stares out at the stark white yard. It snowed last night, and frost covers the windows. "I'm not sure yet. We'll talk with Papà once we have the list."

I blurt out, "He'll kill you when he finds out you let Pina go to the club."

Dante spins. "And all of you knew, so don't think your asses aren't in trouble. All of us are going to hear it."

"Then don't tell him. Let's figure this out ourselves," I suggest.

"No. Papà might need to speak to the council. There are rules for a reason," Dante states, then adds, "I have to meet the wedding planner. I'll let you know when I have the list."

My brothers and I break apart, each going our separate ways. Without thinking, I go into the garage and hop in my Mercedes-Benz G Class. It's an SUV I drive when the weather is bad. I turn on the engine, pull out of the gate, then head to Pina's.

I'm unsure why I think this will make anything better, but something urges me to talk to her. At the very least, we need to clear the air about last night. While I'm glad she won't be in the club anymore, I didn't speak my mind about the issue because of what happened between us. I would have reacted the same, even if we hadn't hooked up.

It takes longer to get to her condo than normal. The roads are bad. Halfway there, the snow begins to fall again. It creates a thick blanket, giving me little visibility.

I pull up to her building then text her.

Me: *I'm outside. Call security and let me up.*

Pina: *I'm not home.*

Me: *Don't lie. Come on.*

Pina: *I'm not lying.*

Me: *Then where are you?*

Pina: *None of your business. And leave me alone. I have work to do.*

Me: *Are you at your place in Manhattan?*

She doesn't answer me. I take it as a yes and veer out into traffic. All the streets are a mess. I get on the Manhattan bridge and have to come to a stop. There was an accident, and the police closed the other lanes.

By the time I get to Pina's, it's a full-blown blizzard. I text her.

Me: *I'm here and just risked my life, so call security to give me a key card.*

Pina: *Go home, Tristano.*

Me: *No. Look outside. It's a blizzard. I'm coming in so we can talk.*

Pina: *We could have talked last night. You were too immature to stay.*

Me: *Let me up, Pina. If you don't, I'll tell Dante what happened.*

Pina: *Now you're going to threaten me?*

Me: *Okay. That was low. Of course I'm not. But let me up.*

I get out of the SUV and battle the snow. The wind is just as fierce and makes my face feel frozen. I stomp on the rug to clean off my shoes and go to the front desk.

A new security guard addresses me. "Can I help you?"

"I'm here to see Pina dela Cruz." I hand him my license.

He types something into his computer then picks up the phone. "Ms. dela Cruz, a Mr. Tristano Marino is here to see you."

I tap my fingers on the desk.

The guard looks at me and says, "I see. Very well."

My gut drops. She better not have told him not to let me up.

"Ms. dela Cruz will be down shortly," he states.

I groan inside. "Thank you." I go over to the elevator to wait for Pina. The moment the doors open, I step inside and push the close door button.

"Tristano! What are you doing?" she seethes.

"Stop playing games. We need to talk, and we aren't doing it in front of Slim Jim," I assert.

She glares at me. "Slim Jim?"

"Yes. That guy's so thin he isn't scaring anyone away. I seriously hope you aren't relying on him to protect you," I reply.

"I don't need anyone to protect me," she claims.

I grab the key card from her hand then slide it into the slot. I quickly hit the thirteen button, ignoring the goose bumps on my arms.

It's just a number, I remind myself.

"Get out of my building," Pina orders.

I ignore her. When the door opens, I put my arm around her waist and guide her into the hall.

"Tristano—"

"Do you want your neighbors to hear?" I ask, knowing Pina's a private person.

She closes her mouth, giving me more evil eyes.

"You're kind of cute when you're all pissed off," I confess.

"Shut up," she snaps.

I chuckle then get to her door. I wait for her to open it. "We don't have all day."

She angrily shakes her head at me then punches in the code.

Six-Nine-Seven-One, I repeat in my head, memorizing it and pushing the thoughts of the seven out of my mind.

We step inside, and she spins, jabbing me in the chest. "You have a lot of nerve coming here."

"When you finish acting like a brat, let me know," I state.

She puts her hand on her hip. "What do you want, Tristano?"

"Can we sit down and take a breather?" I ask, trying to ignore the erection pressing against my zipper, even though she's giving me a hard time.

She crosses her arms over her chest. "Sorry if I'm not in the mood to entertain. Now, what do you want?"

"Sit down," I command.

"I don't take orders from you. I work for Dante." She smirks.

"Last warning. Sit. Down," I repeat.

She scoffs. "Last warning? I don't know who you think you'r—"

Fuck this.

I pick her up and throw her over my shoulder.

She starts kicking and hitting me. "Let me down!"

I slap her ass. "Stop fighting me." The sound echoes in the room.

It only makes her try to hurt me more. She knees me in the stomach, almost knocking the wind out of me.

I smack her again, walking toward the bedroom but stop dead in my tracks in front of another room.

She beats on my back. "Tristano! I'm going to kill you! Let me go!"

"You have a dungeon?" I question.

She freezes.

I step inside, amazed at what's in front of me. Black, hot pink, and pewter cover the entire room. Restraints hang from the walls and ceiling and are attached to the furniture. Shelves display top-of-the-line sex toys. A display case has floggers and paddles of different sizes and materials. Chains of different widths and lengths hang next to them. One corner of the room has a metal cage with bars from floor to ceiling. The other corner of the room has a stage with a pole and floodlights. Mirrors create a reflection, making the room appear larger.

"This had to cost a fortune," I mutter, impressed at Pina's playroom. Like my brothers, I have my own dungeon in my wing of the house, but Pina's is nothing to sneeze at.

"Put me down, Tristano!" she orders, but her voice is softer.

I obey, sliding her down my body until her feet hit the floor, but I don't remove my arms from around her.

Tense silence fills the air. Neither of us moves as she stares at my chest. Her floral scent reminds me of last night, making me desperate to smell it mixed with her arousal. My pulse pounds hard between my ears. Maybe it's my attraction toward her I can't get past, the freshness of what it was like to have her as mine, or even the room she created, but the urge to talk evaporates. All I want to do is claim her as mine even though I should stop the path we're on.

Unable to stop myself, I tilt her head up. The gold in her eyes bursts into flames, mesmerizing me further. I ask, "When did you build this room?"

Heat flushes her cheeks. She bites on her bottom lip, which is the first time I've ever seen her do that. It's a show of vulnerability, and Pina's usually anything but vulnerable. It makes my testosterone flare hotter.

I stroke her cheek with my thumb, questioning, "Why are you embarrassed?"

"I'm not," she replies, her face turning redder.

"No?" I interrogate, arching my eyebrows and tugging her closer to me.

She takes a deep breath then licks her lips.

"I know you use the dungeon at the club," I reveal.

"So what? So do you," she points out.

"I'm not judging you," I assure her.

She nervously exhales. "Good."

"Why did you freak out on me last night? I've known for a long time you like to submit," I admit.

"Yeah? How did you know that? My sessions are private," she states.

I tuck a lock of her hair behind her ear, and she holds her breath. I answer, "You go into the dungeon. It doesn't take a genius to put two and two together."

She raises her chin then scoffs. "You would think that."

Confused, I inquire, "Think what?"

"Ask me again why I got upset last night," she says.

"Tell me why you hated me after we had what I think was incredible sex," I reply and mean it. Hands down, it was the best I've ever had.

"You agreed to my terms then took over. It was a big lie to get what you wanted," she claims.

Frustration fills me. I question, "What did I do that you didn't like, Pina? Tell me."

She waits a moment then admits, "Nothing."

"Then what's the problem? I'm really confused and want to know."

She studies me, tilting her head.

"Pina, it's not fair—"

"You agreed to my terms, then you took over. I wouldn't have let you come here if you hadn't promised me I was in charge," she confesses.

My chest tightens. I try not to sound whiny, asking, "I understand you like control. But you know as well as I do that there's always a dominant and submissive. The Dom is in charge, not the sub. So why is it okay for other men to take charge but not me?"

Anger flares in her expression. "Look around, Tristano. What do you see?"

To appease her, I glance around the room, then refocus on her, acknowledging, "I see a kick-ass dungeon that I want to play in. With you."

She studies me again.

"What did I say now?" I ask.

"Why do you assume I'm the submissive?"

I freeze. My heart almost pounds out of my chest. I mutter, "It's impossible."

"What? That I can dominate a man?" she asks, as if I've insulted her.

"I know the men who you've taken into the dungeon. There's no way they submit," I assert.

She huffs. "You're very naive, Tristano. I never thought I'd say that, but you are."

I gape at her. Some of the cruelest, most vicious, most dangerous men I know have been in the dungeon with Pina.

She softens her tone. "Ah. Now I see you're catching on."

I step away and gaze around the room again. "So you wanted to have me come here to submit to you?"

"Yes."

"And you have men come here instead of the club? Why?"

She shakes her head. "You're the only one who's been here."

"Why me?"

She shrugs. "I don't know. But I only invited you since you agreed to my terms."

The hairs on my arms rise. I turn toward her. "You know I'm a Dom, not a sub."

"So are a lot of men I take into the dungeon."

"Yeah, well, I'm a Dom."

"How do you know?" she asks.

I grunt and tap my fingers on my thigh. "Because I know."

She puts her hand over mine. "You're nervous."

"No, I'm not," I claim, but there's a strange feeling in my gut I can't describe.

She lowers her voice. "Have you ever tried being a sub?"

"Of course not."

"Then you don't know if you'd like it."

"That's ridiculous. I know I'm the dominant one. And you loved submitting to me, so don't deny it," I argue.

She closes her eyes briefly then reveals, "You're right. I did. I don't know why and it's still confusing me, but I did love what we did and how you made me feel. But it doesn't negate the fact I also like to dominate."

Her truth hangs in the air, making me more uncomfortable. If Pina's a Dominatrix, then this will never work between us. I'm a Marino. We don't submit. We dominate.

She drags her finger down my bicep, creating tingles under her touch. She says, "I've heard of people being switches."

"That's a myth," I state, not willing to believe anyone would be able to move back and forth between roles.

"No, it isn't," she insists. "Want to make a deal?" Challenge lights her eyes.

My stomach flips while my pulse continues skyrocketing.

She bats her eyelids. "What's wrong, Tristano? Scared?"

"No. I don't get scared," I declare.

She smiles and rises on her tippy-toes. She leans into my ear and murmurs, "Then let's play. No one will ever know but you and me. You follow through on your promise to me. Afterward, you get to choose how we have sex again."

My ears perk up. I ask, "Again?"

She nods. "Yes. Any style you want, and I won't get angry with whatever you choose. I promise."

Time seems to stand still. I've never submitted to anyone. I know how to break women and put them back together. In order to submit, she'd have to break me, and that isn't happening. I answer, "I won't submit. It's impossible."

Her smile grows. "Then let me have my way and let's see. After, you get to call the shots."

It's the perfect carrot to dangle in front of me. The notion of having Pina again instantly gives me a raging hard-on.

She reaches for my cock and cups it. "Seems like you're interested."

"Don't be a smart-ass," I command.

She steps closer, tracing my collarbone. "Do you want me to put on something a bit...sexier?" She locks eyes with me like the perfect temptress.

I fist her hair and tug her head back, positioning my face over hers. She gasps, and I peck her on the lips, then ask, "Is that a serious question?"

She swallows hard. "So we have a deal? I'll change, and you undress. I want you kneeling in the cage with your head down when I get back."

I glance at the metal bars. Before I think about what I'm saying, I state, "I want more."

She pins her eyebrows together. "More? What do you mean?"

Nothing's been clear since a few months ago in that meeting. The moment I saw Pina for the woman she is, I was obsessed. But last night changed everything. Now, I feel doomed. The nagging desperation to have her again is only growing.

I kiss her with everything I have, not letting her go until I feel her submit to me. I retreat and ask, "Don't tell me you don't see there's something between us."

Worry fills her expression.

"Stop thinking about the logistics. Just admit to me this isn't something superficial for you. Tell me you know if I walk out of here, you're going to be dying for me to come back."

"Tristano—"

"Admit it, and I'll do what you want. I'll play your game and let you be in charge. But then I want a date. A *real* date, and you can't blow me off. And I get to call the shots after," I assert.

Her lips twitch. "A date?"

"Yeah. Why is that funny?"

Her face turns serious. "It's not. Do you think that's a good idea though?"

I snort. "Is any of this a good idea? Nope. But I think we're past the part of using our brains regarding this matter. Don't you?"

She takes a deep breath and slowly nods.

Happy about her admission, I pat her ass, then kiss her again. "Good. Now go get your sexy outfit on."

"Did you have to cut my other one?" she asks.

"You thought it was hot when I sliced it off your pert little ass," I state.

She rolls her eyes. "It was five hundred dollars."

"Then I guess I owe you a new outfit. Go get changed, and let's get this over with before I change my mind," I demand as my gut sends me mixed signals again.

She points at me. "No changing your mind. You owe me this for breaking your word last night."

"Fine. Go. But you can't utter a word to anyone about this," I repeat.

"I won't! And you'll love it, promise!"

"I doubt that. Get changed," I demand, then pull off my sweatshirt.

"Don't move once you're kneeling. If you look up, I'll have to punish you," she warns.

I've been a Dom long enough to know she's serious. I clench my jaw and stare at her.

She peers at me. "Are you sure you want to do this?"

"This is what you need from me?" I ask.

She doesn't hesitate. "Yes."

"Then get out of here." I point to the door.

She leaves, and I take the playroom in again. I'm not used to being nervous, but I suddenly am.

What did I just agree to?

Take it like a man. It'll be worth it to take her on a date and then dominate her again.

I remove my shoes and pants then fold everything. I stack my items on the top of a table then stare at the cage.

I can't believe I'm doing this.

I glance at the door, debating about leaving.

Suck it up.

Shaking my head, I step into the cage, kneel, and stare at the floor, wondering what I've agreed to do.

6

Pina

NERVOUS ENERGY GROWS IN MY STOMACH. I STARE AT MYSELF in the mirror. The spaghetti strap, black, wet-leather minidress has silver hooks down the middle and along my thigh from my hip bone to the bottom. The same design is on the lower part of the sleeves and neckline. One of the chains fits like a choker and the other drapes slightly below it. My six-inch stilettos have a pointed silver heel and the same black wet-leather look.

I've worn Dominatrix outfits too many times to count. Normally, the moment I step into them, I feel powerful. Today, I feel off.

Why am I feeling like this?

It's Tristano Marino.

I enjoyed him dominating me.

It just means I must be a switch.

Pull it together.

I take a deep breath and turn to see my backside in the mirror. Everything fits perfectly. I look hot. One thing I've always done is take care of myself, so I may be thirty-seven, but I could pass for late twenties. I wrap my matching tool belt-garter around my waist and secure my fishnets. I go to my nightstand and select which items I want to have on me.

I step out of the bedroom, head toward the dungeon, and freeze before I get to the door, leaning against the wall. My stomach's become a roller coaster, continuing to confuse me.

I can't go in there like this.

I'll make him wait longer. It'll add to his vulnerability.

I don't look at the room as I pass it. I go to the kitchen and glance at the time. It's only eleven in the morning, but I need something to calm my nerves. Glancing around the room, I grab a red-blend bottle of wine. I open it, pour a glass, take several sips, and pace the condo.

The large windows have frost on them. Snow falls so thick, I can't see the buildings across from me or the street. Even though I have the heat on, I shiver, then reprimand myself for this sudden inability to be the confident Dominatrix I am.

I drink several large mouthfuls, focusing on the different tastes of cherry, blackberry, and a hint of smoke. My heart rate begins to return to normal.

This is your one chance. Who knows what will happen after we do this.

He doesn't want this.

He agreed though.

I need him to reiterate he's okay with this before I start.

Don't blow this. Do your thing.

Music! He needs to hear music.

I go to the surround sound controls and hit the playlist I previously created. The first song that plays is "You Never Forget Your First Dominatrix" by Dominatrix.

So appropriate, I think, smiling and beginning to calm further. The lyrics begin, and I step two feet over to the video screen. I hit another button, and the playroom comes into view. To my surprise, Tristano is kneeling and keeping his gaze on the floor as instructed. I assumed he'd disobey while I was gone, but he's not.

Good little sub.

He's not little.

Jesus, he's beautiful.

Several songs play while I study his mesmerizing body and decipher my thoughts. There are so many things I've thought about doing to him over the last few months. Now that he's here, vulnerable, and at my mercy, it all feels overwhelming.

I turn the heat up a few degrees in the playroom and wait. Within a few minutes, sweat beads on his skin, turning him into a glistening work of art. I down the rest of my wine and check myself out in the mirror again.

It's now or never.

I flip the switch for the hot-pink strobe lights and go into the playroom. More confidence grows with every step I take. I hit a button on the wall, and restraints lower from the cage. The song ends, and a new one comes on with a faster beat and men screaming in pain. I'm sure Tristano's never heard anything like it. He always plays the opposite when he's in charge, which is women crying out in agony. I study him for several moments to add to his apprehension.

He stays still, but his chest rises and falls faster. Everything about it sends adrenaline shooting through my veins.

Tristano Marino is finally going to submit to me.

I crouch in front of him and reach for his chin, grasping it and tilting his head up. His hardened dark eyes are ones I've seen from many men who I've convinced to allow me to do this to them. I state, "You've obeyed well."

"What now, Pina?" he asks in a flat tone.

A bead of sweat rolls down his cheek near his ear. I lean forward, lick from his jaw to hairline, then murmur in his ear, "I was going to say I'll let you come later, but you just disrespected me, so you'll have to re-earn it."

He cocks his eyebrows. "Oh? How so?"

"I'm Mistress to you. You'll address me as such," I inform him, feeling the power I always do ignite.

He purses his lips.

"I'm waiting."

"Sorry, Mistress."

I trace his lips, cooing, "Subs don't ask questions unless permitted. You know the rules. But I'll give you a pass on that one since this is your first time."

He grinds his molars, and I remind myself he needs to give me consent one more time before I begin. I don't normally ask at this stage, but my gut tells me I need to.

"Stand up," I order.

He rises, and I step closer. I circle my fingers over his hard nipples, challenging, "Do you want to end this? We can stop if you want."

He licks his lips then stands taller. "No. Not if this is what you want."

"Not if this is what I want, *Mistress*," I remind him.

"Sorry. Mistress," he adds.

"I won't ask you again. Once we start, we're not stopping until I say or you use your safe word," I forewarn.

He nods. "I understand, Mistress. Can I ask, what is the safe word?"

"You may. But for you, I think we'll make it a phrase," I assert.

Confusion fills his expression. "A phrase?"

"Yes." I drag my knuckles over his chest, circling his body until I'm behind him. I kiss his back and announce, "If at any time you can't handle it and wish to stop, you need to say, 'I'm a Marino.'"

His body stiffens.

I taunt, "Aw. You don't like your safe phrase?"

He stays quiet.

I slide my hand around him and stroke his cock, threatening, "You need to answer me when I ask questions, or I'll have to punish you."

"The safe phrase is fine, Mistress. Can we please start?" he grumbles, his erection growing harder in my hand.

"There's another rule," I add.

"Please tell me, Mistress."

I kiss the curve of his neck, happy he's already complying, then I work him harder. His jaw twitches as I say, "There's no coming unless I permit you."

His hands ball into fists at his sides. The muscles in his shoulders flex.

I release him and step back to a panel on the cage. I press a button, and the floor beneath his feet lowers. When I'm a few inches taller than him, I order, "Hands behind your head. Spread your legs."

He laces his fingers together and moves his feet toward the sides of the cage. I cuff his ankles then reach up for the other restraints. I secure a cuff around each wrist then raise the floor to the normal position. I push another button, and the sound of the chains rolling into the spool echoes around us.

When there's no more slack, I glance at my toolbelt and select a metal roller. It has spikes, and it'll break the skin if pressed too hard. I've never gone that far, but I've seen other Doms do it. Blood isn't my thing, but Tristano doesn't know that, so I roll it along his spine, asking something I question all my subs about. "How many men have you tortured?"

His shoulder blades pop out. Goose bumps break out on his arms and the back of his thighs.

"Did I stutter? When I ask a question, you answer," I remind him, pressing the ball to the point I know I shouldn't go past.

"Too many to count, Mistress," he states.

I move to the front of his body. "Were they restrained like you are?"

He glances at the ceiling, sighing.

"Look at me," I demand, then slap the side of his ass hard.

His eyes widen, and his nostrils flare. He scowls.

I slap him again then grab his chin. "Is your tongue cut off?"

"No."

"No, who?"

"No, Mistress."

"Then answer my question."

"Yes, many were restrained."

"In your father's dungeon?"

He jerks his head backward. "How do you know—"

"I know lots of things. And you keep breaking the rules. No questions," I scold, then take out my flogger and slap it across his ass three times. Red flushes across his cheek, and he grits his teeth.

I take my hand and rub the spot, but I also glance at his cock, stating, "Your dick just throbbed."

He purses his lips.

I step closer, feeling a high so potent, dizziness hits me. I reach for his shoulder to keep myself stable and press the button. A step rises under my feet. When I'm at eye level with him, I put my lips an inch from his. Tonka bean, cedarwood, and geranium waft in my nostrils. I reach for his cock and stroke it, interrogating, "You've never mixed pleasure with pain before, have you?"

Fire burns in his eyes. Hardness overpowers his expression.

I softly laugh. "You thought only your subs could enjoy you. It surprises you that you're into this."

He continues not to speak.

I work his cock harder until pre-cum slips onto my hand and his chest is heaving for air. I purr into his ear, "I didn't permit you to come. If you do, I'll keep you locked here for a week."

His muscles contract. Hatred fills his eyes, but there's also a weakness. I've never seen it before. Tristano's always an alpha male who charges into danger without hesitation. But now, he's at my mercy.

The power trip I always get when I make powerful men submit reappears. It smolders, ready to burst into flames, but

Tristano hasn't submitted yet. I move my face in front of his and kiss him.

He resists for a moment, probably from pride, but when I slide my hand through his hair, his tongue urgently darts against mine. I work his cock harder, kissing him as if my life depended on it, until his erection throbs in my hand and he's groaning. He yanks the chains, but there's nowhere for him to go.

I retreat several inches from his mouth, working him until he's shaking. But Tristano surprises me, controlling his orgasm past the point I thought he could. I pause my hand and ask, "Do you want to fuck me?"

"Please, Mistress."

Hearing him call me Mistress sends a new wave of power through my bones. I'm also contemplating something I've never done before, which is to end this and let him put me on the O-train. I don't usually have sex with my subs. Sure, I allow them to get me off, but I don't let them penetrate me. I'm unsure why, but it's always fulfilled my needs. Maybe it's the freshness of our encounter last night, but my pussy's throbbing to have him back inside me.

Stay in your role, I reprimand myself.

I drag my hand up his torso then slide my fingers with his pre-cum in his mouth, whispering, "You have to earn it. Now suck."

He shoots me a challenging expression but obeys.

"You haven't submitted yet," I state, pulling my fingers out.

"Mistress?" he questions.

I scoff. "You know you haven't. Until you submit, you aren't coming."

He straightens his shoulders and stares above my head. Another bead of sweat drips down his arm, and I slide my palm over it. He sniffs hard and glances at me.

Memories of the things I've seen him make his subs do float through my brain. I tap the buttons, release the tension from the chains, and uncuff him. He slowly moves his arms to his sides and waits for my command.

I reach up and stroke the side of his head. "Do you want to see me dance?"

He hesitates, studying me.

"Well? Would you like that?"

He admits, "Yes, Mistress. I'd like that."

"Good. Go sit on that chair," I order.

He glances at the hot-pink, curved leather sex chair. His lips twitch, and he walks to it and sits.

"Close your eyes," I instruct.

He shuts them, and I open a drawer, pulling out a cock cage. It's used to stop a man from ejaculating, but it doesn't eradicate the need. Every man I've used it on never wore one before, and I doubt Tristano will be any different.

I take it to him then slip it into the pocket of my toolbelt. I massage his temples and lean over him. "You like it when women dance for you, don't you?"

He locks eyes with me. "Yes, Mistress."

"Have you thought about me dancing for you?" I ask.

He takes a deep breath. "All the time."

"And you like it when they touch you, but only after the pole?" I question.

"You've studied me," he replies.

"I learned from you," I toss back.

Pride swells in his face. "And you liked what you saw, Mistress?"

I peck him on the lips. "Yes. I did."

"Can I ask what you believe I taught you?"

I reach down and cup his balls then stroke his shaft with my thumb. A tiny groan escapes him. He reaches behind him and slides his hand over my thigh.

Intense zings burst throughout my body. As much as I want to end this and let him have me, my ego won't let me. Tristano Marino is at my mercy, and I'm also getting off from it.

I take his hand and move it back to his lap, answering, "I learned to never give up my power. And a sub always needs to break first."

The vein near his eye pulses.

"Ah. You don't like hearing the truth when you're on the receiving end?" I taunt.

"Maybe it's because there's no way you'll break me," he claims.

"Hmm," I huff, smiling. I walk around him and do something else I've never done to a sub. I kneel between his thighs. Arrogance washes over his expression. I lean forward and lick from the base to the tip of his cock.

He groans. "Fuck."

I smirk. "How many times did you think about me doing this?"

"Daily. Multiple times," he confesses, placing his hand on my head and pushing me back toward him.

I softly laugh, take his entire cock in my mouth, then suck on the cap.

"Jesus," he mumbles, moving my head over him.

It's another surprise. I thought I wouldn't like any man controlling my head when I went down on him, but everything about it creates a new set of endorphins for me.

You're the Dom, not him.

But this feels right.

Get back into your role.

I jump up and point to the restraints on the armrests. "Hands there so I can dance for you."

Amusement floods his face. He arrogantly secures one wrist in a cuff and then places the other in the second cuff, waiting for me to close it.

I snap it shut, cage my body over his, then kiss him before muttering, "Are you ready for me to dance?"

"Yeah, baby girl."

I wag my finger in front of his face. "Mmm, mmm, mmm. How do you address me?"

He grins. "Sorry. Mistress. You're smoking hot in your outfit, by the way."

Flutters explode in my stomach. I kiss him again then lean down and cuff his ankles to the chair.

"Did you think I'd go somewhere?" he teases.

I sit on his lap and put my arms around him then assert, "You haven't submitted. You still think you're in control."

"Mistress, I believe you prefer it when I'm in control," he argues.

"Oh? Really?" I ask, tilting my head.

He leans forward and darts his tongue out of his mouth, licking my lips, suggesting, "Why don't you stay right here and dance on my dick? I promise you that you'll feel better."

I laugh and then caress his cheek. "Aw. You really do need to submit. But don't worry, I'll help you."

More cockiness appears in his expression. "If you want to bring your pussy to my face, I'll be more than happy to lick it."

My butterflies go nuts and my insides clench.

Pull it together!

"Maybe later," I tease, kissing him again and then rising. I pull out the cock cage.

"What is that?"

"A cock cage."

The color drains from his face. "You aren't—"

"Do you want to use your safe phrase?" I ask, batting my eyelashes.

He licks his lips and clenches his jaw.

"No?" I challenge.

He stays quiet.

"Last chance," I offer.

He shoots me daggers with his glare.

I unclasp the cage then secure it over his erection. When it's in place, I ask, "How does it feel?"

"How do you think?" he barks.

"Aw," I pout. "Is that any way to speak to your Mistress?"

He scowls.

"Do you want me to leave you here for a bit to think about your answer?" I threaten.

He releases an angry breath. "No. I'm sorry, Mistress."

I smile then pat his cheek. "Good boy." I go over to the surround sound then flip to a playlist I know is the type of music Tristano makes his subs dance to. I go over to the pole and mimic all the moves I know turn him on, slowly taking my outfit off.

When his face is red and he's breathing hard, I go over to him, tracing his skin displayed between the metal. I sit on his lap and slide my arm around his shoulders, stroking his scalp. I lean into his ear, "What's wrong, baby?"

"Get this off me, Pina. Let me make you feel good," he states.

"Did you forget who I am?" I remind him.

"I'm not playing your game anymore. Release my dick. Now."

I smile, peck him on the lips, then reply, "Okay. But you have to say the safe phrase."

7

Tristano

MY ERECTION FIGHTS TO ESCAPE THE CAGE, BUT IT'S impossible. The need to release is so strong that I don't ever remember feeling so desperate to come.

Pina's sexy striptease only makes me want her more. She knows exactly how to dance to showcase all her curves. Like most guys, I'm visual. It doesn't take much to affect me, but watching Pina on stage, utilizing the pole to tease me, then taking off her clothes in the slow fashion I like, is fascinating. It's also made everything about this cage a hundred times worse.

I never knew Pina studied me while I was at the club in the dungeon. Part of me loves that she took an interest. The other side of me curses myself for agreeing to this charade. She knows what she's doing, from the little dose of punishments she gave me right down to the restraints. And Pina has something many dominant men never learn.

She knows how to fuck with your mind.

It's everything I'm into, whether with a sub in a playroom or torturing a man in Papà's dungeon. But this situation is fucked-up. I'm a Dom, not a sub. I'm also a Marino, so this goes against every fiber of my DNA. Marino men take action. They don't allow themselves to be in a helpless situation. So I should quit this now, but my ego won't let me.

Pina gives me a challenging look, waiting for me to say the safe phrase, "I'm a Marino." I have to give her more credit. It's the ultimate mind fuckery. She knew exactly what she was doing using that phrase, knowing I wouldn't be able to cave and say it.

Instead of bowing out, I ask, "What's the fun for you if I can't use my dick?"

She smirks then shifts on my lap until she's straddling me. The faint scent of her arousal flares in my nostrils, and I groan inside. All I've thought about since I saw her in her leather outfit was eating her pussy.

She releases the wrist restraints and slides her arms around my shoulders. I palm her ass and tug her closer with my forearm. Her lips twitch, her expression turns innocent, and she chirps, "I haven't given you your lap dance yet. That's what you like, correct?"

My pulse increases. I can't deny my love for them. And a woman like Pina... well, shit. After last night, she became my dream woman. But the way she just moved her body during her striptease solidified it. Now, I'm kicking myself for never noticing it all these years.

Still, I haven't forgotten the cock cage around my most precious commodity. I demand, "Take it off and let me show you some new tricks."

She laughs. "I think you forgot I'm in charge. Not you."

I groan then fist her hair and tug her head backward. She gasps, and I lean over her face. "Did you forget how good I made you feel last night?"

Her breath merges with mine. Her hard tits tease my pecs. The gold in her eyes swirls with the brown, making my dick ache worse. She stays quiet as the music pounds around us.

Neither of us blinks. The hip-hop rapper belts out his song, and Pina uses it to her advantage. She grinds her hips against me, torturing me further. She states, "You need to learn to submit."

Fuck this. This game of hers has gone too far. Maybe she gets off dominating men, but I saw how much she was into submitting to me. And it's time to flip this situation to how things are supposed to be. One thing Pina's done is underestimate my ability to get others to do what I want.

I give her a chaste kiss then slide my palms to her ass, pick her up, and sling her legs over my shoulders.

"Tristano! Put me down," she screams.

"Not until I'm done with you," I state, then bury my face in her pussy, holding her tight so she can't escape. Her salty-sweetness bursts on my tongue. I think I might die a happy man right now, even with my cock in the heinous contraption.

"Tristano!" she says again, swatting my head.

"You want to dance, you dance on my face," I order, then start flicking my tongue on her clit.

"Tri...oh fuck!" she cries out, her body submitting to me, curling around my head. Her hands grip my hair, and whimpers fly out of her mouth.

Sweat drips down my face. My heart races and my cock aches to be free, but there's no question about who's in control right now.

I am.

It's how it's supposed to be.

And I may have agreed to this play session, but she'll never break me. I'll always figure out a way to make her submit. I know I confused her last night, but she enjoyed how we were together. Today, I'll prove it to her again.

Pina's body begins trembling, growing strong until she cries out, "Oh God, oh God, oh God!"

I lean forward, keeping her pressed to my face, and bite on her clit.

"Tristano!" she moans.

I reach to my ankle and unlatch the restraint then the other. My mouth never leaves her pussy. I sit back, reposition my arms around her back, and slide my hand into her tool belt until I find the key. For another minute, I rotate between licking, sucking, and biting her.

She turns limp in my arms. Her cries turn hoarse. Our sweat mingles, and her body violently convulses.

I unlock the cock cage. My erection springs free, and the relief is instant but short-lived.

I need to be inside her.

I rise, toss her over my shoulder, then lay her on the bed. I cuff her hands to the headboard and then hit the button to release the slack on the chains. Gripping her ankles, I tug her to the end of the bed, hug her shins to my chest, and plunge into her.

"Oh!" she barely breathes.

I thrust fast for a few strokes, then slow it down, realizing I'm going to explode if I don't.

Control. Gain control! I reprimand myself.

Pina's face flushes. Her chest rises and falls fast as she pants, trying to catch her breath. Her pouty lips are in an O, and I know exactly how this will end.

I growl, "You think you can break me?" I thrust fast, then slow, repeating the pattern when she doesn't answer.

She locks eyes with me, and I know she's on the verge of flying over the edge. I bark, "Don't you dare come!"

She swallows hard, closing her eyes. I pound into her, going as deep as I can. She pulls the chains, but there's no slack to be had. Her knuckles turn white, and she begs, "Please. Oh God! Please!"

"Please, who?" I demand.

"Sir! Please, Sir! I-I-I can't...oh!" She blinks hard.

I slow it way down.

"Oh...oh...Sir! Please!" she pleads, her walls gripping my shaft torturously.

It's all too much for me. The time I spent in the cock cage made every sensation more powerful, yet I'm not ending this until she does what I want.

And she's going to love every minute of it. She's even going to admit it to me.

"You want to come?" I ask harshly, then wipe the sweat off my forehead.

"Please!" she begs.

"Then I want the truth!"

"Wh—" She licks her lips, panting. "What truth?"

"What do you prefer? Dominating me, or me dominating you?"

She locks eyes with me.

"Don't you dare lie!" I warn, pushing my thumb against her clit and circling it.

She replies, "Please."

"Who do you prefer to be the dominant one, Pina? There's only room for one of us. Decide. Do you want to dominate, or do you want me to? Hmm?" I demand.

Her lips tremble. Her eyes glisten.

"Pina!"

"You! I...please!" she cries out.

"Come," I order as I circle her clit faster and thrust as fast as possible.

She comes within seconds, screaming my name, her eyes rolling and convulsing so hard on me, it takes all my willpower not to release into her.

When her orgasm subsides, I pull out of her. I release the restraints then yank her into a sitting position. I hold her head next to my erection, commanding, "Be a good girl and show me how badly you want me."

She takes all of me in her mouth. My head hits the back of her throat, and it's bliss. After everything she's done to me, I feel completely unhinged. It's a similar feeling when I've killed someone.

On a normal day, that'd scare me. But all I can think about is that Pina dela Cruz, the most confident and in control of everything woman I know, is sucking my cock, fully submitting to me.

She admitted she preferred it.

I wrap her hair around my fist and palm her head, not showing her any mercy, thrusting into her mouth like the world's coming to an end.

It doesn't take long. To test her further, I reduce the pressure on her head so she can retreat and warn, "I'm about to come."

She passes my test. She doesn't flinch, swallowing all of me as so much adrenaline attacks me that I struggle to keep on my feet. Endorphins create the most powerful high I've ever had. And Pina keeps her lush mouth over my cock, milking me dry.

I retreat then lie on the bed, pulling her into me. Neither of us speaks, both trying to find our breath. A long time passes before I scoot down the bed so I'm at her eye level. I tuck a sweaty lock behind her ear and study her face, searching for any sign of the anger or confusion she had the previous night.

She bites on her lip and furrows her eyebrows.

"You okay, baby girl?" I ask.

She hesitates.

"Is that a no? Something's wrong?" I fret.

She shakes her head. "No. I'm... I'm okay."

I stroke her cheek then peck her on the lips. "You sure?"

She turns away and stares at the ceiling.

My gut flips. The last thing I want is Pina pissed at me again over how we have sex. I cage my body over hers and pin her wrists to the headboard.

She gasps, "What are you doing?"

"Don't go backward," I say.

She scrunches her face. "Backward?"

I nod, grinning. "Yep. Don't get pissed at me. Besides your little stint where you were mean to my cock, we just had a really good time."

She huffs. "You broke your word again. I didn't think Marinos went back on their promises."

I sigh. "Pina, I'm not a submissive. I don't know how you got those other men to submit, but it's not in me. You should know this."

She stays quiet.

"You just admitted you wanted me to be the Dom," I point out.

Her eyes glisten. She blinks hard then turns her head.

I force her to look at me and soften my voice. "Why does this upset you?"

She slowly shakes her head. "I don't know."

I cautiously ask, "But you weren't lying earlier? You prefer me to dominate you?"

She closes her eyes and groans.

"What's that about?" I ask.

She opens her eyes. "Nothing."

"No, tell me," I insist.

She stays silent.

I lean into her ear and murmur, "Do I need to tie you up and make you spill it?"

She stifles a laugh and pushes my chest. "Stop it."

"Not until you tell me what I want to know," I say.

"See! This is exactly the issue," she claims.

"What?"

"Get off me."

To mess with her, I say, "No."

"Tristano!"

I groan and roll off her. I lean on my elbow, facing her. "Chill out, baby girl. Now tell me what this issue is, because I'm clueless right now."

"Obviously," she mutters.

"Sue me. Now start talking," I demand.

She tilts her head, giving me an exasperated look. I stay quiet, waiting. She finally states, "I don't cave to the Marinos."

I jerk my head back, insulted. "What does that mean?"

"Don't get all bent out of shape. You asked me and I answered," she asserts.

I sit up and face her. I tap my fingers on my thigh. "Fine. Tell me what you mean."

She sits up, too, then puts her hand over mine. "Everyone bends over backward to do exactly what you and your brothers say. I've never let any of you push me around," she admits.

My chest tightens. "So you think what we do in the bedroom somehow changes your interaction with my family?"

She shrugs. "I don't know. Does it? I mean, it's a bit convenient that the day after I sleep with you, I get banned from the club."

Rage boils my blood. "Biagio isn't someone to take lightly. If he wants something or someone, he'll do everything in his power to get his way. And you should have told Dante or one of us about the others."

She hugs her knees to her chest. "Dante's never wanted me in the club."

"No, he hasn't. But can you blame him? It's not the safest place to hang out, and you know this. It was only a matter of time before something like this happened. Frankly, I'm surprised it took this long with a woman like you," I confess.

Her eyes turn to slits. She fires back, "What does that mean?"

"Don't get all insulted. You're sexy as fuck, and you don't let anyone push you around. Plus, you're Dante's right hand. Lots of men would want to get with you," I state.

She stares at me, but her irritation doesn't disappear.

I suggest, "Maybe you should stop thinking we're out to get you and remember we're all on Team Pina."

Her lips twitch. "Team Pina?"

I grin. "Yeah. You want me to get T-shirts and hats made?"

She slaps my shoulder with the back of her hand. "Ha ha!"

"I will," I threaten.

She covers her face and shakes her head.

I remove her hands and palm her cheek. "Listen to me. You've always been part of our family. Do you not know this?"

Her expression softens. "I know."

"Okay. Then trust this is in your best interest. You know what the Abruzzos are capable of, and it's not worth the risk," I declare.

"It's still not fair. You guys get to do whatever you want. Yet all the women in your family have to abide by your parameters. Now I have to follow suit, and I'm not even related to you."

"What's the big deal about the club? You have your own dungeon here, and it's way better than any of the club rooms, so why fight us on this?"

Her face falls. "Easy for you to ask when you go there all the time and aren't banned. And it's just as dangerous for you. Don't tell me it isn't. I may not have been there when you guys shot up the place to rescue Brenna, but I know how many casualties there were."

She has a point, but the club represents many opportunities for my family. We get to find out what other crime families are up to. We learn about men's weaknesses and strengths. At times, we flip the closest advisors of our enemies. "I'm not going to deny what you say, but not going to the club isn't an option. You know why we go."

She scoffs. "Don't act like you haven't all used it as your fucking ground since you were eighteen."

My gut flips. I cringe inside. I can't fault her for saying that, but it still sounds horrible, especially when she's sitting next to me naked and the room still smells like sex. After some thought, I finally reply, "I'm not eighteen anymore, nor are my brothers."

"All of you still act like it at times," she declares.

I groan. "Pina, are you, of all people, going to hold this over my head?"

"What are you implying?"

"You work for Dante. You've been going to the club for years and partaking in activities of your choice. It's no different than what we've done."

"Or are still doing," she states.

I grind my molars, unhappy she's tossing all our indiscretions in my face.

"Don't pout," she orders.

"Then stop acting like you're a saint and I'm the devil," I order.

She sighs and looks at the bed.

Several moments pass. I debate which direction to take this conversation and finally break the silence. "I can't do anything about the club. It's for your protection. But I promise you, I'm not going to treat you any differently outside of the bedroom than I have in the past."

She inhales deeply.

I hold up my pinky. "Pinky promise."

She tilts her head but bites on a smile.

I wiggle my finger. "Are you going to leave me hanging all day?"

She laughs and hooks her pinky around mine.

I lean forward and kiss her then ask, "So are we good now? Can you relax and trust me?"

Tense silence fills the air. She swallows hard.

Hurt, I question, "You don't trust me?"

She nods. "No, I trust you."

"Okay, then why the hesitation?"

She gets on her knees and puts her arms around my shoulders. "Nothing has changed. I don't want Dante to know about whatever this is between us."

I don't know how to categorize Pina and me, so I'm not ready to rush out and tell Dante anything. And I definitely don't want to do it until she's comfortable. So I slide my arms around her waist and tug her closer. "You have my word. Everything between us stays a secret until you say otherwise."

"You promise?"

I arch my eyebrows. "Do you want my pinky again?"

She smiles. "No. I'll take your word."

"Good, because I've never lied to you, and I'm not looking to start," I vow.

Her body relaxes, and her eyes light up. "Thank you. Do you want to take a shower?"

I toss her over my shoulder and rise.

"Tristano," she says on a laugh, slapping my ass.

I walk through the condo and go into the bathroom attached to the bedroom. I set her on the counter, fist her hair, and tug her head back. I lean over her and ask, "How many times do you think I can make you come today?"

8

Pina

Monday

Nicki Minaj rapping "Boss Ass Bitch" tears me out of my sleep.

Groaning, I fumble for my phone, hit the snooze button, then snuggle back into Tristano's warm body.

He tugs me closer, pressing his lips to my forehead. In a sleepy voice, he imitates Nicki, singing, "I'm a boss..." ass bitch, bitch, bitch..." the chorus.

I reach for his mouth and put my palm over it. "Shush."

He chuckles then tries to bite my fingers.

"Ugh!" I whine then try to get away from him.

He flips me on my back, caging his muscular frame over me. A twinkle grows in his dark eyes. He moves his lips an inch from mine, ordering, "Call off work today."

"What? No," I reply. It's not in my nature to play hooky. Besides, Dante will probably show up on my doorstep if I don't go into the office. He's messaged me a dozen times over the weekend asking me to call him about the list I sent regarding the men at the club who have shown interest in me.

Not that I'm at my primary residence. The blizzard continued wreaking havoc in Manhattan. Still, I didn't plan on Tristano staying all weekend, nor did we discuss it. It just naturally happened.

Neither of us left the condo all weekend. We had more sex than I've ever had, in less than forty-eight hours. We cooked food, binged a reality program about celebrities eating hot wings while being interviewed, and listened to each other's playlists. His brothers blew up his phone the entire time, but he ignored them.

Tristano kisses the curve of my neck, claiming, "One day won't hurt."

I smirk. "Says the man who also takes orders from Dante."

His body stiffens, and he puts his face in front of mine, scowling.

"What did I say?"

"I don't take orders from Dante."

I scoff. "Since when?"

His expression hardens. He rolls off me and stomps into the bathroom.

I get up and follow him. He turns on the shower, and I reach for his arm, asking, "What's going on?"

He steps under the water and picks up my body wash.

I twist my hair, secure it with a claw clip, then move in front of him. "Why are you pissed?"

He squeezes soap into his palm then sets the bottle down. While washing himself, he answers, "I'm not Dante's minion."

"I didn't say you were," I point out, unsure what's going on, but it's clear I've hit a nerve.

He sniffs hard, takes some shampoo, and lathers his hair. "Think what you want, Pina." He closes his eyes and lets the water run over his head.

I step closer to the stream of hot water. I slide my hands up his chest and lace my fingers behind his head. "I don't understand why you're upset right now. Everyone takes orders from Dante, including me. Does that mean you think I'm his minion?"

Tristano clenches his jaw, spins me so I'm under the water, then responds, "Of course not. It's your job."

"But?" I push and reach for the body wash, adding, "You're not the firstborn. There's a hierarchy established. You don't have to be all touchy about the subject."

"Thanks for the 101 on how my family works. Glad you've been paying attention," he seethes, then steps out of the shower.

I rinse off, shave my armpits, then turn the water off. I reach for a towel and wrap it around my body, following Tristano to the sink.

He takes the toothbrush I gave him and puts paste on it.

I slide in front of him. "Hey!"

He grinds his molars and locks eyes with me.

I admit, "I'm not sure why you're upset."

Several tense moments pass. He finally confesses, "It sucks being the youngest male in my family. You chose your position, I didn't."

My pulse creeps up. "You don't like the family business?"

He sighs. "Didn't say that."

"Then what's the issue?" I press.

He glances at the ceiling then back at me. "I'm the last on the totem pole, and I can't do anything to change it."

His admission surprises me. I always assumed Gianni got the unlucky straw since he's only a few minutes younger than Dante. Now that Tristano's voiced his feelings, I can see how it would be difficult to be in his shoes. I've always wanted to be someone in charge. Even though Dante's my boss, I've learned how to take control in the office. Over the years, we've established our boundaries, and Dante knows not to cross certain lines with me. If it has to do with my duties, I call the shots. But as Tristano stated, I chose this position. He didn't get to pick his.

I reach up and cup his cheek, trying to focus on the positive. "How many men answer directly to you, working on your projects?"

He shrugs. "Dozens."

"And how many men are under them?"

"Hundreds. And you already know this, so what's your point?"

"Seems to me you have lots of power. Any of those men would love to be in your shoes," I assert.

He steps to the side of me and turns the water on and replies, "Forget I said anything." He brushes his teeth.

I grab my brush and add paste to it. I continue, "I'm not disregarding your feelings. I can see how it would be annoying at times."

He grunts, keeps brushing, then spits in the sink. He mumbles, "Try almost every day." He opens the bottle of mouthwash and takes a swig.

"I can sympathize," I offer, then brush my teeth.

He swishes, spits, then sits on the counter, studying me.

I finish then ask, "Why are you looking at me like that?"

"Doesn't it ever get to you?"

"What's that?" I take a capful of mouthwash.

"Taking orders from Dante. Hell, taking orders from my brothers and even me at times."

I swish, then spit, wipe my face, and step in front of him.

He palms my ass and arches his eyebrows. "Well? Does it?"

"I don't work for you and your brothers. Anything I do for you three is because you beg me to help," I chirp.

Amusement fills his expression. "I'll remember to add some extra desperation in my plea the next time I need your assistance."

I laugh, teasing, "That might give me extra motivation to put your project ahead of Dante's."

His face turns serious. "Okay, so what about Dante? Don't you wish you could call the shots sometimes?"

I bite on my smile and stroke the side of his head.

"Why aren't you answering?" he asks.

"Nine times out of ten, I do call them. Sometimes it sucks—like when all of you gang up on me."

"We don't gang up on you," he claims.

I huff. "Really? What would you call the meeting at your house on Saturday morning?"

His face darkens. "Protecting you. That isn't the same thing."

I roll my eyes. "I guess we'll have to agree to disagree."

"Pina—"

"I don't want to hear your excuses, Tristano. It is what it is, but that isn't the majority of my day. And I think if you try to focus on the things you're in charge of, you'll realize how much power you have independent of your brothers." I push out of his grasp, adding, "I need to get ready so I'm not late."

He stays quiet, watching me put on my makeup. After a few minutes, he pats me on the ass and leaves the bathroom.

I finish my makeup, put my hair in a messy bun, then go into my closet. I put on a black dress, a hot-pink scarf, and knee-high boots. I step into the bedroom, and Tristano's on the phone.

He stands in front of the window, staring out the glass, speaking in Italian.

I didn't know any language except English when Dante hired me. I quickly learned the Marinos often communicate in Italian, so I took it upon myself to learn it. While I barely speak words out loud, I fully understand conversations.

No one knows my little secret. Maybe it's not ethical to hide it from them, but they've also never asked me if I'm fluent in Italian. So I've not lied. Plus, I can often help Dante fix things he wouldn't ask me to do for whatever reason. I always find a way to explain why I did something so he doesn't know I can understand his conversations.

Tristano barks in Italian, "He knows the rules. This was a blatant disregard. Papà should have convinced the council to take away his membership, not allow this stall tactic."

My gut flips. The memory of Biagio's palm on my ass and the scent of his stale cigarette breath makes me cringe.

Tristano seethes, "That's not good enough, and you know it. He shouldn't have agreed to another meeting." He taps his fingers on his thigh. His shoulder muscles flex through his T-shirt. He shakes his head then spins, catching me watching him.

I move to my dresser and open my jewelry box, pretending to debate about what to wear.

"Papà should have done better on this. You know he's not going to stop. If he's shown interest, we need guards on her."

The hairs on my arms rise. I don't doubt Tristano's talking to one of his brothers about me. It wouldn't be the first time Dante added a bodyguard to watch over me, but it's normally when the family is on high alert due to some outside threat.

It always seems silly when my driver also serves to give me a layer of protection, but I learned years ago when Dante decides I need a bodyguard, it's best not to argue. Plus, I know what the Marino enemies are capable of doing to women. I'm not looking to be their next victim.

I put my earrings on, and Tristano says, "I'll be back soon, and we can look at who's available."

I add a bracelet and turn.

Tristano slides his phone into his pocket. He steps forward. "I have to go."

"Everything okay?" I ask.

"Yep." He leans down and tilts my chin, kissing me until his phone buzzes. He groans, glances at it, then pecks me on the lips. "You still owe me a date."

My butterflies spread their wings, but I'm also worried. Plus, I don't know what this is between us. Sure, we had a great time, but this can't go anywhere.

I should end this now.

Instead of doing what I know is the smart thing, I ignore the nagging voice in my head and ask, "Don't you think it's risky to go out in public together? What if someone sees us?"

Hurt passes in his expression, but it disappears so fast, I think I imagined it. "Don't worry. I'll make sure no one sees us."

"How?" I question.

He grins. "That's my secret. I need to go. I'll call you later." He gives me another panty-melting kiss and then squeezes my ass.

I watch him leave my unit then wait ten minutes, worried. If I text my driver to take me to work, he might see Tristano. So I pace my family room, reliving the weekend and trying to contain my smile. When it's been long enough, I slide into my coat, text my driver I'm ready, and head downstairs.

The cold wind slaps my cheeks the moment I step outside. I get into the SUV, pull my phone out of my purse, and text Dante.

Me: *Are you coming to the office this morning?*

Dante: *I'm already on my way.*

Surprised, I glance at the time. Dante usually comes in either late morning or early afternoon if he's not working out of his home office.

Me: *Well, aren't you motivated on this cold Monday morning.*

Dante: *We need to talk.*

I groan. Whenever Dante needs to talk, it usually involves some sort of lecture. I'd bet money it's regarding the club.

Me: *And to what do I owe the pleasure?*

Dante: *We'll discuss this in person.*

Me: *Fine. If you want me in a good mood, I'll need my favorite drink.*

Dante: *It's in my hand.*

I smile. At least I have Dante trained. There's a coffee shop halfway between his house and the office. It has the best salted-caramel latte on Earth. He made the mistake of bringing me one years ago. Now he knows if he wants to butter me up, he better bring the drink. And the coffee shop is out of my way, so I don't have it often.

Me: *I'm ten minutes away. See you soon.*

I scroll through my messages that I ignored over the weekend, respond to a few texts, then click on a voicemail Chanel left Saturday afternoon.

She chirps, "Hey, girl. Call me ASAP."

I tap the button, and her phone rings four times.

She groggily answers, "Hello?"

"Morning! Sorry I didn't call. I just got your message."

She groans. "It's only seven."

"Yep. And Monday. It's a workday," I tease.

"I don't have a normal job, remember?" she grumbles.

"Doesn't Zara have school?" I ask. Zara is Chanel's daughter.

"Snow day," Chanel replies, then yawns.

"Lucky her. So what's going on?"

"What do you mean?"

"You asked me to call you ASAP," I remind her.

"Oh. Duh! Sorry! Of course. So, you know Zara's birthday is coming up, right?"

"Sure. I already got her present. I just need to wrap it," I admit.

"That's sweet of you. What did you get?"

"Not telling you."

"Really?"

"Nope."

"Give me a hint."

"Sorry!"

Chanel whines, "You're no fun!"

I smile as the SUV parks in front of my office building. "Hey, I just got to work, and Dante's on his way in, so let's get back to why I needed to call you."

Chanel yawns again. "Since when does Dante grace you with his presence so early?"

"Today. So...?" I push. I love Chanel, but she can get off track easily. And Dante's SUV just pulled in front of mine.

"Zara's delusional," Chanel claims.

"How's that?" I ask as my driver opens my door. I slide out and step into the frigid air, trotting toward the entrance.

"She wants a tattoo for her birthday."

I groan. "She's too young to put something on her body for the rest of her life."

"That's what I told her!" Chanel exclaims.

I nod at the doorman and step past him into the warm building. I swipe my key card and push past the metal gate, saying, "Let me guess, she's not listening."

"You got it. I swear she just wants to push me. Now that she's turning fourteen, she also wants a credit card," Chanel informs me.

The elevator opens and Dante orders, "Hold it, Pina."

I hold in my groan, wishing I could avoid whatever conversation he has planned. I hold the door and tell Chanel, "Did you tell her to get a job?"

"Of course."

"What did she say?"

"That all the kids in her class already have tattoos, and it's not fair she doesn't," Chanel answers.

Dante nods and punches the code for our floor.

I scoff. "Just because the other parents want their kids to be spoiled brats doesn't mean she has to be."

"Yes! I said the same thing!" Chanel blurts out.

"So, what's the problem?" I ask.

"Should I get her one?"

"Umm, no!"

Chanel exhales loudly. "But if all the other kids have one..."

"Seriously? If all the other kids were doing drugs, would you tell her it's okay?" I question.

"Of course not!"

The elevator stops on our floor. The doors open and Dante motions for me to go first. I step out and say, "Well, there's your answer. Did you figure out what you're doing for her party?"

"Not yet. I'll let you know this week."

"Okay. Stick to your guns. And I'll talk to her about the tattoo if you want," I offer.

"Awesome! I was hoping you'd say that! She listens to you more than me."

"Not surprising. You're her mom. She's not supposed to prefer your advice," I claim.

"Good point."

"Listen, Dante's here. I've gotta run."

"Okay. Thanks."

"Bye," I say, then hang up. I take the coffee out of Dante's hand and go directly to my office. If he's going to lecture me, I'm sitting at the desk. For some reason, it makes me feel more in control. I take a sip of my favorite drink and then smile. "Thanks."

"No problem. Was that Chanel?" Dante asks.

"Yep."

"Has she had any problems at the club?" he interrogates, his face hardening.

"Well, let's just get right into it," I chirp, setting my cup on my desk and taking off my coat.

Dante plops on a chair across from mine. He pushes the pads of his fingers together and, in a stern voice, warns, "Don't make light of this, Pina."

I toss back, "Don't make this bigger than it is."

Frustration fills his expression. I take a deep breath, telling myself to chill out a bit. When Dante wears that look, I shouldn't press his buttons too much. He shakes his head. "You're wrong."

I sigh. "What do you expect, Dante? It's a sex club. People go there wanting one thing. Everyone besides Biagio backed off when I made it clear I wasn't interested."

"This is exactly why you should have never been going in the first place," he claims.

Annoyed, I snap, "Is there a point to your visit? I have work to do."

"Don't get pissed at me," he asserts.

"Then don't act like a broken record. You already banned me. What else do you want?"

"Until I say, I'm adding security to you. If Biagio tries to contact you or you see him anywhere, you let me know immediately," Dante declares.

"Is this necessary? My driver—"

"It's not negotiable," Dante interjects.

We lock eyes, each challenging the other, but this isn't a battle I'll win.

"Any questions?" Dante asks.

"Who's going to be the fly on my back?" I smirk.

"Tristano's going through our men to see who the best fit is," he answers.

"Fine. Send me a memo." I turn on my computer and pull files out of my desk drawer.

"It's probably going to take a few days. We need to move our guys around," Dante adds.

"Well, I won't hold my breath," I mutter.

"Until we figure out who we can utilize, your driver is on high alert. He'll be stationed outside your condo door, too," Dante informs me before he rises and leaves the room. When the door to my office shuts, I put my hands over my face and groan.

I knew Tristano's conversation was about me. It's not a surprise Dante's adding security to me, yet I still don't like it. I'm a private person. I like to keep my personal life away from the Marinos. They influence enough of my choices.

It's exactly why I need to cut off whatever this thing is between Tristano and me.

9

Tristano

Friday

My patience is running thin. Pina's ignored most of my messages all week. The last one she sent to me stated it wasn't a good idea for us to be anything but professional and that I needed to forget about last weekend. It pisses me off, but instead of moving on, I only want her more.

When I left her condo on Monday morning, I couldn't get my mind off her. I kept replaying the entire weekend. I hadn't meant to stay that long, but it felt right. Now, it's like we've taken ten steps backward.

Why can't I forget about her?

I don't chase women.

She needs to stop ignoring me.

Papà's had me dealing with different issues all week. It's prevented me from going to Dante's office or knocking on her door at night. But every text I send her has gone unanswered in the last two days. It's making me feel crazy.

I got home at five this morning and met my brothers for our morning workout. No amount of punching the boxing bags reduced my frustration. If anything, it only made me more determined to figure this issue out today.

I step out of the shower, dry off, then get dressed. It's seven thirty, and Pina should be at work. The rest of the staff doesn't get in until nine, but she likes to get there earlier. Dante already confirmed he's working from home today, so I text Flex to meet me out front.

On my way out, I run into Papà. He asks, "Where you off to?"

"I'm meeting Rubio at the docks," I lie.

Papà arches his eyebrows. "Is there an issue or shipment arriving that I'm not aware of?"

"No."

"Then what's the meeting about?"

Irritation fills me. Lately, Papà's drilling all of us about our activities. I accuse, "Are you going to start micromanaging me now?"

He crosses his arms. His eyes turn to slits. "When my sons return to obeying my orders, I'll not ask questions."

"I just spent my entire week obeying your orders," I point out.

"Do you want a medal?"

Anger sears through me. "Are we done here?"

"No. You haven't answered my question. What's the meeting with Rubio about?" he demands.

I rack my brain, scowling at him.

"Tristano, I want an answer. Now," he states.

"We're going through the upcoming shipment and route to the new buyer," I fib.

"It's not for three weeks."

"Yeah. I'm trying to be proactive. Is that a problem?" I seethe.

Papà studies me, and I do everything in my power not to flinch.

When he doesn't speak, I hurl, "So it's a problem?"

He sniffs hard. "No. Go on. Let me know what the new plan is when you get back."

"Fine," I snarl, adding a visit to Rubio to my list of things to do today and cursing myself for creating that lie. I just added a big project to my day. I push past Papà and go outside. The remnants of the previous weekend's blizzard are still on the ground but almost completely melted. Salt covers the steps and driveway to keep people from falling. My boots crunch over it as I walk.

I get into the front seat, and Flex nods. "Boss. Where are we heading?"

"Dante's office, then the docks," I reply.

"Got it," he says, veering toward the gate.

I sit back in my seat, glancing at the text messages I sent Pina. Every unanswered one makes my gut drop. Reading them makes me feel like a desperate teenager who can't take a hint.

But we're good together. She knows it, and I know it.

Dante probably freaked her out somehow.

Flex interrupts me, asking, "Guess who's back in town?" He glances at me, and I can faintly see his eyes through his sunglasses.

"Who?" I ask.

"Callie Langford."

I whistle. Callie and Flex used to date in high school, then on and off until she moved to California. I question, "Why's she in town?"

Flex glances over his shoulder then moves into the other lane before veering onto the expressway ramp. "Don't know."

"How do you know she's back?"

His lips twitch. "She texted me."

"Did you see her yet?"

"Not yet. Was hoping you didn't need me tonight?"

I review my schedule in my head then respond, "Unless something changes, I don't."

"Thanks."

"How long has it been since you saw her?" I ask.

He lowers his voice. "Too long."

Right now, I understand that feeling. I've not seen Pina in a few days. It's been years for Flex and Callie, and I'm fairly certain he's not over her. "How long is she in town?"

"Not sure," he says, then guns the engine, whizzing past several vehicles and weaving in and out of different lanes.

We don't talk for the rest of the trip. He pulls up to Dante's office building, and my stomach flips. I have limited time before the rest of the staff arrives, so I hightail it inside and through the building.

When I step off the elevator, I see Pina's back in the glass. She's in the conference room, lost in her work. Papers and file folders are strewn all over the table. Her laptop is open, and she's highlighting something.

My dick strains in my pants. I'm unsure what it is about this woman, but just looking at her affects me. I debate about what to do then sneak into the room. I lean over her, sliding my hands down her arms until my armpits rest on her shoulders. Her body stiffens, and I murmur in her ear, "You owe me a date."

She freezes, breathing deeply.

I kiss the pulse that's throbbing in her neck.

She snaps her head toward me. "What are you doing?"

"Reminding you that you're mine," I arrogantly declare.

She scoffs. "Yours? I think I made it clear this isn't happening again." She pushes her chair back. I retreat a step, and she rises and spins, blurting out, "You shouldn't be here. Someone is going to see us."

"They aren't in for another hour," I assert as I grab her hips and place her on the table. I lean over her until she's flat on the wood.

"Tristano!"

I slide my hands over her cheeks and kiss her, parting her lips with my tongue and darting it around her mouth until her body submits. She laces her fingers in my hair and a tiny whimper fills the air.

I kiss her some more then stare at her.

Her chest heaves, and her golden-brown eyes widen.

I repeat, "You owe me a date."

"This isn't a good idea," she says again, but this time, it sounds weak.

"I'll pick you up at seven tonight. Assuming you'll be at your normal place? Or should I go to Manhattan?" I question.

"We can't—"

Crap. Not seven!

"Make it eight. And I'm not leaving until you agree to see me tonight. If you try to ditch me, I'll show up here next week when the entire office is engrossed in their work. Don't test me, Pina," I threaten.

In a hurt voice, she asks, "You'd do that to me? After you promised to keep it between us?"

"Promises go both ways. You owe me a date. Don't make me be a cocksucker," I warn, then step back and pull her into a sitting position.

She glares at me. "You're already one."

I grunt. "Fair enough. But it's your choice which version you want. I'll see you at eight."

She jumps off the table and shoots daggers at me with her glare. "You aren't going to bully me into seeing you."

I arrogantly smile. "If that's how you see it, I can't help you. I'll see you tonight, or I'll see you next week. Again, you're choice." I turn and leave the room.

She follows me. "Tristano! This isn't appropriate!"

I push the button for the elevator then glance at her. "Stop overthinking everything, Pina. We're going on a date. I'll make sure no one knows or runs into us."

"How?"

"Don't worry about it. I'll handle it," I vow.

"This isn't smart. We need to stop."

The elevator opens, but I ignore it. I spin her so she's against the wall and close the gap between us. She gasps, and I hold both her cheeks. "Admit you missed me."

She stays silent.

"I missed you," I confess.

She pins her eyebrows together.

"I know you missed me. You want to know how?"

She still refuses to speak.

I rub my thumb over her lips, admitting, "I felt it in your kiss. Right now, I see it on your face. So we're going out tonight.

I'm picking you up at eight. No one will know, but I'm not backing down about this." I peck her on the lips then push the button for the elevator again.

"Tristano—"

I kiss her again, this time, I put everything I have into it. Endorphins flare in my cells. She returns my affection and the elevator dings. I retreat and wink, then say, "See you tonight." I step into the elevator and hit the button to close the doors.

She gapes at me as the doors shut. The elevator drops to the ground floor, and I go to the SUV, feeling like I'm walking on air.

Everything I felt last weekend is real. Kissing her confirmed my obsession isn't delusional. The chemistry between us isn't something you can fake.

I open the passenger door and get in the SUV. Flex pulls out into traffic. "Docks, right?"

"Yeah."

He glances at me then asks, "Why do you look so happy?"

I take my phone out of my pocket. "Do I?"

"Yep."

"Huh." I call Rubio.

He answers, "Tristano, what's up?"

"I'm heading your way. We need to go through the new routes," I inform him.

"Today? It's not for a few weeks," he states.

"Papà wants a report by the end of the day," I announce.

There's a moment of silence. Rubio finally asks, "Is there something he's concerned about?"

"No. Just wants me to be proactive," I lie.

"Okay. See you soon."

"Later," I reply, then hang up.

Flex guns the engine, cuts someone off, and a horn blares. He questions, "Your Papà on a rampage again?"

I shrug. "You know how he gets ideas in his head. So where are you taking Callie?"

"My place." He grins.

"Wow. Straight at it, huh?" I tease and hold my fist out.

He bumps it and adds, "I'm cooking her favorite meal for her. She said she missed it."

I chuckle. "So she's gagging for it, huh?"

Arrogance washes over him. "Can't blame the woman for missing the real thing. I doubt half those Hollywood A-listers can even get it up."

"Is that who she's dated the last few years?" I inquire.

"Not sure, and I don't care. She's back, and I plan on reminding her what she's been missing," he confides.

I nod, understanding that statement. It's less than a week since I had Pina. I'm feeling half-crazy, so I can only imagine what Flex has felt over the years.

He reaches for the dial and turns the music up. Hip-hop blares through the speakers, adding to my good mood. By the time we get to the docks, the sun shines bright, making it the first day in a long time it isn't gray. The water sparkles and I decide to take Pina somewhere warm on our date.

I get out of the SUV and text her.

Me: *I hope your pussy's ready for my tongue tonight.*

Pina: *Is that part of your blackmail stunt?*

Me: *Bet you won't tell me to stop.*

Pina: *You're annoying. Stop texting me. I have work to do.*

I chuckle then type another message.

Me: *You're super predictable.*

Pina: *Apparently, you can't follow directions.*

Me: *Do you have to get the last word in?*

Pina: *Silencing my notifications now.*

Me: *Ah, you do need the last word.*

Pina: *You can't help yourself, can you?*

Me: *Save your energy so you can beg me later.*

Pina: *Beg you to leave the date, you mean?*

Me: *Baby girl, when you fall in love with me, don't forget I'm the one who saved us.*

Pina: *FAT. CHANCE.*

Me: *It's inevitable. You'll see.*

Pina: *You just continue to get more annoying.*

Me: *I have work to do. See you at eight.*

I take my phone and put it in my pocket. It vibrates from another text, but I ignore it, stepping inside the office. "Hey, Rubio."

He nods. "Tristano. Flex. You're out early this morning."

"We're high achievers," Flex claims.

Rubio arches his eyebrows. "Is that what you tell yourself?"

"Every day. I can give you lessons if you want," Flex taunts.

"Let's get this done. I've got shit to do," I state.

Rubio grabs a file off his desk. "I started working on this last week. I think there needs to be two options. We don't have all the police data and won't until it's closer to shipment time. Frankly, I'm surprised Angelo wants this when we don't know the coordinates yet."

I shrug and cross my arms over my chest. The last shipment was too close for our comfort. Police were everywhere, and nothing was as normal. Our contacts on payroll claimed the chief changed things at the last minute. After that, Papà decided we needed fresh routes for all shipments. However, it requires aligning things with our police contacts in other counties. "Me, too, but let's give the old man what he wants. We'll confirm closer to the date which route we'll take. What are the options?"

We spend several hours going through possible routes and each of the counties and local districts that could cause issues. Rubio makes a copy of the file. I leave and take it to Papà.

He opens the file and thumbs through the pages.

"Rubio, Flex, and I triple-checked all the police entities we'll need to work with on each route," I tell him.

He reads some more then looks up. "This is good work, Tristano."

Pride and surprise fill me. My father hasn't given me a compliment in months. I hate how I actually care about his approval, but I do. I reply, "Thanks."

"If you had to choose today, which route would you take?" he asks.

"Plan A."

"Why?"

I step closer and tap the summary. "Fewer cops to organize. It's a few miles longer, but overall less possible exposure."

He rises and pats me on the back. His lips twitch. "So you do listen."

Insulted, I huff. "Seriously?"

He chuckles, goes to the bar, and pours two shots of sambuca. "Since when did you lose your sense of humor?" He hands me a glass then clinks his to mine, adding, "Salute."

"Salute." I down the liquor. It coats my throat in a slow burn then hits my stomach. I question, "Do you need anything else? I have plans this weekend."

"Oh? Where are you off to?" he inquires.

"Quick trip to the Caribbean. I need some sunshine," I state.

"Who are you going with?"

"Just a girl I'm seeing. You don't know her," I lie.

He studies me then says, "Have a good time."

"Thanks." I leave his office and go to my office in my wing. Then I turn on my computer and pull up several high-end New York boutiques.

Several items catch my eye, so I place orders. I text Flex to pick everything up and take it to my private jet. Then I call my travel agent, Barry.

He answers, "Tristano! What's going on, bro?"

I scratch my jaw, replying, "Hey, man. I need a place in the Caribbean for the weekend. Something top notch."

"Boys' weekend or are you bringing a woman?" he asks.

I chuckle. "It's a woman. I need something secluded but with options to do things around wherever we are. I want all the amenities and something full service."

"Any particular island?"

"Don't care. Surprise me. But I need it tonight through Monday morning."

"Let me see what's available. I've got a few places in mind you'll love," he states.

"Great. Just book it and shoot my pilots a text with the information," I instruct.

"On it!"

"Thanks." I hang up and glance at my watch.

Three hours.

Since I ordered clothes, there's nothing to pack. Plus, I always keep a toiletry bag with several outfits on the plane for myself. I call Flex.

"What's up?" he answers.

"I'm going to send you a list of toiletries. Can you pick those up and deliver them with the rest of the items?" I ask.

"What time are you leaving?"

"A little after eight."

"Done. Anything else?"

"No. That should do it. Thanks." I hang up and text him a list of bathroom items I know Pina uses. Then I pace the room, trying not to look at my watch every five minutes.

Food.

I send instructions to my flight attendant about what I want her to serve and decide it's time to shower. I shave, brush my teeth, and spray on some cologne.

My patience runs out, so I text one of our standby drivers.

Me: *I need to leave in ten minutes.*

Pedro: *I'll pull the SUV up.*

I glance around my bedroom suite, wondering if there's anything I'm missing. I can't think of anything, so I grab my wallet and leave.

Gianni stops me in the hall. "Papà said you're going on a trip?"

"Need to get out of town for a bit," I admit, which isn't a lie. Ever since deciding to go away today, New York feels like it's closing in on me.

"Where are you off to?"

"Not sure. Told Barry to pick a place."

Gianni chuckles. "Sounds like something you'd do."

"Good thing I'm not an uptight control freak like you."

"Whatever. Have a good time. You back Sunday?"

"Maybe Monday. See you later." I fist-bump him and leave.

When I get in the car, Pedro asks, "Where to?"

My gut sinks. What was I thinking? I can't have Pedro take me there. He'll tell Papà.

"Hold up," I reply, then text Flex.

Me: *Need you to meet me at Sizzlers.*

Flex: *Are we going drinking?*

Me: *No. Need your discretion. How far are you?*

Flex: *Not far. Five minutes maybe?*

Me: *Okay. Wait for me. Leaving now.*

I tell Pedro, "Sizzlers."

"I went there last weekend. Those waitresses are something else," he informs me.

"I heard, but I'm meeting Flex there," I reply, then say nothing else until he drops me off. I get directly in Flex's SUV.

"So what's going on?" he asks.

My chest tightens. I told Pina I wouldn't tell anyone, but I can't keep this under wraps without one of my drivers knowing. Flex is my most trusted man. I turn and state, "This is between us. No one, and I mean *no one*, can know."

He nods. "You know I've got your back."

"Okay. I need you to take me to Pina's, then drop us off at Teterboro."

Silence fills the car. He cocks his eyebrows at me then asks, "You're seeing Pina?"

I don't say anything.

He whistles then pulls out into traffic, warning, "You better not let Dante catch you two."

10

Pina

THE CLOSER IT GETS TO EIGHT, THE MORE I FREAK OUT, PACING my condo.

What am I doing?

I need to call this off.

He'll tell Dante.

No, he won't.

What if he does?

I'll go and not let him touch me.

Memories of him pinning me to the conference room table and kissing me won't disappear. My butterflies spread their wings, and I reprimand myself.

Stop feeling attracted to him.

How?

Ugh!

I return to the full-length mirror, picking apart any imperfection I see and trying to correct it. I flick a piece of lint off my dress and peer closer at my face. My eyeliner is a tad uneven, so I move into the bathroom and carefully swipe a Q-tip on my lid. The black line evens out, and I take a deep breath, looking for more flaws.

The doorbell rings, making my pulse skyrocket. I glance at my watch then go to the front door. I open it and attempt to ignore the raging flutters in my stomach, declaring, "You're early."

Tristano drags his eyes over my body, pausing on my cleavage on the way down and up. His dark eyes swirl with fire, which only makes my nerves heighten. He cocks a brow at me and states, "You don't like it when people are late."

Damn him for knowing so much about me. I can't deny that tardiness drives me insane. Ye,t him pointing out he understands this only unsettles me further. It's a reminder we shouldn't be doing this, so I blurt out, "This isn't smart. Let's forget about last weekend and move forward."

He shoots me an exasperated look, then steps inside, shuts the door, and spins me so fast I gasp. He pushes me against the wall, palms my chin, leans down, then puts his lips against mine, challenging, "I'll make you a deal."

Blood pounds between my ears. As I take his bait, my voice is weak. "What's that?"

He pecks me on the lips then below my ear. Tingles burst throughout my spine. He licks my lobe then murmurs, "One date. If you have a good time, we keep seeing each other. If you have a bad time, we stop." He walks his fingers to my belly button then moves lower. He stops above my slit.

My heart beats so hard, I'm sure he can feel it. I hold my breath, swallowing hard, feeling like this is a trap.

He kisses my jaw until his provoking stare is back on me. "What's wrong, Pina? Afraid you'll have to keep seeing me?"

I square my shoulders and lift my chin. "Don't be so cocky."

"Then you agree? Or are you too scared?" he taunts.

One date, and I can end this.

God, his body feels good against mine.

Stop! Not helping!

Why does he smell so freaking good?

Ugh!

His lips twitch. "Never pegged you for a woman who won't accept a challenge."

"I'm not," I claim, stepping to the side of him and heading toward the door. "Let's go." I grab my evening bag off the table then reach for the knob.

Tristano's fast on my heels. He grabs the side of the door above my head and puts his palm on my ass.

I hurry out of his grasp and head toward the elevator, my head spinning with anticipation that I need to somehow shut off. But it's impossible.

He steps next to me, sliding his arm around my waist and tugging me into his warm frame. His lips brush the side of my forehead as he claims, "You're going to love where I'm taking you."

"Where are we going?" I ask.

"It's a surprise."

My chest tightens. "How do you know no one will see us?"

Arrogances washes over him. "Pina, give me some credit. You need to trust me."

I tear my eyes off his chiseled face, focusing on the silver metal of the elevator door. I admit, "That's not easy for me."

He snorts. "Yeah, I know, Ms. Control Freak."

I smirk. "Spoken like someone who can identify."

The doors open, and he guides me off the elevator and through my building. The cold air slaps my face, and we rush toward the SUV. The moment I slide inside, more panic erupts.

How could he be so stupid?

Why didn't he drive?

Flex glances at me in the rearview mirror. His expression is just as cocky as Tristano's. I hold myself back from lunging across the seats and slapping him. He nods. "Pina."

I hit the button to close the divider window.

Tristano slides in then slams the door.

I hurl, "Trust you, huh?"

His face falls. He holds his hands in the air. "Calm down."

The SUV pulls out into traffic. I reach for the door, and Tristano grabs my hand, pulling me back. "What are you doing?"

"I should have known better that you wouldn't keep this between us," I seethe.

"I am. And jumping out into traffic isn't going to keep anything secret," he points out.

I snarl, "How could you tell him?"

"Pina, calm down," he repeats.

"Don't tell me to calm down again," I warn.

"Flex isn't going to tell anyone. You have my word," Tristano declares.

"Sure he won't!"

"Flex doesn't talk. And he promised me, so chill out," Tristano orders.

"If you screw up my career—"

"Do you really think I'd do that?" he accuses.

I breathe through my anger then demand, "Tell me right now where we're going. If you're taking me anywhere I'm not comfortable with, I'm not getting out of this vehicle."

Tristano sits back in the seat, licks his lips, and tilts his head.

"Answer me," I command.

"I'm taking you out of New York," he announces.

I freeze, staring at him.

His arrogance grows. "Still want to accuse me of being stupid?"

"What are you talking about?" I ask.

"We're getting in my jet and flying away from here. No one will know. Flex isn't telling anyone, and neither will my air staff. And you know they understand confidentiality, so stop worrying."

I don't say anything, debating in my head whether I should get on the plane or not.

"Did you prefer we go out in New York?" he asks.

Begrudgingly, I admit, "No. This is better."

"I took all the necessary precautions. I'm not trying to harm you. I'm not that kind of a dick," he asserts.

I release an anxious breath, confessing, "I know you aren't."

"You do?"

I nod. "Yes."

He picks up my hand and kisses the back of it. "Good. Can you stop worrying and trust me, then?"

I bite my lip, still uneasy about this scenario.

"Really?" he hurls, with hurt all over his voice.

Guilt eats at me. I subconsciously reach for his thigh and reply, "Okay. I trust you."

He studies me.

"Can we change the subject?" I ask, not wanting to dwell on this anymore. If I do, I'm going to be paranoid all night.

"Fair enough," he agrees, then glances out the window. "At least traffic isn't bad."

"So, where are you taking me?"

He chuckles. "You can't stand the suspense, can you?"

I try to stop my smile. "I'm just curious."

He leans closer, tucks a lock of my hair behind my ear, then declares, "I'm taking you on the best first date you've ever been on."

My butterflies reappear. I try to stay cool. "Is that so? Pretty big claim to make."

He puffs his chest out. "You'll see."

We speed along the highway, weaving in and out of traffic. I haven't ridden with Flex a lot, but he handles the SUV in the same manner as my driver. We arrive at Teterboro in record time. Tristano's jet is waiting on the runway.

He gets out of the SUV, reaches inside for me, and helps me out. He says, "Thanks, bro. See you later."

"Later," Flex replies, then takes off before I'm halfway up the staircase.

We get past Tristano's flight crew and settle on the couch. His attendant, Danika, appears and hands me a glass of champagne. She gives Tristano a beer and asks, "Can I get you anything before we take off?"

"I'm good, thanks," I reply.

"Same," Tristano adds.

She smiles. "Did you want to know where we're going?"

"Yes," I say at the same time Tristano answers, "No. The pilot can announce it when we land."

I gape at him. *He doesn't know?*

Danika says, "Very well," then leaves.

"You don't know where we're going?" I ask.

Tristano chuckles. "Only the vicinity."

"Will you tell me what we're going to be doing?"

"Nope!"

"Ugh! You're impossible!"

He shifts in his seat and holds his bottle next to my flute. "Relax. Salute."

I decide to go with the flow and clink his beer. "Salute," I respond, then take a sip. The semi-sweet bubbly drink tastes delicious. I have another mouthful and then put my drink down, asking, "How long is the flight?"

He shrugs, and amusement lights up his features. "Don't know."

The pilot announces, "We're all cleared for takeoff. Please buckle up. There's due to be some turbulence in the first ten minutes or so. Danika, please halt all services until I turn off the seat belt sign."

I tap the side of the couch. One thing I hate is turbulence. I've flown to many places with Dante, but it still makes me jittery.

Tristano slides his arm around me and turns my head toward him. Mischief gleams in his eyes. "I think we should play poker," he suggests.

I furrow my eyebrows. "Poker?"

"Yep. Winner takes all."

"Sorry. I don't gamble. It's a waste of money."

He jerks his head back. "Are you serious?"

"Yep."

"But you went to Vegas last year with your friends," he states.

I scoff. "So? There's more to do in Vegas besides gamble."

"Sure. But you didn't walk by a slot machine and play a few rounds?"

I shake my head as the plane speeds down the runway. "Nope."

Doubt fills his face. He asks, "What's that all about?"

"Not gambling?"

"Yeah."

The feeling I used to get as a child appears. I hate it. No matter how successful I become, it always creeps up at unexpected times. I answer, "I wasn't raised like you."

"Meaning?"

"You know."

"No, I don't. Why don't you clarify?" he demands.

The plane levels in the air, shaking, but not as bad as I've experienced in the past.

I blurt out, "I wasn't raised with a silver spoon in my mouth."

"What are you insinuating?" Tristano questions in a defensive voice.

"Don't get offended."

"How am I supposed to take that?"

"Like the truth," I reply.

He scowls.

I put my hands in the air. "Don't get pissed at me for answering your question."

He exhales deeply. "Fine. Explain how my privileged life makes you not able to gamble when you're in Vegas."

I can't help but snicker. "You did grow up privileged."

"So? Does that make me a bad person?"

"Not at all. But I grew up poor. There were times we didn't have food. It took everything I had to build the life I now live. The last thing I'm going to do is waste my hard-earned money gambling," I confess.

Tristano's anger disappears. "I'm sorry."

My pride overpowers my other emotions. "It's fine."

Silence fills the jet, aside from the overhead bins rattling. I try to think of how to change the subject, but nothing comes to me. All I keep thinking about is being a young girl and having nothing.

Tristano breaks the silence. His voice is soft as he states, "I bet that was hard for you."

"It was what it was," I reply.

He strokes his thumb on my thigh, asking, "This is why you're so freaked out about Dante finding out about us. Isn't it?"

My discomfort grows. I hate showing any form of weakness. I try at all costs not to speak about how I grew up. I love my parents, and they worked their asses off to provide for us. It wasn't their fault we had no money. And something about Tristano pinpointing my issue with Dante makes me feel super vulnerable. I spin in the seat as much as I can with the seat belt on. "Can we change the subject?"

He pins his gaze on me, studying me like I'm a specimen under a microscope.

It adds to my nerves. I beg, "Please."

He finally caves. "Okay. So tell me what you did in Vegas if you didn't gamble."

Relieved he's moving on, I answer, "I saw a lot of shows and spent most of the time in the pool. It was nice to feel the sun in winter."

His face lights up, and I'm unsure why. He smiles. "Yeah, it is. I feel like this winter is never going to end."

I groan. "Agreed. It's been the worst."

His grin widens. "So you like sunshine, swimming, and what else?"

My flutters reignite. I've known Tristano for what feels like forever, yet we've never talked like this. It makes me realize how much I don't really know him. Everything about his question feels like a first date, which I know we're on, but I have conflicting feelings.

Where can this go?

What if it could work?

It can't.

Instead of answering, I flip the conversation on him. "Nothing exciting. Besides gambling and boxing, what else do you do?"

His lips twitch. "Why are you dodging my question?"

"I'm not," I lie.

"Bullshit."

My anxiousness grows as it hits me that I've made a huge mistake. I underestimated Tristano. He seems to be able to read me better than Dante. And he can get to the root of issues quickly.

How did I never notice this before?

He laces his fingers through mine, sending zings straight to my core. He asks, "Are you going to avoid my questions all weekend?"

I snap my head toward him, panicking. "All weekend?"

His eyes widen but quickly return to normal. He sniffs hard, assesses me, then asserts, "You won't want to go home tonight. Just trust me."

"You can't say that when you don't even know where we're going," I point out.

The typical Marino cockiness flares on his expression. "Of course I can."

"You didn't tell me this was a weekend thing."

He purses his lips. "And your point is?"

The urge to slap him festers in my veins. I accuse, "Don't be an ass. You knew I'd be upset."

"You won't be. Trust me," he repeats.

"Stop telling me to trust you when you can't even be honest about what we're doing!" I hurl.

"It's a surprise. You're going to love it and never want to return home," he claims.

I groan, putting my hands over my face. This is the issue with doing anything with Tristano. He's a Marino. Whatever they want, they get. There's no asking for permission, either. They take what they want, don't apologize for anything, and figure they can manipulate their way through any scenario. "I'm not one of your ditzy women, Tristano!"

He scrunches his face, questioning, "Did I ever say you were?"

"You didn't have to. You thought you could steamroll over me to get what you want," I accuse.

He crosses his arms, seething. "You seem to have a lot of notions about me. I never knew you thought I was such a dick. Anything else you'd like to tell me?"

I unlatch my seat belt, jump off the couch, and the plane rolls to the right. I fly into Tristano's lap.

He slides his arms around me, reprimanding, "When the seat belt sign is on, you keep it on."

"Don't tell me what to do," I argue, pushing against his chest.

He holds me tighter. "Stop fighting me, Pina. My plane, my rules."

I roll my eyes. "You're just like your brothers."

His face hardens. "You seem to have numerous opinions about us. What else do you have to say?"

I glare at him.

"Go ahead. I'm listening," he goads.

"Let go of me," I order.

He holds me another moment then finally releases me, turning me so I'm back in the seat. He buckles my seat belt and demands, "Don't get up until the light is off."

"Didn't know you were such a rule follower," I mutter.

"It's for your safety. And good to know you think so highly of my brothers and me," he declares.

My gut drops. *What am I doing?* I quickly reply, "I don't think bad about any of you."

He snorts. "Could have fooled me."

I glance at the window across from me, trying to calm my racing heartbeat. The turbulence dies out, and the seat belt light dings.

Tristano unbuckles his seat belt then trudges toward the front of the plane.

Crap! What have I done?

No matter what my fears are, I shouldn't insult him or his brothers. They've been nothing but generous and fair to me over the years. Plus, one of the reasons I've succeeded so much is because of how they don't settle for anything less than agreement. If it were an ordinary day, I'd approve of everything they do to get what they want.

This is screwing with my head.

I release my seat belt then go to the front of the plane, taking a seat next to Tristano. I softly say, "Hey."

He clenches his jaw then locks eyes with me.

I put my hand over his, admitting, "I didn't mean for that to sound how it did."

He huffs. "Sure, Pina. Whatever you say."

"I mean it. I-I don't know why I said that."

He turns toward the window, mumbling, "Well, it's true, isn't it?"

Silence fills the air, answering his question. I shift in my seat. "Tristano."

He slowly meets my eyes.

Once again, I feel super vulnerable, but I deal with it so I can try and make this right. I state, "What you and your brothers do is nothing short of admirable."

He scoffs. "Don't lie to me now."

"I'm not."

He says nothing and turns back toward the window.

We sit in silence for a while until Danika appears. She beams as she asks if we're ready for dinner.

Tristano glances at me with an arched eyebrow.

I smile at Danika. "That would be great. Thanks."

"Coming up," she replies, then leaves.

Tristano firmly asserts, "I'm only going to ask you this once, Pina. Whatever you answer decides what happens tonight."

Nerves fill my chest. "Okay. What is it?"

His expression darkens. "Do you want to stay on this date, or do you want me to have the pilot turn the plane around?"

11

Tristano

EVERY SECOND PINA DOESN'T ANSWER ME FEELS LIKE A lifetime. She wears her don't-mess-with-me expression, which could intimidate any gambler. Whenever she looks at me like this, I can't tell what she's thinking.

"Well? Should I tell the pilot to turn around?" I ask again, tapping my fingers against my thigh.

She exhales deeply and shakes her head. "No. It's not necessary."

Part of me is unsure whether I should be relieved or not. I'm used to women throwing themselves at me. There's never a challenge dating any of them. Nothing is easy with Pina though. It's good when we're together, but it's like I have to fight for each moment.

And that confuses me.

I should hate it, yet deep inside, I'm digging the obstacles she puts in front of us. Every time I figure out how to make her cave to what I want, I get a burst of adrenaline—except for now.

"Are you sure?" I question.

She doesn't hesitate. "Yes."

To make a point, I reply, "So you want to stay on this date with me, knowing I'm not bringing you home until the weekend is over?"

I rarely see nerves on Pina's face, but they pop up at my question. My stomach flips.

She's going to back out.

Twelve excruciating seconds pass. She leans back into the seat, opens her tray table, and smirks. "I didn't have any exciting plans this weekend, so that works."

My insides relax. I pull my table out and mumble, "Sounds like you have an awesome social calendar."

She huffs, as if she's insulted. "I have an amazing one."

"Says the woman who has nothing going on this weekend."

She arches her eyebrows. "So you canceled your plans to kidnap and take me out of the country?"

Danika saves me from answering. She chirps, "Hope you're hungry. These portions are huge!" She lifts a silver lid and places a plate on Pina's table.

A mix of colors fills the plate. Indian spices flare in my nostrils before Danika sets my meal in front of me.

Pina's eyes light up. "Is this from the Indian grocery store near my work?"

"Sure is," I boast, happy I choose the right dinner.

Pina leans closer to me. "You know I love that place."

"So you've said only a thousand times over the years," I point out.

Danika pours champagne for Pina and a beer for me. She asks, "Need anything else?"

"I think we're set," I state.

"Yes, all set. Thank you," Pina echoes.

"Very well. If you change your mind, let me know." Danika lowers another tray table and places a basket of garlic naan on it. "Don't forget this," she says, then disappears.

Pina glances at her plate filled with saag paneer, chicken tikka masala, and lamb rogan josh all over a bed of basmati rice. "Mmm," she moans, inhaling deeply.

I chuckle. "You're so predictable."

She shrugs. "You can't get my favorite meal and claim I'm predictable." She takes a bite of lamb and groans. "So good."

"Seems like I can," I claim, suddenly hungry and shoving a forkful of chicken in my mouth. The earthy Indian spices mix with ginger, turmeric, coriander, and cumin. I wash it down with a sip of my beer.

"If only all of New York knew how good this food is," Pina declares.

"It is crazy they make it in a grocery store. This is better than any five-star Indian restaurant in the city," I admit.

"Right!" Pina practically shouts, then eats the saag.

I pick up a piece of the garlic naan and add a scoop of rice and the lamb rogan josh. We eat in silence, and I pat myself on the back for getting dinner right.

Pina puts her fork on the table, drinks half her champagne, then turns in her chair. She tilts her head. "Do you really not know where we're going?"

I swallow my beer and shake my head. "I have no idea."

She studies me a moment then says, "That's so unexpected."

Unsure how to take her comment, I inquire, "Meaning?"

The gold in her eyes brightens. "Dante would never go anywhere without having every last detail planned."

I grunt. "Well, I'm not Dante." I finish my beer and then push the call button.

"I never said you were," Pina claims.

"Mr. Marino. Can I get something for you?" Danika asks, magically appearing.

"Another round," I order, motioning to our drinks.

She smiles. "Can I take your plates? Or are you still working on them?"

I pick up my plate and hand it to her, announcing, "I'm finished. Thank you."

She takes it and asks, "Pina, what about you?"

"Oh, I'm finishing this. In fact"—she reaches for my plate—"why don't you leave this here? It's a sin to let food this good go to waste!"

"Okay. Two drinks coming up. And have at it," Danika teases, setting my plate next to the basket of naan. She leaves.

"You aren't going to eat that," I claim.

Pina snorts then shoves a large piece of naan dripping in tikka masala sauce in her mouth. She groans, chews for what seems like forever, then swallows. She chirps, "Watch me."

"You'll feel sick if you eat all that," I warn.

She rolls her eyes. "Are you the food police?"

"No."

"Then let me overindulge in my Indian in peace," she demands.

Danika reappears with drinks. She sets them down and asks, "Can I get you anything else?"

"Maybe a barf bag for Pina," I taunt.

Pina elbows me in the rib cage.

"Ow!" I grimace.

"Don't be disgusting," she orders.

Danika snickers. "I guess I'll hold off on the bag. If you need anything else, I'm your girl!"

"Thanks, Danika. Any clue where we're going?" Pina inquires.

Danika holds her hands in the air. "Sorry! I'm under strict orders to zip my lips."

"Just give us a tiny hint," Pina says, holding her thumb and pointer finger an inch apart.

Danika glances at me.

"Under no uncertain terms are you to tell her anything," I relay.

"Sorry, Pina," Danika states, then turns and goes to her area of the plane.

"You're no fun," Pina pouts.

I chuckle. "You're more like Dante than I am."

"Am not," she claims.

"Are too," I insist.

An exasperated sigh comes out of Pina. "And how do you figure I'm like Dante?"

My lips twitch. I try to stop them, but it's impossible. "Should I pull out the list?"

"Ha ha! Funny," she states, then rolls her eyes. "I'm nothing like your brother."

"Oh, quite the contrary," I assert.

She puts her naan down on the plate. She pushes the tray away and turns toward me. "Okay. How am I like your brother?"

Amused, I take a few mouthfuls of beer. "Number one. Dante is a control freak. *You* are a total control freak. And don't even argue you aren't."

She rolls her eyes. "Fine. What else?"

"You're both bossy, demanding, and manipulative," I point out.

"Manipulative? I am not!" she insists.

"Sure you are."

She scoffs. "Says the guy who didn't tell me our date was the entire weekend. How do you figure I'm demanding?"

I slide my arm around her and lean into her ear, murmuring, "It's a skill, baby girl. Don't be so offended."

She turns her face toward me, questioning, "And you don't think you have all those qualities?"

I grin. "Of course I do. But I use them selectively. You and Dante use them on a daily basis."

Her eyes turn to slits. She hurls, "Is there anything else you want to tell me about myself?"

"Why are you so insulted?"

She glares at me. "Is that a serious question? Did you even listen to what you said about me?"

I retrieve my arm and sit back in my seat. "You wouldn't be able to make all the things happen if you weren't. I'm giving you a compliment."

"Manipulation is not something anyone should be proud of," she claims.

"Why? I'm okay with my skill set," I boast.

"Good for you." She finishes her champagne and stacks her plate on top of mine. Then she rises and picks the tray up.

"What are you doing?" I ask.

"Well, I'm not being manipulative," she asserts.

I point to the plates. "I thought you were going to down all of that."

"Lost my appetite," she states, then hurries to the front of the plane.

"Pina," I call after her, but she ignores me and disappears behind the curtain.

I finish my beer, amused but also kicking myself she's pissed at me again. So far, if I had to rate this date, I'd give myself a C-minus. I'm always an A-plus kind of guy. Yet it seems like every step I take forward pushes me two steps back with Pina.

So much for impressing her with her favorite meal.

At least I have all weekend to get back on her good side.

I kind of like her pissed off at me. Gives me a challenge.

I'm officially fucked in the head.

I put the tables back where they belong and wait for Pina to reappear. Several minutes pass until she struts toward me with Danika on her heels.

"Miss me?" I tease.

Instead of sitting down, Pina ignores me and goes into the other room. The door shuts, and I glance at Danika. "She's super pissed, isn't she?"

Danika bites on her smile then shrugs. "Sorry, boss. I can't comment on that."

"No? Then what did you discuss?"

Danika's eyes widen. "She asked me if I was happy with you or if I'd like to join Dante's crew since his flight attendant is retiring soon."

My pulse increases. Danika's been with me for years. She's discreet, works hard, and is perfect at her job. I study her closely, try to stay cool, and ask, "And what did you tell her?"

She smiles, replying, "I said thanks for the offer, but I'll be staying here for as long as you're willing to employ me."

Relief fills me. I shouldn't be surprised, but no one has ever tried to steal my staff. I have a hard enough time finding the right men to train for the business. All of my brothers have had someone they hired and put their faith in, only to have those people betray our family. I wish I could say I've never had it happen with men I've chosen, but I can't. The last thing I need is to have Danika, who's always been loyal and discreet, jump ship for Dante.

I sniff hard and nod. "As long as you can work, you've got a position with me, Danika."

"Thank you, Mr. Marino. Is there anything else I can get for you?" she asks, then picks up my empty bottle.

"No, thanks," I reply, wait for her to leave, then sit back in my chair and stare out into the darkness. My heart rate finally returns to normal, and I pull my phone out of my pocket. I email my accountant.

JANINE,

SEND A TWENTY-FIVE-THOUSAND-DOLLAR BONUS TO DANIKA AS soon as you read this. Put on the memo, "Thank you for your continued service."

SINCERELY,

Tristano Marino

I TOSS MY PHONE IN MY POCKET THEN HEAD INTO THE NEXT room. Pina's sprawled across the couch, reading a fashion magazine. She crosses one ankle over the other, displaying her silky-smooth legs. I say a little prayer of thanks she wore a dress. I lift her legs, slide under them, then warn, "Don't ever attempt to steal my staff again. That's not cool and crosses the line."

She doesn't look up from her magazine and casually asks, "How big of a loyalty bonus did you send Danika?"

I freeze, not even breathing.

How does she know I did that? Does she somehow have access to my email?

She drills her eyes into mine. "Well?"

I search for words, finally questioning, "Did you hack into

my account?"

She scoffs. "I'm not a hacker, Tristano."

Blood pounds between my ears. "Then how did you know I sent Danika a bonus?"

She glances back at her article and turns the page. She asks, "What do you think Dante does every time you or your brothers attempt to steal me? Hmm?"

My pulse pounds harder. I slide my hand up her thigh until it's cupping her pussy. She inhales sharply, holding her breath. I point out, "That was manipulative."

"Was it ten grand or more?" she inquires.

"More," I confess.

"Hmm." She smiles and then returns to reading.

I lean closer to her. "What does 'hmmm' mean?"

"Nothing."

"It must mean something. Do tell," I demand.

She places the magazine on her stomach and smirks. "I didn't know you would feel so threatened."

"Bullshit. You knew exactly what you were doing," I accuse, but to my surprise, my dick hardens. Pina's the smartest woman I've ever met. The fact she just played me, and I fell for it, turns me on. I doubt any other woman could get away with doing that to me. I'd hate them, for sure. Yet something about Pina doing it sends a rush of adrenaline through my bones.

She tilts her head, widening her golden-brown orbs. "Sorry."

I hold in my chuckle. "No, you aren't. And you just cost me twenty-five big ones."

"Glad to know you aren't cheap." She bats her eyelashes.

I trace her slit with my middle finger. She squirms. It's only an inch, but I notice it. That small action fires all the testosterone in my body. I ask, "Have I ever been cheap with you when I've asked you to do a job for me?"

Her face hardens. "No."

I push my thumb past her panties and make a circling motion, continuing to slide my middle finger over her slit. "Then why would I be anything less with my full-time employees?"

She sits up as if there's a fire, shoving my hand off her.

"What did I do now?"

"This is the precise reason we need to stop this," she claims, swinging her body around, so her feet are on the floor, and crossing her legs.

I groan. "Not this again. Can we get past this whole you-work-for-Dante issue?"

She furrows her eyebrows. "But I don't just work for Dante, do I? I also work for your other brothers and you."

I shake my head. "No, you don't."

"I don't?"

"No. You're on Dante's payroll," I justify, knowing it's not entirely true but wanting to get past her worries.

She scoots as close to the wall as possible. "How often have you hired me to do something for you?"

"It's not the same thing," I claim.

"Answer me."

I sigh. "A lot. Why?"

"And how much do you pay me?"

"What's your point, Pina?"

"My point is that I also work for you. And now we're doing things we shouldn't be," she frets.

I reach for her and tug her onto my lap.

"Tristano!" she exclaims, pushing my chest.

"Can you stop freaking out for a minute?" I ask.

She clenches her jaw. Red crawls up her cheeks.

I wonder if it's anger or embarrassment. "What are you worried is going to happen?"

She looks away.

I turn her chin so she's facing me. "Tell me. What do you think Dante will do? He's not going to fire you. He can't operate without you. So what is it?"

Her lips quiver. She swallows hard.

"Pina?" I urge.

She takes a deep breath then states, "You don't know what I've been through... What I've done to get where I'm at."

"Then fill me in," I demand.

Moments of tense silence fill the cabin. I force myself to wait for her to speak. She finally says, "I didn't grow up like you, Tristano."

I tuck a lock of her hair behind her ear. "So you mentioned. Tell me more about how you grew up."

She licks her plump lip, hesitates, then admits, "I wasn't lying when I said we grew up without food. My parents were always working, but nothing they did was ever enough. We got evicted so many times I lost track."

My chest tightens. The vision of Pina as a little girl moving all the time and going to sleep with a hungry belly makes me feel ill.

She continues, "I fought to get where I'm at."

"You've done well. It's because you're talented," I claim and mean every word.

She shifts on my lap. "Yeah, I am. But I didn't get here by sleeping with my boss."

I sniff hard, hating the predicament I've put her in. If I were a man of higher ethics, I'd let her go for her own sake. But I'm not that man. I'm a man who seizes what I want. Ever since that day in the conference room, all I've wanted was her. So I tug her closer and state, "No one would ever accuse you of anything of the sort. We all know how hard you've worked. Even my papà sings your praises, and he doesn't do that with hardly anyone."

"Exactly! What would your papà think of me if he found out?"

My gut flips. I blurt out, "Papà would be angry at me. Not you."

"You don't know that."

"Yes. I do," I insist.

She shakes her head. "Dante will throw a fit. You know he will."

"So what? He'll get over it," I claim.

Pina scrunches her face. "Dante respects me right now. I don't want to lose that."

I cup her cheek. "You won't. I'll make sure that never happens."

"I know your brother better than you do. He won't ever look at me the same," she says sadly.

"Pina—"

A loud ding interrupts me. The pilot says, "Please put your belts on. There's turbulence ahead. But on another note, we should be landing in the next hour."

I debate about ignoring him, but safety's always been my thing. I slide Pina off my lap, reach to secure her seat belt around her, then press my lips to hers. I retreat and assert the only thing that comes to my mind, "You owe me a date. If you want to end things after this weekend, I'll let you go." As I say the words, it feels like a steel fist is squeezing my heart.

She says nothing, and I sit back in my seat, buckling my own seat belt. No matter what, I'm making sure she has no option but to tell me she wants to keep seeing me. I'm not sure how, but I'm going to figure it out.

12

Pina

"Welcome to Nassau," the pilot announces. The plane's wheels hit the ground, and the sound of the brakes fills the cabin.

Excitement fills me. I've never been to the Bahamas, but I love the other Caribbean islands I've visited. For the last hour, I've tried to forget about my career fears. Tristano's right about Dante. I doubt he'd fire me, but I don't want him to change how he treats me or for him to have a different opinion about me.

I decide it's best to forget it for the weekend. Right now, there's nothing I can do to reverse the situation I'm in. A deal's a deal, and I agreed to Tristano's terms. When I get home, I'll make it clear we can't continue whatever is going on between us.

I turn toward him, beaming. "A weekend of sunshine. Good call."

Arrogance spreads across his expression. He rises and reaches for me, tugging me to my feet, asserting, "We're going to have fun, baby girl. Trust me."

Whenever he calls me baby girl, I get a little jolt of a high. It's strange since I've never had anyone give me a pet name. Nor would I ever have thought I'd like a man to call me that, but I do. It's another example of how the things I assumed I knew about myself, I don't. Between my love of submitting to him and crossing the professional line I've always had, I suddenly wonder if I ever knew myself. There are so many questions floating through my head ever since our first encounter, and all they do is spin faster the deeper I fall for him.

I'm not falling for him.

This is pure lust.

After this weekend, it's ending.

"Let's go," he directs, guiding me out of the plane and to the private car waiting on the runway.

It's pitch-black outside and after midnight. There are barely any lights on the runway. I wish I could see the turquoise water, but it'll have to wait until morning.

The driver pulls away from the jet. Tristano laces his fingers between mine. He leans close to my face. "Are you ready to run around naked all weekend?"

"Funny," I reply.

He cocks an eyebrow. "Who said I'm joking?"

I climb over him, resting my knees next to his hips. I slide my arms around his shoulders and pout my lips. "Aw. I was looking forward to swimming."

His eyes twinkle. He glides his hand over my spine. Tingles shoot straight to my loins. He murmurs, "Who said we wouldn't swim?"

"Are we going to a naked resort?" I ask, trying to bite on my smile.

He shrugs as more mischief fills his expression. "I have no idea."

I tilt my head. "You really didn't know where we were going?"

He grins. "Nope."

"Wow. I'm impressed," I admit.

"Why is that?"

"I don't think your other brothers would ever do anything spontaneously. They don't like surprises. I thought you were the same, but I guess not," I confess.

"I can assure you I'm not," he states. His eyes swirl with fun and something else I'm unsure about, but it's like a demon fighting with his inner happiness. It's mesmerizing, making me want to peel back more of Tristano's layers. And it strikes me further that after all these years of working with the Marinos and thinking I knew them so well, I really don't.

Tristano is suddenly a mystery I want to unravel. I always thought of him as Dante's youngest brother. In my eyes, no

Marino was as sharp as Dante. Not that any of them are stupid, but I've witnessed Dante's brilliance since I was eighteen. Now, my gut's screaming at me that I've severely underestimated Tristano. His ability to trust whoever he delegated to set up our trip intrigues me. While Dante has full confidence in me, he wouldn't be able to handle not knowing where he was going. Yet, Tristano seems nothing but calm and confident in wherever it is we end up.

I shift closer to him and stroke the side of his head. I tease, "I can see you're a lot more fun."

He grunts. "You're just learning this?"

I wince. "Sorry."

"Don't tell me you thought Dante was the most fun," he adds.

I shake my head. "Nope."

"Then who?"

I cringe, admitting, "Massimo."

"Ugh. I should have known," Tristano groans.

"Well, I've changed my mind. You're definitely the fun one."

His lips twitch. He fists my hair, tugs my head back, and leans over me. My pussy clenches as he asserts, "I should punish you for being so misguided."

My pulse creeps up. I've seen Tristano punish his subs at the club. I've used his techniques on men. I never considered anyone using them on me, nor did I think I would enjoy it. Something about Tristano teaching me a lesson is suddenly appealing.

I've lost my marbles.

Why does the thought of his palm leaving a red mark on my ass excite me?

Yep. I've for sure gone crazy.

I provoke, "What would you do to me?"

His eyes darken, sending a shiver up my spine. He studies me like he's searching for some secret within me. I swallow hard, and he answers in a low voice, "Telling you takes the fun away, don't you think?"

I bite on my lip, trying to steady my breath.

He drags his knuckles over my cheek, questioning, "If you were going to punish your sub, how would you do it?"

Adrenaline kicks in, zinging through my cells. My mouth turns dry, and my heart rate speeds up. All of it confuses me again.

Why am I getting excited about domination when my loins are screaming for him to make me submit?

His lips graze mine. He orders, "Answer me."

My blood boils hotter. I shift my hips, letting his erection push against my clit. I hold in a groan and reply, "It depends."

"On what?"

"How badly he's behaved."

Respect and approval enter Tristano's eyes. He kisses me, but it's brief. He retreats when my tongue hits his, and he says, "Tell me what you'd do for a minor punishment, to the most hardcore."

My butterflies spread their wings. I fill my lungs with fresh oxygen several times. Visuals of punishments I've given powerful men flood my memory. My voice shakes. "I'd start with floggers, then move to paddles."

"Give me something not so vanilla," Tristano goads.

Nerves annihilate me. If I were under a light with the police interrogating me right now, I might feel calmer. I'm anxious for his approval, but there's something else I can't put my finger on. His warm breath merges into mine. A car's headlights fill the space we're in, highlighting his chiseled features. I clench my thighs against him, adding, "If he deserved something stronger, I'd put a cock cage on him, make him kneel, then have him eat my pussy while I whipped him."

Tristano's lips twist. He sniffs hard and asks, "Is that what you wanted to do to me?"

"I-I don't know."

He scoffs. "Don't play dumb with me, Pina. Now isn't the time to get bashful. Besides, I do the same thing while making my subs blow me."

"You do?" I ask, surprised. I've never seen him do that while I observed him at the club.

"Yeah, but I do other things to them while they're doing it," he states.

My pulse beats hard in my neck. "Like what?"

He unzips the back of my dress and slides his warm hand down my spine. I inhale deeply and press closer to him.

Arrogance, confidence, and dark dominance explode on his face. It's so sinfully attractive that I wish I could take a snapshot to view it anytime I want. His voice deepens, as if it's not already sexy enough, and he replies, "I won't answer your question."

"Why not?" I whisper.

He observes me for several moments, adding to the tension that makes me feel like I might explode. He finally leans into my ear and swipes his tongue on my lobe.

I whimper, unable to control myself. I've become putty in his hands. It's nothing I'm used to, but there's no way to stop it. I'm at his mercy, and he's fully aware.

He murmurs, "Tonight, my baby girl. Everything you want to know, you'll soon find out."

Chaos erupts in the farthest part of my soul. Instead of running or wanting to be the dominant one, I'm already submitting, dying to experience whatever he wants to do to me.

My body relaxes against his. A throbbing sensation hits me everywhere. I'm so wet, I wonder if I'm going to leave a stain on his pants.

And maybe he's some super god with magical powers because the look of approval he gives me tells me he fully understands what's happening within me. Perhaps he even gave my body subconscious orders that it's obeying, even though that must be impossible.

His lips graze my ear as he asserts, "You're going to submit to me in ways you haven't before. When we leave this island, you're going to be so addicted to me that you won't be able to stop yourself from craving what I can give you."

My fears mix with anticipation so fast, they're soon blended into unrecognizable pandemonium.

What if he's right?

No, I'll prove him wrong.

What if I can't?

He grunts, dragging his knuckles down my spine, insisting, "There's nothing to be afraid of, baby girl. I'll make sure nothing changes with work."

Can he read my mind?

I attempt to deny his statement, lying, "I'm not thinking about that."

He holds my head in front of his face, sternly ordering, "Don't ever speak untruths to me, Pina. I'm not the dumb younger brother."

His comment surprises me. I blurt out, "I never said you were, nor did I ever think you're stupid."

The back door opens. I hadn't realized the car had parked or the driver had gotten out. Tristano glances at the driver then releases me. I scramble off his lap and straighten my dress over my thighs.

Tristano orders, "Give us a minute." He shuts the door, zips my dress, then pecks me on the lips. He opens the door, steps out before reaching in to help me out, then leads me toward the entrance.

A man stands behind a podium. He grins, saying, "Welcome to Nassau! I'm Cornelius. You must be Mr. and Mrs. Marino?"

I open my mouth to object, but Tristano tugs me closer and, before I can speak, replies, "Yes. And I'm afraid my wife is very tired. Is there any way we can skip whatever you normally do and go directly to the room?"

His wife?

Why do I like the sound of that?

I need to snap out of it!

"Most certainly, Mr. Marino. I'll have Gulliver take you to your suite." He motions to a man behind us then hands us a fruity cocktail. He asks, "Have you eaten, or would you like me to arrange to have food sent to your room?"

"I'm good. Pina?" Tristano questions.

"No, thank you," I state.

"Very well. Gulliver will take you to your suite." He gestures to a golf cart waiting nearby.

"Thank you," Tristano says and whisks me over to the vehicle.

We slide into the back seat. Gulliver turns and says, "Welcome to Sugar Dreams. Sit tight. Your room is the most secluded on the resort, so it'll take a bit longer to get to."

Tristano slides his arm around my shoulders. "No problem."

Gulliver turns on reggae music, shifts the gears, and accelerates. The warm ocean breeze, crashing waves, and Tristano's hard body make the moment perfect. We pass the different parts of the resort, which are all lit up. Pools glow with pink and purple lights. There's an outdoor dance club, several bars, and restaurants. All are full of smiling guests.

It instantly puts me in a better mood. I lean into Tristano and glance at him, saying, "Looks like a nice place."

He nods. "We'll explore it all tomorrow."

My butterflies flutter harder. I confess, "Not a bad place for a date."

Pride sweeps his face. He wiggles his eyebrows, saying, "Just one of the perks about dating me."

I laugh. I never thought about dating any Marino, but Tristano is full of surprises. Curious, I ask, "So who booked this place?"

Tristano rubs his thumb over my bicep, answering, "Barry."

"Really?"

"Why do you sound so shocked?"

I shrug. "Barry screwed up the last trip Dante had me book with him."

"How?"

"Long story, but Dante said I'm not allowed to use him again. Didn't he tell you? Don't you all talk about everything?" I ask, surprised.

The look I saw earlier returns. Tristano glances into the darkness and lowers his voice. "No. I'm usually the last one to know anything. And there are lots of things they don't tell me."

Something about his admission feels vulnerable. I place my hand on his thigh then state, "Well, it seems like you have your secrets, too."

He locks eyes with me. The emotions swirling in his orbs make me think he's hurt. "Not really. Only you. And that's your choice."

My chest tightens. I open my mouth to speak, but the golf cart stops and Gulliver announces, "This is it."

Stars twinkle and the full moon shines, shedding a ray of soft light over a detached cottage. Candles flicker in the windows. Brick pavers lead to the entrance. A deck sits on the ocean side of the building, boasting a private pool and hot tub.

"Wow. This looks amazing." I beam.

"Glad you approve," Tristano says and grabs a suitcase off the cart.

"Mr. Marino. I have it," Gulliver declares, pulling the handle up on the other suitcase.

"It's okay. I can take this one," Tristano claims, then motions for me to go ahead of him.

"But you are a guest," Gulliver points out.

"It's all good."

"I could lose my job," Gulliver frets.

Tristano pulls out a wad of cash and waves it in front of Gulliver. "This is for you. And I won't tell if you don't, but it's stupid for me not to help."

In all my years working for the Marinos, I've never seen any of them lift a finger when any staff was around. It didn't matter if it was at their house or on trips.

I've never paid that much attention to Tristano.

Is this normal for him?

The respect I have for him grows. It's not that the other Marinos treat people badly, but they display their air of authority wherever they go. I always assumed Tristano was like his brothers.

I assumed wrong.

He's different.

How did I never see this?

"Sir, you don't need to carry that," Gulliver continues.

"Chill, Gulliver. We're almost inside anyway," Tristano orders.

Gulliver finally caves. "Yes, Mr. Marino."

"You can call me Tristano. Seems wrong to be so formal in the Caribbean, don't you think?" he questions.

Gulliver scrunches his face. "Umm..."

Tristano reaches in front of me and turns the doorknob. We all step inside a small entryway, and he pats Gulliver on the back, asking, "You want a drink before you head back?"

Gulliver's eyes widen. "No, thank you, sir."

"Okay. Suit yourself," Tristano replies.

"Can I show you around your cottage?" Gulliver asks.

"Please," I answer, touched that Tristano is being so cool but also sensing Gulliver's panic.

He releases a tense breath. "Thank you, ma'am. Please follow me."

He holds another door open, and I step through then freeze, exclaiming, "Wow!"

Soft Caribbean music fills the air. Teal, orange, and white give color to the walls, drapery, and other decor. A tranquil waterfall covers an entire wall. Turquoise and other blue tiles mimic what I imagine the ocean looks like. An oversized king bed faces a glass wall. A small dining and living area flow into the bedroom. The bathroom boasts a two-person shower, jacuzzi tub, and dual sinks.

"Can I unpack your belongings?" Gulliver questions.

"Nah. We got it," Tristano replies.

More anxiety floods Gulliver's expression. "Are you positive, sir? It will only take a few minutes. I would be happy to assist."

"No. We—"

"We'd be happy to have you help us," I interject.

Tristano furrows his eyebrows. "We would?"

"Yes. Let the man do his job," I assert, sensing that Gulliver might have a heart attack if he leaves without helping.

Relief floods his face. He replies, "Thank you, ma'am," then rolls the suitcases into the walk-in closet.

Tristano opens the fridge and pumps his hand in the air. "Yes!"

"What?"

He takes two Red-Stripes out of the fridge, sets them on the counter, and opens a drawer. He shuffles through it, pulls a bottle opener out, pops the tops of the beer, then hands me one.

"I don't drink beer," I state.

"Why not?"

I shrug. "Never really got into it."

He grunts. "Try it. Thousand dollars says you love it."

"Thousand bucks?" I double-check.

"Yep. But you have to be honest. I'm ready to take your money," he booms.

"Fat chance," I state, then clink his bottle and take a large mouthful.

Tristano does the same then stares at me, waiting for my reaction.

I take another sip then wince. "Crap."

Tristano chuckles. "You love it, don't you?"

I put my hand over my face and moan. "This is why I don't gamble."

"Ha! Told you!"

"Don't rub it in," I say, taking another sip of the faintly sweet and very cold drink.

"Gulliver!" Tristano shouts.

"Jeez," I say, but I also laugh.

Gulliver races out of the closet. "Yes, sir?"

"What time are you off?" Tristano asks.

Gulliver answers, "As soon as I return, sir. You're my last drop-off tonight."

Tristano nods. "You like beer?"

"Yes, sir."

Tristano grabs two beers out of the fridge, steps forward, then slides them into Gulliver's pockets. "Great. Have a few drinks when you get home."

"Sir. This isn't necessary," Gulliver states.

Tristano leans closer to him. "Bro, you need to relax. I insist you take the beer. Now, I know you want to help me, so I'll tell you how you can assist me."

"Please do, sir."

Tristano points at me. "See this woman?"

"Yes."

Tristano wraps his arm around Gulliver's shoulders. "You've been awesome, but you need to leave so I can show her what's up. You know what I'm saying?"

Heat flies into my cheeks. I cover my mouth, trying to stop my laugh from escaping.

In a serious voice, Gulliver replies, "Understand, sir."

Tristano walks him to the door. "Thanks. Now get your ass back on the golf cart. I'll see you tomorrow."

13

Tristano

GULLIVER LEAVES. I LOCK THE DOOR AND RETURN TO THE MAIN room. Pina stands in front of the window, staring out into the darkness and drinking her Red Stripe. I step behind her, circle my arm around her waist, and lean into her ear, admitting, "I thought he'd never leave."

She spins. Amusement fills her expression. "I thought he was going to have a heart attack."

I grunt. "Dude needs to chill."

Pina tilts her head and arches her eyebrows. "He values his job."

"So? He can still relax a bit. All that formal stuff is for the birds."

She points out, "He probably doesn't have the luxury of screwing up like you do."

"What does that mean? I don't have that luxury. You, of all people, understand how important it is I don't mess up," I declare.

Silence grows between us. Pina never blinks, and neither do I. It's one of the things I've always respected about her. Most women, and many men, back away when challenged by my brothers or me. Yet Pina steps right up to the plate when controversy rears its head.

She narrows her eyes, asserting, "People who aren't rich don't have the options you do. If you screw up, your papà isn't going to kick you out of the family business and leave you on the street, penniless."

I scoff. "Are you that naive after working for Dante all these years? Papà won't stand for mediocrity."

"That's not what I'm saying. You don't know the resort's rules or what Gulliver is facing. I know you're trying to be nice to him, and there isn't anything wrong with what you did. I'm just telling you that he probably needs his job and can't afford to take any risks," she claims.

"But I can?" I ask.

She smiles then slides her hands up my chest and laces her fingers behind my neck. "I'm not trying to insult you."

"You aren't."

"Then why are you so defensive right now?"

My heart pounds harder. "I'm not," I insist.

"Are you sure about that?"

I sigh then confess, "I know I grew up rich and have opportunities others don't. But I still work hard and have to be accountable."

"Tristano, I never said you didn't. I know the hours you and your brothers put in, which doesn't include what I'm not privy to."

The silence grows between us before she adds, "I'm sorry if I've upset you. I just know what it's like to not have a lot and to worry it'll be taken away."

I freeze for a moment, processing what she said. Then I ask, "You worry about losing your job? How can that be when you know Dante can't deal without you?"

Her face falls. She answers, "I haven't worried in a long time until recently."

The hairs on my arms rise. "You mean since we got together?"

She licks her lips then nods. "Yeah."

"You're worrying about nothing," I claim.

"Maybe. Maybe not."

I place my hands over her cheeks, firmly stating, "You are, baby girl."

She lifts her chin and squares her shoulders. "Let's not discuss work for the rest of the weekend."

My anxiety begins to diminish. "That sounds like a really good plan."

Her face lights up, making my heart do a double take. She smiles, and the entire world seems to disappear. She chirps, "Deal. Now, what should we do for the rest of the night?"

My cock hardens. All the thoughts I had on the plane while Pina and I discussed what we've made our subs do intensifies. I don't like thinking about her dominating other men. I know I shouldn't care. I have a past, and so does she, but the jealousy I felt while she mentioned what she used to do to her subs hasn't totally subsided.

Her pussy is mine to lick, not other assholes!

It's not my business.

Fuck if it isn't.

She needs to be punished for letting others do that to her.

I glance around the room, looking for anything to restrain her to, but my options are pretty limited.

Fuck it. I'll make her submit with nothing but my body.

She deeply inhales, waiting for me to answer. The clock in the room ticks louder. My erection strains against my zipper.

I step back, dragging my eyes over her form-fitting, chocolate-brown minidress. She smoothes the fabric over her stomach, but nothing is out of place. Her cleavage is low enough to make any man drool, but it's not trashy. The curve of her waist could be on a sculpture. Even her knees are sexy, which I've never noticed on any woman.

I slowly trail my eyes up her body, noticing too many things that make me harder, adding to my anticipation. Her chest rises and falls faster. I reach for her shoulder then swipe my index finger over her collarbone.

Her bottom lip quivers. The faint sound of her breathing fills the air. Golden desire-filled fire erupts in her orbs, but it surprises me. It's the same look she gives me when she's about to submit, yet it's always when we're in the middle of our activities. There's normally a window of time where she grapples with her confusion over her need to obey.

I step forward until she's against the glass. Her body heat soaks into my skin. A combination of roses, lilacs, and lavender floats through the air, almost making me dizzy. She glances up, holding her breath.

I swirl my finger over her dress until her nipple hardens under my touch.

Her voice cracks on my name. "Tristano?"

"What's up, baby girl?"

She swallows hard. "Those things we discussed on the plane..." She licks her lips and wrinkles form on her forehead.

I wrap her hair around my fist until there's no slack. My cock throbs against her stomach at the notion of her sucking me off while I do naughty things to her.

But it quickly disappears. The thought of another man going down on her while at her mercy creates an entirely new problem for me.

What if she has an urge to dominate again?

She won't. I'll make sure she only wants to submit.

She's a switch. At some point, it'll happen.

She's always going to remember them.

She needs to only think about me if she ever has these urges again.

Fuuuck!

I make a new decision. I order, "Don't move." I leave her at the window, go into the closet, and fish through the built-in drawers.

There we go!

What am I doing?

No matter where I go, I always have a suitcase of items I keep on my plane. It allows me to be anywhere and do what I want to do. Anytime I use anything with a new woman, I have Danika replace the items, but they're always identical pieces.

Anxiety creeps through my bones as I stare at the tools. These are all my favorites, and I'm an expert at using them. But it's always when I'm in charge, not others. The fact I'm even contemplating this is crazy.

After a few moments, I pull out a flogger, run my fingers over the black braided leather, and glance at myself in the full-length mirror.

I'm not a sub.

It's me, or she's going to seek out others.

Time to suck it up.

At least she doesn't have her cock cage.

I grab the flogger and handcuffs, leaving the other toys in the drawer. Another minute passes as I give myself one final pep talk, then return to Pina.

She glances at the items. A pink flush deepens in her cheeks, and I almost change my mind.

This is for her, not you, so deal with it.

I close in on her, caging my body around her so she's pinned to the glass. I tilt her head and lock eyes with her, stating, "I think it's time we changed it up a bit."

She pins her eyebrows together. "Wh-what do you mean?"

I kiss her neck, then jaw, then briefly on the lips, admitting, "I can't stop thinking about other men eating you out."

"Sorry. I shouldn't have told you," she whispers.

"Yes, you should have. We don't need secrets between us," I declare.

She slides her hands through my hair. "Let's forget I said anything."

"I can't, baby girl," I confess, then kiss the curve of her neck.

She closes her eyes, whispering, "Just...just make me submit to you."

Do it.

Don't be a pussy.

It's another guy or me.

I lean into her ear, murmuring, "I want you to punish me."

She freezes. I'm sure she can hear the sound of my heart beating against my chest. Or maybe it's hers. Either way, time seems to stand still.

I add, "I want to eat your pussy while you punish me."

She opens her mouth and then shuts it. Confusion fills her expression. She blurts out, "I don't understand. You aren't a sub. I think we established that fact."

No, I'm not.

But she needs this.

A strange feeling fills my chest, and I don't know what to make of it. Maybe it's apprehension, but part of me thinks it's excitement. It perplexes me as much as she looks confused right now. Still, I challenge, "Show me how you dominate. Make me fully submit to you."

She studies me, staying quiet, as if she's afraid to speak or move.

I take her hand, wrap it around the flogger, and curl my fingers around hers. Sniffing hard, I place the cuffs in her other hand and then demand, "Make me submit, Pina."

After another tension-filled moment, she squares her shoulders. Her face slightly hardens, and she asserts, "I'm Mistress to you. Do you understand?"

I step back and nod. "Yes, Mistress."

She glances around the room then spins. "Remove my dress."

A cloud drifts by, allowing the moon to shine through the night sky. My stomach flutters as I push her hair over her shoulder. I reach for her zipper and slowly pull it down while kissing her neck. The fabric falls to the floor, and goose bumps pop out on her arms.

She spins and wags her finger. "Did you have permission to kiss me?"

"No, Mistress."

"Then why did you?" she asks.

I glance at her purple-and-gold lace bra then reprimand myself when my dick pulses against her stomach.

Her lips twitch. "Answer me."

"It's hard not to," is all I give her.

She points to the bed. "Strip and kneel facing the mattress."

I step back, reach for the back of my shirt, and pull it over my head. Her eyes drift over my torso. I release my pants, step out of them, then kneel in front of the bed.

"Bow your head, sub," she orders.

Blood rushes to my brain. I obey, staring at the floor. She steps next to me, staying quiet. Her floral perfume flares in my nostrils, making my urge to have her expand.

Too much time passes. A mix of demons plagues me, making me wonder why I agreed to this. The nagging feeling of excited anticipation grows. It's similar to when I make my subs stay kneeled, and it throws me for another loop.

Her pussy. I need to be the only sub in her memories eating it.

But I'm not a sub.

The tension is too much. I finally look at her, saying, "Mistress?"

Golden flames burst in her eyes. She crouches next to me, questioning, "Did I tell you to speak?"

"No, Mistress."

"Did I permit you to look up?"

"No, Mistress."

She grips my chin, drilling her piercing gaze into mine. "What has to happen now that you've disobeyed me?"

My mouth turns dry. A craving for water annihilates me. The back of my throat feels raw. It's a question I know how I would demand my subs to answer, so I state, "There have to be consequences."

Her lips curl. She scans my body then leans closer. Her breath teases my ear. She murmurs, "You want to be punished, don't you?"

Without hesitation, I reply, "Yes, Mistress."

"And on a scale of one to ten, with one being a minor infraction and ten being major, what do you rate your disobedience?" She runs her finger over my shoulder.

Tingles race down my spine. Testosterone flares in my blood. All I can think about is eating her pussy. I respond, "Ten."

Her eyes turn to slits. "Ten?"

"Yes."

"When I ask you a question, I expect you to not lie to me," she warns.

I shift on my knees, ready to get off the tile floor since the thin rug doesn't do much to create any sort of substantial padding.

"Did I say you could move?" she asks calmly.

"No, Mistress."

"Spread your arms and grip the corners of the mattress."

I stretch my arms as far as possible and squeeze the bedding.

She rises and puts one stiletto next to each of my knees. Adrenaline rushes through my body. I restrain myself from reaching for her. If I don't lick her soon, I'll go crazy. She tugs my head back so I'm facing the ceiling. The sweet smell of her arousal only makes things worse. I hold in a groan as she asserts, "The punishments you receive, you earn. Now, what's our safe phrase?"

Loathing fills me. She wants to use the same tactics as before, knowing it's not in me to say it to tap out. I swallow my pride, hating the words as they come out of my mouth. "I'm a Marino."

She runs her thumb over my lips, leans down, and gives me a brief kiss. "Good boy. Now, chin on the mattress."

Fresh oxygen fills my lungs, yet I barely feel it. I do what she says and wait.

More excruciating time passes. I'm about to cave when she turns around, ordering, "Don't move. Take your punishment like a man."

My fingers dig into the bedding right as the flogger hits my bare back. It's so light I get cocky, thinking the wrong thoughts.

This isn't a big deal. Pina doesn't have it in her to hit me harder. I should have known.

Another five slaps at the same intensity hit my skin. I continue maintaining my position, growing more arrogant.

This is a piece of cake.

I can be her sub from time to time if she needs it.

She asks, "What's the safe phrase, Tristano?" The sound of the leather on my back echoes in the air.

I grit my teeth, not wanting to even say it again. Everything about that phrase makes me more determined to play her game and win.

"Answer me," she demands, keeping control of the flogger.

I stay quiet.

"For every second you don't respond, I'm adding more time to your punishment," she threatens.

Unable to control my ego, I glance behind me, egging her on. "Is this all you got?"

She purses her lips, puts the flogger on the bed, then sits down. Her fingers weave through the side of my hair. She purrs, "Are you ready for your real punishment, sub?"

My lips twitch. I attempt to stop them but can't. This is ridiculous. I'm a Marino, alright. That means she can't make me submit. I can pretend to appease her, but it's not in my genes. And I'm ready to get to the pussy licking, so I do what I know will result in a punishment. I move between her legs and drag my tongue from her inner knee up her thigh.

She gasps but quickly recovers, pushing my head away from her. She declares, "I think you have a problem with authority."

No shit.

"Sorry, Mistress," I apologize, but it doesn't sound genuine.

Instead of looking angry, she tilts her head, cooing, "I think it's time I gave you a gift."

I dip my head toward her pussy and sniff.

She pushes me away again. "Tsk, tsk, tsk. You're not very obedient tonight."

I kneel as straight as possible and grin. "Sorry."

She smirks then gets off the bed. I watch her strut to the table. She picks up her purse and orders, "Face the bed, sub."

I obey, still smelling her arousal, ready to show her what she's been missing all these years.

She slinks behind me, caging her warm body around mine. Endorphins swirl inside me. She glides her palm over my cock and caresses my shaft, murmuring in my ear, "So hard, sub."

"Only for you, Mistress," I proudly state.

"You know what I thought about when we talked on the plane?" she questions.

My erection is so hard, it could compete with steel. I grip the mattress tighter, trying to ignore it for the moment. I ask, "What was that?"

She flicks her tongue on my lobe, and I almost lose it. She answers, "I thought about how I wanted to punish you."

"Punish me, then," I demand.

Her hot breath tickles my ear. She softly laughs then says, "I thought about you eating me."

"Yeeeees," I groan.

Her other arm circles me, and I lean into her, inhaling all of her as pre-cum seeps out of my cock. She pecks me on the nose, then lips, murmuring, "With this on."

It happens so fast that I don't realize it. She must be a pro, and I've definitely underestimated her. My cock strains against a cage, and I burst out, "What the fuck, Pina!"

"Tsk, tsk, tsk," she reprimands, rising quickly then slapping me with the flogger harder than before. "Such an outburst! Is that any way to talk to your Mistress?"

I grit my teeth. "Get this thing off me."

Satisfaction fills her expression. She widens her eyes and challenges, "Did you need your safe phrase?"

I clench my jaw.

"Well?" she asks.

I stay quiet.

"Do you want me to continue?" she challenges.

I sniff hard and straighten my back. Unable to tap out, I order, "Go on."

She steps back and pats me on the head. "Good boy." She flogs me several more times then slides her hand between my legs and tickles my balls.

"Pina," I groan as my erection tries to free itself from the metal.

"Who am I?" she demands.

"Sorry. Mistress. Please..."

"Please what?" she asks, licking my spine.

Oh fuck.

Sweat pops out on my skin. I try to contain my breathing. The urge to come makes me dizzy.

"Please what?" she repeats in a firmer tone.

"Please, baby girl. I need to come," I admit, sounding desperate.

She slides in front of me, spreading her thighs so they touch the outside of my shoulders. Her sweet scent flares in my nostrils. With an innocent look, she coos, "Did you want to come or do something else?"

14

Pina

Tristano's tongue swipes his lips. His eyes dart back and forth from my face to between my legs. I planned on flogging him softly for hours until he cried out his safe phrase. It's how I normally break my subs. They're powerful men and think my gentle slaps are nothing, until hours pass and it gets to be too much. It's a technique I learned independently, not by watching anyone. And I'm proud of my ability to slowly torture them until they fall to pieces.

However, my plan's short-lived. I knew Tristano was trying to go directly to what we discussed on the plane. I tried to hold off, but I got so wet from watching him wear the cock cage while I flogged him that it felt impossible. Plus, the thought of his tongue on my pussy is driving me insane. It's been almost a week since he's done it, and every night I obsessed about it while in bed, smelling the faint residual of his cologne on my pillows.

I may not have flogged him for hours, but right now, he's acting like a squirrel, unable to focus on any one part of my body. I've seen it before, and satisfaction grows within me. He's two steps from submitting, so I dig deep and slide as close to his face as possible. I hold his head an inch from my pussy, asking, "What will it be? Come or eat me?"

Desperation lines his voice. He sniffs hard, grinds his molars, then replies, "Your pussy."

I lean toward his face. "So let me make this clear. I'm giving you a choice to remove the cock cage, but you'd rather keep it on and eat me? Is that correct?"

He glances at my throbbing clit, licks his lips, then nods. "Yes."

"Yes, who?"

He swallows hard. "Yes, Mistress."

Tristano Marino is my sub.

I pat him on the head then smile. "Then let's get on with it, shall we?"

He lunges his mouth toward me, but I retreat to the mattress, ordering, "Whoa! Stay in position!"

Confusion and frustration flood his expression, turning into a scowl.

I get off the bed and repeat, "Get in position or state your safe phrase."

His shoulders tense. He stretches his arms as far as possible and grips the bedding.

Armed with a new resolve to break him, I pick up the flogger and return to my soft slaps. I create an X pattern, approving of the red marks growing brighter on his back and ass cheeks. I start with ten, rub his skin with my palm, then tickle his balls while rubbing my nipples on his back. After, I repeat the pattern but increase the number of slaps each time by five.

Every now and then, I stand to his side and turn his head. "Lick me," I order.

He always groans, swiping his tongue on my clit like a dog at the water bowl. And as much as I want to have him keep going, I pull away.

For over an hour, he takes it, not flinching during the flogging. Yet, I don't miss his knuckles turning white or the way his shoulders stay taut. And I have to give him credit. Very few men I've dominated get as far as he has without protesting.

I allow him to lick me again, but this time, when I pull back, he quickly wraps his arm around my hips, tugging me back to him.

"Let go, sub!" I demand.

"Let me finish," he pleads.

My hand flies to his balls. I cup them and squeeze. I grab his hair and position his face toward the ceiling. A deep groan flies out of him, and more sweat pops out on his skin.

"You have a safe phrase," I remind him.

"Please, Pina," he mumbles, a wild and crazed look filling his orbs.

"Please, who?"

"Mistress."

"And what do you want, sub? Tell me."

He takes several shallow breaths.

I grab the flogger and slap his back.

"No more!" he says.

Adrenaline flows through me. Tristano Marino, on his knees, begging me and about to tap out, is like a dream I never knew I had. It's like everyone I've ever dominated has been a practice session leading up to this moment. And something about it is stunningly beautiful to me. I reply, "I don't understand what that means. Use your safe phrase if you need to."

He closes his eyes. "Pina—"

"'I am a Marino' is all you have to say! And I'm not your—"

He grabs my hips, tosses me on the bed, and lunges over me. He takes a pair of handcuffs and restrains me to the headboard.

"Tristano!"

He pushes the back of my thighs and orders, "Thighs on your chest!" His face dips to my pussy, and every notion I ever had about what it's like for Tristano to eat me flies out the window.

His mouth and fingers become a hurricane, violently swirling around, flicking me, sucking me, and teasing me until my skin is soaked with sweat and fluids.

"Oh God! Please!" I beg, forgetting everything about how I'm supposed to be the one in control. My legs shake so much, they dip several inches.

He pushes them back, pressing his forearm against them, growling, "You submit to me, baby girl. Do you understand?"

"Yes," I cry out, not able to deny him if I tried.

"Why?" he barks, then dips back to my body, flicking me so fast, I get dizzy.

"Yes! Don't stop!" I demand.

"Why do you submit to me?" he repeats, then tosses the cock cage on the bed next to my head.

I should have brought the one that locks, quickly goes through my mind, but then his tongue teases me further.

"I'm going to come! Oh God! Don't stop! Please," I beg again.

"Answer me!" he orders, lunging over my body and positioning his face a few inches from mine.

My heart pounds fast. Our breaths merge, both of us struggling for air.

"Tell me why you submit to me," he says again.

I blurt out, "Because I love it!"

He sniffs hard, nodding. "That's right, baby girl." He thrusts into me until his pelvis hits the back of my thighs.

"Oh!" I gasp, seeing stars. Our bodies meld together. His cock glides faster and faster until I cry out, "I'm coming!"

He slows down, torturing me. The dark flames in his eyes burn hotter as he studies me.

"Oh God," I moan, wondering how I ever lived without his body in mine. Nothing's ever felt so good or right.

"Fuck, Pina! Admit you love us together," he demands, increasing his speed.

I stare at him, barely able to keep my eyes open. Every pleasurable sensation I've ever had seems to spiral around me. It's like a high I know I'm always going to have to chase. How could it ever be possible to reach again?

"Tell me," he growls.

"I-I oh God!" I scream as a new wave of euphoria pummels me.

"You're mine, Pina. Tell me the truth! Tell me you want more of me," he orders.

My raspy voice barely gets out, "Yes! More of you."

"Because we're good together. Admit it!"

"Yes! Us. Together," I moan, unable to see anything but white stars.

He kisses me deeply, and it's like an out-of-body experience. If any more of him could be inside me, I'd take it. I've never had so many zings bouncing in all my cells.

He pushes my legs so my ankles are near my ears. He scoops his arms under my body, holding me tight to his chest and

MAGGIE COLE

reaching one arm to fist my restrained wrists. His erection slides against my walls, creating more sensations I've never felt before.

My whimpers fill the room. The tremors in my body get more intense. Adrenaline floods me so much, it feels like I'm floating.

"Fuuuuuuck." He grunts, and his cock shoots his seed in me for what feels like forever. It swells forcefully, stretching me into a new reality.

Our bodies convulse against one another. The sound of our cries and the smell of sex tornados through the room. I pull on the cuffs, but there's nowhere to go. He squeezes my wrists tighter and groans.

When it's all over, his body continues to shake. At first, I think it's mine, but I realize he's affected as much as I am. It takes a long time for us to regain our breath. He finally rolls off me, releases the cuffs, then pulls me into his chest.

My heart's still not back to its normal rhythm. Goose bumps pop out on my skin from sweating, then cooling off. His warm skin is as wet as mine.

He strokes my hip, murmuring, "I don't think I've ever come that hard before."

Surprised, I tilt my head. "Yeah, that was intense."

He cocks an eyebrow. "Have you ever come that hard before?"

My pulse creeps back up. Something about admitting that to him seems like a red flag.

"You can't answer me? Or are you scared to tell the truth?" he challenges.

My chest tightens. "Why would I be scared?"

His arrogant grin widens. "You'll have a harder time saying we shouldn't be together."

I nervously scoff. "Why is that?"

"It's difficult to let go of something once you know how good it is and have admitted it," he claims.

I should deny his statement, but I can't.

"So? Are you going to confess? The sex we have is the best for both of us?" he presses.

I take a deep breath and lock eyes with him, divulging, "Yeah, it's the best."

Satisfaction ignites. He flips me on my back and cages his body over me, grinning.

I laugh. "What are you doing?"

His face falls. He drags a finger through a lock of my hair then tucks it behind my ear. Then he cups my cheeks, studying me. It's sweet and makes me feel super vulnerable.

My butterflies flutter fast. The voice in my head tells me to roll off the bed and run. Tristano and I aren't a long-term possibility. It can't work.

Maybe it can.

No, it can't.

It's going to hurt to give him up.

I could keep him.

No, I can't.

He rips me out of my debate and announces, "You're not anything like I thought."

"What does that mean?" I ask defensively.

"Chill. Nothing bad."

I release a tense breath. "Okay. So what does it mean?" I ask softer.

He pecks me on the lips then admits, "It means I really like you."

My heart swells and sinks, fighting with my brain. I wish I could turn it off. I open my mouth and then shut it.

Hurt fills his expression. "You don't like me?"

"No! Of course I do!"

"Then why did you just look like you wanted to crawl into a hole and die?"

I cringe. "I didn't mean to."

"But you did. So what was that all about?" he presses.

Blood pounds in my brain. I confess, "I really like you, too, Tristano."

His face hardens. "But?"

"You know the but."

He shakes his head. "You're worried about things that aren't going to happen."

I close my eyes and try to shut off all my fears.

"Pina, look at me," he demands.

I obey, blinking hard and wishing I didn't feel so emotional all of a sudden.

He kisses my forehead, nose, then lips. He adamantly states, "I won't let anything happen. I promise."

I stay quiet, processing his words and wondering how that's possible.

"You don't believe me, do you?"

"It's not that. I just—"

"You're just in your head."

I nod.

He kisses me again, but it's not a peck this time. It's another out-of-body experience that leaves me whimpering in his arms. He retreats and grins. "I know you felt that."

"What?" I ask.

"Don't play dumb."

For some reason, I feel shy, which isn't something I'm used to. I softly agree, "Okay. I felt it."

His lips twitch, and he declares, "Good. Now that we got that out of the way, do you think there's pizza at this resort?"

I laugh. "Pizza?"

He rolls off me, rises, then pulls the covers over me. "Yep. I need the biggest pizza they have. Maybe some goat cheese garlic knots, too."

"Well, don't get specific or anything," I tease.

He kisses me on the forehead. "You keep the bed warm. I'm going to find a menu somewhere in this place."

I point to the desk. "Or you could start with that binder."

He glances at it then beams at me. "See now. That's why I need to keep you. I'll never be searching for menus." He picks it up and jumps on the bed, thumbing through it. After a few seconds, he pumps his arm in the air. "Pizza! No goat cheese garlic knots, but they have pretzel bites with cheddar cheese. That'll do."

"Are you that hungry?" I ask.

He dramatically jerks his head backward. "After that workout we just had?"

My stomach growls. "Guess you're right."

He wiggles his eyebrows. "Okay, well, I know you love pretzel bites. If memory serves, you prefer your pizza with parmesan crust, mushrooms, and black olives."

"Wow! Have you been stalking me?" I tease but am also impressed he's paid attention.

When did he pay attention? We haven't had pizza together in a long time.

He picks up the phone next to the bed and hits the speakerphone and another button. It rings, and a man answers, "Good evening. Is this Mr. or Mrs. Marino?"

I almost correct them, but Tristano tugs me closer and answers, "Both."

CARNAL

Like last time they called me Mrs. Marino, I like it. I wonder what it would be like to be his in that way. Then I reprimand myself for even contemplating such a thing.

The man replies, "Great. I hope you're enjoying your stay so far?"

"Yes, everything is perfect," Tristano states, winking at me.

My flutters take off again.

The man asks, "What can I do for you?"

Tristano says, "We need to order food. Can I do that through you?"

"Yes, sir."

Tristano's hand strokes my torso. "We need an extra-large pizza with parmesan crust, mushrooms, and black olives. Also, can we get two orders of pretzel bites with extra cheese sauce?"

"Two?" I question.

He nods.

"Right away, sir. Would you like anything different than what's in your fridge?" the man asks.

"Pina?" Tristano inquires.

"Was there water in the fridge?"

"Yeah."

"I'll have that."

"We're good on drinks," Tristano replies.

"Very well. Is there anything else I can get you?"

"Nah. That'll do."

"It'll be about thirty minutes."

"Perfect. Thanks." Tristano hangs up the phone.

I rise and attempt to pull him off the bed.

He arches his eyebrows. "Where are we going?"

"We have time before the pizza arrives to shower."

"Good call." He gets up and follows me into the bathroom, slapping my ass.

"Hey!" I laugh, turning on the water.

"Don't 'hey' me. I should beat your ass after you flogged me as long as you did," he states.

I wince. "Sorry."

He shakes his head. "No, you aren't."

"Maybe just a little," I offer, holding my thumb and pointer finger close together.

Tristano tilts his head. "You, Ms. dela Cruz, are one bad bitch."

"Hey! I only did what you would have!" I claim, stepping into the shower.

He follows me in. "No. I wouldn't have flogged you softly. I would have added some more strength to those little slaps."

I bite my lip and shrug my shoulders. "But it wasn't bad, right?"

Amusement fills his expression. "Don't act like you don't know what you were doing. But honestly, paybacks are a bitch, baby girl. The next time I flog you, I'm using your technique on you."

My stomach flips. There's no way he's fibbing. I blurt out, "But you broke me last weekend. It won't be as challenging."

He smirks. "We'll see about that."

I ignore the anxiety reigniting in my chest and let the water soak my hair. We both do our thing in the shower then get out and dry off. It isn't long before we're eating pizza and pretzel bites. Tristano has more beer, and I have water.

"What did you want to be when you grew up?" Tristano asks, then pops another pretzel bite full of cheese into his mouth.

I don't hesitate. "Successful."

He finishes chewing and downs it with a mouthful of Red Stripe, then replies, "Well, that's a given. But what did you want to do?"

I pick a mushroom off the pizza, eat it, then answer, "There wasn't anything specific. I just knew I wanted to not struggle like my parents did. Was there something you wanted to be?"

His eyes light up. "A fireman."

"Really?"

"Why do you look shocked?"

I shrug. "Not sure."

"Well, I love fire and thought it would be cool to go down that pole. The trucks are badass, too."

"Why didn't you do it?"

His face darkens. He lowers his voice. "You know how it is in my family. Our paths are created at birth."

I scoot closer to him. "Do you like what you do?"

He pauses, as if thinking over my question. After a moment, he stares at me. In a calm tone, he states, "You know my family better than anyone."

I nod, not able to deny it.

He continues, "So you know the devil's in me."

I blurt out, "Is this where you tell me all the things you've done in your papà's dungeon?" His eyes widen, and I put my hand over my face, groaning. "Crap."

"How do you know about the dungeon, Pina?"

I peek from under my fingers, slowly admitting, "Your brother tells me a lot when he's drunk and depressed."

Tristano moves my hand off my face. "What are you talking about?"

"Let's forget I said anything."

"No. Tell me how you know about the dungeon."

Nerves fill me. I confess, "Dante used to get really upset about Bridget. A long time ago. Like when she was in Chicago and before they got together."

"And?"

The hairs on my neck rise. I shouldn't be telling Tristano any of this, but I don't see a way out. "He would get drunk and come into the office. I worked a lot of late nights. He'd lie on the couch, telling me his sob stories and eventually fall asleep. I'd come in the next day, and he'd be gone."

"So, what do you know about the dungeon?" Tristano demands.

"Just stuff," I casually reply.

Tristano's face reddens. "Pina, I want to know right now."

"Why? You can't tell Dante!"

He exhales loudly.

"Tristano!"

"Fine. But I still want to know."

"Why?"

"Because I do."

I decide there's no way of getting out of this. I cave. "First of all, I've never told anyone, so chill."

"Well, that's good to know," he sneers.

"Don't be like that, or I'm not telling you."

He looks at the ceiling then finally back at me. In a softer tone, he says, "Go on."

I rack my brain for all the conversations I've had with Dante and decide less is better. "So it's no secret you kill your enemies, so don't freak."

Tristano's eyes widen.

"Look, I know you torture men there, and honestly, I don't have a problem with it. They all deserve it," I state and mean it. An enemy of the Marinos' is an enemy of mine.

"And?" he presses.

I get on my knees and straddle him, pushing my fingers through his hair. "Should I tell you what I know about you?"

"Go on."

I try not to smile but can't suppress it. "I know you like to be creative with different tools."

"You find that amusing?"

"Well, you did use a potato slicer. I mean, that was pretty creative," I confess.

Tristano's expression makes me laugh.

"Don't be so serious," I accuse.

"Pina, what happens down there is serious. Men die."

Silence fills the air. I finally break it. "Yes. I know."

"You don't think it's horrible what we do?" he asks.

I contemplate how to answer his question and finally respond, "You say you have the devil in you, but those you slaughter are the true devils. So, no, I don't judge anything your family has done."

He stares at me. My anxiety continues to grow. He demands, "You never breathe a word of this to anyone, okay?"

I nod. "I swear you're the only person I've ever discussed this with besides Dante."

His entire face gets so dark, it scares me. He adds, "Good. You need to keep it that way."

"I will," I vow. "Let's change the subject."

More tension surrounds us until he grabs a piece of pizza and shoves it in my mouth.

I shriek, laughing.

He pins me on the floor and smears the slice on my breast. His eyes light up as he says, "Damn. Guess I have some more body parts to lick."

15

Tristano

A Few Days Later

The plane lands and the fasten-seat-belt light goes out. I kiss the top of Pina's head, gently stating, "Wake up, baby girl."

We left at midnight to get back to New York in time for her to be at work at her normal time. Almost as soon as the plane got in the air, she curled into my chest and fell asleep. I didn't have the heart to wake her and make her move to the bedroom.

She softly moans. Her eyelids flutter open and shut a few times. It makes me smile, feeling even happier than I had the past few days, which I didn't think was possible.

We spent the entire weekend enjoying the ocean, snorkeling, kayaking, sunbathing, and laughing about crazy things. I told

Pina things I've never discussed with anyone. And every revelation she revealed only made me fall deeper for her.

"We landed?" she groggily asks.

I grin. "Yep. Back to reality."

She groans then yawns. "Can we just go back?"

I chuckle. "I wish." My butterflies kick off. "So? Does that mean you had a good time?"

She reaches for my cheek and tenderly caresses my jawline. "I had a great time. Thank you."

Giddiness fills me. I lean closer to her face. "You know what that means, then?"

She bites her lip. Nerves fill her expression.

"The deal was if you had a good time, we keep seeing each other. If you had a bad time, then we stop. Don't tell me you're going back on your promise," I add, my chest tightening.

She takes a deep breath and then releases it. She turns more in her seat and replies, "I'm not going back on my word. But, Tristano, I'm not ready to tell Dante or anyone else anything."

I have mixed feelings about keeping us a secret, but I know why Pina feels strongly about not telling my family. So I consider this a win. I'll help her come to terms with telling my family over time. I kiss the back of her hand and promise, "Understood. I'll let you decide when the timing is right."

"You will?" she asks.

"Why do you seem surprised?"

She shrugs. "I don't know."

"Well, don't worry about this," I instruct as I rise and hold my hand out to help her stand.

She takes it, and I tug her into me. She looks up and says, "It really was a great weekend."

"It was. Come on. I better get you to your place so you can get to work." I lead her off the plane and onto the snowy runway.

The cold air tortures us. I instantly wish I could go back to the warm sunshine. I battle snowflakes to guide Pina to the vehicle.

Flex opens the back-seat door and says, "Shit. You two are tan. Where did you go?"

"The Bahamas," I reply.

Pina slides into the SUV, saying nothing.

I fist-bump Flex then get in. He shuts the door.

Pina frets, "Are you sure Flex isn't going to say anything?"

I put my arm around her. "Yes. Stop worrying."

Flex gets in. "Where to?"

"Pina's," I answer.

He nods then puts the SUV into gear. "So, what's interesting in the Bahamas?"

"Everything," I state.

He grunts. "Want to be more specific?"

Pina jumps in, "The Blue Lagoon was amazing."

"Like from that old movie?" he questions.

"It's a private island you have to take a half-hour ferry ride to, but it's worth it. The water's pristine," she informs him.

"More so than the resort water?" he inquires.

Pina thinks a moment. "No. It's just different. You have to see it to understand, I guess. And it's cool because no one lives there."

"If only they let us stay longer than two hours," I add.

Pina beams. "Yeah. Agreed. It was still awesome though."

I stretch my legs as far as possible. "Flex, you see Callie this weekend?"

"Sure did."

"How'd it go?"

He chuckles. "So good I dropped her off this morning from our Friday night date."

"Callie Langford?" Pina questions.

Flex boasts, "The one and only!"

"How long is she in town?"

"She was supposed to leave this week, but she's extending her stay," he claims.

"Ohhh! Give us the deets," Pina orders.

He veers onto the expressway ramp and speeds up, declaring, "I don't kiss and tell, Pina."

"Sure you don't," she teases.

"Nope. I don't. That's how you know your secret is safe with me, too," he points out.

She shifts in the seat and lowers her voice. "Thanks."

"No problem." Flex weaves through the morning rush hour traffic but not as aggressively as usual due to the snow.

We stay quiet the rest of the ride. When we pull up to Pina's building, I get out and walk her to her unit.

"You didn't have to come all the way up here," she states, unlocking the door.

I push her inside, shut the door, and pin her against it. She gasps, and I put my lips an inch from hers, admitting, "I had one of the best weekends ever with you."

The gold in her eyes ignites. Her lips twitch, and she replies, "Me, too."

I continue, "And I did have to walk you up here because it wouldn't be appropriate downstairs."

She arches her eyebrows. "What wouldn't?"

"This." I lean closer and part her lips with my tongue, kissing her with everything I have, not wanting to leave but knowing I have to.

She whimpers, clasping her arms tighter around me.

I retreat, stating, "I'll call you later to arrange date number two."

Her face lights up. She nods. "Okay."

I give her a chaste kiss then step back. "Enjoy your day." I leave her condo, feeling like I'm walking on a cloud of sunshine even though it's freezing outside. I get into the front of the SUV.

Flex whistles.

"What?" I question.

"You two look super...how should I say it?"

"Super what?"

He glances at me. "Involved."

Involved. I try to process that word and what Pina and I are to each other. I'm unsure what I'd call us. Are we a couple now even though we're a secret? If we aren't a couple, then what are we?

"Wrong word?" Flex asks.

"No. Involved is fair," I reply, then try to change the subject. "So tell me about your weekend with Callie."

Arrogance lights up Flex's face. "It was good. We were at my place all weekend."

"So, no details?"

"Are you going to tell me about you and Pina?"

"Okay. Next topic," I assert.

He chuckles. "Fair enough."

I glance at the traffic around us, inquiring, "I assume nothing crazy happened since Papà and my brothers left me alone all weekend?"

"Quietest one in a long time. I won't lie, I kind of enjoyed it," Flex admits.

"Yeah, me, too." I pull out my sunglasses and lean the seat back to a forty-five-degree angle. I close my eyes and announce, "I need to catch some Zs. Wake me up when we're home."

He accelerates, replying, "Done."

As hard as I try, I don't sleep. I keep my eyes shut, remembering different pieces of my perfect weekend. While it's still not ideal I fell for Pina, what's done is done. Now that we opened Pandora's box, there's no going back. The weekend only solidified that we're good together. And I've never felt so connected to a woman before. I don't know if it's because of Pina and my long history or what it is, but everything about us feels different.

When we get to the house, Flex taps my shoulder, announcing, "Home sweet home, boss." He parks in front of the steps.

I adjust the seat and slap Flex's hand. "Thanks for the ride, bro."

"Anytime."

I get out, pass the guard, and go into the house. It's barely five thirty. Everything is quiet. I go to my bedroom and change into workout clothes. I go to the gym, and my brothers and Papà are already there.

"Look who's back," Massimo booms.

Dante, Gianni, and Papà turn.

"How was the sunshine?" Massimo questions.

"Awesome. Wish I could have stayed," I confess.

"Don't blame you, bro," he adds, then motions to the squat machine.

I help him add weights as Papà asks, "Where did you end up going?"

"Bahamas."

"Ah. I took your mamma there once. She loved it."

My heart swells and also hurts thinking about Mamma. She died way too early. I'd give anything to hug her once more. I nod and reply, "I can see why. It's an amazing place."

"Who'd you go with?" Dante inquires.

My chest tightens. I didn't think about these things. I quickly lie, "Flex."

"I thought you were going with a girl?" Papà questions.

My anxiety grows. I'm not used to lying to my family. I shrug, adding another weight to the machine. "I did. But Flex came at the last minute."

"Don't tell me you're into threesomes with him, bro," Gianni taunts.

"Shut up. We each had a woman with us," I fib.

"Thank God. I wouldn't ever be able to look at Flex or you the same," Gianni claims.

"Whatever," I mutter, then stretch my arms. "So, it was a quiet weekend?"

"Yep. No one to chase down and toss into the dungeon," Dante states.

I glance at him, biting my tongue, wanting to ask how he could be so loose-lipped to tell Pina about the dungeon. If Papà knew, he'd kill Dante.

"What?" he asks.

"Nothing." I jump on the treadmill and hit the program buttons.

"We do have a new problem to discuss," Papà announces, stepping on the elliptical next to me.

I hold in a groan. Of course there would be an issue the second I return from paradise. I was hoping to work out and get a few hours of sleep. Not sure what's happening, but my gut says I won't be getting any daytime rest. I face Papà, responding, "Yeah? What's that?"

"Jacopo Abruzzo called a meeting for the heads of the families," he reveals.

My stomach drops. The only thing anyone calls that type of meeting for has to do with the sex club.

"Probably trying to smooth over his asshole son's mistakes," Gianni sneers.

"It's at noon. Tristano, I want you to go with me," Papà asserts.

Shocked, I ask, "Me?" I've never been to those meetings. If Papà takes anyone, he always takes one of my other brothers. It's mostly Dante since he's next in line.

Papà nods. "Yes."

"Why?"

"Does there have to be a reason?" he questions.

"Yeah. You don't do anything without having a reason," I state.

Papà chuckles. "Fair enough."

"So? What's the reason?" I repeat, curious why I'm finally getting a seat at the table after all these years.

Papà takes a swig of water then replies, "Because you're ready."

An odd feeling fills me. I'm unsure what that means, nor did I know that before now, Papà didn't believe I was capable of attending these meetings. Part of me is interested in seeing what it's like, but the other part is insulted that he didn't have faith in me.

"Don't get too excited. It's normally boring as fuck," Gianni claims, selecting a speed rope.

Papà scowls at him. "Keep your comments to yourself."

"What? I want to kill half the men in there. The others I see enough of. If I never have to go to another meeting, I'm good," he declares.

Papà shakes his head then addresses Dante. "Take note of this. Someday, when all the pressures are on you, keep this little admission of your brother's in your head."

Gianni groans and then starts jumping rope.

I finish my workout, shower, and attempt an hour's nap, but I can't sleep. I text Pina.

Me: *Are you tired?*

Pina: *Not too bad. Did you sleep on the plane?*

Me: *Not really.*

Pina: *Can you now?*

Me: *Nope. Papà has me scheduled for a meeting.*

Pina: *Have fun with that.*

Me: *I'm sure it'll be stimulating. How's work?*

Pina: *The same.*

Me: *When can I see you again?*

Pina: *When do you want to?*

Me: *Tonight.*

Pina: *Don't you want to sleep?*

Me: *Why don't we order in? We can have a low-key night.*

A few moments pass. Little dots appear as if she's typing. Then they disappear. I wait, holding my breath, then finally type back.

Me: *You can use me as a pillow.*

Pina: *Ha ha! Sorry, I was debating.*

My gut drops.

Me: *Don't tell me you're having second thoughts about us.*

Pina: *No. That's not it. I was going to say, why don't we go to my place in Manhattan. I'll cook you dinner.*

I grin like a schoolboy.

Me: *What time?*

Pina: *Seven?*

Tell her eight.

Get over the seven. It's an extra hour with her.

Me: *Perfect. See you then.*

I pump my fist in the air and jump out of bed. It's time for me to meet Papà downstairs. I find him in his office and knock.

He looks up from his desk. "You have your Glock?"

"Of course," I reply.

"Make sure you leave it in the SUV," he orders.

"Okay. Ready to go?"

He rises, puts a stack of papers in a folder, then walks toward the door. "Yes."

We go to the front entrance and step out into the cold winter air. His driver is waiting and holds the door to the back seat open. He nods and says, "Boss."

Papà pats him on the shoulder. "Achille." Papà gets in, and I follow.

He turns toward me. "It's important you don't lose your cool today, Tristano."

"Why would I?"

Papà hesitates then answers, "Things can get heated. The more we don't react, the better."

I take my Glock and slide it under the seat. Anger flares as the vision of Biagio palming Pina's ass pops up in my mind. I inquire, "Jacopo's going to try and downplay what Biagio did, isn't he?"

"Probably."

"I thought you already met about it."

"We did."

"So why call another meeting?"

Papà crosses his arms. "There's a reason I didn't take your other brothers, especially Dante."

"Which is?"

Papà pins his dark gaze on mine. "The security footage wasn't available when we met. Tully suggested we reconvene to review it."

I lower my voice. "Then why is Jacopo calling the meeting?"

"That's what I don't understand, either. He must have something up his sleeve. Whatever it is, I need you to keep your cool. Dante's too close to Pina to deal with this how we need to," Papà states.

Guilt eats at me about keeping my relationship with Pina a secret, but maybe it's for the better right now. If Papà knew about us, there's no way I'd be allowed in the meeting. And it's refreshing to actually do something I'm normally not allowed to.

We don't talk the rest of the ride. When we pull up to the restaurant, we go inside. The hostess takes us to the back and into a private room. A few dozen men fill the space. All the heads of the families are here, including Jacopo and Biagio.

Across the table from them, Tully and his son Brody nod at us. There are two empty seats. Papà sits next to Tully, and I take the other seat.

Several servers place crocks of French onion soup and plates of Caesar salad in front of everyone. There are bottles of wine on the table, but most of the men drink hard liquor. Papà orders two sambucas, and we get served quickly.

As soon as the servers disappear, Sergio, the head bouncer of the sex club, shuts the door. He taps on his glass and the room turns quiet. He pins his deadly gaze on each of us, taking his time to assess everyone. He finally states, "The club cannot exist if rules are not followed."

All the men in the room except Jacopo and Biagio nod.

Sergio crosses his arms, scowling at Biagio. "We need to finalize the consequences for what occurred at the club. Let's review the recording again before we discuss what those shall be."

Biagio's face hardens and the vein near his eye twitches.

Sergio motions for Kelso, another bouncer, to turn on the TV. He obeys and hits play.

Pina's face appears on the screen. My hands turn to fists and my heart thumps harder as Biagio steps behind her. He grabs her ass, and shock fills her expression. She turns, and he closes the gap between them.

Rubio appears, followed soon after by Dante and Gianni, but I can't tear my eyes off Pina's scared expression. My pulse skyrockets, making my insides shake with rage. I glance at Biagio's arrogant face and almost rise, but Papà puts his hand on my thigh.

I turn toward him. He doesn't look at me, continuing to watch the footage.

When the video is over, Kelso turns the TV off. Tense silence fills the air. Papà and I leer across the room at Jacopo and Biagio.

Sergio speaks first. "It's clear Biagio was out of line. This unacceptable behavior cannot be tolerated. I put forth to the council that he has a three-month suspension."

Biagio snorts. "Fat chance."

"You were out of line," Szymon Kowalczyk, head of the Polish mafia, accuses. While the Kowalczyks aren't what I'd call our allies, I also wouldn't call them our enemies. We do business with them from time to time, but nothing formal has ever been created between our families.

Jacopo states, "As were the Marinos."

"Excuse me?" I seethe, still wanting to kill Biagio as soon as possible for putting his grimy hands on Pina.

Papà taps my kneecap under the table, not flinching.

Jacopo's sinister grin widens. He holds what resembles an old handbook in the air. "If we're following rules, we need to follow all of them."

The air in the room turns stale. It's so quiet, you could hear a pin drop. Sergio accuses, "We don't need to play games, Jacopo."

"Oh, I'm not." He opens the handbook, and a bookmark falls out. "It's all highlighted here."

"What is?" Sergio asks, taking the book from him.

Tully answers, "It's the original handbook from when our fathers created the rules."

Biagio grabs a breadstick, sits back in his chair, grins, then shoves half of it in his mouth.

"So what?" I blurt out.

Papà digs his nails into my knee.

I avoid looking at him. "It's very clear no one is to touch other families' women. Dante stated from day one Pina is a Marino."

"Yes. That's in there. But so is rule fifteen-twenty-eight-A," Jacopo declares.

"Which is what?" Szymon interjects.

"Read it," Jacopo instructs Sergio.

He clenches his jaw, scanning the page. Time seems to stand still until he reads, "Any man, for whatever reason, caught aggressively confronting an enemy family gets an automatic one-month suspension."

"That's right!" Jacopo exclaims, jumping up. He points to the TV. "You all saw the Marino men aggressively confronting my son."

"You have to be kidding me," Brody mutters.

Papà claims, "My sons were protecting Pina. If Biagio hadn't—"

"It doesn't matter. The rule clearly states 'for whatever reason.' So I'm fine with my son taking his punishment, but the Marinos must also," Jacopo declares.

The room turns silent. Everyone seems to be staring at Sergio. I grip the edge of the table to stop myself from lurching across it and pummeling Biagio and his father in the face.

Sergio continues to stare at the handbook then finally looks up at Papà. "The rules must be adhered to."

Papà nods. "Agreed."

Sergio says, "Your two sons and the other men in the video will need to take a one-month suspension."

"That's bullshit," I blurt out.

Papà glares at me. "It is the rule." He turns back to Sergio. "However, I ask the council to support your recommendation. Biagio should have a three-month suspension."

"I second," Tully declares.

"Third," Szymon calls out.

"My son should receive the same punishment as the Marinos," Jacopo suggests.

"Agreed," Biagio states.

"One day, I hope for your father's sake you learn to shut the fuck up," Bram Wilson, head of the Scottish mafia, states.

Biagio gives him a look of death.

Sergio nods. "Then let's vote. All those in favor of Biagio getting a three-month suspension, hold your hand up and say aye."

Most of the room holds up their hands, shouting, "Aye," including Abruzzo allies.

"Opposed, hold your hand up and say nay," Sergio instructs.

Fewer than six men take that option.

"It's settled, then. The Marinos on the tape get a month's suspension. Biagio gets three. And I will also put this out here while we're all in the room. Any more trouble from you, and it'll be an indefinite suspension," Sergio warns Biagio.

I barely taste my food. I spend the rest of the meal scowling at Biagio, wanting to kill him. When he smirks at me, it's settled. One day soon, he's going to meet his maker.

16

Pina

A Few Weeks Later

"Don't get upset with me," Tristano states.

The scent of garlic butter fills the air. I turn off the stove and move the saucepan to the unlit burner. "This is the third time you've done this to me."

He throws his hands in the air. "What do you want me to do, Pina? Until Dante and Gianni are allowed back into the club, it's all on Massimo and me."

I cross my arms, glaring at him. "I've made you dinner three times. Not once have you eaten it. Every time, you leave me with a kitchen full of hot food to run off to the club."

"You know I don't have a choice."

"Do I?"

His eyes widen. "What does that mean?"

I scrub my face, frustrated and angry.

"Well, don't stop talking now," he hurls.

"Fine. I'll tell you. You banned me from the club, but you're constantly there. Gee, I wonder why," I sneer.

"Working. I'm there working, and you know it," he claims.

"Oh, I'm sure you're working it. Especially with lipstick marks near your ear!"

His face turns red. He steps closer and lowers his voice. "I told you, Chanel hugged me and kissed my cheek, just like she always does. End of story. You can ask her if you don't believe me."

My emotions stew inside me. I don't believe Chanel would ever do anything with Tristano or he with her. However, I hate that Tristano's there without me.

He declares, "I don't know why you even want to go to the club. We can do everything at your place in Manhattan or here."

I stay quiet, my heart beating faster.

His face darkens. "Are you not happy with us? Do you need to do what you used to there?"

I sigh, admitting, "No. Of course not."

"You sure?"

"I just said no."

"Then why are you fighting with me about this? You know I don't control when Papà gives me orders. And what would you do if you were at the club with me? It's not like you'll let me tell anyone about us. Unless you changed your mind?" he questions.

It's another sore spot. Last week, Tristano wanted to take me to a new restaurant opening. I said no. It would have meant outing us to his entire family. I reply, "I'm not ready for that."

"How convenient for you," he mumbles.

"Don't do that," I order.

"Don't be a hypocrite, Pina. I'm sorry I can't stay for dinner. I'll come back after I do my job and eat it then," he claims.

"Don't bother," I snap, then pick up the saucepan and toss the contents down the drain.

"What are you doing?"

I turn on the water and rinse the remaining liquid off the metal. I answer, "I'm not hungry anymore."

"That wasn't necessary."

I scoff. "I doubt you spending all your nights at the sex club is necessary, either."

"Are you serious right now?"

"Do I look like I'm joking?"

Tristano shakes his head. "Okay, Pina. Have it your way. See you later." He turns and walks toward the door.

Fear pummels me, but my ego doesn't let me tell him what I'm feeling. I follow him. "What are you saying, Tristano? Be very clear."

He opens the door, glances back, and says, "I'm not letting you accuse me of doing things I haven't done. Since we got together, I've not touched another woman. I have no desire to. But I'm not going to shirk my family responsibilities. You work for us. You know the nuances of the job."

Guilt crashes into me. I can't argue his statement. I do understand how the Marino family works. If Angelo orders you to do something, you don't argue. I'm not being fair to Tristano, but the thought of him going into the club makes me feel ill.

I have no reason not to trust him, but knowing what goes on there and what he's done in the past doesn't give me any peace. Women throw themselves at all the Marinos, and Tristano is no different than any other man. I'm sure it takes a lot of willpower for him to pass on every woman who hits on him.

My silence angers him. He scolds, "Really, Pina? Wow. Good to know what you think of me." He steps out into the hallway.

I grab his bicep. "Wait."

He shrugs out of my grasp. "I'm going to be late. Have a nice night."

"Tristano!" I call after him, but he disappears down the stairwell instead of waiting for the elevator.

I go inside, shut the door, then lean against it, slightly banging my head.

Why did I have to do that?

I hate him spending so much time at the club when I can't go.

But then the Marinos would know about us.

Maybe it wouldn't be as bad as I think.

Nope. No way. Dante will never forgive me.

Then where is this going?

The more time I spend with Tristano, the more my fears nag me. I'm trying not to fall for him, but it's proving impossible. Besides the last-minute cancellations, which always happen when I'm cooking him dinner, everything between us seems to get better. He's funny, doesn't seem to have any issues being emotionally available, and our chemistry is unlike anything I've ever experienced. Plus, right when I think sex can't get any better, he proves me wrong.

When I close my eyes at night, I see my future with him. It scares me more than anything. I wish I could get past the "working for Dante" issue. It would be a lot easier to let the world know we're together. I know my pride's in the way. Yet, I can't figure out how to not care about Dante's thoughts and how he'll treat me at work if he ever finds out.

The anxiety of keeping Tristano and me a secret isn't fun, either. Whenever Tristano comes into the office, I stress over whether I'm acting like my pre-Tristano self toward him or not.

Upset, I decide to clean up the kitchen and go to bed. I'm no longer hungry and I'm also mad at myself. I never throw food away. It's a cardinal sin since I grew up hungry all the time.

I curl up in my bed, feeling exhausted but unable to sleep. Throughout the night and into the morning, I check my phone for a message from Tristano. It never comes, and at four thirty, I text him.

Me: *I'm sorry. I hope things went well for you last night.*

He doesn't reply. The message says delivered, making my thoughts spiral out of control again. Some of the subs he used to have sessions with pop into my brain, and I cringe.

Since I can't sleep, I shower, grab a yogurt, and head to the office. I take my usual spot in the conference room and spread my files all over the table. I get lost in my work for hours.

The other staff members arrive around nine. I clean up the space and go into my personal office. My intercom buzzes.

"Pina, you have a delivery," Megan, our newest receptionist, states.

"What is it?" I ask, racking my brain over what I could have ordered.

"I think you need to come out here to find out," she chirps.

I turn the speaker off and groan. Megan is super dramatic. Everything is always a big deal. However, she's proved herself worthy over the last few months, so I've kept her on board.

I trudge out toward the lobby. When I turn the corner, I freeze.

The largest bouquet of roses I've ever seen sits on Megan's desk. Since they take up so much space, I can't even see her face. They're red, and while some people put no thought into the color of roses, I know what every color represents. Red signals romance, love, beauty, and courage.

My pulse pounds harder, and a grin I can't control forms on my face. I ask, "Are these for me?"

Megan rises, wiggling her eyebrows and dangling a tiny envelope in front of me.

I snatch the envelope out of her hand and am relieved to find out she didn't open it. I pick up the vase and take everything to my office. I open the card, and my heart skips a beat.

PINA,

I'm sorry I ruined your dinner. If it means anything, it smelled really good before you tossed it down the sink. (That's supposed to make you laugh, so don't hate me more.)

Let's have a do-over, but I'll do the cooking. Meet me in Manhattan at eight.

Love,

You Know Who

P.S. - Yes, I know what red roses stand for.

MY BUTTERFLIES GO CRAZY. I SMILE SO BIG, MY CHEEKS HURT. Does he really mean it? Does Tristano love me?

I lean into the flowers and take several deep breaths. Then I pick up my phone and call him. It goes to voice mail.

I leave a message, stating, "Hey. It's me. I just got the gorgeous flowers you sent. Thanks. Ummm... I'll see you tonight. Bye."

I hang up just as Dante knocks on my door. He booms, "Damn, Pina. Someone rob a florist?"

Heat flushes my cheeks. I reply, "Ha ha."

He steps closer. "Who's the lucky guy?"

My pulse picks up. "No one you know," I lie.

He arches his eyebrows. "Maybe it's time I meet him."

"Are you my dad now?"

"Not old enough."

"Then don't make comments like you are."

He bends over and inhales. "This is a lot of roses. And they're all red."

"So what? Why are you here so early?" I ask, trying to change the subject.

He smirks. "Oh, we'll get to that in a moment. Does this guy know what the color of roses means?"

"Probably not. You only know since I educated you," I declare.

He grunts. "Good point."

"So? You're here because...?"

Dante sits in a chair. I take my position behind the desk and wait. He presses the pads of his fingertips together, studying me.

It makes me nervous that he knows something. I clear my throat. "What's going on? Is everything okay?"

He waits another moment then says, "Pack a bag."

"Why?"

"I'm sending Tristano and you on a trip," he announces.

My gut flips. I stare at him.

"What's wrong?" he questions.

I clear my throat. "N-nothing. I'm confused."

"Tristano will fill you in," he states, then glances at his watch and rises. "I need to go. Bridget's waiting in the car."

Does he know about us?

What's going on here?

Panic tornados through me. I follow him out of the office. "Where are you sending us?"

"You can pick. Take the day off tomorrow if you want," he adds, confusing me further. He pushes the elevator button.

I reach for his bicep. "Dante, this is bizarre. Why are you sending me on a trip with Tristano?"

"You'll see."

"Can you give me some details, please?" I beg.

The elevator door opens. He steps inside, spins, and shakes his head. "I can't right now. Tristano knows what's going on. Try to have some fun. You work too hard."

"Bridget's having a bad effect on you," I point out.

"Oh? Why?"

"You're too chipper," I assert.

He chuckles. "Guess I am. Bye." He waves as the elevator doors shut.

I stare at the silver doors, trying to get my thoughts in order. Dante's sent me on trips before, but there's always a clear assignment. And it's never been with any of his brothers.

Does he know?

I race to my office and call Tristano. It goes to his voicemail again. "Ugh!"

I text him.

Me: *Dante just told me we're going on a trip. What's this about?*

Tristano: *I'll tell you in the car. Pick you up in an hour.*

Me: *An hour?*

Tristano: *Yep.*

Me: *I need to pack.*

Tristano: *No, you don't. Trust me.*

Me: *Does he know?*

Tristano: *No. Chill out.*

Me: *I'm so confused.*

Tristano: *As I said, chill out. Everything is fine, baby girl.*

Me: *You'll tell me as soon as I get in the car what's going on?*

Tristano: *Promise.*

I release an anxious breath then try to clean up any remaining work issues. It doesn't help my nerves. I pace my office and then decide I need fresh air.

I go to the lobby, step out of the building, and run right into a hard chest. "Sorry! I—" My mouth turns dry.

Biagio's lips curl. "Pina. Long time no see."

"What are you doing here?" I hurl.

He steps closer and moves me to the side of pedestrian traffic.

"Don't touch me!"

"Calm down," he orders, then closes the space between us.

I retreat until I'm against the wall. "Get away from me!"

He grabs my chin so tight it hurts.

"Stop!" I cry out.

"You're trouble, aren't you?" he asks.

"Back off!" I shout, trying to push him away, but he's a thousand-pound stone that's unmovable.

He seethes, "You cost me money."

"Stop touching me!"

He leans so close, I can smell his cigarette breath. I swallow the bile creeping into my throat. He threatens, "When someone takes money out of my pocket, there's a debt to pay."

My voice shakes. "I've done no such thing. Now, move!"

"You got me banned from the club for three months," he announces.

"That isn't my fault," I claim.

He snorts. "From where I'm standing, it's clearly your fault."

"I'm telling you for the last—"

"Fucker!" Tristano barks, grabs Biagio's shoulder, and yanks him away from me. Biagio spins, and Tristano lands a right hook on his face. Blood bursts from his nose, and he rushes at Tristano. Flex grabs the back of his coat and tugs so hard, Biagio loses his footing. He slides on the slippery pavement and goes down on his back.

"Take care of this thug," Tristano orders to security guards running toward us. He swiftly leads me to the SUV, and we hop inside.

Flex jumps in the driver's seat and squeals out. Horns blare, and the sound of cars crashing fills the air.

I spin in my seat. Four cars crashed. One is spinning on the road. Smoke comes out of the hoods.

Tristano palms my cheeks. "Are you okay?"

I nod. "Yes."

"Did he hurt you?" he frets.

"No. I'm... I'm okay."

Tristano slides his arm around me, holding me close. "What did he say to you?"

I glance up. New fears ignite within me. "He says I cost him money. And that I have a debt to repay."

"Fucking asshole," Tristano seethes, then takes his phone out of his pocket. He swipes the screen then holds it to his ear.

"Who are you calling?" I inquire.

He holds his finger in the air. "Dante, Biagio just cornered Pina outside your building."

Flex veers sharply to the left, and I slide closer to Tristano.

He growls, "I knocked him out. Security is dealing with it. We're on our way to Teterboro." He kisses the top of my head and then states, "She said she's okay, but he claims she has a debt to pay for losing him money."

My gut flips. If Biagio thinks I cost him money, he's not going to back down until he gets whatever he wants from me.

What does he want?

I shudder.

Tristano tightens his arm around me. "Tell Papà. I want him dead, Dante."

I glance up.

He listens to whatever Dante is saying then says, "I'll keep you posted." He hangs up then tugs me onto his lap. "Are you sure you're not hurt?"

"Positive."

"I'll kill him," Tristano snarls.

"Bro, what time's your flight? There's an accident ahead," Flex informs us.

Tristano glances at his watch. "In an hour."

"Okay. I'm taking the long way. Otherwise, we'll be sitting here all day," Flex states.

"Do whatever you need," Tristano orders, then closes the divider glass. His voice softens. "I'm sorry that happened."

"It's not your fault," I insist.

He sniffs hard and clenches his jaw.

Several moments pass before I ask, "Want to tell me where we're going?"

"Where do you want to go?"

"I'm not following," I chirp, just as confused as in the office.

Tristano's lips twitch. "We can go anywhere you want. Name it, and we'll go."

"Am I on a hidden camera reality TV show or something?" I question.

He chuckles. "Nope. But speaking of hidden cameras, we will be doing something discreet."

"Such as...?"

Tristano glances at the closed divider window then back at me.

"What's going on?" I ask again, getting more frustrated by the minute.

He says, "You can't tell anyone what we're going to do. Only Dante, Gianni, and I know."

"Know what?"

He tucks a lock of my hair behind my ear. "We're taking Massimo's plane."

His admission only adds to my bewilderment. "Instead of yours?"

"Yes."

"Is something wrong with your plane?"

He shakes his head. "No. But Massimo thinks there is."

"Can you get to the meat of this trip? At the rate you're going, I'm going to have wrinkles by the time I learn whatever is happening here."

"But you'll still look sexy as fuck," Tristano claims.

My flutters take off. I place my hands on his cheeks. "Tell me what is going on here!"

His face darkens, and his voice turns serious. "We need to bug Massimo's plane."

17

Tristano

FOR MONTHS, MY BROTHERS AND I VOICED OUR CONCERNS over Massimo's current girlfriend, Katiya. We're all convinced she's an Abruzzo and playing him. She was even involved in my sister Arianna's kidnapping. As time has passed, Massimo's gotten increasingly sketchy. So Dante, Gianni, and I decided to have him followed.

It's a strange feeling to even consider my brother could betray us, but he's changed, growing more and more attached to Katiya and not listening to anything we have to say. Plus, he always seems to be hiding stuff, which isn't like him.

I can't see him turning to the Abruzzos, but I think everyone is on edge with all the traitors we've recently found in our family.

It makes my stomach flip thinking about all this, but there's only one way to know what's going on with Massimo. So I told him I needed to borrow his plane while mine got serviced, informed my pilots and Danika, and gave his team time off.

Pina's eyes widen. "Why would you bug Massimo's plane?"

My chest tightens. I stare at her, unable to even say it out loud.

But I don't have to. She's smart enough to figure it out, and it only takes a moment before I can see the lightbulb going off in her brain. "This has to do with Katiya, doesn't it?"

"Yeah."

Pina cautiously asks, "And what are you hoping to find?"

"I *hope* I find nothing," I declare.

She opens her mouth, shuts it, then tilts her head. She lowers her voice and questions, "And what are you scared you might find?"

My stomach rolls faster, like a ball free-falling down a hill. "Don't make me say it."

She arches her eyebrows. "You think Massimo would betray you and join the Abruzzos?"

"Do I think? No. Is it possible? Anything is at this point."

She scoffs. "No. Not Massimo. You're crazy thinking such thoughts!"

I hold my hands in the air. "I know. Like I said, I don't believe it, but there's too much going on." Flex pulls up to the runway, and I open the door as soon as he stops. Jumping out, I reach in for Pina.

Shock still fills her expression. She takes my hand, and I guide her into the plane.

Danika greets us, chirping, "Where should I tell the pilots you want to go?"

"Where do you want to go, Pina?"

She gapes at me. "Ummm...?"

"It's your call," I add.

Pina glances at the runway then turns back. "Okay. Let's go somewhere warm."

"Where?"

"Florida?"

"What part?"

She takes out her phone, swipes the screen, then studies it. She looks up, beaming. "Miami."

"Done. Good choice," I praise.

"I'll reserve your hotel and let you know when the flight plan is approved," Danika states, then hands a glass of champagne to Pina and a beer to me.

"Thanks." I lead Pina to the middle of the plane, and we sit on the couch.

She takes a sip of her bubbly drink then scoots closer. She puts her fingers on my shoulder, fretting, "How did I end up on this plane with you?"

"Don't freak out," I instruct.

She releases a breath. "Then tell me why Dante paired me up with you on this. It's not like you couldn't do it alone."

I take a swig of beer and admit, "I convinced him I had a job for you, but I needed to oversee it. I also said it was important to do it today. So I told him he could give you a quick trip wherever you wanted to go and also work on the plane while I bugged the place."

"And he fell for that?" she questions, her voice full of doubt.

"Yep."

"What am I supposed to be working on?"

"Helping me code the new shipments. I don't trust my new assistant yet, and Dante knows how important it is to be correct," I add.

"So, where are the forms?" She glances around the room.

I grin, confessing, "In my safe. I did them yesterday. And don't breathe a word to Dante that I told you about bugging the plane. He'll go apeshit."

She nods. "Understood. Can I see what we're using to bug this plane?"

My gut churns. I reach into my coat pocket and pull out three tiny metal pieces.

She picks one and holds it in the air, squinting. "It's so small."

"Yeah. It'll pick up a whisper."

"Wow! It's amazing what technology can do. Plus, you'd have to be looking for it to find it," she adds.

"Exactly."

She puts it back in my hand. "So, where are we planting these things?"

My chest tightens. Everything about this feels wrong, but Massimo isn't acting like himself. If he ever finds out, he's going to kill us. I glance around and assert, "We need one in each of the three rooms." I point to the chair across from us. "That seat will work, probably five or six in the front cabin, and then the bedroom." I rise and go to seat eight then take a safety pin out of my pocket. I put the record button in the on position and crouch down to attach it to the bottom of the seat.

"Should I do the one in front?" Pina asks.

"No. I'll do it when Danika's back here talking to you. I don't want her to see anything," I reveal, feeling more guilty.

"Understood," Pina replies, then rises. She steps in front of me, slides her hands up my chest, and laces her fingers behind my neck. She looks up at me, smiling. "Hi."

Our disagreement from the previous night races back to me. I blurt out, "I'm sorry I couldn't stay for dinner."

She nods. "I know. I'm sorry about how I acted."

I circle my arms around her, feeling vulnerable but admitting, "You realize you're all I think about, right?"

She bites on her smile. The gold in her eyes flares against the brown.

My heart swells. What I thought in the beginning was just an itch I needed to scratch has proved false. I can't imagine her not being mine anymore. Every moment I spend with her only confirms it further, even when we have our disagreements.

She reveals in a soft voice, "You're all I think about, too."

My pulse pounds hard in my neck. I blurt out, "I love you."

She inhales sharply. Time seems to stand still as tension builds between us.

I add, "Don't freak out."

She swallows hard. "I'm not. I love you, too."

Adrenaline shoots through me. I tug her closer, grinning like a schoolboy. "You do?"

She nods. "Yes."

"Good. Then why don't we—"

"Excuse me for interrupting. The flight plan has been approved. We'll be in the air in about five minutes," Danika states.

I pin my gaze on her. "Thanks. I need to talk to the pilots really quick." I release my arms from around Pina.

She chirps, "Hey, Danika! Can you give me your opinion on something?"

"Sure. On what?"

Pina takes a seat on the couch and pats the cushion next to her. "Pop a squat. I need to pull some bathing suits up so you can tell me what to order." She opens her purse and takes out her phone.

"I need to get things ready for takeoff," Danika claims.

"It'll just take a minute. Please!" Pina begs, holding her hands in a prayer pose.

Danika nervously looks at me.

"Go ahead. If you don't help her, she'll be jittery the entire trip," I tease.

"Hey!" Pina exclaims.

I chuckle. "I'll be back soon." I go into the other cabin, shut the door so it's only open halfway, then crouch near seat five. I do the same thing I did to seat eight in the middle cabin then peek my head into the cockpit, inquiring, "All settled in? Anything you aren't familiar with that I should be concerned about?"

Jeffrey and Matthew, two former Air Force pilots, turn their heads. Jeffrey says, "It's a few years older than yours, but nothing we can't handle."

"Great." I nod and return to the middle cabin.

Pina sees me and claims, "I'll get that one, then. Thanks so much!"

Danika rises. "No problem. Is there anything I can get you before we take off?"

"I'm good," I answer.

"Me, too," Pina declares.

Danika smiles. "I'll finish preparing for our flight, then." She leaves.

I shut the door and then sit next to Pina. "Thanks for covering."

Pina feigns a yawn. "No problem. All in a day's work."

I chuckle. "So, what suit are you getting?"

She pulls up a thong bikini. It's dark purple with a maroon flower pattern.

"Nice," I state, trying not to drool, imagining how she'll look in it.

"Don't worry. I got you the matching Speedo," she declares.

I grunt. "Speedo?"

"Yep."

"I'm more of a trunks kind of guy," I state.

She pouts, dragging her finger over my shoulder. "But you'll wear it for me, right?"

I lean back in the seat. "Are you serious? You want me to wear a Speedo?"

"Yep."

"Why?"

She shrugs. "I don't know. Something different for you to try. It'll make you step out of your comfort zone."

"And why would I need to do that?"

"To appease me." She smirks.

I cross my arms. "Is this a joke?"

Her face turns serious. "Nope."

CARNAL

"Fine. If it makes you happy, I'll wear it. But if you breathe a word to anyone at home, you're in trouble," I threaten.

Amusement floods her expression. She bats her eyes, innocently purring, "Does that mean you'll have to punish me?"

I lean over her, buckle her seat belt, and then put mine on. I reply, "Don't look so excited about the possibility."

"Who? Me?" she taunts.

"Don't play innocent." I take several large mouthfuls of beer and ask, "Why did you pick Miami?"

She turns in her seat, putting her knee on the couch. "The weather is usually a guarantee."

"Have you been before?"

She answers, "My sister and I went for a long weekend. It was a few years ago."

"You stay on South Beach?"

She rolls her eyes. "Duh! Is there anywhere else to stay?"

I rub my jawline. "I'm not sure."

The pilot comes over the speakers. "Please buckle up. We're ready for takeoff." In less than a minute, we're racing down the runway.

The plane lifts, eventually reaching the desired altitude and leveling off.

Pina scratches her throat. I've noticed she does it when she's trying to figure something out.

I roll my head, facing her. "What are you thinking about?"

She drills her gaze into mine, hesitates, then asks, "Why was Biagio near Dante's office building?"

The hairs on the back of my neck rise. "I don't know."

She pins her eyebrows together. "Was he there looking for me?"

I sniff hard, not wanting it to be true or scare her but not able to deny it. So I answer, "I'm going to find out."

There's a ding, and the seat belt sign turns off.

She unbuckles herself and flips off her heels. She turns so her back's against the wall and hugs her knees, confessing, "Not once have I ever worried about anyone when I was at the club. The rules were in place, and I always felt protected. After today, I'm questioning my safety."

I scoot closer to her and put my hand on her knees. In a firm voice, I vow, "No one, especially that thug, will harm you."

She doesn't look convinced, and I hate it. I don't want her to feel unsafe. She gazes out the window then says, "Dante told me he was working on security for me."

"We're moving men around, but we just discovered more traitors," I seethe.

Pina's face turns as angry as I feel. "Why do you think that keeps happening?"

"We shouldn't have ever allowed our organization to get this thin," I mutter, pissed that Papà keeps waiting for Giuseppe Berlusconi, the head of the Mafia in Italy, to fulfill his commitment to send more men. My father's loyalty to Giuseppe isn't one my brothers and I mirror. None of us understand why Papà continues to allow Giuseppe to give him orders. The last time the fat prick visited our home was before Mamma died. He didn't even come to her funeral, and it didn't go unnoticed by my brothers and me.

Pina puts her forehead on my hand. "Ugh. I don't want to feel like this."

"Hey. I don't, either, but it's important you listen to your gut." I pull my phone out of my pocket and swipe the screen then press the button for Dante.

"Who are you calling?" she asks.

I hold my finger in the air.

Dante answers, "Tristano, did you do it?"

"Yeah. One more to go, but I'll finish in a moment. I'm calling on another matter," I state.

His voice deepens. "What's wrong?"

I stroke the side of Pina's knee and lock eyes with her. "Did you sort out Pina's security?"

He sighs. "No. I've been in a meeting with Bridge and the wedding planner, but we still don't have anyone to move right now."

"Biagio assaulted Pina. We need to sort this out ASAP!"

Dante growls. "Yeah, I know, trust me. But you know the situation."

I tap my fingers on my thigh then assert, "Until we can find the right security, I'll watch her. It's not safe for her to be unguarded."

Dante clears this throat. "I agree. But you can't do it on your own. You have responsibilities, too."

He has a good point. I go through options in my mind and then state, "I'll arrange with you, Gianni, or Massimo to watch her if I can't. You've got so much security during the workday that she'll be fine without any of us there. It's mostly if she steps out of the building and on nights and weekends."

Several moments pass. He replies, "My next few weekends are packed with wedding stuff and the kids' activities. But I can skip some things to help out."

"Don't do that. I can handle it," I claim.

He hesitates, igniting my nerves.

I relay, "My schedule is pretty open, but I can let you know if I need backup."

"Are you sure? I know it's a lot to ask, but you're right. We can't leave her a sitting duck for the Abruzzos to go after."

"Yep. No problem. You keep your schedule. It's just temporary anyway until we figure out who we can move to guard her," I casually add.

Dante lets out a frustrated breath. "Okay. Thanks. I appreciate it. I'm going to be home in about ten minutes. I'll discuss this with Papà as well."

"Sounds good."

"So, where did Pina pick?" Dante questions.

"Miami."

"Sunshine and saltwater. I'm jealous," he admits.

I chuckle. "Have fun with the snow. I'll talk to you tomorrow." I hang up and toss my phone on the couch.

Pina says in a distressed tone, "Dante wasn't suspicious of you volunteering to look after me?"

"Nope. So don't make it an issue," I order.

She stares at me.

I tug her onto my lap. "I'd tell you if you had anything to worry about, so don't freak out."

"I'm not," she claims.

I grunt. "Yeah, right. You're two steps from having a mini panic attack."

Her lips curl. "Am I that predictable?"

"Totally."

She groans and covers her face with her fingers. She peeks through them and winces. "Sorry."

I remove her hands and kiss her then mumble, "You know what's awesome?"

"What?"

I grin. "I get to stay at your place, and I don't have to lie about it."

Her face falls. "I'm sorry. I-I wish I could get over my fears about telling Dante."

I hold my breath, studying her.

She nervously asks, "Why are you staring at me like that?"

I take another minute to collect my thoughts and reveal, "Pina, I don't want to hide forever."

"I know. I don't, either. I swear," she claims.

I tuck a lock of her hair behind her ear. "Then tell me you're closer to coming to terms with this."

"I am. I promise," she pledges.

I have a nagging feeling that she'll never tell Dante about us. Yet, this is the first time she's admitted she's considering it. So I cut her some slack and state, "Good. As long as we get there sometime soon."

She smiles, but I don't miss the fear in her eyes.

A sharp stab pierces into my heart. I rise with her in my arms and walk toward the bedroom, announcing, "We have some equipment to test out."

"Oh?" she questions, biting her lower lip.

I toss her on the bed, shut the door, then attach the bug to the bottom of the mattress. I open an app on my phone and put it in front of her face. "You know what this is?"

"No."

"It's how I can record everything said on this plane."

Her face turns red. She gets on her knees and slides her palms on my chest. She smirks. "And is there something in particular you want to hear?"

I sniff hard, shaking my head.

"No?"

"No, baby girl." I lean into her ear, lick her lobe, and assert, "You're the one who needs to hear it."

"What's that?"

Zings fly through my body. "What you sound like when I punish you."

18

Pina

Several Months Later

"Shit!" Tristano mutters.

"What's wrong?" I ask, waking up and sitting up in bed. I glance at the clock. It's almost two in the morning.

He scrubs his face and rises. "I have to go."

My pulse creeps up. "Where?"

"Don't ask," he replies, then goes into the closet.

I get out of bed and follow him. He pulls a pair of designer jeans off the shelf. Over the last few months, Tristano's kept more and more things at my main place and the one in Manhattan. I cleared out a few drawers at each condo for him. It's rare we're apart at night except for when he's handling work issues. I accuse, "You're going to the club, aren't you?"

Tristano's face hardens. He glances at the ceiling then at me, staying quiet.

His silence tells me everything. My chest tightens. Anger builds, and I cross my arms.

"Don't look at me like that. You know I have no choice," he claims.

I turn and leave the closet, snapping over my shoulder, "Have fun with all the skanks."

He follows me. "Seriously?"

My insides quiver. I hate the thought of Tristano being at the club without me. The Marinos have kept my ban in place. I trust Tristano in every aspect of our relationship, yet every time he has to go to the club, all I can envision are the women who are probably hitting on him. He says he does his job and leaves, but it still doesn't eliminate my jealous episodes. I reply, "It's two in the morning."

"I'm getting tired of having to defend myself for things I haven't done," he declares.

My gut flips. The rational side of me knows it's not fair. However, I've not figured out how to accept our situation. And the longer we continue to hide our relationship, the more it seems to eat at me.

Yet, I can't seem to agree to tell Dante. It's creating more issues between us. Several times, Tristano's given me deadlines. They always come and go. We fight it out—it usually leads to some heavy makeup sex—and then things are back to normal for a few weeks.

My frustration gets the best of me. I crawl into bed, tuck the covers under my chin, and hug the pillow. Then I mutter, "Have a nice night."

"Stop acting like this," he demands.

"Go do whatever it is you have to do. I'm going to sleep," I fire off and shut my eyes.

Tense silence fills the air. Tristano finally states, "Fine. Be that way. Papà sent his driver over to make sure you're safe. He'll be standing guard in the living room, so make sure you're decent when you leave the bedroom." The sound of the door shutting hits my ears.

I fight the urge to crawl out of bed and race after him with the itch to hold my ground. Instead of falling asleep, I toss and turn the remainder of the night.

Before the sun rises, I work out in my building's private gym. I shower, get ready, and arrive at the office before six. As much as I try not to look at my phone, I can't help checking to see if Tristano's reached out.

I stay past five, after the other staff members have left. All day I was distracted, which didn't help my production. I go to the conference room, spread my folders over the table, and get lost in my work.

"There you are," Dante's voice booms.

I jump and spin in my chair.

Tristano follows his brother, sitting on my right. Dante sits on my left.

The flutters that ignite whenever Tristano's in the room erupt. It feels like it's been forever since I saw or spoke with him even though it was only yesterday. But the flutters are also mixed with nerves. It happens anytime Dante or his other brothers are around. I try to appear confident, asking, "Why are you two here?"

"We're going on a trip," Tristano declares, pinning his dark eyes on mine.

My mouth turns dry. I swallow hard, arching my eyebrows in question, and gripping my pen tighter so I don't reach for him.

Dante announces, "Tristano said you needed a quick getaway."

"Sorry?" I question, focusing on Dante as my heart pounds harder against my chest cavity.

Tristano casually answers, "I can guard you while taking care of some family business. You'll get a few days in the sun."

I glance between the brothers.

Dante scratches his jaw. "We're low on men. It'll help out if you go with Tristano. Otherwise, I'll have to insist you stay at our place until Tristano's back."

"So you'll lock me in the compound?" I tease, but nothing about the Marino estate is anything less than extraordinary.

"I stopped by your place and packed some things," Tristano states.

My pulse skyrockets.

Is he crazy?

Dante's sitting right here.

I snap, "You went through my clothes?"

He sits back, sniffs hard, and shrugs. "What's the big deal? It's just clothing."

"Seriously?"

Dante interjects, "We don't have time for you to get upset. You need to go." He stacks the folders on the table.

Confused, I watch him, taunting, "I think you've spent too much time with Bridget."

He freezes. "Why is that?"

"Since when do you pick up my folders?" I question, pointing to them.

He grins, continues stacking them, then pins his dark eyes on me. His lips twitch. "Should I file these or put them on your desk?"

"Don't you dare touch my file cabinet!" I warn.

"See. This is why you should come work for me, Pina. I have much better skills than Dante when it comes to filing. You wouldn't have to worry about me messing your system up," Tristano claims, winking.

My panties melt, and I shift in my seat.

"Watch it," Dante threatens. His face turns red like it always does whenever one of his brothers attempts to steal me.

"So, where are we going?" I inquire.

Dante rises. "Bora Bora."

I jump up. "Is this a joke?"

He chuckles. "No. Why?"

I lift my chin. "It's kind of far. How long will we be there?"

Dante and Tristano exchange a glance.

"Don't keep me in suspense," I add.

Tristano's face hardens. He stands and answers, "Until the job's over. We need to get moving. Grab your purse and whatever else you want to take."

"What's the job?"

Another uneasy look passes between them.

"This has to do with Massimo, doesn't it?" I ask. Ever since we bugged his plane, he's gotten closer to Katiya. It's driving Tristano crazy. Dante hasn't said anything to me about it, but Tristano and I seem to talk about everything.

Dante breaks his gaze with Tristano and says, "We have proof Katiya is working for the Abruzzos."

My gut drops and I gape at him. It's always been an assumption, but now that we know it's real, it seems extra disheartening. I blurt out, "Does Massimo know?"

Tristano sniffs hard. "That's what we're going to find out."

Tense silence fills the room until Dante orders, "You two need to go. Bora Bora isn't exactly close by. Pina, make sure you keep him on task."

I groan as if annoyed, but I can't deny I'm excited to go somewhere new. Plus, alone time with Tristano where we can go out and not worry about being seen sounds good to me—assuming he's not still upset with me.

He doesn't look it.

Maybe he's acting in front of Dante.

I sneak a peek at him but don't get any answers. He's not changed his demeanor since they walked into the office.

"Like I need a babysitter. I'll be in the lobby," Tristano states.

"Have a good trip," Dante says, then goes into his office.

I step into mine, grab my purse and coat, and meet Tristano at the elevator.

His hand is on the metal, holding the door open. I join him in the elevator. He hits the close door button, then the G, and leers down at me. Tension fills the small space as he asserts, "You can apologize anytime now."

I scoff. "Excuse me?"

Arrogance washes over his expression. "You were out of line last night."

Heat flushes my cheeks, but my stubbornness won't allow me to agree. I tilt my head, asking, "How many women offered to fuck you last night?"

He scowls. "Knock it off, Pina."

"Knock what off? Trying to learn the truth?"

He grinds his molars. The elevator stops and the doors open. He slides his palm on my back and marches me through the lobby and into the cold outside.

Flex is waiting with the SUV and opens the back door. His mirrored sunglasses hide his eyes, but his lips make me want to smack him. His expression is like he's shouting to all of New York that he knows our secret. "Pina."

"Save it," I mutter, then get into the back seat.

Tristano follows, and the door shuts.

Flex gets in the driver's seat. "Where to, boss?"

"Teterboro," Tristano answers, then hits the button for the divider window to close. He turns to me, his eyes black slits.

My stomach flips. I sit taller and try not to flinch under his stare. I'm wrong and know it, but something about admitting that to Tristano is hard for me. He's a Marino. I've spent my adult life learning not to cave to them so they don't push me around.

He lowers his voice, "What do you suggest I do when Papà orders me to handle business at the club?"

The air in my lungs turns stale. I know he has no option but to go, yet I hate how I feel thinking about him there with all those women prowling around for his attention.

"Well?" he demands.

I stay silent, unsure how to solve our dilemma.

"We need to figure this out, Pina. It's not going to change. Not because I don't want it to, but because you know it's not how things work in my family," he claims, then clenches his jaw.

Guilt shoots through me. It's no secret that Tristano resents being the youngest. He doesn't have the authority Dante has, and being the last in line normally means he's always trying to prove himself. I cave a little, admitting, "I know you don't have a choice."

He slides closer to me. "Then why can't you remember that when I get called away?"

I close my eyes and take a few deep breaths. I open them and confess, "I hate thinking about all those women throwing themselves at you."

"They don't," he declares.

"I don't believe that."

"Why? I go inside, do my job, and get out. It's not like before," he insists.

I turn in my seat, putting my knee on the cushion, adding, "That seems impossible. I know those women."

He places his hands on my cheeks. "Listen to me, Pina. I don't care about them. There's one woman I want, and it's you. We have to get past this."

My heart swells. I get teary-eyed and slowly nod. "I know. I'm sorry."

He firmly asserts, "I love you, Pina. Only you. Understand?"

A tear falls. I swipe at it, and his finger hooks around mine. I reply, "I love you, too."

He stares at me a moment then tugs me onto his lap, hugging me. I return his affection, happy to be back in his warm embrace. He murmurs in my ear, "I get extra points for convincing Dante to let you come with me."

I softly laugh then retreat, revealing, "I've always wanted to go to Bora Bora. Have you been?"

"Nope."

"So, what are we doing there?"

He swallows hard then answers, "Following Massimo and Katiya."

The hairs on my arms rise. "Why? Did you hear something from the surveillance?"

Tristano shakes his head. "No. But he's flying halfway around the world with her. Dante thinks something is going on."

"Or maybe he's taking her on a romantic getaway," I suggest.

Tristano shrugs. "I don't know. Either way, it's our job to find out."

The SUV parks on the runway in front of Tristano's jet. He opens the door, helps me out, then guides me into the plane.

Danika greets us. "We're clear to leave in two minutes. Do you want a drink, or should I tell the pilots to get in the air?"

"I'm good," I reply.

"Me, too. Let's get going," Tristano adds, then leads me to a seat. He orders, "Put your seat belt on."

I do it then look at him in question.

"What?" he asks.

"It's strange how you're so into safety."

"Why?" He slides his hand over mine.

"Dante hardly ever puts his seat belt on when we fly."

Tristano grunts. "He'll learn one of these days."

"What do you mean?"

He shuts the window shade and confesses, "When Papà gifted me this plane for my twenty-first birthday, I took my friends to Vegas."

I lean close to his head, rubbing my hands together and chirping, "Oh! Tell me all the deets! Did you fill the plane with strippers and get so drunk you puked on them?"

He wrinkles his nose. "That's disgusting."

"Says the guy who uses kitchen tools to torture people," I mumble.

Tristano's eyes light up. "I forgot to tell you about the pizza cutter."

My eyes widen. Something about Tristano's twisted mind intrigues me. Every now and then, I'll get information from him about what he's done, and it's fascinating. It should scare me that he's capable of such violence, but it seems to have the opposite effect. All his confessions only make him more attractive to me. I blurt out, "That's a bit deranged, even for you."

He grunts. "You don't know deranged."

I drag my fingertips down his cheek. "Sure I do."

He turns and bites my fingers.

"Ow!"

He chuckles. "As I was saying, I took my friends to Vegas. Well, on the way back, there was a horrible thunderstorm. None of us listened to my pilot's warning to put on our seat belts."

"What happened?" I ask.

He traces a scar on the bottom of his forearm. "See this?"

"Yeah."

He points to the overhead bin. "One of my dickhead friends left the bin open. His knife was out. The plane hit a bad patch of turbulence when I knocked back another shot, and I flew. The knife did, too. It hit the floor at the exact same time as I did, and my forearm slid on it."

"Ouch!" I exclaim.

"Tell me about it. But I learned my lesson. From then on, it was safety first," he declares.

"Did Dante not get the memo?" I ask.

Tristano shrugs. "Obviously not." He yawns.

I peer closer at him. His eyes are slightly bloodshot, and he looks tired.

How did I miss it?

"Babe, when did you sleep last?" I ask.

He yawns again. "Maybe two days ago."

"Have you eaten?" I question.

"Not recently."

"Okay. As soon as the seat belt sign is off, you're eating. Then we're going back to the bedroom and sleeping," I order.

He cocks his eyebrows. "Sometimes you're cute when you're bossy."

I bat my eyelashes. "I'm always cute."

He leans closer and kisses me. "Agreed."

I grin. "Then it's settled. Food. Sleep. Then Bora Bora."

19

Tristano

PINA'S EYES WIDEN. SHE HOLDS HER HAND OVER HER MOUTH, stifling her laugh.

Massimo's flight attendant Chanel says, "I like to watch sex. Women and men are both beautiful. Any more questions?"

"I could have told you that," Pina mutters.

Sometimes I forget how good of friends they are and that they've spent hours together hanging out at the sex club.

Massimo answers, "No, Chanel. You've been very helpful. Thank you."

Chanel chirps, "In that case, have a great week in the Maldives."

We slept little, but I'm no longer tired. Most of the trip was spent listening to Massimo and Katiya's sexual games.

Apparently, they're into letting other people listen and watch their activities, which is new to me. But then again, I don't really talk to my brothers about all their kinks.

Not long after we left, Massimo redirected his pilots to the Maldives. I'm unsure why, but Bora Bora quickly got discarded.

The scuffling of them leaving the plane comes through my phone. I exit the app and toss my phone on the bed, informing her, "We'll be landing soon."

We leave the bedroom. Within a few minutes, the pilot comes over the loudspeaker to announce we're landing.

"Wow! The Maldives doesn't disappoint!" Pina declares when we step out of the jet. Turquoise water sparkles around the tiny runway.

We get into the car, and as soon as the driver takes off, I palm Pina's pussy.

She inhales sharply and turns her head toward me. The gold in her eyes brightens before she slips her sunglasses on.

Unlike my brother, I'm not into broadcasting anything between Pina and me. I may have displayed my Dom skills at the club, but I didn't see any of those women as my future.

I'm going to marry her.

She has to let me tell my family about us.

When we leave this island, she'll agree.

During the plane ride, I exercised all my self-control. I carefully studied Pina's expression as we listened to all the dirty shit my brother made Katiya do. I assumed we'd spend the flight engaging in our own sexual activities, but hearing my brother's voice stopped me, even though I was hard as a rock watching her get turned on. Now that we're away from that, I lean into her ear, murmuring so the driver can't hear, "Why's your pussy so hot?"

Her cheeks flame with red. She squirms against my hand.

I unzip her pants and slide my fingers under her panties, stroking her.

A tiny gasp fills my ears.

"Look at me," I demand in a low voice, working her clit in slow circles.

She obeys. Her lightly tinted sunglasses display her fluttering eyelids. Her chest rises and falls faster.

I lick her lobe, increasing the speed of my fingers, uttering, "Who owns your pussy?"

She closes her eyes and her breath turns ragged. Her voice cracks as she barely gets out, "You do."

"That's right, baby girl. And when we get home, you're letting me tell my family about us," I proclaim.

Her face hardens. Little wrinkles form on her forehead from her pinning her eyebrows together.

I bring her to the edge. Her body trembles, and I slow back down. Nibbling on her neck, I order, "Tell me you understand."

She stays quiet.

I speed up again, and she whimpers.

"Answer me," I demand.

"Please," she whispers, frantically circling her hips.

I take my other hand and hold her thighs. "You aren't allowed to come until I permit you. Now, tell me we're coming clean."

"I..." She blinks several times as I pinch her clit then slide my pointer finger inside her. She mumbles, "Oh shit."

I roll my thumb on her clit and swipe my finger around her walls, taunting, "You want to come, baby girl?"

"Please," she begs, her skin on fire.

"Tell me you agree," I command, working her harder than before.

"Trist—" Her mouth hangs open.

"Say it," I repeat, slowing down.

She puts her hand on mine and buries her face into the curve of my neck. I barely hear, "I agree."

My ego soars. Finally, after all these months, we'll be free. Then I can marry her and officially make her mine.

"Good girl," I praise, then release my hands from her thighs and fist her hair, tugging her head back. I kiss her, gliding my tongue into her mouth when her lips part.

She moans, her body convulses, and she frantically returns my kisses.

I don't let up, even when her whimpers turn louder and there's no way the driver doesn't know what's going on. And maybe I'm more like my brother than I thought because something about him knowing she's mine and I'm the one who knows how to please her makes me harder.

Just as she's coming down, the car stops. The driver clears his throat and announces, "We're here."

I retreat, release her, and shove my fingers in my mouth, licking her arousal off them.

She turns toward the opposite window, catches her breath, and zips her pants.

Arrogantly, I get out of the car and reach in for her.

She ignores me, pushing the other door open and jumping out.

My gut drops.

Here we go.

She's going to backtrack now.

For the next few minutes, I barely listen to the resort host speak. He hands Pina a coconut with some drink inside it. I decline one, and we get on a golf cart.

"We need to talk," I announce.

Pina sucks on her straw then finally pins her gaze on mine. She seethes, "You aren't forcing me to do something by using sex to get me to agree."

"Forcing you with sex? Do you even know what that sounds like?" I hurl.

"You know what I mean," she states.

"Choose better words. You make it sound like I did something nonconsensual with you," I accuse.

"That's not what I meant, and you know it," she insists.

I grunt. "Don't backtrack. It's unbecoming."

She scoffs. "Don't you dare try to get me to agree to do something I'm uncomfortable with via sex!"

"You could have told me to stop," I assert.

"Ugh! You're missing the point!"

"No, you're trying to keep us hidden forever. What's the real reason, Pina? Are you embarrassed by me?" I ask.

She jerks her head back. "Is that a serious question?"

Hurt, I answer, "What do you think?"

She smirks. "Of course I'm not embarrassed by you. But I do think you're acting like a manipulative jerk."

I cross my arms and scowl. The golf cart stops in front of an overwater bungalow. I state, "Sorry, I forgot to mention we're meeting my brother. Can you take us to Massimo Marino's place?"

The driver nods. "Sure." He picks up a walkie-talkie, finds out which one it is, and then takes off.

Pina stares at the water.

It only makes my insecurities grow. I lean into her and state, "I'm not going to stay your little secret forever. We either move forward, or everything between us ends."

She snaps her face toward me. Hurt, surprise, and anger fill her expression. "So now you're giving me an ultimatum?"

Guilt eats at me. I didn't want to force her to come clean. I wanted her to do it on her terms. I reply, "I can't keep hiding. I love you, and my family will be fine."

"You don't know that," she claims.

"Yes, I do," I firmly declare as the golf cart stops.

The driver points. "That's it."

Pina shakes her head and jumps out. We both mutter, "Thanks," and make our way down the dock.

I pull out my phone and dial Massimo. He sends me to voicemail, so I call again.

He barks, "Make it fast, Tristano."

"Pina and I are on your dock," I announce.

Silence fills the line. He peeks around the bungalow and freezes. He bellows, "What the fuck are you two doing here?" He trots toward us with Katiya in tow.

My gut flips seeing her. I pretended to like and accept her, but she's an Abruzzo. The fact my brother insists she's not and continues seeing her breaks my heart.

Please don't be a traitor, I silently pray.

We meet in the middle, and Massimo repeats, "I asked you what you're doing here. And why are you with Pina? No offense, Pina," he says, glancing at her.

She waves her hand. "Dante owed me a vacation. Tristano said he needed my assistance. I make things happen."

"What are you here to make happen?" Massimo seethes.

I try to get him alone, ordering, "Let's talk in private."

Massimo only gets angrier. He demands, "Spit it out, Tristano."

All the emotions over Pina's and my disagreement mix with the ones about Massimo possibly betraying us. My defense mode kicks in, and I cross my arms, challenging, "I want to know what's going on. Why are you and Katiya halfway around the world?"

"One, it's not your business, little brother. Two, you could have called to ask me this. Three..." Massimo glances at the ladies then snarls, "How did you know where I was?"

I sniff hard, not flinching but trying to figure out what to say.

I should have rehearsed this better.

It was fine before Pina distracted me.

"Tristano," he barks.

I firmly reply, "Answer my question first."

Massimo's eyes turn wild. He announces, "I'm on vacation with my fiancée. Now, talk!"

My chest tightens. I blurt out, "Your fiancée?"

Massimo warns, "Yeah. And you better not say one disrespectful word about her."

My pulse skyrockets. I angrily accuse, "Are you crazy?"

Massimo lunges at me, grabbing my shirt. It takes me by surprise, and he pushes me backward. I yell, "Get off me!"

"Do not disrespect her!" Massimo shouts.

I jab him in the chest and claim, "She's working for Leo!"

I expect my brother to be horrified. He can't be an Abruzzo now. He just can't! But instead, his hands turn into fists. He threatens, "Little brother, you're one step from getting punched off this dock."

I push back. "It's true! She's trying to find out all the details about our business contacts!"

Massimo surprises me again. He claps slowly. "You haven't told me anything I don't already know."

Horrified, I question, "Why are you with her, then? Tell me you haven't turned against us, Massimo."

His face turns maroon with disgust. He roars, "Turned against you? And done what? Joined the Abruzzos?"

I stay quiet, but my heart beats so hard, I'm sure everyone can hear it.

Massimo seethes, "You believe I would ever be part of that family?"

I grit my teeth, repeating, "Then why are you here with her?" I glance at Katiya, who looks like a mouse caught in a trap.

Massimo seethes, "We're on vacation. Not that it's your concern."

"Have you lost your marbles? She's an Abruzzo," I growl.

He reaches back to punch me, but Katiya grabs his arm.

"Sorry! I tried to keep her away!" Pina blurts out. I assume she's referring to the few times she tried to sabotage their plans. As good as Pina is, Massimo found a way around her obstacles.

Massimo freezes. His eyes widen as he shakes his head. "You're here to trick Katiya?"

I protectively pull Pina to my side.

"Well...umm..." Pina looks guiltily at both Katiya and Massimo.

"Goddamn it, Pina! You work for Dante! Not Tristano!" he reminds her.

She winces.

More surprise fills Massimo's face, and the blood drains from his cheeks. "Dante knows why you're here?"

Cringing, she replies, "He is my boss. Sorry to be the bearer of bad news, but honestly, Massimo. What the heck are you doing?" She puts her hand on her hip and arches her eyebrows.

God, I love this woman. She's not easily intimidated, and most women would be hiding in a corner right now the way Massimo's reacting.

He fumes, "Fuck off, Pina. And mind your own business."

I warn, "Don't talk to her like that."

"Or what? You're both out of line," he asserts.

"You just admitted she's an Abruzzo trying to betray us," I snarl, scowling at Katiya.

He pulls her to his side, roaring, "So what?"

Pina gasps.

My insides shake. So this is it. The truth I didn't want to believe. I step closer.

"I didn't want to!" Katiya interjects.

Disgust fills me. "Sure, you didn't. And now you're going to fuck with my brother's head some more."

"No! I—"

"Don't waste your breath on him," Massimo instructs, then adds, "I'm only going to tell you one time. I know all about it. She didn't betray us and is as much of a victim of Leo as Arianna or Cara were to the Abruzzos."

"How is that?" I seethe.

"None of your business," he claims.

His attitude makes me angrier. "I beg to differ."

"Beg all you want. Get the fuck off my dock," he demands, then spins with Katiya.

She tugs on his arm. "Wait."

He mutters, "What?"

"We have to sort this out," she insists.

He shakes his head then throws daggers at Pina and me with one look. "No. We don't need to sort anything out. I'm done. And tell Dante I'm done with him, too."

"Massimo! Don't say that!" Katiya cries out.

"Yeah. If you're through with the family, she can't get what she wants," Pina interjects.

Massimo wags his finger at her. "You're about to go into the water with Tristano."

I lunge forward, shouting, "Don't threaten—"

"Ludis Petrov and Leo Abruzzo both owned and raped me. Leo tossed me out when I got too old for his tastes. He put me up in a brownstone, made me work at the library, and for a long time, I didn't know why. I swear to you, I had nothing —and I mean nothing—to do with Arianna's kidnapping except to give Donato the key. I had no idea what he was going to do!" Katiya maintains.

"Sure, you didn't," I state, but I'll feel horrible if it's true. Still, can it be?

"You're an asshole." Massimo glowers.

"Takes one to know one," Pina mutters.

"Excuse me?" Massimo says, as if shocked.

She tilts her head. "Really? Every one of you and your brothers are assholes."

"Gee, thanks," I mumble.

She chirps, "Sorry. Just telling the truth."

"We are not assholes," I proclaim.

"Of course you are," she states.

"Fine. We're assholes. Whatever. But you sure like our paychecks," Massimo adds.

She smirks. "I earned every single one of those."

"Didn't claim you didn't," he answers.

She gives him a snotty look and then turns toward Katiya. "Can you finish, please?"

"You aren't buying this, are you?" I utter, scrubbing my face in frustration.

Pina ignores me and nods to Katiya. "You were saying?"

She takes a deep breath. "For a long time, I worked in the library, thinking he forgot about me. But Leo's always watching. He has eyes everywhere."

"Don't doubt that," Pina states.

"Right. So, besides Donato, I never had to deal with him. But then...well..." Katiya nervously locks eyes with Massimo.

He interjects, "I wouldn't stop going into the library to ask her out. Leo found out, and he wanted Katiya to learn about our jewelry contacts."

"And you were going to do it, weren't you?" I accuse.

He tugs Katiya closer to him, declaring, "No. She told me right away. We've been playing Leo the entire time."

I stay quiet, processing all of this. Did she really get raped? It's not out of the Abruzzos' or Petrovs' characters. Why did Massimo not feel he could tell us?

He asks, "Isn't that right, dolce?"

She squares her shoulders and lifts her chin. "Yes. Massimo is correct."

I study them briefly, asking, "How exactly were you playing Leo?"

"It involves me killing him, not that it's any of your business. All you need to know is that I knew about her association with the Abruzzos all along. She was helping me. Now drop it."

Hurt and still confused, I inquire, "Why didn't you tell us?"

Massimo admits, "Because I'm going to kill Leo, and you know how Papà is lately about making moves on high-ranking crime family members. I wasn't going to risk him saying no."

"You could have told us. We could have helped you," I claim, but I can't blame him. He's right about Papà.

Massimo adds, "And risk Dante going to Papà? No, thanks. But I do want to know how you knew I was here. The only possibility is you followed me."

My chest tightens. I grind my molars, wishing I hadn't done what I did.

He hurls, "Are you serious? You followed me?"

No one speaks.

He demands, "You've been following me? And Dante knows about this? What the fuck, Tristano?"

"You've been making bad decisions," I remind him.

His eyes darken. "You put trackers on me? Do you have my plane bugged, too?"

"Seats five and eight, and the bedroom," Pina admits.

He gapes at her. "You little—"

"You heard us in the bedroom?" Katiya frets.

"Nope! There was too much interference, but we did hear some rather interesting things in the main cabin." Pina smirks.

Katiya's cheeks turn red.

Massimo shakes his head at Pina, snapping, "Hope you enjoyed the show."

"I actually think Chanel is the most interesting character," she admits.

"What?" Massimo asks in shock.

"Sure. She's into girls...but not. I wonder if she's ever been to the club. I bet she's watched a lot of things," Pina states, which is bizarre since she's always there with Chanel.

"What club?" Katiya questions.

It becomes clear what Pina is up to when she dramatically opens her mouth then replies, "What? Massimo didn't take you to the club yet? Especially with what you're into?"

"Meaning?" Katiya pushes.

Pina's smirk grows, but it's also laced with disgust. She turns to me, and my gut drops. "Ask him. He was there just the other night."

Frustrated, I snarl, "I told you I had to go for work."

She puts her hand on her hip. In an annoyed voice, she answers, "Sure. I could work on Fifth Avenue at two in the morning, too. Would you like that?"

I groan. This is getting old. I ask, "How many times—"

"This is the thing about men in their thirties. You only know how to play," she argues.

I slide my hands in my hair and tug on it. "Are you kidding me? This is getting old, Pina."

"Are you two fucking?" Massimo asks with a shocked voice.

We freeze. I can actually feel the blood draining in my cheeks.

"You are!" he shouts, as if he won the lotto.

I sniff hard, willing Pina to admit she's with me.

She spins and claims, "I never confirmed that."

"You didn't deny it, either," Katiya mumbles.

"You don't have a place to talk. This is about you two and your issues. Not—" She snaps her mouth shut.

Katiya glares at them. "Not about you two?"

"Kind of hypocritical, don't you think?" Massimo says to Katiya.

She nods. "Totally."

Uncomfortable silence fills the dock. Massimo breaks it by saying, "Dante's going to kill you."

"Shut up," I bark, not needing him to acknowledge Pina's fears.

He chuckles. "Come on, dolce. We're on vacation. Just ignore them while they sit on their high horses."

She lifts her head higher, and they return to the bungalow.

Pina glares at me.

"Guess the cat's out of the bag," I cockily state.

"You're such an ass."

"No, I'm not. And you love me, so let's have a good time and not worry about it," I declare.

She grabs my arm. "Tristano! Please! I'm begging you. Tell them not to say a word. I'm... I'm not ready to tell Dante."

"Pina, I'm tired of hiding."

She scrunches her face and lowers her voice. "Give me a little more time. Please. We can convince Massimo and Katiya not to say anything for now. I promise it'll be soon, just..." She swallows hard. "Give me another month. Please."

"Why do you need a month?"

She squeezes her eyes shut. "Let Dante get past the wedding. I-I don't want him stressed before it. Please."

"This isn't—"

Massimo yells, "Well? Are you coming for a drink or not?"

Pina shoots me a look of death then marches toward them.

I follow her, not happy.

"Sit," Massimo orders, pointing to the chair.

We obey.

Massimo hands me a beer and the ladies another coconut drink. He takes a sip and then announces, "Tomorrow at this time, Katiya will be my wife. You will treat her with respect.

You will apologize for your rude behavior. You will not ever again have me followed. Do you understand?"

I stay quiet and scowl. I'm pissed I didn't trust my brother. I'm disappointed in myself for bugging his plane and other things I've done. But most of all, I don't want to hide anymore.

He picks up his phone, threatening, "Should I call Dante right now?"

"No! Please don't!" Pina begs.

"I don't care. Call him," I order, then take a mouthful of beer. I turn and glare at Pina.

She shakes her head. "Massimo. I'm begging you."

"What's it going to be, Tristano?" he threatens.

"Tristano," Pina pleads.

It's only a month.

Too long.

I'll make her promise me again that she won't back out this time.

I cave then pin my eyes on Katiya. "I'm sorry for being rude."

She offers a tiny smile. "It's okay. I promise you, I hate the Abruzzos as much as you do."

Pina reaches for my hand and squeezes it. I glance at her, and my heart hurts for too many conflicting reasons. I clench my jaw and stare at Massimo. "Put the phone down."

"Tell me you won't have me followed anymore," he repeats.

"Fine," I agree, but I'm ashamed I did it in the first place.

He drops his phone on the mattress. "How long were you following me?"

"A few months."

"A few months!" he seethes.

I hold my hands in the air. "Easy."

Massimo demands, "So the person following me wasn't an Abruzzo? It was our men?"

"Luca, actually," Pina mumbles.

"What? You had Luca on me? Are you kidding me?" he explodes. Luca's our cousin and one of our best men. He's usually reserved for the toughest jobs.

I jump out of my seat. "You would have done the same thing. You weren't acting rationally."

"Fuck off," Massimo hurls.

Tense silence fills the air.

Katiya questions, "How did you know Leo wanted me to find out info about your contacts?"

Pina scoots her chair closer. "Tristano got it out of one of his men."

"Who?" Katiya asks.

"Tommy," Pina answers.

Katiya gapes. "He told you? No way!"

"He didn't have a choice. Tristano made him," Pina informs them.

Massimo accuses, "You shooting your mouth off?"

It's not something I can deny. Pina knows things she shouldn't because of Dante and now me. Still, I hurl, "Shut up."

"I'm not stupid. I know all about the dungeon but not from Tristano," Pina states.

Abhorrence fills Massimo's expression. He snarls, "What are you talking about?"

"Oh, please! Don't try to cover it up. Do you know the number of times I had to pick Dante up off the couch over the years? He was always drunk and moaning over Bridget and whatever he was up to that week in the dungeon," Pina claims.

"Dante? Drunk and talking? No way," Massimo scoffs.

I nod. "Yep. Pina knows more about our family than we do."

"Then why are you telling my brother?" he growls.

She jumps. "It's...it's only Tristano!"

He points at both of them. "You two are idiots."

Pina threatens, "I'll remember that next time you want concert tickets, or an impossible reservation, or—"

"Knock it off, Pina! I'm not in the mood. Tristano, you better tell me how you got Tommy to rat out Leo," Massimo demands.

My lips twitch as I reply, "He went to Katiya's brownstone two nights ago. When she didn't answer, he used a key to get inside."

"And?" Massimo asks.

"I picked him up. It didn't make sense he was there with a key if she's not an Abruzzo."

Massimo arches his eyebrows. "Then what?"

Satisfaction fills me. I lick my lips and relay, "Pizza cutter."

"I personally can't use one anymore," Pina cringes.

"Why?" Katiya asks.

"Well, he likes to—"

"No reason. Forget you heard anything about it," Massimo states, glaring at Pina.

"Long story short, Tommy sang like a canary and will no longer be of use to anyone," I proudly announce. I'm happy to see that piece of shit dead.

Katiya takes a deep, shaky breath.

Massimo slides his arm around her. "You okay?"

She nods. "Yes. It's a relief but hard to believe."

"Oh, believe it! He's—" Pina takes her hand and pretends to slice her neck.

Katiya shudders, and Massimo reprimands Pina again. "Knock it off."

Pina rolls her eyes then glances around the bungalow. "Can you have the butler bring my bag? I could at least be getting a tan right now."

"They're in our place," I state.

"Your place? Let's get back to this little issue you two have," Massimo says.

Pina rises and drops her T-shirt and shorts, showcasing her lace bra and thong.

"Pina," I growl.

"What? It's no different from a bikini," Pina claims, then grabs Katiya's hand. "Let's go for a swim. Let the brothers talk. Don't forget to give him the box."

"What box?" Massimo asks.

I hold up my finger, indicating for him to wait a moment. Earlier today, our jeweler, Ettore, asked me to give this to Massimo. Part of the rush to follow him was to try and stop him from proposing to Katiya, but now that we know the truth, he should have it.

"Three, two, one," Pina says, pushing Katiya into the water and diving in.

"Pina!" Massimo shouts, then rises and steps to the edge, but Katiya bursts through the surface, laughing.

I stand, reach into my pocket, then pause. "Let's go inside a minute."

"Fine." Massimo leads me through the slider wall and crosses his arms. "You and Pina? Seriously? Isn't she a tad old for you?"

"Shut up, dickhead. She's only a few years older," I state.

"Dante's going to kill you, no matter your age gap," he repeats.

I'm so over worrying about Dante. I have enough issues with the amount of authority he has over me. He's not going to dictate my relationship with Pina. I snort. "That's rich when you're what...fifteen years older than Katiya? And I'm not scared of Dante."

"Then tell him."

"I would, but Pina won't let me," I confess.

He grunts. "Sucks to be you, then. Now, where's this box?"

"Are you sure you want to marry Katiya?" I question.

"Man, are you trying to disrespect her again?" he booms.

"No. I'm just asking. How do you know she's the one?"

He sighs, admitting, "Never been so sure about anything in my life."

I study him for a moment then pull out the ring box. "Then you should have this. Ettore gave it to me before I left."

Massimo opens the box, and his eyes light up. A sense of calm washes over his expression, and it hits me.

This is what it's like to get the woman you want.

I vow that within a month, as soon as Pina lets us tell Dante and the rest of my family, she'll be wearing my ring.

20

Pina

Later the Next Day

A LIGHT SPARKLES SO BRIGHTLY IN KATIYA'S EYES THAT I CAN'T help but feel a pang of jealousy. Her form-fitting, sheer white, strapless dress has ruched panels and shows off her cleavage. It's island chic, with a slit running up the skirt, displaying her thigh. She looks like the perfect bride. Happiness radiates off her.

Marriage wasn't ever something I dreamed of as a little girl. While my other friends planned their fantasy weddings, all I could think about was how I could make my way in the world so I didn't have to stay poor. Now that I'm with Tristano, I keep visualizing marriage and kids. Every time I do, I reprimand myself. I can't even tell Dante about us, so it seems impossible. But I know my window of time to figure that issue out is getting smaller.

Since learning the truth yesterday, I've given Katiya a chance. And I can't find any fault with her. I like her and see why Massimo is so head over heels for her.

There are only seven people on the beach—a DJ, a photographer, the wedding officiant, and the four of us.

"You may kiss your bride," the officiant permits.

Massimo kisses Katiya, bordering indecent.

Tristano steps next to me and slides his arm around my shoulders. He leans in, murmuring, "As soon as dinner's over, I'm taking you back to the room."

My butterflies expand in my belly. I glance up, my lips curl, and I suggest, "Maybe we should utilize the deck on our bungalow."

Tristano grins. He drags his knuckles down my arm, asking, "Did you see the hook on the overhang?"

Zings fly through my body. I nod, whispering, "Yes."

His lips brush my ear as he asserts, "I'm going to tie you to it, eat your pussy, and make you come so many times, you beg me to stop."

I swallow hard, squeezing my legs together as he tugs me closer.

He continues, "When that happens, I'm going to—"

"Let's go," Massimo booms.

Tristano kisses my neck, leads me to the car, and we all get in to go to dinner. We pull up to the valet area, but as he reaches for the door, Tristano shoves the lock down and shouts, "Go! Go now!"

The hairs on my neck rise. I glance out the window, but I don't know why he's freaking out.

Massimo fumes, "Tristano, what in God's name—"

"Get down!" Tristano shoves my head to my knees and cries out, "His men are here!"

For the next twenty minutes, I pray for our lives. We weave in and out of traffic, and Tristano jumps to the front. He forces the driver to get in the passenger seat while the vehicle is speeding down the road. How he manages to exchange places without us crashing amazes me.

The smell of urine fills the small car. I inch my window down to help me breathe, trying not to puke from the harsh ammonia smell. I don't dare lift my head, scared I might get shot from the bullets being fired.

Tristano manages to ditch them and heads toward the private airport. When we pull up, Massimo's plane is on the runway.

We race inside it, and within minutes, the pilot takes off.

Tristano tugs me into him. Concern laces his expression. He frets, "Baby girl, are you okay?"

I nod, snuggling into him. "Yeah. How did you do that?"

"What?"

"Take over driving while we were going that fast?"

He shrugs, and Massimo holds out the phone, stating, "Dante wants to speak to both of you."

My anxiety sparks. It shouldn't since Dante knows were here together, but why does he want to speak with me?

Massimo must sense my worries. He mumbles so Dante can't hear, "It's fine."

I breathe a sigh of relief.

Tristano rises and grabs the phone. "Let's take this in the back."

I follow him, and once we're in the bedroom, he shuts the door and holds the phone to his ear. "Dante."

I bite my lip, cross my arms over my chest, and stare at Tristano.

"I told you yesterday that we believe her. You need to let this go before we get home. She's part of our family now. Plus, she was put through as much trauma as Bridget was," Tristano declares.

Goose bumps break out on my skin. I can't imagine what both Katiya and Bridget have been through.

"Yeah, she's right here," Tristano replies, then hands me the phone.

I take it and hold it to my chest, whispering, "What does he want?"

Tristano shakes his head. "Don't know, but stop freaking. He doesn't know anything."

"Shh," I scold.

He steps forward, fists my hair, and tugs my head back.

I gasp. No matter how many times he does that to me, it still makes my knees turn weak.

He murmurs in my ear, "Talk to my brother so we can get busy."

I stifle a laugh. "Get busy?"

He squeezes my ass. "Yeah. Now talk." He releases me.

I hold the phone to my ear. "Hey, Dante."

"Pina, you're okay?"

"Yes. All good. Still able to run circles around you," I chirp.

He chuckles. "Good to know. Hey, Bridget wants to know if you can get us a meeting with Silvio Blatchford."

"The florist?"

"That's the one."

I reply, "Sure. Is this for the wedding?"

"Yes."

"Why isn't your wedding planner doing it?"

Dante groans. "She's not on good terms with him at the moment."

Tristano tears off his shirt, displaying his inked, ripped torso. He wiggles his eyebrows at me.

Tingles dance down my spine.

"Pina? You there?" Dante asks.

"Yeah. Sorry. Think we hit a brief patch of turbulence. All good now. Tell Bridget I can call as soon as I'm back. But how's that going to work if your planner and he aren't on good terms?" I inquire.

Tristano drops his khaki shorts and his belt clangs on the floor. He spins me and unzips my sundress then pushes the spaghetti straps over my shoulders. It falls to the floor, and he drags his knuckles up my back while kissing my neck.

Endorphins explode in my body. I close my eyes and lean into him.

Dante's frustrated voice fills the line. "No idea. But for what I'm paying her, she can deal with it. If Bridget wants to work with Silvio, then that's who she's going to work with."

Tristano slides his hands over my hips, under the sides of my panties, and forces them outward. The thin material snaps, and he cups my pussy.

I quickly tell Dante, "Have fun with that. See you soon."

"Thanks. Later." He hangs up.

"See? Nothing to worry about," Tristano states, then, in a swift move, flips me onto the bed.

"Tristano!" I laugh, pushing my palms on his chest.

He cages his body around mine, secures his fingers around my wrists, then pins them above my head. His face dips toward mine, and his tongue parts my lips.

Fireworks explode in my cells. I instantly submit to him, which is something that happened a while ago. I realized it the other day, which created more questions I've internalized.

I no longer even attempt to be dominant. It's like he fucked me into submission so many times, I lost the desire. The mere thought of trying to seems like an injustice. All I do is crave to be at his mercy.

Every flick of his warm tongue against mine creates scorching fire, burning through my veins. His fingers clasp tighter around my wrists. His other hand slides between us, stimulating my nipple.

I arch into him, thrusting my hips toward him, but he holds me off.

His hand slides to my hair. He forces it under my head, lacing his fingers through my locks and keeping my face in front of his. He declares, "I'm going to marry you."

I freeze, my pulse skyrockets, and my heart swoons. We've never discussed marriage.

Is he being serious or just nostalgic from watching Massimo get married?

"I'm serious," he assures me.

Joy fills me, but then all my fears kick in. I open my mouth then shut it.

I need to get past this.

How?

"Don't do that," he warns.

"Do what?" I ask, but I know what he means.

"Think about your job and insecurities right now."

Insecurities? Is that what I have? If that's the case, am I only imagining how bad it'll be telling Dante?

"Tell me I'm your future, Pina," he demands.

I blink hard, acknowledging the only thing in my heart. "You're my future."

Relief fills his face. He enters me in one thrust, filling me with his body, exiting me, then pushing deeper until I see stars.

"Oh...oh..." I cry out, tightening my legs around him and trying to grasp something, but he still has my wrists pinned.

"No more excuses, baby girl. After the wedding, we tell everyone. Don't make me regret you," he asserts.

"Regret...me?" I ask, my mouth forming an O as a tidal wave of adrenaline hits me.

He stops thrusting, leering at me. "I'm in love with you. I want to be free. I want my family to know about us. And I want to spend my life with you. So don't make me regret loving you, Pina."

My eyes fill with tears. I swallow hard, nodding.

Why can't I get past my fears?

I can't lose him.

I'll tell Dante when I see him next.

"I love you," I proclaim.

He resumes thrusting, dips his head to my neck, and sucks on my collarbone.

"Tristano, I... I...oh God!" I moan. My eyes roll back, a burst of white light flares in my vision, and endorphins consume every nerve in my body.

"Fuuuuck," he mumbles in my neck. His cock pumps hard, stretching me farther, adding more pleasure to my high.

Turbulence hits, shaking the plane. A loud rattle hits my ears, and I barely hear Tristano and me trying to catch our breaths.

He stays inside me, releasing my wrists and curling his arms under my body. The warmth of his body merges into my skin.

I clutch his shoulders tightly. An aftermath of electric zings slowly fades.

The reality of what just happened hits me. He pecks me on the lips, turns us on our sides facing each other, then cocoons his leg and arm over my body. He drags his finger over my forehead, tucking a lock of hair behind my ear. Bright flecks dance against the darkness of his orbs.

I confess, "I don't know why I'm so scared, Tristano."

His fingers caress my cheek. "I don't, either, baby girl."

I tear up. "I do love you. Please believe me."

He inhales deeply and pulls me closer. "I do, but I'm tired of hiding."

I nod, tears dripping down my face. And I hate that I'm crying. I normally have control of my emotions. Right now, I have none. "I think about this. All the time."

"Listen to me. We need to come clean. My family will welcome you with open arms. Trust me. Besides, you know they love you already," he claims firmly.

"Dante and your Papà..." I swallow the lump in my throat. I worked so hard to earn their respect. The line I crossed with Tristano is so unprofessional, I don't see how they'll ever think of me the same again.

"Love you and will get over it," he insists.

I close my eyes, muttering, "You don't understand."

Anger laces his voice when he orders, "Don't go back on your word, Pina. If you do, I can't stay."

I open my eyes then freeze.

Tension grows between us. The engine's whirring fills the room, adding to the strained silence.

He adds, "I want to marry you, and I won't continue doing this in secret anymore."

Panic grips me. My former thoughts to tell Dante today reappear, but I chicken out. I beg, "You said you'd give me until after the wedding. Please!"

Tristano clenches his jaw.

"I just need until then. He's already stressed about the wedding. Please. I promise I'll tell everyone," I vow.

Tristano palms my cheek. "I'll keep my word. But don't test me on this. We either move forward, or there's no point to us continuing this."

My gut flips so fast that I have to swallow down bile. The thought of losing Tristano is unbearable. I hold his face, pledging, "My future is with you. I promise after the wedding I'll tell everyone."

He studies me a moment. Every second that passes makes my chest tighten further. He finally responds, "Good, baby girl." He kisses me, and I put everything into it, trying to show him how much he means to me.

We settle under the covers and sleep the rest of the flight. When we land, the driver takes the four of us to the Marino estate. Everything is fine until we get inside. Dante steps out of his office with his papà and Gianni. Massimo swiftly guides Katiya past them and up the stairs. The Marino men's hardened expressions aren't anything I'm not used to seeing, but something makes me nervous about it today.

"Tristano! We need to talk after we meet with Papà. You, too, Pina," Dante claims, then motions for him to go into the office.

Angelo steps forward and hugs me. "Pina, I'm glad you're all right."

"I'm fine," I assure him, hugging him back while willing myself to keep my emotions together.

He kisses me on the cheek. "Excuse me while I deal with things."

"Sure."

"Make yourself at home," he adds, then glances at Tristano.

Tristano stares him down until he goes into the office. Then he turns to me and pats me on the back in assurance before following the three men into the other room.

The door shuts, and I pace the hallway until Massimo comes barreling down the stairs. He cautiously asks in a low voice, "What's going on?"

"Dante wants to talk to Tristano and me."

"About what?"

"He didn't say." I glance at the ceiling and take several slow breaths.

What if Dante knows?

Maybe it would be best if he did.

What am I saying? He's going to be so disappointed in me.

Massimo pulls me to the corner of the hallway, questioning, "Why don't you just get it over with and tell him?"

"No," I insist.

"Why not? If you and my brother are an item, then just—"

"Who said we're an item?" I blurt out but instantly regret it.

He crosses his arms, scowling. "You slept with Tristano, and it's just fun and games?"

My heart beats hard, and I try my best to give him my poker face.

Why is this so hard for me?

"Tell me you aren't that stupid," Massimo seethes.

"Why don't you ask your brother that?" I hurl.

"Meaning?"

I huff. "You know Tristano."

What am I saying?

His eyes turn to slits. "Still not following."

I glance around the Marino palace, feeling like I'm going to cry. This is their life, not mine. I don't belong here. *What was Tristano thinking when he said he wanted to marry me?*

I spout more nonsense. "This is a conversation you should have with your brother, not me. I'm not the one with the issues."

"What issues?"

"End of conversation," I claim and brush past him.

"Pina!" he growls.

I glance over my shoulder and glare at him. "Stay out of it, Massimo."

He holds his hands in the air. "Fine. I have enough of my own problems."

"Yeah, you do," I mutter, hating myself for making statements that sound like Tristano is anything but loyal and dedicated to me.

Why can't I just tell everyone and stop worrying about what they'll think about me?

Time seems to drag by. I return to pacing the hallway, pissed at myself for being so weak. *How can I be so strong in every part of my life except for this?*

When Tristano and Dante finally step out into the hallway, my stomach is in knots. Both brothers look equally upset.

"What's wrong?" I ask, trying not to look at Tristano too long but trying to get a read on the situation.

Dante motions at the same corner where Massimo and I spoke. We make our way over, and he seethes, "That bastard Biagio showed up at the docks today."

The blood drains from Tristano's cheeks. "He crossed the line?"

Dante steps closer and glances behind his shoulder then lowers his voice. "He told Rubio to give us all a message."

"What?" I ask, touching the wall to steady myself. I had forgotten about Biagio. Crossing into the Marino territory at the docks means he's not going to back away. It's a crime family unspoken rule that you don't trespass at the docks.

Dante stares at Tristano, sniffs hard, then states, "He's coming after all of us."

"Let him try," Tristano sneers.

"You aren't the one I'm worried about," Dante asserts.

My stomach somersaults so fast, I get dizzy. I reach for Tristano's arm and grasp it.

Dante continues, "Giuseppe sent new men. They arrived this morning. His top guy is Guido. From now on, he goes everywhere you do, Pina."

My eyes dart between Dante and Tristano.

"We don't know this guy. I'll continue guarding her," Tristano states.

Dante shakes his head. "Papà knows him. He says he's one of the best. You'll resume your other duties."

"We can't risk anything happening to Pina. I can do my job and watch her. I've been doing it for months," Tristano claims.

"Guido will take over security for Pina. He's more qualified than you are," Dante claims.

Tristano jerks his head backward. "Are you fucking kidding me?"

Dante's eyes turn to slits. "No. He's guarded Giuseppe for years."

"If he's so good, why did that fat fucker send him here?" Tristano seethes.

"Do not disrespect Giuseppe," Dante orders.

Tristano scoffs. "When did you become Papà?"

"Shut up, Tristano." Dante turns to me. "Pina, you'll be safe. You go nowhere without Guido, understand?"

I gape at him. If Guido is going to guard me, how will I see Tristano? I keep glancing between the brothers.

"Pina?" Dante pushes.

"Tell him," Tristano demands.

I gasp, shocked he's doing this after promising to give me until after the wedding.

Dante crosses his arms. "Tell me what?"

Tristano arches his eyebrows at me.

My insides quiver. I lock eyes with Dante, open my mouth, and then shut it.

"What?" he asks.

Tristano grinds his molars.

My mind spins with what to say. I finally state, "There have been too many traitors. I don't want anyone to guard me except Tristano, your other brothers, or you."

From the corner of my eyes, I see Tristano's face fall.

I concentrate on Dante. He sighs and puts his hand on my shoulder. "Pina, besides Bridget, her kids, and my family, you're the most important person in my life. Hell, you're part of our family. I wouldn't have anyone protect you who I wouldn't have protect Bridget, her kids, or my sister. Guido is the best. His track record and loyalty are impeccable. You'll be safe with him."

"So I get no say in this?" I question.

"I'm sorry, but you're going to have to trust that I know what's best for you," he declares and walks away.

Tense silence grows. Tristano shakes his head at me when Dante is out of sight, scowling. "Why didn't you tell him?"

"I—you said I had until after the wedding," I claim, but it sounds weak.

Tristano's face darkens. "How am I going to see you now?"

"We'll figure it out," I say.

Tristano scoffs then lowers his voice. "Sure, Pina. Have a good time with Guido." He turns and walks away.

"Tristano!" I call after him.

He looks back at me. All I see is his disappointment and hurt.

And I want to crawl into a hole and never come out.

21

Tristano

A Few Weeks Later

SINCE RETURNING FROM THE MALDIVES, I'VE BARELY SEEN Pina. The new guy, Guido, never leaves her side. A few days ago, I went over to her condo. I always claim I have business to discuss with her, but it doesn't allow me to spend the night. Within minutes of arriving, Papà called to tell me I had to go to the club. All it did was add to Pina's and my already stressful situation.

Not seeing her every day is driving me crazy. And Papà knows about us. Somehow, he figured it out. He won't disclose how, but he called me out on it a few weeks ago. He told Massimo and me that Dante and Gianni were picking up Leo Abruzzo and Fat Tony to bring them to the dungeon. Massimo and I were upset he didn't disclose it to us, and I stated it was unfair.

My comment set Papà off. His eyes turned to dark slits. He jabbed me in the chest, barking, "Unfair? Don't you dare talk to me about disclosure! Or did you already fully inform your brother of your personal affairs?"

Goose bumps popped out on my skin. I stayed quiet, wondering how he knew.

Papà put his hand on my cheek. "You need to grow up. Real men don't hide things from their family—especially a woman."

"This isn't only about what I want," I stated.

"Pina is like a daughter to me. If you mistreat her—"

"Are you serious? You think I'd do that?"

He didn't say anything.

"Thanks a lot," I seethed, staring him down.

Massimo moved the subject back to Leo and Fat Tony. Yet, I wasn't off the hook with Papà. A few days later, he ordered me to his office, demanding I tell Dante about Pina and me. Then he interrogated me about our relationship.

It was a hard lecture to swallow, but I can't even blame Papà. He's always thought of Pina as a second daughter. So his questions about how I'm treating Pina, warning me to not hurt her, and wanting me to tell my brother aren't completely out of line.

All it's done is create more tension between us. And it freaked Pina out. The distance between us has grown. Not being able to see her as freely as I used to only makes it harder to help her release her fears.

Tomorrow is Dante and Bridget's wedding. Her time to keep this a secret is coming to an end, yet the closer we get to it, the more closed off she's become toward me. All day, her text messages have been brief. She claimed she's busy tying up loose ends so Dante can enjoy his honeymoon, but I'm not buying it. And now, I'm walking into the rehearsal dinner, and she's not on my arm next to me. I promised her I'd wait until after the wedding, but the thought of pretending all day we're nothing to each other only adds to my frustration.

As I step into the room, her golden-brown eyes lock on mine. She's toward the back with the women. My brothers are close with Papà, huddled together but in jovial spirits.

All I want to do is go over to her and kiss her. I curse myself for ever agreeing to her wishes. I walk toward the table, and she rises and then bolts to the bathroom.

I say my hellos, tell everyone I need to use the men's room, then walk right into the women's room, not caring who's there.

The bathroom attendant's eyes widen. She stutters, "S-sir, this is the women's room."

Pina spins. "Tristano, what are you doing in here?"

I pull a few hundred-dollar bills out of my pocket and hand them to the attendant. "Step outside for a few moments."

Her eyes dart between the money and me. "I-I can't. I'll get fired."

"I own part of this restaurant. You won't," I assure her.

She pins her eyebrows together, as if she's not sure if she should believe me or not.

I step closer and glance at her name tag. "Shirley, my name is Tristano Marino. I assure you I have the authority to make sure you never get fired. Take the money and step outside."

She still hesitates.

Pina loudly sighs. "He's telling the truth, and he's as stubborn as a bull. Just do what he says so we can all get past this little spectacle."

I scowl at her. "Really?"

She purses her lips and puts her hand on her hip.

The attendant clears her throat then takes the cash. "Thank you, sir."

I tear my glare off Pina. "You're welcome. Thank you for your dedication to your job."

She nods then leaves.

I lock the door.

Pina fires, "What are you doing in here? Are you trying to cause Dante extra stress the night before his wedding?"

I close the space between us, replying, "Enough. This has gone too far. Everyone knows except Dante. It's time to fess up. I don't want to spend the rest of the night, nor the wedding, pretending we aren't together."

She crosses her arms. "We already discussed this."

"And things change," I point out.

"It's not that far away. Just leave it," she demands.

I palm her cheeks, firmly holding her face so she can't look away. I insist, "I want to have fun this weekend—with you. Dante will be fine. Trust me."

She stays silent.

I lean closer. "I miss you. So much. Now, let's go out there and come clean."

Her bottom lip trembles and she blinks hard.

"Come on, baby girl. This has gone on longer than it should have, and we both know it," I insist.

She squares her shoulders. "We had a deal. Don't you dare change it on me now!"

Anger flies through me. I seethe, "Aren't you sick of hiding?"

"Of course I am!"

"Do you really love me?"

"You know I love you," she claims.

"Then prove it. Go out there right now and come clean to Dante," I order.

She gapes at me.

It only adds to my vexation. I accuse, "You're never going to tell him, are you?"

"Of course I am."

"I don't believe you."

"I will," she maintains.

"Then do it now."

Her face turns red. "No. We agreed—"

"No, you convinced me, and I was stupid enough to go along with it. Enough is enough, Pina. I miss you. I'm tired of hiding. The last thing I'm going to do is spend the weekend pretending we're just platonic!" I explode.

She pushes my chest. "We aren't doing this here. I'm going back to my table. When Dante's back from his honeymoon, that's when we'll tell him."

"No. It's now, or you can keep me your dirty little secret forever," I state.

She freezes. Tense silence fills the air. She finally replies, "You don't mean that."

"I do, Pina. I've been patient long enough. It's come-clean time, or we're done," I proclaim.

Hurt fills her expression. A few moments pass, and she stands taller, then steps away from me. "I'm not going to take ultimatums from you, Tristano. We had a deal. If you can't follow through, then that's on you." She turns on the water and washes her hands, avoiding me.

My insides shake so hard, I swallow down bile. I stare at her until she pulls at the towels then quietly say, "Fine. You made your choice."

"Tristano—"

"No! I'm done," I assert, then leave the restroom. I go directly to the bar, order a shot of sambuca, and down it. For the rest of the night, I avoid Pina, go through the motions, then leave as soon as possible.

I get in the front seat with Flex, and my phone vibrates. I glance at the screen.

Pina: *You aren't being fair.*

Me: *You made your choice.*

Pina: *Don't do this. I love you.*

Me: *People who love people don't hide them.*

Pina: *Just stick to the deal we agreed to.*

Me: *Deals are meant to be broken when they no longer make sense.*

I shove my phone into my pocket and ignore the vibration from her new message. As soon as Flex drops me off at the house, I go into the garage and get on my motorcycle. The snow has finally melted. Spring is in the air, and the weather is warmer than usual for this time of the year. I grab my helmet, snap it in place, and then get on the bike.

For hours, I ride around the city, flooring it while on and off the expressway. No matter how fast I accelerate, I can't keep the emotions from expanding in my chest. Anger mixes with grief.

I've lost her.

She doesn't love me enough to get past her insecurities.

Why did I let myself get into this situation?

I pull over to the side of the road, remove my helmet, and stare at the dark water. It's a full moon, displaying more light than normal. My phone vibrates. I ignore it, and only a few moments pass before it goes off again.

I groan then grab it from my pocket. I have several missed calls from Pina, two from Papà, and a slew of text messages.

Pina: *Tristano, call me. We need to talk.*

Papà: *Where are you? Call me immediately.*

Massimo: *Dude, shit's going on. Call Papà before he has a stroke.*

Pina: *I love you. Please call me. I'm getting worried now.*

Gianni: *Get your ass home, little bro.*

Pina: *Stop ignoring me.*

Dante: *This is the night before my wedding. I don't need this stress. WHERE THE FUCK ARE YOU?*

"Fuck!" I shout, then send one text to Pina.

Me: *Don't contact me again unless you're ready to tell Dante. And if it's not tonight, then don't contact me after. I mean it, Pina. Make up your mind. You either want me, or you don't.*

I press the button to call Papà.

He barks, "Where the fuck have you been?"

"Riding my motorcycle. I just got the messages. What's going on?" I reply, biting my tongue from telling him off. I'm not in the mood to be ordered around tonight.

"Get your ass home," he orders.

"Fine." I hang up, put my phone back in my pocket, and gun the engine. I speed back to the house and go directly to Papà's office.

"About time you got here," Gianni quips.

"Shut up," I mutter, glancing around the room. Tully's smoking a cigar. His four sons, my brothers, and Luca are there. The hairs on my neck rise. I ask Papà, "What's going on?"

His face turns a deeper shade of red. He sneers, "Those Abruzzo thugs sent your brother a wedding gift through the O'Connors."

I turn toward Tully. "How did they do that?"

He takes a long drag of his cigar, puffs a circle of smoke in the air, then answers, "His messenger dropped it off with my guards at my gate."

"Why would they send it to you?" I question.

Tully exchanges a knowing look with Brody then replies, "The dumbass sent a message to your papà meant for us. He got them mixed up."

"Dumb fucks," Gianni mumbles.

My gut flips. "What did they send us?"

Papà motions to his desk.

I gaze down, and it feels like a knife slices through my heart. Photos of Pina doing her daily activities fill the desk. She's working, shopping for groceries, getting in the SUV, and even a few in her condo. I blurt out, "How did he get these?"

Dante picks up a piece of paper and hands it to me. "Motherfuckers need to die. Tonight."

I read the letter.

. . .

Dante,

Best wishes on your nuptials. Don't worry, I'll take care of her while you're gone with your new bride.

Biagio

Blood boils hot in my veins. I repeat, "How did he get these photos? Are the office and her house bugged?"

"I just finished scrubbing them. There are no bugs," Luca states.

A chill runs through my body. I claim, "Then we have another traitor."

"No shit," Dante growls.

"Well, who is it?" I demand, getting more agitated every second that passes.

"We're trying to figure that out," Papà answers.

"It's got to be Guido," I accuse.

Papà's eyes widen. "He's one of Giuseppe's best men."

"Then why did he send him here?" I hurl.

"To help us out," Papà claims.

"Bullshit. He's here, Pina's in danger, and now you're all standing around twiddling your thumbs while he's watching over her." I point at Dante. "I told you not to let him guard her and that I'd continue to monitor her."

"You heard Papà. He's Giuseppe's—"

"I don't give a fuck, Dante! Jesus! You're all blind. I'm going over to Pina's to ensure she's safe." I motion around the room. "All of you are idiots sometimes."

"Watch your mouth," Papà warns.

"Pick that bastard up," I snarl. I leave the office and call her.

"Tristano! Where've you been?" she frets.

"Listen to me. Where is Guido?" I ask.

"In the hallway. Why?"

"Do not let him in. You let no one inside but me, understand?"

Fear laces her voice. "Why? What's going on?"

"I'm leaving the house now. I'll be there soon. Get your gun out of the safe, and if he tries to come inside, shoot him," I order.

"What? Tristano, you're scaring me. What's he done?"

"Promise me you'll do what I say," I bellow.

"Okay. I'll get my gun now."

"Good. I'll be there shortly," I say and hang up.

A text pops up.

Papà: *Do not do anything to Guido. Luca and Gianni will pick him up.*

Tristano: *If he attempts anything, I'm killing him.*

Papà: *You don't know it's him. If it's not, we need to know who it is, so don't do something you'll regret. If it is him, we need to get as much information out of him as possible.*

I hate that Papà is right. All I want to do is pull out my Glock and shoot him when I see him.

Me: *Fine.*

I turn on my bike, weave through traffic like a crazy man, and get to Pina's in record time. When I step off the elevator, it takes all my willpower not to kill Guido on the spot.

It has to be him.

But what if it's not?

Who else would it be?

When I approach him, he says in his thick Italian accent, "Tristano. First Luca, now you. Is something going on I should know about?"

I fake it as best as I can. "No. I need to pick up some files Pina has that Dante needs before he leaves for his honeymoon."

Guido whistles and shakes his head. "If I were getting married, I wouldn't be worrying about work the night before."

"Yeah, well, you're not Dante." I pull out my phone and call Pina.

"Tristano," she answers, her voice full of worry.

"I'm here. Let me in," I order.

The door unlocks. I slide inside then lock the dead bolt behind me.

She throws her arms around me. "What's going on?"

"Not here," I state, then move her to the back of the condo where her bedroom is so I'm far away from Guido.

"Please. Tell me what's going on," she begs.

"Biagio sent photos of you to Dante."

The color drains from her face. "What photos?"

My lungs tighten to the point the air turns stale. "Pictures of you all over town, in the office, and here."

She gapes at me then swallows, questioning, "Guido is working for them?"

"We aren't 100 percent sure. But my money's on him," I claim.

She glances at her door. "Then why are we here?"

"Luca and Gianni will be here shortly to pick him up," I tell her.

Fear floods her expression. I hate it. This should never have happened. If only we had come clean, Dante wouldn't have been able to insist Guido guarded her.

I tug her into my arms. "Everything will be okay. I'm not letting anything happen to you."

She hugs me tightly. "I'm sorry about earlier. Don't hate me."

"I don't hate you."

She tilts her head up. Her eyes fill with tears. "I don't know why I'm doing this."

"Then stop doing it."

A tear drips down her cheek. She squeezes her eyes shut, whispering, "How?"

I palm her cheek. "Go to the wedding with me. We'll tell Dante and Bridget. It'll be fine."

"I don't want to ruin his big day," she claims.

"You won't. Just trust me."

She hesitates.

I state in a firm voice, "Pina, if you love me, you have to trust me on this."

She slowly nods. "Okay."

My heart stops. "Okay, as in, you'll go to the wedding with me, and we can come clean to everyone?"

More tears fall as she keeps nodding.

"I need to hear you say yes," I demand.

She locks her eyes on mine. "I love you. So, yes."

22

Pina

MY EYES FLUTTER OPEN, TAKING IN THE DARKNESS. I don't know what time it is, and I couldn't have been asleep very long, but I strangely don't feel tired. Maybe it's the reality that we're finally going to make peace with the Dante situation. I'm still uncertain how he'll react, but at least Tristano and I will be free.

His warm body curls around my back. He kisses my neck, murmuring, "You know what we should do?"

I spin into him. "What's that?"

He grins. "Take a shower, then go for a ride during sunrise."

"On your bike?"

"Yep."

My mother's warning about motorcycles being dangerous flies into my head. I admit, "I've never been on one."

Tristano gapes. "For real?"

"Yeah. My mom isn't a fan. She drilled the danger into my brain," I confess.

"But you want to know what it's like, right?"

I bite on my lip, cocking my head.

"Am I wrong?"

I shake my head. "No. I always wondered what the big deal was with motorcycles."

Tristano's cocky expression intensifies. He jumps off the bed, slides his arms under my body, and picks me up.

I laugh. "What are you doing?"

He walks toward the bathroom, stating, "We're showering, then going for a ride."

My flutters expand. "We are?"

"Yep." He turns on the water, kisses me for several minutes, then sets me on my feet. He slaps my ass, demanding, "In."

I obey, and he follows me under the spray. The warm water flows over us, and he tugs me against his body with one arm and fists my hair with the other. His lips mold against mine. Our tongues collide like two hurricanes fighting for power. He takes two steps, moving me backward until I'm against the wall, then spins me so I'm facing it.

My body presses against the cold white tile. His warm frame against my back is a stark contrast, making me shiver. He pins my wrists above my head, against the wall. His other arm circles around my waist. He yanks my ass in the air and thrusts inside me.

"Oh God!" I cry out.

His mouth teases the curve of my neck. Tingles race down my spine and through my legs, electrifying my entire body. "Do you know how happy I am that we're not going to hide anymore?"

I close my eyes, enjoying the sensations of his body in mine and try to shut up the nervous Nelly in my head. I can't let my fears sabotage our relationship anymore. I don't just want Tristano. I want a life with him. Last night, when he wouldn't return my texts or calls, freaked me out. It was a glimpse of how life would be without him. And I don't want to return to life without Tristano. I answer, "I'm happy, too."

He slides his fingers between mine, holding them flat against the wall. His other hand dips lower, rolling over my clit. He declares, "I'm going to fuck you all day today. When you're getting ready with Bridget and the others, I'm calling you to my wing."

Steam thickens the air, creating a cloud around us. I whimper, loving every part of his body owning mine.

He rubs me faster and continues, "When we get to the church, I'm going to fuck you some more."

Adrenaline shoots through me. "Oh...oh...oh God!" I moan. Convulsions rip through me.

He growls, "That's it, baby girl. You squeeze your tight pussy around me."

"Tristano... I...oh..." I barely get out as he thrusts harder and keeps my orgasm going.

He licks my lobe then sucks on it before stating, "At the reception, I'm finding a dark corner. You're going to come so many times today, you're going to smell like sex for days. It's going to drive me nuts. Now, do that thing you do." He moves his hand to my hip and tugs.

He doesn't need to say anymore. I circle my lower body, matching the urgency of his thrusts and grip.

"Fuuuuck," he growls, pounding into me harder.

All hell breaks loose in my body. The wall becomes a blurry sheet of whiteness. Endorphins attack all my cells. My knees buckle, and my cries echo against the tile, merging with his loud grunt.

He holds me tight as our bodies convulse against one another. His cock stretches my walls, pumping into me like a machine gun firing a full round.

For several moments, he keeps me sandwiched between him and the wall while we try to catch our breath. He finally spins me.

My back presses against the tile. He slides his hands over my palms, kissing me like he didn't just have me. I wrap my arms around him, returning his affection, wishing we could stay here all day and never lose this moment.

But all things have to end. He finally retreats. We wash then dry off. I plug in my hairdryer, and after I dry it halfway, he comes into the bathroom, dressed. He hands me a pair of leather pants and my leather coat.

I turn off the dryer and smirk. "Are you trying to make me look like I belong on a motorcycle?"

He kisses me on the head. "You'll thank me later when you don't have windburn. We should get going, or we'll miss the sunrise."

I put my hairdryer down. "Okay. We're coming back here so I can look semi-presentable and get my dress and stuff, right?"

"I'll have Flex pick everything up and take it to the house," he replies.

My butterflies kick in. I slide my arms around his shoulders and lace my fingers around his neck. "What do you think Dante is going to say?"

His face hardens. "Don't tell me you're trying to backtrack on—"

"No! I'm not. I promise!" I claim.

He lets out a tense breath. "Okay. Good." He stares at me.

"So, what do you think he'll say?" I repeat.

He shrugs. "Not sure. Whatever it is, don't worry about it. Everything will be fine, and he'll get over it."

I take a deep breath, smile, and nod. "Okay."

I rise on my tiptoes, peck him on the lips, and he pats my ass. He orders, "Get dressed, and we'll go."

I obey, and within minutes, we're in my parking garage. My chest tightens as my mother's warning screams at me inside my head. I ignore it, listen to Tristano give me directions on which way to lean when he's turning, and put on the helmet.

"Do you always carry two helmets?" I question.

He gets on the bike then pats the back of the seat. "Nope. I had Flex drop it off."

"When?"

"An hour ago."

"Poor Flex. He was probably sleeping," I say.

"Nah. He's got insomnia half the time," Tristano replies, then slides his helmet over his head.

"He does?"

"Yep. Okay, hold on, baby girl," Tristano instructs.

I circle my arms around his waist, lean as close to his body as possible, and he revs the engine.

"Eek," I squeal, and an excited, nervous energy races through my bones.

He pulls out of the garage and onto the street. The darkness is fading as the pink sky turns brighter. We race through the empty side streets, past several exits on the expressway, and over a few bridges. We get to the west side of Manhattan, and Tristano parks the bike and leads me along an elevated railway track.

The sun is barely visible. The modern art and sculptures throughout the area look different at this time of the morning. We stop, and I take in the breathtaking view, blurting out, "This is beautiful."

Tristano says nothing. I turn to look at him and inhale sharply.

He's down on one knee, holding up a brilliant ring. His chiseled features look extra sharp against the rosy hues of the morning sky. He kisses my hand and holds it, stating, "You drive me crazy, Pina. Most of the time, I'm unsure whether I should spank you or kiss you."

I laugh, my eyes welling with tears. Tristano had mentioned marrying me, but while I wanted it, a part of me thought it would never be possible. We haven't even come clean to Dante yet, but everything seems within our reach now.

He continues, "I'm done hiding. There's only one woman I've ever truly loved or wanted. It's you. And even though you've driven me to the brink of insanity over the last few months, I'd do it all over again in a heartbeat if it means I get you. But I don't want another day to pass where you're not in my bed and the world doesn't know you're mine. So, baby girl, make me the happiest man and tell me you'll marry me."

Tears fall down my cheeks. I step closer and slide my palms on his cheeks. "I love you, Tristano. I do. So much."

The sky turns pinker behind him. His eyes sparkle, and he asks, "Does that mean you'll marry me?"

I laugh through my tears. "Yes, I'll marry you." I kiss him.

The happiness on his face is priceless. If I could bottle it up and keep it forever, I would. He takes the ring, slides it over my finger, and rises. He declares, "Thank God it fits."

I kiss him again then look at the ring. Diamonds surround an enormous round sapphire in an intricate pattern. It hugs my finger as if it were always meant to be there and has a sense of familiarity. I question, "How did you know I love sapphires?"

A semi-sad expression appears on his handsome face. He answers, "I heard you tell my mamma years ago. It was at one of the Christmas parties when Papà gave it to her."

Goose bumps pop out on my skin. I glance at the ring and then back at him. "This was your mamma's?"

He nods. "She loved you like a daughter."

I wipe my cheek, choking up. Tristano's mom was an amazing woman. She used to take me aside and give me pointers on how to deal with Dante when I first started. "And I loved her."

He confesses, "I didn't know what I would ever do with this when Papà gave it to me. The moment I knew I wanted to marry you, I thought of this gem. I had it redesigned, but it was her sapphire."

I kiss him again then state, "I love it. And you. Thank you. This means a lot to me."

A soft smile fills his lips. He tugs me close to him and spins me. The sun rises, and we stand in silence until it's fully visible.

His stomach growls, and I laugh. He kisses the top of my head. "Let's get going. Papà has a big breakfast planned this morning."

Nerves reappear, but I push them away. Nothing is going to stop me from marrying Tristano. I'll have to live with whatever happens between Dante and me.

We get back to the bike, and he groans.

"What's wrong? Regretting asking to marry me already?" I tease.

He chuckles. "Fat chance. I left my phone at your place. Do you mind if we stop back and get it?"

"Sure."

We get on the bike, go to my place, and get his phone. We get back on the bike and take off toward the Marino compound.

Halfway there, Tristano yells, "Hold on, Pina. I think someone is following us."

The hairs on my neck rise. "Who?" I fret and glance behind us at a black van. My anxiety grows. It looks like the same van that's always on my street.

"Not sure," Tristano booms, then guns the bike and turns down a side street.

I hold on to him as tightly as possible. He weaves in and out of the traffic for ten minutes then finally slows down. "I think we lost whoever it was," he claims, veering onto another street.

We ride in silence for a few more minutes. I almost relax when the black van appears in his mirror. I shout, "He's back!"

Tristano guns it but so does the van. We run a red light, but a truck pulls in front of us. Tristano has no choice but to slow. The van accelerates as Tristano races between the truck and another car.

Horns blare, and the morning light becomes blinding. Tristano veers left, and my gut sinks when the van moves closer.

"They're right on us," I scream.

"Hold on!" he orders, and the bike shoots forward.

We zoom up a hill, and the van gets smaller in his mirror. I yell, "We're losing them!"

He speeds up even more, and the van disappears as we streak down the hill. We're almost to the bottom when another black van comes barreling off a side street and rams into us.

Our bodies fly off the motorcycle and it skids across the pavement. I scream as gravity increases my descent back toward the ground, and my limbs flail in the air. I barely hear the noise around me. Tristano falls to the ground first before my body slams into it. Then everything turns black.

23

Tristano

Two Weeks Later

A BEEPING SOUND GROWS LOUDER IN MY EARS. I ATTEMPT TO open my eyes, but it's too bright. Then pain sears through my body. I groan, but my throat is so dry, it feels like it's cracking.

"Easy, son," Papà's voice orders. Warmth hits my arm, and I realize he's squeezing it.

"P-Papà?" I say, blinking again.

"Come on, bro. You can do it," Massimo claims.

I try to keep my eyes open, but it's too hard. I begin to fall back asleep when I hear Dante.

He declares, "The doctor said he'll be in soon."

"He's trying to wake up," Gianni informs him.

Doctor?

What's he talking about?

The beeping continues. I rack my brain, trying to figure out what's happening and why I would need a doctor. Visions of Pina and me in the shower flood my mind. It shifts to me kneeling, proposing, and her accepting. Then, we're racing through New York on my motorcycle. A black van appears, and I'm sailing through the air.

My eyes fly open, and I try to sit up, but I can barely move.

Papà holds me down. "Stay still, Tristano."

My voice cracks. "Pina! Where is she?"

Papà's face hardens. He stays quiet.

Dread fills me. I glance at my brothers, swallowing down bile and asking a question that I think might be the cause of my death. "Is she dead?"

No one speaks. The expression on their faces creates new panic within me. My insides quiver and my eyes tear up. I stare at Dante and whisper, "She's dead?"

Papà answers, "We don't know."

I snap my face toward him, creating a sharp pain in my neck. I wince, confused and interrogating, "What do you mean, you don't know?"

Papà takes a deep breath then states, "Do you remember what happened?"

"A black van was following us. I'm assuming it was the Abruzzos. We got hit, and all I remember is flying through the air. Now, tell me where Pina is," I demand.

"They took her," Dante says.

My stomach violently flips. I reach for it, but my torso and shoulder erupt in shooting pain.

"Easy. You have broken ribs and a torn shoulder," Gianni asserts.

"What do you mean they took her?" I seethe through gritted teeth, closing my eyes to help contain the dizziness.

Papà answers, "As soon as she hit the ground, they picked her up and put her in one of the vans. Then they took off. Luca's gone through all the city cameras, but they disappeared somewhere in Brownsville."

More fear fills me. I declare, "That's one of the most dangerous neighborhoods in New York. Pina doesn't belong there."

Papà nods. "Yes. We're doing everything we can to find her."

I explode, "Then why are all of you here?"

"Easy," Papà repeats.

"Get out of here and find my fiancée," I order.

"Your fiancée?" Dante asks.

A knife cuts through my chest as I attempt to breathe. I lock eyes with him. "We've been together for months."

"I already know. You could have told me," he claims.

A moment passes before I admit, "She didn't want you to treat her any differently."

"You could have told me," he states again.

"We were going to tell you before the wedding. Please. You need to find her," I beg, trying to sit up, but I'm too weak.

Papà holds me down again. "Tristano, stop moving. You're not in good condition."

"Why are you all here? It's Pina. Go find her," I bark.

Papà motions to my three brothers. "Your brother is awake now. He's right. Get with Luca and help in the search."

"It's Biagio. Pick him up," I growl.

Anger flares on Dante's expression. "Luca said he's got five guards around him at all times. You know his father's estate is off-limits. He's been hiding out and lying low."

"I don't care. Pick. Him. Up," I demand.

"Go. Now," Papà orders my brothers.

One by one, they all leave, stating phrases I don't even hear. When they're out of the room, I close my eyes, declaring, "I need to get out of here."

Papà leans closer. The smell of his expensive aftershave flares in my nostrils. "You had a nine-hour surgery. The medical team put you in an induced coma. I'm waiting for the doctor to give me the okay to have you moved home. It'll be an easier recovery for you if you're in your own bed. Plus, I can only control the security so much here."

I lick my lips, but everything is dry, including my tongue.

"Have some water," Papà orders, holding a Styrofoam cup with a straw a few inches from my face.

I take a few sips then get emotional, confessing, "I need her back. You can't let them hurt her."

Papà's expression turns deadly. He vows, "We'll get her back, son."

"Now. You need to find her now."

"We're doing everything possible."

"Papà, I can't live without her."

He puts his hand over mine. "We'll find her. I promise."

Someone clears their throat. I glance at the doorway. A man I've never seen before, in a white coat, walks toward us.

"Doctor. Just who I wanted to speak with," Papà states.

The man says, "Good to see you're awake, Mr. Marino. I'm Dr. Keinman. How do you feel?"

"Fine. I'm ready to go home," I claim.

Seriousness fills his expression. "I'm sure you are, but you had a long operation and we just took you out of your induced coma. It would be best for you to stay for another few days under our observation."

"I've already talked with our primary physician. He has a medical team waiting at our house, along with the equipment required to monitor Tristano's recovery," Papà replies.

The doctor's eyes dart between us. He warns, "Your son's condition is very serious."

Papà rises. "I'm aware and can assure you that I wouldn't approve of him coming home if the situation at my house was not appropriate. Our family physician handpicked the team of doctors and nurses who are at my house as we speak. And they're all the best of the best."

Dr. Keinman arches his eyebrows.

"Present company excluded," Papà adds.

Dr. Keinman chuckles then turns toward me. "Mr. Marino, if you insist on going home, I'll release you based on the conditions your father has discussed. But I would prefer you to stay."

I try to sit up again, and the pain accelerates through my abdomen. I grimace. "I'm good to go."

The doctor's voice grows stern. "You need rest, Mr. Marino. Your team of doctors need to make sure you move to prevent blood clots, but it's imperative to your recovery that you don't overdo it."

"I'm fine," I insist.

"If you cannot follow orders, I'll have to insist you stay here under our supervision," he threatens.

"I'm not—"

"He'll do exactly what is required. I'll make sure of it," Papà states.

Silence fills the air.

"The situation at home is as good as here. You have my word," Papà asserts.

Dr. Keinman sighs. "Okay, Mr. Marino. But don't make me regret this."

"I won't," Papà replies.

Dr. Keinman studies me a moment then squeezes my foot. "You got lucky, Mr. Marino. An accident like that could have been much worse. I wish you a speedy recovery."

I sniff hard, not saying anything. Until I get Pina back and make sure she's okay, I'm unsure if still being alive is a good thing.

"Thank you, doctor," Papà says.

The doctor takes one more look at us then leaves the room. It takes another hour to get discharged and then wheeled out of the hospital. I try to walk, but Papà orders me to sit in the wheelchair when the doctor insists.

Neither of us talks much on the way home. My body hurts everywhere, but it's nothing compared to the pain I feel in my heart. I clench my fists tight, attempting to settle the constant shaking in my gut, but it doesn't help.

Papà finally speaks. "We'll find her, Tristano."

I turn toward him. "I want him picked up."

"We'll get him. I give you my word," Papà vows, his dark eyes replicating how my soul feels right now.

The driver goes through the gates and parks at the front of the house. Papà's main guard for the house opens the back door. He greets, "Good to see you, Tristano. Boss." He nods to Papà.

I grunt, fight through the pain, and get out of the SUV. I refuse to let anyone help me walk up the stairs and into the house, but the six steps make me dizzy. I grip the rail, pushing myself to continue. Once inside, I glance at the grand staircase, overwhelmed. Still, I move toward it.

Papà grabs my arm, suggesting, "Don't be a fool. Take the elevator."

Putting my ego to the side, I obey, slowly moving to the tiny lift.

Papà follows me and pushes the button. The elevator moves up. The doors open, and he motions for me to go first.

Every step I take results in excruciating pain. I turn the corner to my wing and almost run into Bridget.

"Tristano! I'm so happy you're home!" she exclaims, tossing her arms around me.

I inhale a breath between clenched teeth, which only creates more pain in my ribs.

She winces. "Oh crap! I'm sorry."

Guilt eats me. "How was the wedding?"

She tilts her head and gives me a sympathetic smile. "We postponed it."

"Shit. I'm sorry, Bridget," I offer.

She shakes her head. "Don't be. It's fine. Let me help you to your room. Silvio is there with the medical team."

Papà adds, "If you're okay taking Tristano to his room, I'll go handle some issues that need to be taken care of."

"That works, Angelo," Bridget chirps, leading me down the hall.

I walk into my bedroom suite and freeze. When Papà claimed an entire medical team was at our house, he wasn't kidding. Nurses, doctors, and a lot of equipment fill my room.

Silvio, our family doctor who's taken care of our family for as long as I can remember, gives me a big smile. He instructs, "Tristano, come lie down. I'll introduce you to the medical team."

"I'd rather sit," I say, then gingerly make my way to the armchair.

"Very well, then," Silvio replies, waiting for me to settle. He introduces the men and women in the room, but I barely hear their names. All I want to know is if Pina's alive and where she's at.

The team fusses over me for several minutes, checking my vitals, helping me get resituated in the chair, and handing me my medication. I stay quiet through most of it, wishing all of them would disappear. When it gets to be too much, I lock eyes with Silvio. "I think I'm good for a while. Can I have some privacy now?"

He studies me then states, "We'll check on you in a while."

"All of you?" I question. The number of people in my room seems absurd.

Bridget sits on the couch across from me, smirking. "Your Papà might have gone a tad overboard."

I grunt. "Guess it's nice to know the old man still loves me. But, seriously, Silvio. Send all the unnecessary professionals home."

His face falls. He shakes his head. "Your injuries are serious, Tristano. I would not have let your Papà bring you home without a full team."

I scrub my face, instantly regretting it. My ribs hurt so badly, I didn't realize my face was bruised. I ask Bridget, "Can you bring me a mirror?"

"Sure." She gets up and leaves the room.

I refocus on Silvio. "I'm going to rest now. Thank you all for your service." I glance at each staff member.

Silvio assesses me then commands, "You heard the man. Everyone out. Nikki, recheck his vitals in thirty minutes."

I groan. "Not necessary."

"Don't argue, or I'll send you back to the hospital," Silvio threatens.

"Try me," I warn, but the thought of moving off the chair makes me shudder.

The room slowly empties until it's just me. Silence only feels good for a moment. The hole in my heart grows, and I close my eyes, fighting too many emotions.

What is my baby girl going through right now?

There's no way she isn't hurt. I was driving faster than I would have with Pina on the back, but I didn't see any other option. I mutter, "How fucking stupid could I have been?"

"Don't beat yourself up," Bridget softly orders.

I open my eyes, asserting, "I shouldn't have taken her on my bike."

She sits on the coffee table in front of me and grabs my hand. "You didn't know Biagio's men were following you."

I turn toward the window, wanting to cover the sun. Darkness fills me, and I'm scared it may never be light again.

If she doesn't come home to me, it won't be.

I mumble, "I should have taken precautions."

"Tristano—"

"Don't mom me, Bridget! There's nothing you can say to change the situation."

She sighs then hands me a mirror.

I take it and stare at my beat-up face. It's bruised but nothing more than if I were in a boxing match and got my ass kicked.

Bridget pulls a phone out of her pocket. She holds it toward me. "Here. I got you a new one since yours was destroyed in the accident."

"Thanks." I grab it from her.

She continues, "I had the phone company transfer everything on your cloud to it."

"I appreciate that," I say to be polite, but I couldn't give a rat's ass about my phone.

Tense silence fills the air. She finally rises. Her blues glisten as she softly declares, "Your brothers will find her. I know they will."

The knot in my gut twists. I swallow the lump in my throat then say my worst fear out loud. "What if she's dead?"

A tear falls down Bridget's cheek. She swipes at it and squares her shoulders. It reminds me of when Pina does it, which only hurts my heart more. In a firm voice, Bridget asks, "Do you feel she's dead?"

I stay quiet, contemplating her question.

She adds, "When Sean died, I could feel it."

"You were there," I remind her. It's a shitty thing to do since it was such a traumatic experience for her. I quickly say, "I'm sorry. That was out of line."

She takes a deep breath. "When someone you love dies, you feel it. Whether you witness it or not, you know they're gone. So what do you feel?"

I ponder her statement then reply, "I think she's alive, but I don't know if it's just my wishful thinking."

Bridget nods. "Okay, then. She's alive."

"How can you be so sure?" I ask.

Bridget smiles. "I just am." She places her hand on my shoulder, kisses the top of my head, then adds, "I'm here if you need anything." She leaves and shuts my door.

The quiet soon gets to me again. Too sore and drugged to get up, I turn on my phone. When Pina's text messages and the photos we took all pop up, I sigh in relief. Then I torture myself, spending hours re-reading all our messages and staring at our photos.

A nurse comes into the room to check on me. After going through the motions, she leaves. I return to my phone then freeze when I see the date.

It's been two weeks?

I force myself to get up and go downstairs to Papà's office.

He looks up when I enter. "Tristano. What are you doing down here?"

"What's the status on Pina?"

He doesn't answer.

"Where is she, Papà?"

"We will find her."

"It's been two weeks," I seethe.

He rises. "Yes. I told you that you were in an induced coma. The doctor was worried about your brain swelling."

"Why haven't you found her if it's been two weeks?" I bark.

Papà holds his hands out. "Calm down. This isn't good for your recovery."

I slam my hand on the desk. A sharp sting jolts through my rib cage. I wince and boom, "I don't give a damn about my recovery. I need you to find her."

"We're doing everything we can."

"Not good enough," I snarl.

He moves around his desk and places both palms on my cheeks. "Son, I know you're upset. You need to focus on your recovery. When we find Pina—*and we will locate her*—she'll need you strong."

My insides shake harder. I'm a man on the verge of cracking, and I've never experienced anything like this before. I manage to get out, "What's he doing to her? Right now, Papà. What's he putting her through?"

Papà's face darkens. He sniffs hard and replies, "You can't focus on that. The only thing you can do right now is get your strength back. I promise you, we will find her."

I say nothing, too afraid if I speak, I'm going to break down.

When I asked Pina to marry me, I knew that she was my life. Nothing has ever hurt like this, and I've never been scared until now. This seems like a cruel punishment. I wonder if it's penance for everything bad I've ever done.

24

Pina

Two Months Later

"Don't move too fast," Tracy advises, tucking a piece of her gray hair behind her ear. She's the nurse who's taken care of me since I woke up. Biagio and Kiko come and go, but Tracy always seems to be there.

As much as she's helped nurse me back to health, I'm unsure what to think of her. Whenever I try to get to know her, she flips to her cold personality. The first time it happened, I was shocked. As time passed, it became a game for me. I was bored and lonely. Trying to figure out Tracy was the only thing I could do to help pass the time. So, every day, I tried to learn something personal about her.

I didn't do very well. She's as tight-lipped as anyone I've ever met.

Not that I remember a lot of people.

Flashes of my past will pop up in my mind at random times. For each episode, I try to figure out who the people were, what I was doing, and which part of my life that memory belongs to. Pieces of what I think are my childhood appeared first. I was hungry, studying, or moving homes.

After the first episode, I asked Biagio why my family wasn't visiting me. I was sure the people in my visions were them. His answer made me wish I had never asked.

He told me they were all dead. He said the man who kidnapped me killed my family.

It sent me into a tailspin of depression, even though I still can't remember a lot about them. Biagio would visit and attempt to comfort me, but it didn't help. Every time he touches me, my skin crawls. Something about him makes me not want to trust him. I can't put my finger on it, but it's just a feeling I have.

Maybe if I had a memory of him, it would help. Yet, I remember nothing about our relationship.

After a few weeks, my flashbacks morphed into other things. I was in a beautiful office, working. Dark-haired men who I assume are brothers spoke Italian. Christmas parties with hundreds of people, birthday celebrations, and other events would feel so real, it made me long to experience them again. And it's always with the same people.

All of it adds to my confusion. Every memory I have is like looking through a window but not understanding the whole story. And the current visions I'm having make my heart ache, but I don't know why.

There are more and more flashbacks of the two brothers. It started with who I think might be in charge. I also think he's a twin because there's another guy who looks like a replica of him. Yet, different emotions pop up when they are both together. Something tells me I like the twin who I believe might be in charge a little bit better. There's no reason for my intuition. It's just a strange feeling I can't shake.

Then there's the man I think is the youngest of the brothers. Sometimes the way he looks at me makes my heart skip a beat. His chiseled cheekbones and intense eyes haunt me.

It makes me feel guilty. Biagio has been nothing but sweet to me. He'll come at strange times, and there's never any warning. Sometimes, I wake up and see him sitting in the chair, staring at me. It used to freak me out, but I'm slowly getting used to it.

Over the last few weeks, I've been able to move around more. Three times, Biagio tried to kiss me. It wasn't his normal kiss on the head or cheek or peck on the lips. He shoved his tongue in my mouth, and each time, I pulled away, cringing.

He got angry with each incident. He barked, "Are you ever going to love me again?"

I couldn't answer him. On the one hand, I felt horrible for hurting him. He rescued me and kept me safe from the man, Tristano, who kidnapped me. Yet, I don't feel anything but repulsion when he touches me. Plus, he smells like cigarette smoke, his overbuilt, steroid-enhanced body is unattractive to me, and something about him makes my subconscious scream for me not to get close. Those things make me question how I could have ever loved him enough to get engaged.

Engaged.

My stomach flips. I glance down at my hand. A gorgeous sapphire with diamonds surrounding it sparkles on my ring finger. It's incredible that it didn't get destroyed or lost in the accident. Every time I see it, I can't help but think it's perfect. And if I still have it and it feels like it was made for me, then isn't that a sign I need to tap into whatever I used to feel for Biagio and move forward with my life?

So much confuses me. When Biagio gives me his wounded expression, I tell him, "I'm sorry. I still don't remember anything about us."

My words only hurt him further. He'll scowl at me like I'm destroying him.

Maybe I am. I don't want to, but when he kisses me, my skin crawls. I wish it didn't, yet I don't know how to stop it.

Regardless of my errors, Biagio has been good to me. While his aura screams danger, I don't feel scared around him. Perhaps it's because he's done everything to take care of me.

Kiko is another story. Something about that guy makes me terrified to cross him.

I asked Biagio once, "Why do you send Kiko here?"

Biagio replies, "When I'm out of town, I need to make sure you're okay."

"But I have Tracy," I stated.

Biagio slid his arm around me. I wanted to shake it off but had already hurt him once that day. "Tracy needs to be accountable, too."

"She's doing her job," I insisted.

"Yes. But would she if we weren't watching her?"

His question only added to my confusion. *Don't nurses usually do their jobs?*

As if her ears were burning, Tracy came into the room with my medicine. "Sorry to interrupt, Mr. Abruzzo. I need to give Pina her shot." She stuck it in my arm and then left.

I rubbed my skin over the incision site. "I don't understand why I need this shot. I'm feeling a lot better."

"Doctor's orders. I need to go," Biagio said, rising.

Panic filled me. As much as I feel strange around Biagio, I get nervous when he's not here. There's no one else to connect to, and besides, he loves me. I may not feel it toward him, but he tells me all the time. So I tugged on his arm, inquiring, "Wait. Why can't I go home with you?"

"I've told you that it isn't safe."

"When will it be?"

"Soon. Very soon." He kissed me on the forehead and left, which was good. Like all the other times I got my shot, I quickly fell into a deep sleep.

Today, he showed up around breakfast and told me he was taking me home. At first, I was excited. Then, he whisked me through the house and into the garage. I got into the SUV and felt like I couldn't breathe.

Tracy claimed it was a panic attack. I don't know if I've had them in the past, but it felt like I was having a heart attack. Halfway through the journey, I found my breath.

And now, I'm in front of a mansion. The gray stone feels cold even though the sun is shining. I'm not even wearing a jacket it's so warm, but I still shiver.

Biagio pushes Tracy out of the way. He slides his arm around me, stating, "Let's get you inside so you can rest."

I lift my chin, claiming, "I'm okay."

"You aren't," he insists.

"No, I am," I argue.

He sniffs hard and grinds his molars.

Something about it makes me fearful. I quickly soften my voice and add, "I'm excited to be home. Can you show me around?"

He relaxes then leads me up the steps and past several thugs with machine guns.

I swallow hard, trying to display confidence, but it's hard. If I'm with Biagio, they're surely there to protect me. But if that's true, why do I think they'd kill me in a heartbeat?

Biagio leads me through the grand house. The finest of materials are everywhere. Marble, real metals, precious art, and luxurious fabrics adorn the place. There are so many rooms, I get overwhelmed. We get closer to the staircase, and Biagio knocks on a door.

"Come in," a gruff voice states.

Biagio opens the door, and the hairs on my arms rise. A salt-and-pepper-haired man with similar facial features as Biagio sits behind a desk, but unlike Biagio, he has a potbelly. A cigarette burns in an ashtray to his right.

I refrain from coughing even though the smoke suffocates my lungs.

The man arches his eyebrows, as if we're bothering him.

"Papà, Pina's home," Biagio announces, but the typical confidence he usually has seems fake. He turns to me. "Meet my father, Jacopo Abruzzo."

His father slides back in his chair then presses the pads of his fingers together. He orders, "Spin."

My insides quiver. I gape at him, hoping this is a joke.

Jacopo takes a drag of his cigarette then leers at me with his beady eyes. He snarls, "Do I need to repeat myself?"

I tear my gaze off him and refocus it on Biagio.

"Go on," he urges.

"Wh-why do I need to spin?" I question.

Jacopo slams his hand on the desk, barking, "Because when I say to do something, you do it!"

I jump. My lips tremble and I blink hard to stop tears from falling.

"Go on," Biagio says in a softer tone.

I turn around in a circle and then stare at his father.

"Slower," he demands.

I take a deep breath and slowly turn.

When my butt is facing him, he shouts, "Freeze."

I obey, closing my eyes, wondering what the hell is happening. Did I really agree to marry a man whose father is checking out my ass?

"Is she still swollen from the accident?" he asks.

I spin. "Excuse me?"

"Did I say you could turn around?" he challenges.

I glance at Biagio.

He slides his arm around me. "She's still recovering. Give her a pass, Papà."

Jacopo doesn't tear his eyes off me. He takes another drag of his cigarette then blows the smoke in my direction. I refrain from coughing, willing myself not to show him any weakness. He stubs his cigarette out in the ashtray and points at me. "You have a week to lose ten pounds."

I gape at him. "S-sorry?"

"You heard me. My son won't marry a fat woman. Your engagement party is next Saturday night. You'll lose ten pounds, or there will be consequences," he adds, then pulls a folder out of his drawer.

I'm too shocked to move.

Jacopo looks up. "Is there a reason you're still here?"

"We were just leaving," Biagio claims and guides me out of the office and into his wing of the house.

As soon as the door to the bedroom suite shuts, I turn to him. "What was that?"

He sniffs hard. "That's my father."

I gape at him.

He pulls a metal case out of his pocket. "Just do what he says and everything will be fine." He lights up a cigarette and inhales.

I wave my hand in front of my nose, coughing.

It doesn't faze Biagio, nor does he even try not to blow smoke in my direction.

I blurt out, "I can't just lose ten pounds in a week. And I'm not fat."

He stays quiet.

"You think I'm fat?" I ask.

He flicks ashes into a tray then locks eyes with me. "If my father thinks you are, then you are."

I jerk my head back, glaring at him. Several moments of tense silence pass, with neither of us flinching. I finally break it, saying, "I would never agree to marry someone like you."

Maroon explodes on his cheeks. He lunges toward me until my back is against the wall, squeezing my jaw and tilting my head until our faces are inches apart.

"Ow! You're hurting me!" I cry out.

"This isn't pain, darling. Keep running your mouth, and you'll see what it's like for me to hurt you," he seethes.

Tears fall down my cheeks. I hate myself for showing him any weakness.

He leans closer and brings the cigarette near my eye, suggesting, "It would be a shame for you to lose your sight, wouldn't it?"

My lips tremble harder, and tears fall faster from my eyes. I whisper, "Please. Don't."

He doesn't move for what feels like forever. The smoke grows thicker as the white paper disappears into ashes. He finally releases me, stepping back. He warns, "Don't push me, Pina. I'm the boss. If my papà says to do something, you do it. If I give you an order, you do it. Understand?"

I clench my jaw, my pride not allowing me to speak.

A crazed look fills his orbs. He reaches for my hair and tugs it hard, hurting my neck. "Do you understand me?"

"Y-y-yes," I cry out.

He holds me in the same position, his face inches away, his smoke-laden breath merging into mine.

Bile rises in my throat. Unable to help myself, I toss my cookies all over him.

"What the fuck, Pina!" he shouts.

I run to the door I assume is the bathroom and hug the toilet.

"Goddamnit!" he curses, then trots into the bathroom and strips. He turns on the water and steps into the shower.

I don't move until I hear the water turn off. Then I sit against the wall, putting my head between my knees.

"Get up," he orders.

I glance up and look back down. He's naked with a semi. I must have seen him undressed before, but it doesn't sit right with me. My emotions get the best of me, and I uncontrollably sob.

"Jesus." He sighs and slides down the wall until he's sitting next to me. He pulls me into his arms and shushes me.

It only confuses me further. How can a man who just threatened to burn my eye out attempt to comfort me?

He murmurs, "I know this is a lot for you."

I keep crying, unable to stop.

"Shh," he continues, then adds, "Don't worry about the ten pounds. I'll let the chef know, and it'll be easy for you."

I choke on a few breaths and wipe my tears. I study him, but he takes it the wrong way.

He tugs me closer. "Everything will be fine. I'll protect you."

"You just threatened to burn me," I blurt out.

He buries my face in his chest, claiming, "You've forgotten how things are around here. It's okay. I'll give you a pass. You'll soon relearn how to act."

How to act?

Is this guy for real?

No way I agreed to marry him.

Then why am I here with him?

I push out of his grasp. "I'm really tired. Can I go rest, please?"

He hesitates then nods. "Okay. Let me show you what side you sleep on."

"What side?" I question in horror.

His face hardens. He crosses his arms, asking, "Why do you look sickened by the idea of sleeping in our bed?"

My stomach churns. I put my hand over it and turn away from him.

He turns my chin back, snarling, "Pina? I asked you a question."

I debate how to reply but finally choose, "I don't remember anything."

"You will."

"But I don't right now."

Quiet fills the bathroom. My insides quiver harder, wondering if he'll hurt me again. I'm relieved when he lowers his voice and declares, "In time, you will."

I stay quiet.

He adds, "But you won't remember by staying out of my bed. You're mine, Pina. You belong to me and with me. Understand?"

A lump forms in my throat. Nothing could sound worse to me. I swallow hard and decide it's best to agree with him for now. "Yes, I understand," I reply, but the only thing clear is that I need to figure out how to get away from him.

If only I knew how.

25

Tristano

"Where is she!" I bark, unable to hold my cool any longer. It's been two months and two weeks since the accident. We're no closer to finding Pina than when I was in the hospital. Every second that passes, my anger overpowers me.

"I don't know!" Mattia Abruzzo cries out. He's a second cousin to Jacopo and the highest-ranking member of the Abruzzo family we've picked up over the last two months.

"You're lying," I seethe, then take the steel claw and slice it down his arm. It's a kitchen tool meant to tear pulled pork or other meats.

"Fuuuuck!" he screams.

My blood boils so hotly, I can't find the control I normally have when torturing men. Spit flies out of my mouth and lands on his face when I declare, "I'm clawing your dick apart next if you don't give me something!" I press the claw on his pecs then slowly move down.

I get below his belly button, and he shouts, "Wait!"

I freeze, arching my eyebrows.

He swallows hard.

"Speak, or I'm doing it," I threaten.

"She was moved to Jacopo's this morning!" he announces.

I snarl, "What else?"

"Th-that's it! I swear I don't know anymore!" he claims.

"Liar!" I accuse, then slice over his cock.

"Fuuuuuuck!" he howls, his voice echoing in the small cell.

Massimo puts his hand over mine, ordering, "Take a break, bro. I'll take over from here."

"He knows more," I insist.

Massimo clasps the claw tighter. "I'll get it out of him. Go tell Papà what he said."

My chest tightens further. Acid burns my esophagus. Since I got home from the hospital, I've recovered from the motorcycle accident injuries. But I can't seem to eat or drink anything without acid burning my stomach and throat. The longer Pina's gone, the worse it gets. Silvio prescribed me some antacids, yet they're worthless.

Massimo murmurs, "If you kill him too soon, we won't get all the information. Now go tell Papà."

I debate a moment then cave. I release the claw to Massimo, leave the cell, and shower in the bathroom. When I no longer have any blood or sweat on me, I dry off and go upstairs.

Papà and Luca are in his office. Luca states, "Word on the street is he took her to Jacopo's this morning."

"Mattia just confirmed," I announce, stepping inside the room and shutting the door.

Papà goes to the window and stares into the backyard. Summer is almost here. The grass is as green as it's ever been. The flowers are in full bloom, and everything screams cheerfulness. All I can think is how Pina loves sunshine. She should be here, but right now, it's like she's a ghost.

Part of me feels relieved she's not dead. The other side of me is worried. Jacopo's house is a fortress. I've racked my mind too many times, wondering how to penetrate his compound without putting her in harm's way. Everything I imagine leaves her hurt or dead.

I assert, "We need to go get her tonight."

Papà spins. "This is not the time for knee-jerk reactions."

"Knee-jerk? He's had her for over two months! What do you think he's doing to her?" I voice, fighting the bile rising in my throat.

"Do you want her killed?" he questions.

"Of course not!"

"Then you need to use your head and listen to me."

"Tell me your plan," I demand.

Papà goes to the bar and pours three shots of sambuca. He downs his and hands one to Luca and me.

I toss it down and grimace with regret. The liquor burns, creating a scorching fire in my stomach. I manage to challenge, "Tell me your plan."

Papà stays silent.

I seethe, "You don't have one."

Luca steps between us. "I have more information for you."

"What?"

He sets his shot glass on the table and states, "I need you to stay calm."

My anger and fear flare. I grit my teeth, snarling, "About what?"

Luca's eye twitches. He announces, "Jacopo is throwing Biagio and Pina an engagement party on Saturday night."

My stomach churns, and the air turns stale in my lungs. "Engagement party? What the fuck are you talking about, Luca?"

"The hostess at Bella Bella told me. Jacopo has the entire restaurant for the night. If you want her back, that's the best place to make our move," he claims.

"It's a week away," I reply.

He nods. "Yes. But I doubt he'll take any chances and let her out before the party. Once they make it public, she'll be off-limits to anyone else."

"Over my dead body," I vow. All the crime families can fuck themselves. I'll be damned if I'm following some rule that turns Pina into Biagio's property. I add, "There's no way Pina agreed to marry him."

Luca and Papà exchange a glance.

Goose bumps pop out on my skin. "What?"

Papà nods to Luca. "Tell him."

My gut dives further. "Tell me what?"

Luca takes a joint out of his case and lights it up. He takes a long drag, holds the smoke in his lungs, then slowly releases it before he says, "There's something Guido said before he died."

Hatred and guilt overpower me. I knew I should never have let Dante assign Guido to Pina. Luca tortured him for hours before he finally admitted he was a traitor. I sniff hard. "And?"

Luca offers me the joint. I normally don't smoke unless it's night and I'm out partying. Lately, I need it to keep me from taking my Glock to the Abruzzo estate and killing as many men as possible before they take me out. I inhale a lungful of smoke as Luca answers, "He was almost dead when he mumbled something about Biagio creating a shot that causes amnesia."

"What does that mean?" I ask, taking another hit.

Papà interjects, "We think Biagio could be using it on Pina."

I freeze.

Luca steps closer and lowers his voice. "We don't know anything more. He died shortly after. But you should be prepared."

"For what?" I ask, feeling sicker by the moment.

"She may not remember you. Or any of us."

"Bullshit. She wouldn't forget me," I claim.

Papà points to the chair. "Sit, Tristano."

"I'm fine."

"Now," he orders.

I hand the joint back to Luca and plop in the armchair. "If you're going to lecture me, save it."

"That's not what this is," Papà claims.

"No? Then what is it?"

He sighs. Concern fills his face, and that scares me more than anything. He hesitates then replies, "You need to be prepared that she may have agreed to marry him."

"There's no way in hell she'd do that," I seethe.

"If she doesn't remember any of—"

"She wouldn't," I insist, then rise. "You two twiddle your thumbs. I'm going to get Pina back."

"Sit down," Papà barks.

"I'm not listening to this—"

"You found her?" Dante asks.

I spin. It's no secret I feel and look horrible, but Pina's absence has had a similar effect on Dante. I curse myself for not going to him instead of Papà.

"She was transferred to Jacopo's this morning," Luca states.

Dante clenches his jaw. His eyes turn into dark slits. He locks eyes with me.

"You ready to get her?" I ask.

He glances at Papà.

"Are you serious right now? You're going to ask Papà for permission to save the one person who's been more loyal to you than anyone?" I accuse.

"It's not like that, and you know it," Dante claims.

"Bullshit!"

"You can't just shoot your way into Jacopo's. You'll die, and she might, too," he declares.

"Saturday night at Bella Bella's," Luca says.

"What's that?" Dante questions.

I snarl, "Biagio and Pina's engagement party."

Dante's eyes widen. He slowly shakes his head. "No way she'd marry him."

"She won't have a choice," Papà quietly asserts.

I stare at the ceiling, wishing there was a simple solution and wondering what she's gone through. Even if I get her back, will things ever return to normal? Has he done things to her she'll never be able to forget?

Luca breaks the silence. "I'll put a plan together for Saturday."

"That's a week away," I restate.

"It's the best option we have," he claims.

"You're all cowards," I declare.

"Tristano—" Dante starts to rebuke.

"If you ever cared about her, you'd help me," I state.

He crosses his arms. "You know I care about her."

"Funny way of showing it," I mutter, shoving past him and leaving the office. I storm up the stairs and run into Arianna and her baby girl, Nicoletta. Killian and Liam O'Malley had business with Tully, and they dropped her off yesterday.

"Hey! You okay?" Arianna asks.

"Waa!" Nicoletta screams.

"Shh, it's okay," Arianna coos, caressing Nicoletta's head.

She screams louder.

"Hey now. What's wrong?" Arianna asks, then yawns.

The only thing that's given me any relief from my suffering is Nicoletta. Plus, my sister looks exhausted. I hold my hands out. "Give her to me."

"It's okay. You look like you're in the middle of something," Arianna claims.

I take the baby. "Go take a nap. I'll take care of Nicoletta."

She farts. It's loud and long. I'm pretty sure by the smell of it that she pooped her pants.

"Oh, baby girl," Arianna frets.

I freeze. *I need my baby girl back.*

What's he doing to her?

Does she even remember me?

Arianna tries to take Nicoletta from me.

"I said I have her," I repeat, then shove past my sister and go into her bedroom suite.

Nicoletta cries louder.

She follows. "Tristano—"

"I said I have this," I bark.

Arianna's eyes widen.

Nicoletta's scream turns into a sharp noise that hurts my ears.

I sigh and tell Arianna, "I'm sorry. Let me change her. You take a nap."

Arianna doesn't look convinced.

"I wouldn't hurt her," I state.

"I know that."

"Then go sit down." I motion to the couch.

Her eyes dart between Nicoletta and me, but she finally caves. She plops down on the couch.

I turn to the changing table and put Nicoletta on it. "It's okay, sweetie." I change her diaper as quickly as possible. Her screams turn to little whimpers.

I snap her onesie back in place and pick her up. Her glistening blue eyes tug at my heart. I kiss her on the forehead and say, "There you go. All clean now."

She reaches for my face and tries to stick her fingers in my mouth.

I move my head out of the way and sit next to Arianna, putting my feet next to hers on the ottoman. Nicoletta snuggles into the curve of my neck, and I close my eyes.

Arianna strokes my cheek.

I glance at her.

She softly says, "Any news on Pina?"

My emotions take a toll on me. I blink hard and nod, too choked up to speak.

"You know where she is?" Arianna asks.

I continue to nod.

"She's with the Abruzzos?"

"Yes," I manage to get out. I clear my throat. "She was transferred to Jacopo's this morning. Apparently, she'll be at their engagement party on Saturday."

Arianna's eyes widen. She scoots closer and grips my arm. "Don't do something stupid, Tristano."

I grunt, rubbing Nicoletta's back. "Stupid was when I obeyed Dante."

"What do you mean?" Arianna questions.

I admit, "He ordered me to stop guarding her and put Guido on her. They wouldn't have followed us if Guido hadn't been feeding them information."

"You don't know that."

"Don't I?" I lock eyes with my sister.

She tilts her head, declaring, "This isn't going to help Pina."

"What isn't?"

Arianna turns so her knee hits the back of the couch. She answers, "Blaming Dante or yourself. If the Abruzzos want someone, you and I both know they'll stop at nothing to get them."

I lean my head, resting it against the back cushion. I close my eyes and assert, "Papà should have killed Jacopo when that thug kidnapped you."

"Hmm," Arianna replies.

I roll my head toward her. "What does that mean?"

She shrugs. "Donato died. For that situation, it was appropriate. You know how things work. He can't take out the head of another family—"

"Bullshit. He can do whatever he wants," I declare.

"Language," Arianna chirps.

I groan. "Nicoletta isn't even a year old."

"So? I don't want her cursing like a sailor out of the gate."

I snort. "And how is Killian conforming to this?"

Her lips twitch. "You know Killian. He's stepping up to the challenge."

"How's that?" I ask.

Her face reddens. "Nothing specific. Anyway, I'm trying to make a point."

"And that point would be...?" I arch my eyebrows.

She strokes Nicoletta's head, answering, "There's a time and a place for everything. Whoever is responsible for Pina's situation, they'll pay. You need to be smarter than them."

"Smarter?"

She nods. "Yep. You don't do something stupid like shooting up Jacopo's house."

My heart pounds harder. "Who said I was going to do that?"

She snorts. "Please. You're the brother I've always been closest with. I know how this is affecting you. And right now, you're one choice away from doing something stupid."

I don't say anything, letting her words sink in.

"Go ahead. Tell me I'm wrong," she adds.

I open my mouth and then shut it.

She smirks.

"For someone who doesn't participate in the family business, you sure are well informed."

She grins, teasing, "Which is why you should always listen to me."

"Don't push it," I warn.

Her smile falls, and she lowers her voice. "Don't do something that can get you or Pina killed, Tristano. Listen to Papà and the others. You can't do this alone. You all need to be on the same team."

"Were you a cheerleader, and I somehow missed it?" I taunt.

She ignores my remark and questions, "Do you want to know the smart thing to do?"

I wave my hand. "Go on. Don't stop now."

She sits straighter. "You hit them when they think they're on top of the world."

"Why?"

"Their egos are so big that they think they're untouchable. They won't see it coming. A surprise attack when people are celebrating will always be better than one they're ready for," she points out.

I study my sister for a moment.

"What?" she asks.

I admit, "I think Papà made a mistake."

She pins her eyebrows together. "How?"

"He should have allowed you into the business. You'd be a better ruler than any of us," I state.

She softly laughs. "Nah. I'm not really into blood and gore."

"Then why did you always try to sneak into the dungeon when you were in high school?" I question.

She rises. "Oh, please. You would have, too."

I grunt. "Truth."

She pats my arm. "You sure you're okay watching Nicoletta?"

"Yeah. Why?"

She bats her eyes. "I'm going to do what you say and take a nap."

"Go for it," I reply, then lie flat on the couch, putting Nicoletta on my chest. I continue to process my sister's words.

Hit them when they're on top of the world.

A sense of calm washes over me. It's the first time in months I've felt it. And I suddenly feel very clear about what needs to happen.

26

Pina

A Week Later

ALL WEEK I TRIED TO LIE LOW. BIAGIO LEFT THE MOMENT I got here. He stated that he had to deal with some emergency and went out of town. So I've been left in Jacopo's mansion, under his surveillance.

Every time I see Jacopo, I get nervous. He's beyond mean. His beady eyes leer at me whenever I see him. This morning is no exception.

It's breakfast time and we're in the huge dining room. Several of his men sit around the table. It's full of anything you could ever want for breakfast. The smells waft in my nostrils, making my stomach growl. Even the foods I really don't even like, I would eat right now.

Jacopo has starved me all week, determined to make me lose the ten pounds he claims I should.

For breakfast, I get water and half a grapefruit. I hate grapefruit, but I eat it because it's all I get. Plus, Jacopo might kill me if I disobey him.

My stomach is in knots with hunger pains most of the day. I constantly feel dizzy. And then Tracy will stick the shot in my arm, which makes me even dizzier. So I've been sleeping a lot.

I'm not allowed to eat lunch. For dinner, I get the same thing every night. One tiny chicken tenderloin. It's grilled, and there's no seasoning on it. It's dry, and I choke it down. I'm always grateful to have something in my stomach, but then my gratitude turns into resentment. It's like the small piece of meat makes me hungrier, as if my stomach realizes there's food and needs more. The hunger pains intensify, and I spend the night trying not to throw up from insufficient nourishment.

The sinister satisfaction that appears on Jacopo's face while he watches me eat or when he hears my stomach growl makes me want to cry. He's happy I'm starving.

Right now, he sits at the table with his plate full of bacon, eggs, and homemade toast. His men eat just as much as he does, never once noticing that I'm starving.

I'd kill for a piece of toast, an egg, or something with some substance. Yet, it'll never happen with Jacopo. It makes me wonder if I'll ever eat three real meals again.

I finish my half grapefruit and wait for Jacopo to excuse me. His men are discussing the security for the engagement party tomorrow night. They're speaking in Italian, and I'm sure they think I don't understand what they're saying. I'm unsure why I know Italian, but every word they speak, I know. Something tells me not to let them learn I'm fluent. Today, I half-listen. It's always the same conversations about taking down the Marinos. Plus, all I can obsess over is the platter of bacon next to me.

Every day, I try to stay out of Jacopo's way. I spend most of the time in Biagio's bedroom. It doesn't feel like mine, and nothing is familiar. Still, I've enjoyed being alone without him. He scared me the first day I came here. When he first told me he was leaving, I was relieved. I quickly realized that put Jacopo in charge of me.

Jacopo slams his hand on the table, pulling me out of my thoughts about the bacon. I jump, and he barks, "Pina!"

I attempt not to flinch, lock eyes with him, and answer, "Yes, sir?" It's another one of his rules. I'm to call him sir at all times.

How did I ever agree to be in this situation?

Did I really fall in love and agree to marry Biagio?

His father is ten times worse.

Biagio's just as dangerous. He tried to burn my eyeball out.

I'd give anything to get my memories back, but it's a blank slate with little pieces that quickly disappear.

Jacopo announces, "Frida will be here with the dresses soon. You'll make sure that you're nothing but presentable for tomorrow night. Do you understand me?" I try to breathe in fresh air, but the cigarette smoke is too thick. I refrain from coughing. Anytime I do that, Jacopo yells at me. So I reply, "Yes, sir."

"Well, go on. Get presentable so you don't embarrass me when Frida comes," he orders, motioning for me to leave.

I glance at my designer pants and shirt, wondering what is currently unpresentable about me. After all, I assume either Biagio or Jacopo approved all the clothes in the closet.

"Go," he seethes.

I hold my head high and leave the room. When I get to the bedroom, I close the door and sigh in relief that Tracy isn't here.

She's a pest that never leaves my side. She's constantly in my room, giving me shots. I don't understand why I still have to take them. I don't even understand what the shots are supposed to be doing for me. I asked her, but she won't tell me. She told me any questions about my medical care should be directed to Biagio.

Two days after I arrived, I refused to let her shoot me up with whatever it was in her little vial. That resulted in Jacopo storming into the bedroom, tying me to the bedposts, and Tracy sticking me with the needle. For two days, he kept me there. When I finally got released, I didn't fight it anymore.

If only my memories would come back. I know I don't belong here, but there's no way I can leave. Jacopo's guards are everywhere. Plus, I don't even know where I would run to.

At times, little flashes of memories pop into my mind. But as soon as they come, they go. I keep expecting the flashes to turn into longer memories. I'm sure I'll remember my life then. If I did choose this, I want to understand why. What was it about Biagio I was attracted to? How did we fall in love? Why did I get involved with someone so dangerous?

The other problem is I'll remember something one day, and I can't remember it the next. So when Jacopo released me two days ago, I started writing down what my memories were. And the next day, it made me sicker to know that I didn't remember anything about the previous day's flashbacks.

I stare at the closet and select a Chanel dress, hoping it meets Jacopo's approval. I step into it and reach for a pair of Jimmy Choo heels then freeze.

A familiar man with dark hair and eyes, a chiseled face, and a ripped body—but not from steroids like I'm positive Biagio's is—flashes in my mind. He drags his fingers down my calf and then slides an identical shoe on my foot.

Butterflies burst in my stomach. Tingles raced up my spine. I laugh and say, "Tristano! We're going to be late."

He wiggles his eyebrows. In a deep voice, he declares, "I'm going to take these off later tonight."

"Knock, knock!" A woman's chipper voice drags me out of my flashback.

I step out of the closet and freeze. She's as old as Jacopo. Her jet-black hair is in a perfect French twist. There's no gray anywhere. Her makeup is flawless, and she's so skinny, I wonder how she survives. The formfitting white dress must be a size 00.

That's what Jacopo wants me to look like.

Tristano. That's the name of the man Biagio said kidnapped me before we got into the accident.

Why was he putting my shoe on? It doesn't seem like I was scared of him.

The woman snaps her fingers, and two men roll a rack into the room. It's full of different evening dresses.

"You must be Pina." She beams at me.

"Oh. Sorry. Yes, I'm Pina," I reply, unsure how to react to this woman who appears so happy in this miserable house.

"You must be so excited about your engagement! Congratulations, by the way!"

My stomach churns. "Thank you."

She claps her hands together. "Well, shall we get started?"

"Umm...sure." I walk closer to the rack.

Frida flicks through the dresses, asking, "So what would you say your color is? Is there something that's your favorite? Or should we go with classic black?"

My chest tightens. If I choose wrong, who knows what Jacopo will do to me. Several moments pass as I assess each dress she holds up. I finally question, "What do you think Jacopo would like?"

Her smile falls. She gives me a knowing look, as if she understands how he is and why I'm asking what I am. She takes a sleek, strapless, black cocktail dress off the rack. A gold zipper runs up the front. She holds it up to me, smiling. She claims, "I think this will work perfectly. It's classy. But not too much. Sexy. But you won't look slutty. And Jacopo tends to like black."

Relief that she knows what he likes and his style fills me. I blow out an anxious breath. "Okay, if you think this is it, then this is fine."

"Great!" She claps again, then adds, "Let's try it on. Get your clothes off."

I reach for the dress. "I'll be right back."

"Where are you going, dear?"

"In the closet."

"Nonsense!" She turns to the two men who rolled in the rack and haven't left. "You two. Out."

They don't question her and step into the hallway.

"Come on now. We don't have all day."

I slowly get out of my dress and try on the black one. Frida moves me in front of the full-length mirror. She frowns, "Oh, this is a little big."

My anxiety reignites. I blurt out, "Can you take it in? Jacopo has me on a strict diet. I-I must have lost too much."

She stands taller, pursing her lips. "I see. Grapefruit and chicken?"

It strikes me that she knows what I'm going through. Did Jacopo starve her, too?

I nod. "How—"

"A woman without fat is a woman worthy to stand next to an Abruzzo," she gushes.

My pulse skyrockets. Everything about her statement makes me feel ill.

She gathers the excess material in her hands, saying, "I think we need a couple tweaks. Right around the waist here." She pinches the sides of the fabric, releases it, then goes over to her bag. She pulls out a little case of pins and returns.

For several minutes, she slides them through the fabric before standing back. Her eyes sparkle, and she proclaims, "There you go. You're going to be one knockout in this dress. Look out, Biagio!"

It's a comment that I should respond well to, but reminding me I'm engaged to Biagio doesn't excite me. I still don't even understand how I ever accepted a date with him, never mind agreed to marry him.

As if on cue, the door flies open. Biagio saunters into the room. "Wow, you lost a lot of weight."

His statement pisses me off. I sneer, "I've been on your father's starvation diet."

He shrugs. "Well, you've done well. You look good."

I glance at myself in the mirror again. My curves are almost gone. I look like a strung-out runway model.

Biagio comes over to me and pulls me into his arms. My skin crawls. It's the same reaction I always get, but I hug him back because the last time I didn't was right before he left. He told me if I didn't return his affection, there would be consequences to pay.

Frida chirps, "Look at you lovebirds."

I want to roll my eyes and slap her. Her chipper little attitude was nice at first, but now it's just annoying me. She seems to understand what goes on in this house, yet she still seems happy. That doesn't sit right with me.

Biagio asks, "Frida, are you finished with Pina?"

She drags her eyes over my body. "Yes. I need the dress though."

Biagio crosses his arms and stares at me.

My stomach dives. I say, "I'll go take it off."

He reaches forward and unzips the dress. Then he pushes it over my shoulders.

I swallow hard, feeling exposed and vulnerable.

His eyes scan my body, and my gut flips faster.

He hands the dress to Frida and orders, "Time to leave."

"I'll bring it back tomorrow after the tailor fixes it," Frida states.

I stay quiet, wondering if Biagio will try to burn my eyes out again.

The door shuts. Biagio turns his seedy expression on me. "You look good."

"Thank you. Did you have a good week?" I question, walking toward the closet.

He follows me. "Yeah, it was okay." He takes off his shirt and tosses it on the floor in front of me.

I freeze, close my eyes, then spin. Veins pop out all over his chest and arms. I swear he's on steroids, which isn't attractive to me. But it's also a reminder he could crush me in an instant.

"What are you doing?" I ask.

"We're taking a shower," he proclaims, then drops his pants and wraps his arms around me.

Alarm bells ring in my head. I blurt out once again, "What are you doing?"

Rage flares on his expression, scaring me. He keeps his voice calm, asserting, "I just got home. I've been gone a week. I'm ready for you to show me how much you missed me."

Bile rises in my throat and I swallow it down. "We're not doing this."

His eyes flare. "What do you mean we're not doing this?"

I think fast on my feet and put my hand on his cheek. "We need to wait until we're married."

He laughs. "What do you think I am? An altar boy? No, wait. Do you think you're a nun and I'm a priest?"

I reply, "Well, if I'm a nun and you're a priest, we wouldn't have sex at all."

He grunts, tugging me closer to his muscular body.

I push on his chest. "Biagio, please. I'm begging you. Wait until after the wedding."

Anger flares in his face. "You don't want to fuck me?"

I want to say no, but I refrain. I debate about how to get my way. There's no way I want to have sex with him. I don't know how I'll get out of it once we're married, but I'll put it off as long as I can.

I need to get out of this relationship.

Do I have any choices left?

"Oh, now you're not going to answer me," he seethes.

I step closer and put my hands on his cheeks, lying, "I just want it to be special when we finally do it."

"We've done it before," he claims.

My pulse skyrockets. His statement makes me queasy, but there's no time to dwell on what we've done in the past. I admit, "But I don't remember it."

"Which is why we need to reconnect," he declares.

My heart races so fast that I think it might explode. I soften my voice. "Please. I want it to be special."

He sniffs hard and glances at the ceiling.

I stroke his cheek. "Please."

His dark leer meets mine. "I'll make you a deal."

"What's that?"

"I'll let you have your way."

Hope fills me. "You will?"

Arrogance floods his expression. "Sure. But only until after the engagement party tomorrow night. When we get home, there will be no more excuses."

I blink hard so I don't shed tears, focusing on the vein across his chest.

He lifts my chin. "Did I misunderstand you? Did you say you want to take a shower with me?"

I square my shoulders and feign a smile. "Tomorrow, Biagio. It'll be more special tomorrow night."

The sinister expression reminds me of his father's. I shudder as he fists my hair and shoves his tongue in my mouth.

27

Tristano

"I'll go in with the team and extract her. You're staying in the car," Luca states.

"No way! I'm going in," I argue.

Luca shifts on his feet and glances at Papà. "Listen, Tristano, they know who you are. If anyone sees you, Pina's in grave danger. You need to stay in the car. I'll bring her to you."

"No," I insist. I'm not leaving Pina's rescue to anyone but me. I'm getting my girl and bringing her home.

He gives me an exasperated look.

"You get Biagio. I'll get Pina. And I want him alive," I add.

"It's better for us to shoot him on the spot. You know this," Luca claims.

I cross my arms. "Tough shit. I want him brought back here. It's nonnegotiable. Understand?"

Luca scowls.

Papà interjects, "Luca, Tristano can go inside. But let me be clear, Tristano. Luca is in charge of this operation. I need your head in the game, so keep your emotions out of it."

Keep my emotions out of it.

Like that's possible.

Papà arches his eyebrows at me. "If you can't—"

"Fine. Luca's in charge."

There's a knock on the door. I spin and groan inside. Tully saunters toward us, lights up a cigar, and takes a deep puff.

"Do you think you could come in here and not smoke that shit in front of me?" I hurl, pissed off. Tully has no business being here right now.

Papà barks, "Do not disrespect Tully!"

I glare at Tully, shaking my head.

He chuckles. "Well, you'll be happy when I tell you what I've done."

My gut drops. I snarl, "What have you done?"

Arrogance washes over his expression. "Oh, I made a little phone call to our friends at the police station."

"You did what?" I hurl. The last thing I need is the police and Tully interfering. I add, "Why the hell would you ask the police to come?"

He takes another puff and then blows a circle above his head. "You guys need a diversion. I've instructed the captain to have his men come inside the front."

"Why in God's name would you do that?" I fume.

Papà states, "Tristano, take a breather."

I shoot him a dirty look then refocus on Tully.

He declares, "They'll take the attention off the kitchen and attempt to arrest Biagio."

"For what?" Luca asks.

Tully's lips curl and his eyes light up. "Murder."

"No! You're going to put Pina in more danger. You could get her killed."

"Calm down, calm down," he orders.

"Don't tell me to calm down!"

Tully steps closer. "Either they'll arrest Biagio, and Pina will be left on her own, or he'll try to flee with her toward the back. Either way, it's a win-win."

More rage fills me. "I don't want them to arrest Biagio. I want him in our custody, held hostage in our dungeon while I torture the motherfucker until he dies."

"If he gets arrested, we'll just have to pick him up another time," Tully says nonchalantly. He shakes his head and looks at Papà. "Angelo, tell him I know what I'm talking about."

I hurl, "What, so I can owe you another favor? Well, guess what? I'm sick of your favors. I'll be damned if you use Pina's situation to get ahead."

He holds his hands in the air, claiming, "There are no favors here."

I grunt. "Sure there aren't. You're just going to do this out of the kindness of your heart. Stop playing me for a fool, Tully. There's always favors with you."

He shakes his head. "Not this time, kid. The Abruzzos crossed another line when they kidnapped Pina. So I'm going to help you get her out of there. And I promise there are no favors owed on this."

I still don't trust him. I look at Papà. "You should have consulted me. We don't need him involved in this."

Papà hesitates, glancing between the three of us. He finally states, "There will be a lot of Abruzzos there."

"No shit. Luca and I have this handled."

Luca steps between us. "Tristano, it's a good idea. Let's just let them do it."

"What do you mean let them do it? Since when do we need the police to interfere? Are you on my side or his?" I bark.

Luca glares at me. "Tristano, stop being a bitch. Now, come on. It's a good idea. Tully's right. It'll create a diversion away from where we need to enter the premises."

"We don't need it," I insist.

Luca's face hardens. "Do I need to remind you that your Papà put me in charge? Are you going to be a problem or a help?"

I sniff hard, not flinching. I hate that Papà won't let me take the lead on this.

Papà says, "Tristano? Answer Luca."

I cave. "Fine. Let's go." I leave the office and go outside.

The ride to the restaurant is quiet. I spend most of it staring out the window at the city with the same thoughts that have plagued me since I woke up in the hospital.

What shape will Pina be in after living with the Abruzzos for months?

Will she remember me?

What's Biagio done to her? Will she ever be able to forget about it?

When we're almost there, I ask Luca, "How did you get access to the kitchen anyway?"

He grunts. "I know people. You have to understand, Tristano, I've been in this game a long time."

I snort. "Yeah, you are an old motherfucker."

He chuckles. "Not too much older than you, so careful who you call old. Anyway, I've got my guys in the kitchen. There are two cooks, one dishwasher, and two waiters. They'll back us up."

"What about the other staff?" I question.

He locks eyes with me. "Hopefully, they'll get out of the way when it goes down."

My gut flips. Neither Luca nor I want anyone innocent to die. But if there are casualties for rescuing Pina, I'll deal with my guilt later.

"The hostess is on our payroll, too. She'll let the police through with no issues. I already texted her," Luca states.

"So your guys are carrying?" I inquire.

"Of course."

"Hostess, too?"

He nods. "She knows how to handle herself."

A moment of silence fills the SUV.

He breaks it, adding, "It's best if we don't blow their cover."

"If we blow their cover, we blow their cover," I reply.

He groans and his eye twitches. "Yeah, well I have other shit I have to do with these guys where the Abruzzos are concerned. And normal business needs to go on after we rescue Pina."

I stay quiet. Luca is right, but all I can see right now is getting Pina out unhurt and alive.

He orders, "We're staying in the kitchen, Tristano. They can't see you or me. I'm already skating thin on their trust level right now."

"What does that mean?"

"We'll discuss it another time. Let's focus on this situation," he answers.

I open and close my fist a few times then snarl, "There's no way that thug will come in the kitchen. We need to shoot any Abruzzo we can. They all should die anyway."

"Stop! You know that's not the answer. Use your head. Do you want Pina to get hurt?" Luca seethes.

I scrub my hands over my face. Common sense says to listen to Luca, but I've been on edge too long. I admit, "Of course I don't. I just want my girl back."

He cocks his Glock and affirms, "Yeah, and that's what we're gonna do. But you follow my lead."

The SUV pulls into the back alley of the restaurant. I reach for the door handle, but Luca grabs my hand. He orders, "Wait."

My heart pounds harder in my chest. I grind my molars, tapping my fingers on my thighs. Time stands still until Luca's phone buzzes.

He glances at it then says, "Now we can go in." He gets out, I follow, and the dishwasher meets us at the entrance. He says nothing and motions for us to go through.

As Luca stated, there are two cooks, one dishwasher, and two waiters. The waiters nod to Luca and take a tray full of food through another door.

I rush toward it and look through the square glass. My heart almost stops. Pina's sitting at a table with Biagio next to her. She's as beautiful as always but looks like she lost a ton of weight. I can see her bones. Everyone's eating rich Italian food, drinking expensive wine, and laughing. Yet all she has in front of her is a glass of water and a small piece of chicken.

She's so pale, she looks like she might pass out. Most of all, a scared, unhappy expression is on her face. My heart hurts. I clench my fists at my sides and seethe to Lucca, "I'm going in."

"Hold on!" he commands, grabbing my arm. "You do that, and she's dead."

I take several breaths, but it feels like the oxygen isn't getting to my lungs. It takes everything I have not to storm into the next room. I continue watching Pina, willing her to look at me.

She never does. She keeps staring at her plate.

I'm out of patience when the police storm through the restaurant. And I have to give it to Tully. It's not just a few policemen. There are at least a few dozen of them. They have their riot gear on and guns pulled.

"Whoa!" Jacopo shouts, tossing his napkin on the table and rising. He demands, "What the hell's going on here?"

The captain steps forward, asserting, "We're here to arrest your son."

Biagio jumps up from his seat. "What are you talking about?"

The captain continues, "Biagio Abruzzo, you're under arrest for the murder of Guido Berlusconi."

Biagio's eyes widen. "Fuck off. I've done no such thing."

"Put your hands in the air and step away from the table," the captain demands.

"Get the fuck out of my engagement party," Biagio states, then yanks Pina up next to him.

Three men step in front of Biagio and Pina. The rest of the Abruzzo men rise with their guns pulled.

Jacopo steps in front of him. "Listen, boys, I don't know who you think you are coming in here and throwing out accusations, but I can assure you this is not happening. Now, get your pig asses out of this building."

Two more men form a wall around Biagio and Pina. They begin to move back toward the kitchen.

"Don't move!" the captain shouts.

The sound of guns cocking fills the air. Biagio and Pina continue to get pushed back until they're shoved through the door.

The chefs step in front of me and fire their guns, killing the men who formed the wall. They all drop to the ground and blood pools around them. The restaurant fills with screams.

My brothers rush into the kitchen from the alleyway.

Biagio's eyes widen, and Luca pulls Pina away from him.

He charges at me, but I'm prepared. I slam my fist into his face.

Blood spurts everywhere. His nose moves to the side of his cheek. He takes a few steps back, then regains his balance.

Gunshots fill the air from the restaurant, along with men and women shouting. My brothers fire from behind the safety of the door.

Luca and the dishwasher lunge at Biagio. They restrain him, and Luca tugs a bag over his head.

Pina's shaking in the corner. Confusion and fear fill her expression. I slide my arm around her waist, and she cowers in the corner. Knowing she's scared of me makes my heart hurt, but there's no time to convince her to come with me. I pick her up, and she tries to fight, but it's apparent she's weak.

Gunfire continues on the other side of the door. Massimo, Gianni, and Luca push Biagio outside and into an SUV. Dante and I get into the other one with Pina. Our vehicles peel out of the alley.

Pina scoots as close to the door as possible.

I hold my hands in the air. "It's okay, baby girl. We're taking you home."

Her eyes dart between Dante and me. Her lips tremble hard, and her voice is barely audible when she speaks. "Home?"

"Yeah." I slide closer to her, but she cringes like a wounded animal. I glance at Dante.

He cautiously asks, "Pina, do you remember us? I'm Dante. That's Tristano."

Her eyes burn with golden fire. Any color left on her face disappears. Her entire body convulses, and she stammers, "Tristano?"

Relief fills me. She must remember me. I reply, "Yes. It's me."

A new panic overtakes her expression. She reaches for the door handle and tries to open it.

"Baby girl, what are you doing?" I cry out, grabbing her hand.

She tries to fight me. Her limbs flail in the air, and her fists slam into my chest.

"Pina! Stop!" I order.

She doesn't listen, continuing to hit me.

I wrap my arms and legs around her so she can't try to escape.

She shrieks, "Let me go!"

"Calm down! I'm not going to hurt you," I reiterate.

It doesn't convince her. She screams louder, "Let me go!"

I don't let go and look to Dante for what to do. He has a helpless look on his face.

The entire ride home, she tries to escape my grip. It takes all my strength to hold her at times. It's as if she gets a second wind and attempts to fight; then she'll be worn out within seconds.

Her tears soak my shirt. Makeup runs down her cheeks. We pull up to the gate, and she freaks out again.

"Don't take me there!" she cries.

"Where do you want to go?" I ask, unsure why. There's no way I'm not taking her home. I can protect her there better than anywhere else.

She sobs harder as we drive through the gate. The closer we get to the mansion, the more intense her convulsions become.

We pull up to the front entrance. Papà's main guard opens the door, and she belts out another shrilling noise then attempts to kick him.

Papà steps out of the house. It sets Pina off further.

I've never felt so incompetent. I don't know what to do to calm her.

Arianna and Bridget come outside.

Pina locks eyes with them and almost collapses to the ground. I hold her up.

Bridget cautiously steps forward. In a quiet voice, she states, "Pina, I'm your friend, Bridget. This is your friend, Arianna. Do you want to come to my room with us?"

Tears stream down Pina's cheeks. She glances between the two women, whimpering.

Bridget adds, "It's safe. I promise. We've been your friends for a long time."

Pina glances at me and then at Bridget. "Can you keep him away from me?"

28

Pina

I DON'T KNOW THESE MEN. DANTE AND THE OTHERS SCARE ME, but Tristano frightens me more. Biagio claimed he kidnapped me. And I don't remember him, yet he looks familiar.

If he kidnapped me, he would look familiar.

What if Biagio was lying?

What if he wasn't?

I assume Dante is his brother. He's familiar, too, but I'm still scared. All I want to do is escape everybody so I know I'm safe.

Two women rush out of the house. One resembles Tristano and Dante. The man who came out before them might be the men's father. He has the same dangerous aura that Tristano and Dante have. Still, their danger doesn't feel quite like Biagio and Jacopo's. But I'm so confused about everything happening and not being able to remember anything that I'm not taking any chances.

The woman with blonde hair tells me her name is Bridget and the dark-haired woman is Arianna. She says stuff to try and calm me, but I barely hear her.

The other woman stays quiet. She has a kind face full of sympathy. It makes me realize I'm probably behaving like a wild animal.

Bridget claims she, Arianna, and I are friends. They appear nice and trustworthy. In fact, they're the friendliest people I've seen since I woke up from the accident.

"Would you like to come inside with Arianna and me?" she inquires again, and I realize she's been talking to me but I've barely heard her.

Inside. Is that smart?

I glance around the property. The sun has almost set. A gorgeous pink hue streaks across the sky. The large iron bars enclosing the property loom in the distance.

I'm trapped here, just like at Jacopo's.

I study the women and decide it's better than staying with the men. *Surely, they're safer?*

"Okay," I meekly agree.

Bridget and Arianna step on both sides of me. As I step into the house, another sense of panic rushes through me.

It's overwhelmingly huge, just like Biagio's father's house was. I don't want to be here if it's anything like Jacopo's. I blurt out, "Get me out of here." I turn around to leave, but Tristano is right behind me and I collide into his muscular torso.

He wraps his arm around my waist, pleading, "Baby Girl, please. It's me."

Why is he calling me baby girl?

I shove out of his arms, feeling on edge again.

Bridget puts her arm around my shoulder, ordering, "Tristano, give her some time. Pina, let's go up to my suite, okay? I promise you, everything will be better soon."

I lock eyes with her blues, fretting, "I don't want any of them coming near me."

She keeps her voice soft. "I promise, Arianna and I are the only ones who will go with you."

Hesitating, I glance around the foyer again. All the men are there. Danger emits from them. I want to be able to trust them, but I don't want to make a bad mistake.

"Come on," Bridget says, grabbing my hand.

She and Arianna seem safe.

I cave, letting her lead me to the grand staircase. It's also overwhelming. I'm so weak, I can barely get my feet to move. I take five steps up.

Tristano asserts, "Bridget, let her go on the elevator."

Not wanting to be helpless or show my weakness, I spin, straightening my shoulders. I glare at him. "I'm fine."

Hurt floods his dark orbs. I instantly feel guilty, but I'm unsure why. He lowers his voice. "You're weak. What did he do to you?"

More tears drip down my face.

How do I even answer that question?

Why would I answer him anyway?

Why did he kidnap me from the Abruzzos again?

I keep my thoughts to myself and force myself to climb another step.

Arianna asks, "Do you want to take the elevator? It's just around the corner."

"No, I'm fine," I say, gritting my teeth and somehow finding some energy. But it's true. I'm so weak. I feel like I could pass out at any moment. I grip the railing, pulling myself up.

Bridget and Arianna stay close by me. We go down several hallways. It seems to take forever until we get to a huge suite.

I question, "Where are we?"

Bridget answers, "Your home, sweetheart."

"Home?" I inquire, gazing at the surroundings, yet nothing feels familiar.

"Yeah, your home," Bridget replies.

It just doesn't feel like home. Full of doubt, I mutter, "This is where I lived?"

She glances at Arianna, responding, "Not quite."

"I don't understand. You just told me this is home. Is it not where I lived before I was with Biagio?"

She puts her hands in the air. "I just meant that you're a part of our family."

"I'm related to you?"

"No, not yet. But you agreed to marry my brother," Arianna interjects.

My heart almost stops. I gape at them, shaking my head. "I was supposed to marry Biagio."

Arianna picks up my hand with the ring on it. Her eyes glisten, and she states, "This was my mamma's."

Goose bumps pop out on my skin. I still have no recollection of what she's talking about. I blurt out, "That's impossible. Biagio gave this to me. He told me the story about how he proposed and everything."

Her face hardens. "He's a liar. That was my mamma's. Tristano gave it to you, and you accepted."

More tears slip down my cheeks. I put my hands over my face, admitting, "I'm so confused."

"It's okay. Things will get better soon," Bridget insists, leading me to a sitting area.

Everything's brand new and luxurious. There's been no money spared, just like at Biagio's. I turn to her, inquiring, "Is this your bedroom?"

She smiles. "No, this is Dante's and my wing. It's our guest bedroom."

I take a deep breath, looking around.

"Sit down," Arianna commands, then asks, "Do you want me to have some food brought up?"

My stomach growls as if it can hear her.

When's the last time I ate an actual meal?

I answer, "Please. Just no chicken or grapefruit."

Arianna studies me and then suggests, "How about some lasagna and garlic bread? If I recall correctly, you love our chef's lasagna and garlic bread."

"He just made some cannoli, too," Bridget adds.

The scent of garlic, cheese, and tomato sauce that terrorized me at the restaurant resurfaces, flaring in my nostrils.

"Please," I reply.

Arianna chirps, "Great! I'll be right back!" She leaves the room.

Bridget picks up a blanket and drapes it over me. She hesitates then clears her throat. "I don't want to intrude, but did he harm you?"

Her question makes me sob again. I manage to choke out, "He was mean, threatened to burn my eyes out, and was going to force me to sleep with him tonight."

Bridget tugs me into her. I cry for several minutes, and she murmurs, "I'm glad you're here. We've all been so worried about you."

I retreat from her embrace. "Are you sure it's safe here?"

Her face turns even more serious. "I swear on my children's lives. This is the safest place to be."

"You have children?"

She pulls her phone out of her pocket, swipes the screen, and a photo of a teenage boy and girl pops up. She states, "This is Fiona and Sean, Jr."

"Have I met them before?"

"Yes."

I close my eyes, revealing, "I don't remember them."

She clasps her hand over mine. "Do you remember anything?"

"No. And I don't know why. I woke up from the accident and Biagio and Kiko were there. I was in some dumpy room. I stayed there for a long time. Biagio told me I got in an accident with Tristano when he tried to kidnap me."

"Tristano did not kidnap you," she assures in a stern voice and adds, "He loves you so much."

I open my mouth, shut it, then ask, "Do I love him?"

Love fills her expression. She replies, "You agreed to marry him. But we don't really know the whole situation."

More confused, I ask, "What do you mean?"

She pauses then responds, "You work for Dante. You and Tristano hid your relationship from him."

"Why?"

She shrugs. "I was hoping you could tell me that."

I rack my brain, but nothing pops up.

Is that why Dante looks familiar?

I swallow the lump in my throat, questioning, "So what do I do for Dante?"

She grins. "You're his right hand. He can't survive without you."

"He can't?"

She softly laughs. "Nope. He's going crazy not having you work with him. Plus, you've been with him forever."

I still have no recollection. I doubtfully ask, "Really?"

"Yeah, since you were eighteen. You're the only person he's ever had work for him who stuck around. All of his brothers have tried to steal you, but you're pretty loyal to him."

"I am?"

"Yes! You sure are. And, girl, you run the ship."

Something about that statement makes me happy. "Well, I sound fabulous."

She laughs again. "Yes, you are fabulous."

My smile fades. "Why can't I remember anything?"

She strokes my hair. "Don't worry, Pina. Everything will eventually come back."

I state my biggest fear. "How do you know? What if I can never again remember my life?"

"If that happens, you'll figure out how to deal with it. You're one of the smartest and strongest women I know. Give it some time. But while you're figuring things out, I want to reiterate that you're safe here. Nothing's going to happen that you don't want to happen. Understand?"

I sniffle. "Okay. Thank you."

There's a knock on the door.

I jump.

Bridget pats my hand. "Don't worry, it's just Silvio."

"Who's Silvio?"

She rises. "He's the Marino family doctor."

Wait, what? I'm in the Marino house?

All the things I heard in the Abruzzo household about the Marinos come flying at me, creating more fear.

Bridget asserts, "Yes, but you're safe. We're not the Abruzzos."

Something about Bridget's calm demeanor relaxes me a bit.

The door opens and an older man with gray hair walks in. I pull my knees up to my chest and hug them.

He softly greets, "Hey, Pina, how are you doing?"

Alarm bells ring in my ears. I blurt out, "Don't come any closer!"

He freezes. "I'm a doctor. And I just want to make sure that you don't need any medical attention. Do you mind if I give you an exam?"

Panic gushes through every cell in my body. "No, you're not touching me! Don't let anyone touch me, Bridget!"

She puts her hands in the air. "Okay, don't worry. Silvio, out."

"But—" He starts to object before Bridget cuts him off.

"Out, Silvio. Now!" she demands.

He sighs. "Okay, but I'm here to examine you when you're ready."

"It's not necessary," I assert.

He exchanges a look with Bridget and then leaves. He shuts the door.

She turns toward me. "I promise you, Silvio won't hurt you."

"I don't want anyone touching me."

"I understand. But if you change your mind, I can assure you he's safe."

"Good to know," I murmur, but I have no intention of letting anyone who's male get near me.

Bridget sits down again. "Can you tell me how you feel? Do you have a headache? Does your stomach hurt?"

"I'm just weak. And dizzy. I haven't eaten for so long," I admit.

She furrows her eyebrows. "Why haven't you eaten?"

Shame fills me. I'm unsure why, but I quietly confess, "Jacopo said I needed to lose weight. I was only allowed half a grapefruit at breakfast with water throughout the day. For dinner, I got one grilled chicken tenderloin."

Bridget looks at me in horror. She swallows hard then states, "I'm so sorry."

I shrug and then break down again.

She pulls me into her. It feels so good to have her hugging me. It's like when my mom was alive.

That thought makes me cry harder.

"Shh. It's okay. Everything will be okay. I promise," Bridget coos.

"I wish my family wasn't dead," I cry out.

Her body stiffens. "What are you talking about?"

I glance up, sniffling. "Biagio told me how they're all dead. I can't even remember their funerals."

Bridget's face turns to stone. "Pina, listen to me. Your family is not dead. They're very worried about you. They're actually on their way over."

A chill runs down my spine. "What?"

"Whatever Biagio told you was a lie."

"They...they're alive?" I question again.

"Yes," she assures me.

Arianna comes back into the room, wheeling a big cart. The smell of garlic, cheese, and tomato thickens in the air. My stomach growls and the raw feeling I've had for so long intensifies.

"Come eat," Bridget orders, leading me to the table.

Shocked and relieved over the news about my family, I sit in the seat Bridget pulls out.

Arianna sets a silver-covered plate, a platter of cannoli, and a bread basket in front of me.

I grab a cannoli and take a bite. The pastry melts in my mouth, and I groan. She uncovers the lasagna, and I eat in silence.

I get half the plate of lasagna and half a breadstick in my stomach and then push the plate away. My stomach must have shrunk because I'm full.

My exhaustion sets in. The thought of Biagio's hands all over my body makes me feel dirty and ill. I want to scrub it off. I ask, "Can I shower?"

Bridget rises. "Sure. Let me show you where we keep all the towels and toiletries."

I follow her into the bathroom. She turns on the shower. I wait till it warms up and then step in the water, letting it cascade over my body. I shampoo and rinse it then open my eyes. I stare at the white tile.

A vision of Tristano and me kissing in the shower pops into my mind. I reach for the wall to steady myself. It's so intense and then it disappears. I try to recreate what happened in my mind, but I don't know much more than that little blip.

More confusion plagues me. I get out of the shower, dry off, and go into the other room. Arianna and Bridget are there.

"Your family just called. They're stuck in traffic, but they'll be here in about a half hour," Ariana informs me.

"Can I lie down for a bit?"

"Absolutely," Bridget responds, pulling back the covers on the bed.

"Try to sleep. We'll wake you up when they arrive," Arianna adds.

"Thank you." I slide underneath the silky sheet. Before I shut my eyes, I ask, "Will you promise me nobody will come in here except you two?"

They nod in agreement, which makes me relax further.

Arianna asks, "Do you want the light on or off?"

I ponder her question and answer, "Maybe leave the bathroom light on." I'm unsure why I'm scared of the dark. But I don't know who I am anymore. I don't know what I should or shouldn't be scared of.

Arianna flips the switch to the bathroom light. Bridget turns the bedroom lights off. They tell me good night and leave. The door shuts, and I close my eyes, falling into a deep sleep.

All sorts of flashbacks terrorize me. They're little pieces of information and only leave me with more questions.

Tristano restrains me in a room that looks familiar. I want to say it's a sex dungeon, but am I into that?

A bunch of roses arrive while I'm at a desk. There's a note, but I can't read it.

I'm on a beach. Tristano is rubbing sunscreen on me.

There's a motorcycle, the ring I wear on my finger, and Tristano down on one knee.

I bolt up in bed, a sweaty mess. My entire body shakes. I glance at the clock and can't believe it. I've been asleep for over sixteen hours unless the clock is wrong.

Is my family still here?

I get out of bed and turn on the light. I almost open the door, but then I stop. I don't know who's out there. I don't know where to go in this house. Any move I make could put me in danger.

Am I really in danger here?

I can't be 100 percent sure, so another hour passes while I debate.

The door finally creaks open.

"Who is it?" I shout in alarm.

"It's just me!" Arianna announces and she steps inside with a baby. "I thought you'd want to meet my daughter, Nicoletta."

My heart soars glancing at the tiny baby. "Wow. She's the cutest baby ever. Have I met her before?"

Arianna shakes her head. "No. She's only a few months old, and it's our first trip back home."

"You don't live here?"

She smiles. "Nope. I live in Chicago now."

"Do you like it?"

"Yeah, I do. But it's nice to come home."

I ask, "Did my family arrive?"

"They were here, but you were asleep."

"Why didn't anybody wake me up?"

"We tried."

"You did?"

"Yes, I promise. Bridget and I both tried. Did you get to sleep at all? When you were with Biagio?" she inquires.

"I slept a lot. However, I've been so weak and tired since the accident."

"Maybe it's because of the shot they were giving you," Arianna suggests.

My eyes widen. "What do you know about the shot?"

She shrugs. "Not a lot." She holds the baby toward me.

I take Nicoletta and hold her. She curls into the curve of my neck, and it feels just as good as when Bridget hugged me.

Arianna states, "I don't know a lot about the shot. All I know is that my papà found out Biagio created some sort of shot that makes people lose their memory."

I stare at her in horror.

She takes a deep breath. "I don't know all the details, so I probably shouldn't be saying anything."

"If you know something, you should tell me," I demand.

"You should talk to Tristano," she states.

My pulse skyrockets.

She puts her hand on mine. "He's going crazy. He's been insane with worry for months. Can you just talk to him?"

"I don't remember anything about him. I get these flashbacks from time to time. I started writing them down because I couldn't remember them one day to the next. And I just wanted to remember things, but I couldn't. But there are these moments where I get these visions of him, and I don't understand why or what's going on," I admit.

She shoots me a sympathetic look. "You need to talk to him. He would never hurt you. I'll stay with you while you talk to him if you want."

I walk toward the window, open the blinds, and the sun hits my face. It feels good. The gorgeous yard boasts colorful flowers and dozens of bloomed trees. The grass is as green as green gets, and the pool's open.

Arianna says, "If at any time you want to end the conversation, you can, but I think if you talk to him, it'll fill in a lot of the blanks."

I cautiously ask, "How do I know you all aren't lying?"

She tilts her head. "I think deep down in your heart, you know you're safe here and that we aren't lying."

I think about her words for a few minutes. I finally make a decision. "Okay. I'll talk to him. But can I do it out at the pool?"

She beams. "Yeah, we can arrange that."

29

Tristano

ALL NIGHT, I STOOD OUTSIDE PINA'S DOOR, WAITING FOR HER to come out and talk. I knew it was a small chance she would appear. Not long after she fell asleep, her family arrived. I assumed it'd be a way for me to see her. But she was so exhausted, she wouldn't wake up.

Silvio assured us she was wiped out and that sleep was what she needed most. After her family left, I stayed in the hallway, hoping she'd somehow wake up and remember me. A few times, I tried to go in. I would have just watched her sleep, but Bridget and Arianna wouldn't allow me. And the night dragged by.

Pina never came out. I haven't seen her since Bridget and Arianna closeted her away in Dante's guest room. When the sun rose, I was no closer to seeing her. I had been awake for over twenty-four hours and vowed not to do anything besides get her to talk with me.

It was past noon when Arianna came out of the room and told me she agreed to meet me at the pool. So now, I'm pacing around the sparkling water, wondering what she's going to say to me.

On what feels like my hundredth lap, Pina steps out of the house. My heart swells and butterflies flutter in my gut. She's in a white sundress with red flowers. I bought it for her when we went to Florida.

Over the last two months, I'd go to her condo and sleep. Her pillows still smelled like her. I'd shower and use her shampoo to pretend she was with me. One day, I brought some of her clothes to my house so a part of her would always be with me.

Maybe it was stupid, but it gave me a small ounce of comfort in my darkest times.

I take several steps toward her, and she freezes. I reprimand myself for scaring her and stop.

An uncomfortable silence follows. She looks as beautiful as ever, but she's so thin and frail. And I can see the apprehension on her face. It almost kills me.

Pina takes a deep breath and walks toward me. I stay planted, unsure if I'm supposed to meet her halfway or not. She's almost at the pool when I realize I'm being a coward. So I move forward, slowly, ensuring that I don't scare her off. She gingerly continues making her way across the lawn until she's two feet in front of me. It's farther than I'd like her to be from me, but I'll take whatever I can get right now.

She locks her golden-browns on me, and it's pure torture. The confident Pina who can rule the world if she wanted to, and is always in charge and can command a roomful of powerful men, flashes in those eyes. Yet her fear and insecurities about who I am and who we are swirl around her old self.

I curse Biagio in my mind. I haven't even dealt with him yet. Luca and my brothers restrained him in the dungeon last night. I told them to make him wait. Then I began his long descent toward his death.

Right now, I'm starving him. Bridget told me how his father restricted Pina's diet. So I decided I would only give him half of what she got.

He got a quarter of a grapefruit this morning. Tonight, he'll get half of a grilled chicken tenderloin. And I'll give him water, but he's going to drink it from a hose sprayed on him.

When Pina tells me the full extent of her time with him, that's when I'll begin the real torture. But until I know the full story, I'm too scared to touch him. If I do, I'll kill him too fast and not make him pay accordingly. So it's imperative Pina tells me everything, no matter how horrible the details are.

My gut spins. I've spent too many hours fearful of what he's put her through. I want to know now what he did, but I can see how fragile she is and don't want to spook her again.

"Hey," she says.

My heart swells with love and hurt. All the emotions I felt over the last few months pummel me at once. I swallow them down, replying, "Hey, it's really good to see you. How are you feeling?"

She blinks hard. "I'm better than I was last night."

"That's good," I respond and can't hold back anymore. I step forward and start to reach for her.

She backs up three steps.

I freeze again. "I'm not going to hurt you, Pina. I would never hurt you."

Apprehension fills her expression. She admits, "I don't remember you."

Every ounce of disappointment and hurt I have slaps me in the face. "You don't remember me at all? Is that really true?" No matter what facts I know about this situation, it's hard for me to understand how her mind could be a blank slate when it comes to us.

She bites her lip and looks at the ground.

I sigh. "Why don't we sit down?"

She agrees, walking over to one of the lounge chairs.

I sit in the one next to hers. It's the closest I've been to her since the car ride. I start to reach for her hand but stop myself. She's made it clear she doesn't want me to touch her.

What if she never wants me to touch her again?

I push that thought away because it's too grim for me to consider. I assert, "I know your memory is gone right now, but I'm sure it'll come back."

Fear fills her expression. She inquires, "Will it? Is it true?"

"Is what true?"

She twists her fingers then answers, "Arianna told me that the shot Biagio was giving me was to make me lose my memory. Is that true?"

My chest tightens. The vision of Biagio restrained in the dungeon fills my brain. I respond, "Yes, it's true."

She takes a minute to process the information then asks, "What is it exactly?"

I tell her what I know. "The word on the street is he created a drug he calls 'Forget.' Normally, people take a small amount to try to forget their problems for a few hours. But if he was shooting you up with it daily, it makes me believe that eventually, it'll wear off. Otherwise, what was the point of continuing to dose you with it?"

She closes her eyes. The sun shines hotter, warming my skin. She doesn't open her eyes, and her voice shakes. "Tristano, I want to remember you. I do, but I don't. I only get these little glimpses of you. Well, I should say, us."

She remembers me?

A glimmer of hope ignites in my gut. I sit up and slide my legs toward her chair. "What do you mean? Glimpses?"

She opens her eyes and tears fall. She swipes at them and confesses, "I have these dreams or moments when I'm doing something and your face will pop in my mind. I don't know what it all means. It's never enough to put things together."

I can't hold back any longer. I take a lock of her hair and push it behind her ear. She doesn't flinch, which makes me happy. Yet, I know she still doesn't trust me. "Will you tell me about one of them?" I ask gently.

She sniffles, revealing, "I had several last night when I slept."

I tease, "I'm your dream man. It's why you dreamed about me."

She takes the bait and softly laughs, tilting her head and arching her eyebrows.

That's my girl. Come on, Pina, come back to me.

When she doesn't speak, I ask, "So you did dream about me?"

Amusement fills her expression. A blush crawls up her cheeks. She admits, "I guess you could say that."

"Your sexy little blush is appearing, so I wonder what kind of dream you had about me. Was it dirty?"

She nervously laughs. "Are you always Mr. Funny Guy?"

"I don't know. Am I?"

Silence fills the air. She stares at me.

I blurt out, "Sorry. I was just trying to lighten the mood."

She smiles. "It's okay. It's kind of nice."

"Yeah?"

She nods then hesitates.

"What is it?" I ask.

She twists her fingers again until her knuckles turn white. "This is strange for me."

I acknowledge her statement. "I'm sure it's strange for you. It is for me, too. I've known you since I was in high school."

She swings her legs toward my chair, positioning them between my knees. "Is it true I started working for Dante when I was eighteen?"

"You sure did. And no one else has worked for him since. We've all tried to steal you."

Her eyes sparkle. "That's what I hear. So I'm kind of a badass at my job, huh?"

I rub my thumb over the back of her hand. "You're the biggest badass there is."

She glances at our hands but doesn't pull away, so neither do I.

She lowers her voice. "Do you want me to tell you something about last night?"

I get brave and kiss the back of her hand. "Please."

Her cheeks turn redder. My cock turns hard, and I curse myself. All I want to do is hold her and never let her go, but I'm afraid she'll freak out on me if I attempt it. So instead, I wait for her to speak.

She takes a deep breath and then slowly releases it, claiming, "I had this dream that we were on a beach somewhere. There were dolphins in the background. You were putting suntan oil on me. Did that happen?"

Excited, I pull my phone out of my pocket. "It sure did. Do you want to see the picture?"

"You have a picture of it?"

I try to maintain my cool, but I'm bursting with positive energy. I tell her, "I have lots of pictures of us." I show her the picture on my phone. It's a selfie of us, and the dolphins are flipping in the background. I'm kissing her neck while she's laughing.

She studies it, uttering, "It looks like we were happy."

I assure her, "We were happy. And we can be happy again."

She avoids my eyes. I squeeze her hands. "Pina, please don't give up on us."

She blinks harder, opens her mouth, shuts it, then opens it again. She reveals, "I wouldn't say I'm giving up on us. I just... I just... I can't remember anything, Tristano. You don't understand what this is like."

I glance at the sky then back at her. "You're right, I don't. But what I do know is I love you, and nothing's changed regarding how I feel."

"Everything's changed. I have no memories. I don't know who you are. I don't even know if I should trust you."

Her statement hurts. Maybe I thought her being here erased all the facts of the situation. I jerk my head back. I firmly assert, "You can trust me. I would never hurt you."

She shakes her head. "I'm sorry. I didn't mean for it to come out that way. It's just... I don't know what to think."

Tension grows between us. I struggle with how to break it and finally say, "Fair enough. Tell me another dream that you had about us."

She scratches her forehead and then blows out a big breath of air.

"What's wrong?" I ask.

The red in her cheeks deepens. "Do we...well, do we..." She bites her lip again and stares at the pool.

"Do we what, baby girl?"

She locks eyes with me. "Why do I like it when you call me that?"

I grin. "Because you do. And you love me."

She furrows her eyebrows and blinks hard.

"Sorry. Too much, too soon," I add.

She swipes her cheek and replies, "It's okay. So I had this dream. We were in this room. It's not an ordinary room." She arches her eyebrows.

"Meaning?" I ask.

She studies my face then continues, "It has a lot of, shall I say, handcuffs and other restraints?"

My cock pushes against my zipper. I breathe deep, answering, "That's one of your places, Pina."

"One of my places? How many places do I have?"

I chuckle. "You have a lot of properties that nobody really knows about except me. And I didn't know about it until I started seeing you. But I believe the place you were dreaming of is in Manhattan. You made it into a playroom."

She gasps, throwing her hand over her mouth.

"Why are you embarrassed right now?"

She pins her eyes on me. "Shouldn't I be?"

"No, we go there together."

Confusion washes over her features. "So what does that mean? Do you tie me up or something?"

I chuckle, answering, "I can show you if you want."

Her eyes widen.

I quickly add, "We can save that for later."

She focuses on the pool.

I ask, "Do you want to see some more photos?"

She nods. I show her a photo of the playroom in Manhattan and several of us in the Maldives with Massimo and Katiya.

She points at Massimo. "Is that your brother?"

"Yes, that's Massimo."

"And who's that?"

"His wife, Katiya. They got married a few months ago. It was right before the accident. We were the only ones there," I inform her.

"Why were we the only ones there?" she asks, tilting her head.

"You and I kind of bugged his plane, followed him to the Maldives, and surprised him."

She gasps. "Why did we do that?"

"It's a long story. I'll fill you in later. But do any of these seem familiar?"

Guilt fills her expression. "I'm sorry, Tristano. They don't. I wish they did. I really wish they did."

Disappointment fills me, but I try not to show it. I kiss the back of her hand. "It's all right. We just need to give it some time."

She twists the ring on her finger. "Is it true that this is your mom's?"

I swallow more emotions down my throat, admitting, "Yeah, it was hers."

Pina's forehead wrinkles. "Was? Is she not here anymore?"

I sniff hard. "Mamma died years ago."

She reaches for my cheek, just like she used to. "Oh, I'm so sorry, Tristano. When Biagio told me my family was dead, I felt like I was crumbling. I can't imagine what you've gone through."

I shrug. "It is what it is. But Biagio lied. Your parents and siblings are all fine. They can't wait to see you."

She twists a lock of hair around her finger. "I can't wait to see them, either. But I only remember them from when I was a kid. Do you think they look the same?"

I lace my fingers through hers. "I have no idea. I didn't know them when you were a kid. But I can assure you that you'll recognize them since they're your family."

"What if I don't?"

"Then you don't. But it's not going to stop them from loving you."

"How do you know?"

My voice breaks a little when I reply, "Because it hasn't stopped me from loving you." I blink hard, cursing at myself to keep it together.

She doesn't say anything. A gust of air blows across the pool, making the water ripple. We stare at it as a comfortable silence fills the air.

I blurt out, "Do you want to go out with me?"

She looks at me in surprise. "Go out with you?"

Those damn butterflies in my stomach expand. "Yeah. Do you want to go on a date?"

So much time passes, I think she's going to say no, yet she answers, "Sure. Why not? When?"

"Tonight?" I suggest, then realize I'm pushing it when nervousness fills her expression. I quickly state, "That wasn't fair. I know you're still recovering. It doesn't have to be tonight. But maybe soon?"

She takes a deep breath and then slowly nods. "Okay, I think I'll like that."

"Yes!" I lift my arm in a victory pose.

She laughs, but then she starts to cry.

I can't handle it anymore. I pick her up and place her on my lap. She curls into my chest, sobbing. I hold her as tight as I can.

She wails, "What if I never get my memory back?"

"Shh. You will. You'll get through this, baby girl, I promise. And no matter what, I'll never give up on you."

She lifts her chin and locks eyes with me. "Please don't." She sobs harder.

I hug her tighter, vowing, "I won't. I'll never give up on you, no matter what happens to your memory. And if it doesn't come back, we'll make new memories."

She shakes in my arms. My T-shirt turns wet from her tears.

"Everything will be fine," I say, over and over, trying to calm her, but I wonder if it will ever be the same again.

30

Pina

A Week Later

"And you aren't having any issues eating?" Silvio questions.

Bridgette, Arianna, Cara, and Katiya kept encouraging me to let Silvio examine me, but Tristano was relentless. I finally caved today. I shake my head, admitting, "No. I'm starting to be able to finish my plate again."

His kind smile lights up his face. "Great. You should return to your normal weight soon."

"I hope so. My clothes are too big on me."

He nods. "Continue staying hydrated, and let me know if anything changes."

"Okay. Thank you," I reply.

He packs up his medical bag and pats me on the back. "Glad your memory is starting to stick."

Relief fills me. "Me, too." Over the last week, I've remembered more and more about my flashbacks. And now, the visions are longer with more details.

I keep dreaming of Tristano and me. He gifted me a beautiful journal after we talked at the pool. I'm confident I'm at the point I don't need it anymore, but I guess I do it to ensure I'm remembering things correctly. Plus, every time I look at the black cover with a red rose on it, I get flutters thinking about Tristano. Then I look at the dozens of red roses he's given me daily, and my heart skips another beat.

Every day, I quiz myself on the previous day's flashbacks. Then I try to go back to the ones I had the day before that one. Once I'm confident I'm remembering the visions correctly, I'll review my journal.

Tristano's been amazing with me. All the Marinos have, but the level of care and patience he's displayed toward my issues leaves no doubt in my mind how much he loves me.

And I know Tristano's not a patient person. None of the Marinos are patient people. That's one part of my memory that's come back. Yet, the level of consideration he's displayed hasn't gone unnoticed. Everything is about what he thinks is best for me.

I haven't really gone out of the house except to spend time at the pool. The thought of venturing outside of the Marino compound overwhelms me. Tristano keeps asking to take me on a real date, yet I keep telling him I'm not ready to go out. Every time I do, I see his disappointment, but he'll quickly tell me it's okay and change the subject to something else.

He created a few fun nights for us at home. We've had a game night and a movie night. Two nights my family came over to visit. Last night, we stayed up past midnight at the pool, sitting under the soft glow of the string lights, talking and laughing.

When he walked me to my room, he said, "Let's binge *Sex and the City*."

"You want to watch *Sex and the City*?" I asked in disbelief.

His boyish grin lit up the room and tugged at my heart some more. He stated, "It's your favorite show."

"And you're into that?"

His lips twitched, and he tugged my covers off my bed. "I'm into you. Get changed."

My heart beat faster. I nervously glanced between the covers and him.

He held his hands in the air. "Chill, Pina. I won't try anything, and I'll stay on top of the covers."

Part of me wanted to tell him not to be ridiculous. The other part was relieved. Confused about why I couldn't just kiss him and move forward, I changed into my nightgown and got under the covers.

For the next few hours, I snuggled into him, wanting to pull him on top of me and do naughty things that kept flashing in my mind. But I was too chicken. He attempted to kiss me, but I freaked and buried my head in his chest. Then I fell asleep in his arms, feeling safe and protected. He was still on top of the covers, sleeping peacefully, when I woke up.

I stared at him for over an hour, still fighting the urge to kiss him. Then I chickened out again and got up and showered. When I got out of the bathroom, he had breakfast waiting on the table in the sitting room.

I've had a few meals with the Marino family, but it's overwhelming at times. So I often prefer to eat in my room, yet even that is starting to get old. But I love the private time with Tristano. I'll take a meal with him and no one else around any day.

Dante's patience is another matter. He hasn't come out and said it, but I can tell he's ready for me to get back to work. I'm in a constant debate about if I'm ready or not. Flashbacks of my time in the office come and go. It's not a secret that my job is demanding and stressful. And my gut tells me it's too much right now.

Sometimes I get scared and wonder if I'll ever have my old life back.

Then Dante will come to me in a panic and ask me about different files, how to get the others in the office to get a highly sought-after reservation, or the passwords to different things. They're all issues he knows nothing about, yet I easily rattle off the information without hesitating. When that happens, it gives me more confidence.

Two days ago, I had a call with a couple of the girls in the office. I gave them directions about things they weren't sure how to do. Dante suggested after the call that I return to work. I said I wasn't ready.

A small part of me enjoys watching him realize everything I do for him. I'm unsure why. It's not like Dante doesn't treat me well or appreciate me, but it's been interesting to sit back and watch him. Plus, I've always wondered how he would do if I wasn't there to support him. Now is my only chance to ever know if I'm really worth what I think I am.

So far, I've concluded I'm worth every penny.

There's a knock on my door. I glance over, and tingles race down my spine. Tristano's covered in sweat from his workout. It's only the second time I've seen him like this, but it makes my entire body react. He cautiously asks, "Is everything okay?"

"Pina's doing great. You have nothing to worry about," Silvio assures him.

Relief fills his expression. "Just what I wanted to hear."

"Pina, let me know if you need anything," Silvio states.

"Thank you," I reply.

He pats me on the shoulder, picks up his medical bag, and leaves.

Tristano steps inside and shuts the door. A bit of nervousness washes over him, but it quickly disappears. "I wanted to ask you something."

"Okay." I step closer to him.

He locks eyes with me, inquiring, "What do you think about moving into my wing?"

My butterflies go crazy. I bite my lip and shift on my feet.

He quickly adds, "Don't worry. You don't have to. It was just an idea."

"No, it's okay. I can move."

He hesitates, asking, "Are you sure? You don't have to."

"No, that's fine. Can you show me the room?" I respond.

He grins, grabs my hand, and pulls me out of the bedroom.

I follow him. My flutters go crazy. I know Tristano means well. I want to get back to where we were. I feel like we're getting closer, but there's still so much confusion in my head about things.

Yet, there shouldn't be. He's a great guy. From the depths of my soul, I know that he loves me. And the attraction I have for him is getting stronger and stronger.

I curse myself. I'm almost forty years old. I don't even know why I keep contemplating making a move on him or letting him make one on me.

We venture down the hallway of Dante and Bridget's wing. We turn the corner, and Tristano shows me the different bedrooms.

Strangely, I haven't seen all this before, but everything we've done has been in common areas of the house, my bedroom suite, or near the pool. The one time he tried to show me his wing, I resisted. Now, I'm kicking myself for being so difficult.

Each room is a masterpiece of design. I laugh. "Wow, you really have a lot of rooms."

He shrugs. "Not really. I have to share this wing with Arianna when she comes home. It's not as exciting as Bridget and Dante's."

"I beg to differ," I state, peeking into another bedroom suite. I tease, "This is nice. I like all the pink and purple flowers."

He groans. "That's Arianna's guest bedroom."

"Ohhh! She has her own guest room," I continue to taunt.

He shuts the door and leads me farther down the hall, skipping one bedroom.

I tug on his arm, indicating for him to stop. I ask, "What's behind this door?"

A hungry expression fills his face. Zings erupt in all my cells. He sniffs hard. "We'll look at that room on a different day."

"No way! What's in there?"

He takes a deep breath. "Pina, let's skip it today."

"Why, what's in there?"

His hesitancy doesn't end. He reiterates, "That's a room for down the road."

I tilt my head and pout. "So you're not going to let me see it?"

He assesses me further.

"I can handle it," I claim.

He stays silent, debating what to do.

"Why are you nervous?" I ask.

"I'm not," he asserts.

"Then why can't I see it?"

He caves. "Okay. If you really want to see it, go ahead."

I reach for the doorknob and step inside. I inhale sharply, glancing around the space. The only colors are black, hot pink, and pewter. Sex toys, furniture, and restraints are spread around the room. I cautiously question, "Is this the room you normally restrain me in? The one that's always in my dreams?"

He shifts on his feet, shakes his head, and admits, "No. You've never seen this. I've always had it. When you showed me your place, and we grew closer, I started transitioning it to mimic yours."

I gape at him. "You created this room to look like mine?"

"Yeah. I wanted to marry you. And the moment that I knew in my heart that you were the one, I wanted you to live here. I wanted to surprise you. Maybe it's dumb, but I thought if you had all the things you already have at your place, you'd think of this place as yours."

Tears well in my eyes. I blink hard, but I can't stop them from falling. I stare at him, trying to make sense of everything. Then I step forward so we're inches apart. I open my mouth, shut it, and open it again. I finally blurt out, "I don't know what to say."

He quickly replies, "You don't have to say anything, Pina."

I glance around again, declaring, "This is amazing, Tristano. It feels just like the one in my dreams."

He stays silent, deep in thought.

"Say whatever is on your mind, please," I order.

He reaches for my face then freezes. He drops his hand, stares at the ceiling, and clenches his jaw.

I place my hands on his cheeks.

He slowly meets my eyes, revealing, "This is hard, Pina."

More tears fall. I nod. "I know."

"Most of the time, I don't know if I'm screwing up with you," he confesses.

Panic fills me. "You aren't. You've been nothing but amazing with me."

His jaw twitches. He stares at my lips. Time stands still with the air crackling between us. I think he's going to kiss me, but then he retreats, announcing, "Let's finish the tour. I need to shower."

The rest of the tour is pretty silent. We arrive at his bedroom suite. He announces, "This is my room."

I survey the impeccable black-and-silver room. It's just as big as Dante and Bridget's suite. I beam. "I love it. It's really nice."

"Thanks. If you wanted to change it, you could. Assuming you get to the place where you want to be with me again," he states, and I can't ignore the little bit of doubt in his voice, even though I know he's not doing it to hurt or guilt me.

I shake my head. "No. It's beautiful. And I want to get there again."

He stays silent. The tension grows thicker.

I ask, "So...are you free to hang out today?"

He grins. "'Course I am. Until you're fully recovered, I'm at your service."

I nervously laugh. "You heard Silvio. I'm fine."

He runs his hand through his hair. "I'll take some more time off from work until you're ready to return to your job."

More butterflies fill my gut. I glide my hand over his pecs. "I guess I'll let you take a shower."

He glances down at me. "You can join me if you want."

Sizzles run to my core. I shift on my feet, squeezing my legs together.

Jesus, he's hot.

I need to kiss him.

More electricity swirls around us. I urge myself to make a move, but my body stays planted.

"Sorry. Didn't mean to make you uncomfortable," he apologizes.

"You didn't," I assure him, retreat toward the door, and chirp, "Where do you want me to meet you?"

He hesitates and then motions toward the sitting room. "You can hang there if you want."

I make my way over to the couch, answering, "Great, I'll just be here twiddling my thumbs."

His lips twitch. "No problem. Make yourself at home." He walks into the bathroom and shuts the door.

I pace the room. Everything inside me screams for me to follow him, but I continue to pace.

Why can't I act on my impulses?

This shouldn't be so hard. He's sexy as sin, loves me, and I love him.

I freeze. It's the first time I've admitted to myself I love him. There's no doubt about it. I feel it in my soul.

Stop being a scaredy-cat!

I go to the bathroom and slip through the door. I tiptoe to the shower and stare at his naked, hard body. I strip, take a deep breath, and step behind him.

The water rolls down my body and face. I don't move except to circle my arms around his waist and hug him hard.

His body stiffens. He slowly puts his hands over mine.

My lips tremble as I kiss his back.

He spins, saying nothing, just giving me a look like he wants to eat me for his dinner.

My insides ache. I say, "I'm sorry."

Pushing my hair behind my ear. He asks, "Why are you sorry, Pina?"

I admit, "Every day, I remember more and more about you—about us. I don't want to have this uncomfortable feeling anymore. I don't want you to question what you're doing and feel bad about it. Most of all, I don't want to spend another night in my own bedroom."

His eyes widen. His erection grows, pushing into my stomach. In a low voice, he says, "Clarify that for me."

Nothing is planned. I open my mouth, and words fly out. "I want to stay with you. I don't want to be in any bed except yours."

He clenches his jaw, studying me, then asks, "Are you sure?"

I shake my head hard, confessing, "I love you, Tristano. I don't think I ever stopped. And I'm tired of waiting for my full memory to come back."

He tugs me closer to him. "Are you sure you love me?"

"Yes."

He pushes me to the tile, cups my cheeks, and presses his lips to mine.

I urgently slide my tongue against his, whimpering against him, feeling like I'm waking up from a long sleep.

He mumbles against my lips, "I love you so much, baby girl," and then his mouth continues to own me.

My body submits to his. He palms my ass and picks me up, keeping his lips on mine and carrying me to his bed.

We don't bother to dry off. He places me on my back, cages his body over mine, and pins my hands above my head.

I thrust my hips up, but he murmurs in my ear, "Hold the bars."

His command sends a chill down my spine. I grasp the iron headboard. He nibbles on my collarbone and pinches my nipple.

"Oh..." I breathe.

"I missed your sounds," he mutters, then lowers his mouth to my chest, making his way to my pussy.

A buzzing sensation fills my body. I widen my legs, gripping the bars as if my life depended on it. The moment his tongue hits my clit, I moan.

He eats me out like a starved man, fingering, licking, and sucking me until I'm begging him.

"Please," I barely get out.

"Tell me you'll still marry me," he demands, slowing his pace and licking me while drilling his gaze into mine.

"Yes," I agree, wanting nothing else but a life with him.

"Say it again," he orders, his face darkening.

"Be my husband," I cry out.

My reward is a hurricane of adrenaline attacking my cells, creating an earthquake so deep I continue to shake, even when he slides inside me.

"Yes," I whisper, squeezing the iron so tight, my fingers might break.

He tugs my hair and slides the other arm under me. Heat rises in his cheeks. His dark eyes burn with fire as he states, "Don't ever leave me again."

"I won't," I promise.

"You and me, baby girl. Forever," he asserts, thrusting into me harder.

"For...oh...oh...oh God!" I cry out. Another orgasm rolls through my bones.

"That's it! Clutch that tight pussy around me," he growls.

My body spasms, eyes roll, and everything turns to white stars.

"Let go of the bars," he instructs.

I release them and grip him, holding him as tight as possible, never wanting to let go.

There's no more doubt in my mind. I'm the future Mrs. Tristano Marino. If I never fully get my memory back, it doesn't matter.

He is my future. There's nothing else I need except him. And I know in my heart, he needs me just as much.

EPILOGUE

Tristano

Three Months Later

EVERYONE WE LOVE IS IN THE ROOM. OVER THE LAST FEW months, Pina's fully regained her memory. She returned to work but renegotiated the terms with Dante. After a lot of thought, she decided she wanted to cut back on her hours and enjoy life a little more.

I finally killed Biagio. After starving him and torturing him for so long, Pina told me it was time to put it behind us. So last night, I finished him off with a cheese slicer. Pina actually picked it out for me.

I tug her closer to me. She glances up, her golden-brown eyes shining bright, and smiles. My heart swells with so much love, I can't even describe it. I lean down and murmur in her ear, "After we get home, I'm taking you to the playroom for your surprise."

She takes a tiny inhale, replying, "Do you have a gift for me?"

Nodding, I chuckle, then reply, "You've been bad lately, baby girl. I have a new punishment for you."

She smirks. "Should I be extra naughty tonight?" She bats her eyelashes.

My dick hardens. I drag my finger down the side of her cheek, tuck her hair behind her ear, and assert, "You be as bad as you want, sexy woman. I'll make sure you pay your penance."

She softly laughs. "Well then, challenge accepted."

I squeeze her ass as Chanel runs up to us with her daughter Zara. Chanel chirps, "Hi! I'm sorry we're late."

Pina tosses her arms around Chanel, kissing her on the cheek, and then gives Zara the same treatment. She steps back and holds both their hands, gushing, "You both look amazing!"

"Thanks, Aunt Pina!" Zara says, giving Pina another hug. She asks, "Where's the restroom? I'm going to pee my pants!"

I step back. "Here, let me show you." I guide Zara toward the bathroom and leave the other women.

For the next half hour, I talk to several other people. From time to time, I glance across the room, locking eyes with Pina's.

It's our wedding rehearsal. I felt like this day would never come. I would have married her as soon as she agreed, but she wanted to have ours after Dante and Bridget's, claiming we stole their day when we had the accident. Now that they're officially married, it's finally our time. And I've never been happier in my life. I can't wait to officially make Pina mine.

The DJ cuts the music. He gets on the microphone and says, "If everyone could be seated, it's time for dinner."

I find Pina. We make our way over to our seats. Chanel sits on the other side of Pina and Massimo sits next to me. The servers pass out champagne flutes.

Massimo gets up and makes a speech. In the middle of it, Chanel rises and steps next to him. She interjects, "Since I know the bride the best, I think it's time we discussed the real deets about her."

Pina covers her face and groans, but she's smiling.

Dante yells out, "I think I know her better, Chanel."

"Keep telling yourself that," Chanel sings.

Massimo's eyes light with mischief. He states, "Do tell."

"Oh no," Pina mutters, shaking her head.

Chanel beams at her. "Don't worry, dear friend. I won't tell the embarrassing stuff. Okay, well, maybe I'll tell you a few things."

"Chanel," Pina says, laughing.

I tighten my arm around her and kiss her cheek. She snuggles closer.

Massimo goads, "Do tell, Chanel."

Chanel's expression brightens. She continues, "I thought long and hard about what I should say. I think it's best to discuss the time—" The color drains from her face. She drops the microphone and grabs Massimo's arm.

Massimo catches it. "Whoa. You okay?"

Chanel straightens her shoulders. She leers toward Luca and Zara and seethes, "Get away from my daughter!"

Luca's eyes turn to flames. He steps to the side of the table. "Chanel—"

"Zara, go outside!" Chanel orders then reaches behind Massimo and grabs his Glock. She points it at Luca.

"Mom! What are you doing!" Zara shrieks.

Luca tries again. "Chanel—"

Massimo calmly demands, "Give me the gun."

Red anger fills her cheeks. She never takes her eyes off Luca, gritting her teeth, and stating, "You have three seconds to get away from my daughter."

Ready for Luca and Chanel's story, the final novel of Mafia Wars NY?
READ FLAWED - BOOK FIVE OF MAFIA WARS NEW YORK!

One wild night and failed birth control gifted me with an accidental pregnancy.

I'm not telling the father.

Luca's mesmerizing and charming, but he isn't just a lot older than me.

After our hot night, I found out he's my family's enemy.

So there's no choice.

I'll do anything to keep him in the dark about her.

I disappear for years, leaving him with no trace of where I am.

Except fate isn't my friend when a chance encounter brings him into my life again.

Age has only made him more irresistible.

Still, I know he's wrong for me—for my daughter.

But his wicked ways are too hard to resist...

READ FLAWED - BOOK FIVE OF MAFIA WARS NEW YORK!

CHANEL MOULIN
FLAWED PROLOGUE

Chanel Moulin

14 Years Earlier

Bright light hums from the fluorescent bulbs. Dr. Depeckin glances at his folder, then asks, "Ms. Moulin, what have you been using for birth control?"

My pulse pounds hard against my neck. Heat ignites on my cheeks. There's only one man I've ever slept with, and it shouldn't have happened.

It wasn't even two months ago. He's a lot older than me, stole my breath from the first moment I laid eyes on him. I knew he was a bad boy right down to the faint scar on his right cheek. Yet I felt safe with him. And all I've done since that night is think about him. Not once in my life have I not thought before I acted. I only had half a Cosmopolitan before he swept me away from my friends and onto the dance floor.

By the end of the third song, he was leading me out of the nightclub and into his car. We spent the entire time lip-locked until we got to his place.

Every second of being with him felt right. My body fit with his like I was part of him. His touch lit up all my cells as if he were breathing life into me. Before him, I never thought I was dead. Now, the more time that passes without him, the more numb I become.

My body craves a replay. His few attempts to see me again almost killed me. Sometimes I debate about caving, but I need to stay as far away from him as possible.

It's a mistake I wish I could take back. I didn't know who he was at the time. All I saw was how he looked at me with his dark, brooding eyes and dominant confidence.

God, I was so stupid.

Everything about Luca made me lose my judgment. I've cursed myself ever since. I should have been smarter than to fall prey to him. I'm around powerful, successful men all day. It's not the first time a man looked at me with desire or had a sexy Italian accent. Yet every look he threw my way made my heart skip a beat and pulse quicken.

I knew better than to trust a stranger. My boss and his family are dangerous. My father works for them and is too, I suppose. When I'm working, I'm under their protection. But the night out with my group of friends was far away from their protection.

Luca has all the traits dangerous men have, yet he was honey, and I was the fly. Not once did I stop to find out who he was or think he would hurt me.

He hasn't hurt me.

I can't put it past him.

If my boss or his family knew what I did, I'm sure I'd get fired. It doesn't matter if I didn't know who Luca was or that I'm determined to stay away from him, even though he's mysteriously shown up at the coffee shop I visit or restaurants I eat at.

He's their biggest enemy.

"Ms. Moulin, please answer my question. I'll remind you everything is confidential," Dr. Depeckin says.

I swallow hard, admitting, "I'm not sexually active."

He arches his bushy eyebrows. In a stern voice, he states, "I'm your doctor, Ms. Moulin. There's no need to lie."

My heart thumps against my chest cavity. I blurt out, "I'm not! I don't have a boyfriend, and I work all the time!"

Both of those statements are true. I'm Massimo Marino's flight attendant. The day my father and I arrived in New York from Italy, Massimo's Papà suggested he hire me.

It was a little over two years ago, and I was only sixteen. I had already graduated high school. Guiseppe Berscoloni, the head of the Italian Mafia, had relocated my father to New York to work for the Marinos.

It wasn't the first time I'd moved countries. My homeland is France. My parents and I moved to Italy when I was ten. When my father announced we were coming to the United States, I didn't want to leave. All my friends were in Italy. I knew no one in New York, nor did I know what I wanted to do with my life. When Massimo offered me the flight attendant job, I didn't feel I had a choice. My father would have been extremely disappointed in me if I hadn't taken it.

Regardless of how my career started, I love what I do. I've seen more of the world than I ever imagined I could. Massimo treats me well, pays me more than I ever hoped for, and every day feels like a new adventure.

If only I'd never laid eyes on Luca.

Dr. Depeckin takes a few deep breaths, adding to my stress. "When's the last time you had sex?"

The heat in my cheeks burns hotter. I exaggerate, stating, "It was months ago."

"How long?"

Why is he pushing me about this?

I shrug. "Less than two months ago. But I'm not sexually active right now. And it was only once! I don't sleep around!"

Why did I add that last part?

"Ms. Moulin, did you use any protection?" he questions.

More embarrassment floods me. Visuals of Luca's muscular frame caged over my body, the warmth of his strong arms around me, and the pressure of his lips feels as real as that night. His thick Italian accent, stating dirty phrases in both English and Italian during our encounter, never quiet. I squeeze my legs together, trying to alleviate the ache I always feel whenever I think about him.

"Ms. Moulin?" Dr. Depeckin snaps me out of my thoughts.

"Ummm...I ummm..."

"I'll take that as a no?" he asserts.

I nod, wanting to crawl into a hole and die.

This is so humiliating.

He runs his hand through his graying hair and motions to the desk chair. "Have a seat." He takes the one across from mine.

I obey, preparing myself for the lecture about safe sex. I announce, "I promise I'll be smarter next time."

An expression I can't interpret fills his face. He clears his throat, then states, "That would be a better choice. Now, please tell me if you've experienced any nausea?"

Why would I have that?

I answer, "No."

"Tender breasts?"

I internally groan, wondering if he's determined to continue shaming me, and reply, "No."

He leans closer. "Your form said you don't remember the last time you got your period?"

The smell of his Old Spice cologne makes my stomach churn.

Maybe I should tell him it's time to get a new scent?

I shrug again. "I've never been regular."

A tense moment of silence passes. He studies me, then announces, "Ms. Moulin, you're pregnant."

A nervous laugh escapes me. "That's not funny."

His face turns sterner. "I'm not joking."

Time seems to stand still. Goosebumps break out on my arms. I shudder, shaking my head.

No. No. No.

How did I let this happen?

"Are you okay?" he asks.

More shock fills me. "What do you mean I'm pregnant? That's not possible."

"You had unprotected sex," he points out.

"Once!" I exclaim but understand how ignorant it sounds.

He glances at the ceiling, takes a frustrated breath, then locks his disapproving eyes on me. "It doesn't matter how many times you have sex. It only takes once."

No shit, Sherlock!

My insides quiver. Tears fill my orbs, and I blink hard, but they fall fast.

He softens his tone. "You said you don't have a boyfriend. Do you know who the father is?"

Luca...

Oh my God.

I don't even know the last name of my baby's father.

It doesn't matter. He works for the Abruzzos.

No. No. No.

This is not happening!

I snap, "Of course, I know who he is!"

Dr. Depeckin holds his hands in the air. "I wasn't insinuating—"

"I need to go," I state, jumping out of my chair and grabbing my clothes.

"Ms. Moulin, we need to discuss prenatal care," he asserts.

I toss my shirt over the paper gown and step into my skirt, not bothering with my bra or panties. I shove them into my oversized bag and move toward the door.

He calls out, "Ms. Moulin!"

I yank on the knob. "Thank you." I rush toward the exit sign, barely seeing it through my tears. I toss cash at the front desk, girl. It's probably way more than what I owe, but another second in this office, and I'm going to lose it.

Somehow, I make it through the building. I wipe my face, toss my sunglasses on, and hail a cab. The entire ride is a blur.

Numbness sets in as I climb six flights of stairs, avoiding the elevator so I don't have to see anyone in my building. I get into my apartment, go into the bathroom, and strip.

For a long time, I study my body, cursing myself. The round shape of my belly and my slightly bigger breasts should have given me a clue.

How could I be so naive?

Why didn't I tell him to use a condom?

Why does it have to be Luca's?

I leave the bathroom, pull my bedding back, and slide under the covers. For hours I cry, unsure of what I'm going to do. I'm only eighteen. I'm unprepared to be a mother and especially a single mother. This wasn't my plan for my life.

My parents are going to kill me.

Maybe I should find Luca and tell him.

What am I thinking?

If he's the father, it's his right to know.

Maybe we could be together, and it'll all be okay.

What am I thinking? He's the enemy.

He's my baby's father.

My baby.

Oh my God! What am I going to do!

I will never subject my child to the Abruzzos.

The debate over how I'll manage a baby, my career, and still keep Luca a secret never stops. When morning comes, I still don't have any answers, but there's only one thing I vow to do.

I'll figure out how to be a good mom and protect my child from Luca at all costs.

READ FLAWED - BOOK FIVE OF MAFIA WARS NEW YORK!

READY TO BINGE THE ORIGINAL 10 BOOK MAFIA WARS SERIES? GET TO KNOW THE IVANOVS AND O'MALLEYS!

He's a Ruthless Stranger. One I can't see, only feel, thanks to my friends who make a deal with him on my behalf.

No names. No personal details. No face to etch into my mind.

Just him, me, and an expensive silk tie.

What happens in Vegas is supposed to stay in Vegas.

He warns me he's full of danger.

I never see that side of him. All I experience is his Russian accent, delicious scent, and touch that lights me on fire.

One incredible night turns into two. Then we go our separate ways.

But fate doesn't keep us apart. When I run into my stranger back in Chicago, I know it's him, even if I've never seen his icy blue eyes before.

Our craving is hotter than Vegas. But he never lied.

He's a ruthless man...

"Ruthless Stranger" is the jaw-dropping first installment of the "Mafia Wars" series. It's an interconnecting, stand-alone Dark Mafia Romance, guaranteed to have an HEA.

Ready for Maksim's story? Click here for Ruthless Stranger, book one of the jaw dropping spinoff series, Mafia Wars!

ALL IN BOXSET

Three page-turning, interconnected stand-alone romance novels with HEA's!! Get ready to fall in love with the characters. Billionaires. Professional athletes. New York City. Twist, turns, and danger lurking everywhere. The only option for these couples is to go ALL IN...with a little help from their friends. EXTRA STEAM INCLUDED!

Grab it now! READ FREE IN KINDLE UNLIMITED!

CAN I ASK YOU A HUGE FAVOR?

Would you be willing to leave me a review?

I would be forever grateful as one positive review on Amazon is like buying the book a hundred times! Reader support is the lifeblood for Indie authors and provides us the feedback we need to give readers what they want in future stories!

Your positive review means the world to me! So thank you from the bottom of my heart!

MORE BY MAGGIE COLE

Mafia Wars New York - A Dark Mafia Series (Series Six)

Toxic (Dante's Story) - Book One

Immoral (Gianni's Story) - Book Two

Crazed (Massimo's Story) - Book Three

Carnal (Tristano's Story) - Book Four

Flawed (Luca's Story) - Book Five

Mafia Wars - A Dark Mafia Series (Series Five)

Ruthless Stranger (Maksim's Story) - Book One

Broken Fighter (Boris's Story) - Book Two

Cruel Enforcer (Sergey's Story) - Book Three

Vicious Protector (Adrian's Story) - Book Four

Savage Tracker (Obrecht's Story) - Book Five

MORE BY MAGGIE COLE

Unchosen Ruler (Liam's Story) - Book Six

Perfect Sinner (Nolan's Story) - Book Seven

Brutal Defender (Killian's Story) - Book Eight

Deviant Hacker (Declan's Story) - Book Nine

Relentless Hunter (Finn's Story) - Book Ten

Behind Closed Doors (Series Four - Former Military Now International Rescue Alpha Studs)

Depths of Destruction - Book One

Marks of Rebellion - Book Two

Haze of Obedience - Book Three

Cavern of Silence - Book Four

Stains of Desire - Book Five

Risks of Temptation - Book Six

Together We Stand Series (Series Three - Family Saga)

Kiss of Redemption - Book One

Sins of Justice - Book Two

Acts of Manipulation - Book Three

Web of Betrayal - Book Four

Masks of Devotion - Book Five

Roots of Vengeance - Book Six

It's Complicated Series (Series Two - Chicago Billionaires)

Crossing the Line - Book One

Don't Forget Me - Book Two

Committed to You - Book Three

More Than Paper - Book Four

Sins of the Father - Book Five

Wrapped In Perfection - Book Six

All In Series (Series One - New York Billionaires)

The Rule - Book One

The Secret - Book Two

The Crime - Book Three

The Lie - Book Four

The Trap - Book Five

The Gamble - Book Six

STAND ALONE NOVELLA

JUDGE ME NOT - A Billionaire Single Mom Christmas Novella

ABOUT THE AUTHOR

Amazon Bestselling Author

Maggie Cole is committed to bringing her readers alphalicious book boyfriends. She's an international bestselling author and has been called the "literary master of steamy romance." Her books are full of raw emotion, suspense, and will always keep you wanting more. She is a masterful storyteller of contemporary romance and loves writing about broken people who rise above the ashes.

Maggie lives in Florida with her son. She loves sunshine, anything to do with water, and everything naughty.

Her current series were written in the order below:

- All In (Stand alones with entwined characters)
- It's Complicated (Stand alones with entwined characters)
- Together We Stand (Brooks Family Saga - read in order)
- Behind Closed Doors (Read in order)
- Mafia Wars (Coming April 1st 2021)

Maggie Cole's Newsletter

Sign up here!

Hang Out with Maggie in Her Reader Group
Maggie Cole's Romance Addicts

Follow for Giveaways
Facebook Maggie Cole

Instagram
@maggiecoleauthor

Tik Tok
https://www.tiktok.com/@authormaggiecole?

Complete Works on Amazon
Follow Maggie's Amazon Author Page

Book Trailers
Follow Maggie on YouTube

Are you a Blogger and want to join my ARC team?
Signup now!

Feedback or suggestions?
Email: authormaggiecole@gmail.com

- twitter.com/MaggieColeAuth
- instagram.com/maggiecoleauthor
- bookbub.com/profile/maggie-cole
- amazon.com/Maggie-Cole/e/B07Z2CB4HG

Made in United States
North Haven, CT
03 May 2025

68539045R00288